Bryan Boswell spent most of his working life as a war correspondent and international political writer. He lives in a small white Andalucian mountain village with his wife, an ancient Great Dane and a mature part-Iberian Mastiff that has no claws. He says the location of the village is idyllic but won't name it because he refuses to share its fifteen plus bars.

Tattoo

BRYAN BOSWELL

PIATKUS

First published in Great Britain as a paperback original in 2010 by Piatkus

All characters and events in this publication, other than those clearly in the public domain, are fictitious and any resemblance to real persons, living or dead, is purely coincidental.

A CIP catalogue record for this book is available from the British Library.

ISBN 978-0-7499-4214-4

Typeset in Caslon by M Rules
Printed in the UK by CPI Mackays, Chatham ME5 8TD

Papers used by Piatkus are natural, renewable and recyclable products sourced from well-managed forests and certified in accordance with the rules of the Forest Stewardship Council.

Piatkus
An imprint of
Little, Brown Book Group
100 Victoria Embankment
London EC4Y 0DY

An Hachette UK Company
www.hachette.co.uk

www.piatkus.co.uk

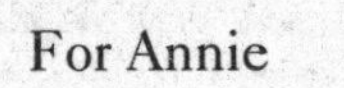
For Annie

Acknowledgements

Thanks to Ian and Janice Paterson, for invaluable advice on Scotland; Rosie Lee, for introducing me to Burnham-on-Crouch; my friends in the *Sierra de Las Nieves*, for eight years of information provided unwittingly by them; Jane Gregory, for persistence; and Emma Beswetherick, for enthusiastic encouragement and the honing of a rough typescript.

Descriptions of the *Masdevallia* family of orchids came, in part, from colour plates in *Orchids in Colour*, by the famed orchid experts Brian and Wilma Ritterhausen.

Prologue

Costa del Sol, Spain.

It was the sobbing, stifled whimper of a child in total despair.

Black. Empty. Devoid of hope, or relief from the pain of life.

The silent corridor soaked up her tears, the helplessness lined its walls. The shadows let the horror hide within itself, as if wrapped in the folds of a shroud.

A choked scream from time to time spoke more of inevitability than of pain. A keening resignation that was muffled by the padding on the door and walls but that pleaded '*enough*, *enough*, *enough*'.

Tabor exited the fourth door, his face pale, bleak eyes staring behind him at the room he was leaving, with its walls of equipment there, ready. Ready and waiting. Leather chokers, some of them fleece lined; gags with wide black leather straps, whips and 18-inch riding paddles. Bondage stocks and head restraints. Hoods and masks and two straightjackets.

For a moment he heard nothing, his mind filled with images of the way these implements would have been used. Then he heard it.

The sobs rolled along the carpet and reached up to his ears.

Begging. Entreating. '*Please. Please help me. Please.*'

It was ten strides to the door and he hit it without trying the knob.

It flew open: there had been no catch or lock fastened and he fell through the doorway, colliding with the hairy man astride the girl.

The man shot forward across the girl's body, smothering her face, then rolled over, the final throes of ejaculation spurting over her as he dropped off the bed and on to the floor.

The girl's breathing was fast and irregular, pulling air into her starved lungs with huge gulps, and the weals and bruises on her face and body were painting fresh hues of blues and blacks in the paleness of her flesh.

She opened her eyes and a momentary spark of recognition flared in them.

Then she closed them and her chest was heaving and alongside the bed the hairy man was pushing himself up, turning to face the intruder who had forced his way into the room.

Tabor took it in at a glance: the girl on the bed, her face ghostly beneath the discolouration of the beating, her hands tied with leather straps to rings on the wall and the iron frame at the foot of the bed but now the other man was on his feet, his face distorted with anger, his hands balled into fists and muscled legs taut in preparation for action.

Tabor hit first. He dived across the bed, pushing the man hard against the wall, hearing his shout of pain as his back scraped against a light switch and he slid down to fall back across the girl.

The man shoved himself up, smashing his fist into the

girl's nose in spite, hearing the bone crunch beneath it, then he was back, reaching for Tabor's throat, his whole body vibrating with the thrill of the pain racing through him. Better than the girl!

Tabor sliced him across the windpipe and the man began to gag. He twisted him around and jerked his knee into the man's testicles, feeling the satisfaction as the bastard screamed out, this time in pure agony when they crushed inside his body. He hit him again: a full forehead butt into the bridge of the nose, simultaneously shooting out with a right hook, punching him, with all of his strength, in the solar plexus.

The man appeared to double over then attempt to straighten up, his eyes glazing, his hands clenching his crushed testicles, but the impact propelled him towards the wall, towards the window. Out of control, staggering backwards, he grasped at the curtains but they ripped from the rail, draping around him, fouling his legs, bringing him to a standstill, whipping his feet from under him.

He was too close and it was too late.

With a scream of terror he fell through the window, the glass shards scraping his face and naked body. Then he was over the ledge and falling, his body twisting, the curtains curling around his legs like a parachute that had failed to open, as he plunged the four storeys to the concrete below.

Tabor didn't wait to see him smash head first into the ground.

He was already reaching for the girl, the tears rolling down his face as he saw her battered body and her eyes, wide in horror and pain, staring at the ceiling.

There was no movement in the features: her chest was still and he could hear no breathing. He took her face gently in his hands and cupped her to him, trying to breathe into her mouth but it was hopeless. It was obvious in the smashed-in nose he had seen before in other places, other times and for other reasons.

He let her sink back into the pillow and reached out to close her eyes. His baby sister.

He looked at her frail body: the skin so pale for lack of daylight. It had seen none of the sun that existed beyond these walls. A body for use, and to be used. She had lost her youthful schoolgirl's figure, and he remembered tales from time past about how the men who used places such as this preferred their children to be skin and bone. It amplified the pain.

Her ribs were showing and her pelvic bones prominent. The flesh was battered and beaten.

But as he stared at her it was the mark that caught his eye.

He looked closer. There, in the groin, where it would normally have been hidden by the girl's underwear, was a highly detailed one-inch tattoo of an intricate flower.

Tabor slumped down beside her, hugged her lifeless body to him and began to cry.

One

Burnham-on-Crouch, Essex. Two years later.

Landon looked away from the corpse inside its body bag, as it was placed on to a stretcher, and turned to DCI Raymond Ellis who had brought him out to this spot, the end of nowhere, Landon thought.

'Have your people found any witnesses yet?'

'Only the man who came across the body,' Ellis answered. 'As I told you in the car on the way over, he was out walking his dog. Why anyone would want to walk a dog in this kind of weather at six o'clock in the morning is beyond me, but it seems he does it every day, rain or shine, light or dark. Like clockwork, he said. Most people have the good sense to stay in bed.'

Landon grunted. It's where he would have preferred to be himself. Although it was now eight o'clock on the bleak Essex coast, it was still no place to be on a Sunday morning. No place for man or beast.

'Do the media know?'

'I put a hold on information until you came. Is it the tattoo?' Ellis asked.

'It's *a* tattoo.'

Too early to be committal.

The wind was still whistling around them and conversation was difficult, with Ellis clearly straining to hear.

'I thought those cases were cold. It's been a long time,' he said. He had never met Landon before and was finding it difficult to glean information from him. Landon, it seemed, didn't share the Essex policeman's trait of normal, relaxed conversation.

'Five months, two weeks, the last one.'

'As I said, cold.'

'Cases are never cold. They lie dormant. We bring this one out from time to time.'

Ellis let the comment pass, but the way he'd heard it from friends in London, DCI Alan Landon and his team had spent nearly two years in all, failing to find anything. There were no clues and the task force that had been assembled was dismantled three times. Now Landon had only his regular unit of four, mostly assigned to other jobs while the Tattoo case lay 'dormant'. As far as Ellis was concerned, that meant the case was cold. He was already starting to regret replying to the message that had been left months ago for all UK forces to contact Landon at New Scotland Yard immediately if anything like the tattoo turned up.

If he hadn't responded to that, Ellis needn't have come out here to the black expanses of the Crouch estuary where it was cold enough to freeze the balls off brass monkeys. He could have left others to do that.

'Hold off on any autopsy for a few days, will you? Give it a chance for any more bodies to turn up?' Landon asked.

'You think there could be more? It looks like a yachting accident to me.' Ellis sounded tetchy. 'The girl was washed overboard. I only called you because one of my men reported the tattoo. We've notified the Coastguard, but it was a bad storm, wreckage could have been blown for miles.'

'Maybe. That's why I want you to wait for more bodies. We don't know anything about the size of yacht she was on, or even for certain if it *was* a yacht – she could have fallen overboard from something like a ferry. It was a big storm. I'd like to wait for some time to see what turns up. If there's wreckage, or more bodies, it could help identify this girl. It could confirm what happened. If there are more girls with tattoos, the comparisons could throw up a new line of enquiry.'

'I don't see how, but please yourself,' said Ellis. 'She won't mind staying in the fridge for a few more days.'

Landon watched silently as the stretcher was carried across the mud banks to where the ambulance was standing on hard soil alongside the river, a good half-mile or more away. She had a serene face. As though she hadn't died in terror at all. Rather as though she'd struggled ashore then given up the will to live and waited for death to bring her peace.

He wondered about the clothing. Often clothing *did* get ripped off in storms but usually something was left – a bra or a pair of knickers at least. Some kind of underwear, but on this body there was nothing. Only the mud where she'd crawled ashore remained on her skin as any kind of covering.

The girl would be fourteen or fifteen. She had the high cheekbones and darker complexion once stereotyped as one of the Slavic races, but that meant nothing these days. She was well built, nourished and could easily have fallen from a sailboat caught up in the storm, as Ellis intimated. Girls liked to top up their tans sun-bathing naked on a yacht deck. It could account for the lack of clothing, but in this weather? Then there was the tattoo.

The bulk of the trumpet-shaped flower was an extraordinary shade of rich golden yellow, deeper than any daffodil he had ever seen, tipped with three slender horns so dark a green they could easily have been mistaken for black. So exquisite was the shading of the tattoo that the base of the flower seemed to sink into a fathomless depth, surrounding the lush green of the hints of leaves that surrounded it.

The tattoo was no more than an inch and half in diameter, but the detail was as fine as that in any book on botany.

And it was placed in exactly the same part of the body as those found on the other dead girls.

But this time things were different. They'd been killed with an ice axe into the brain and acid poured over the tattoo to obliterate all trace. This girl had drowned. No attempt had been made to remove the tattoo and it was clearly visible.

It was the first time he had seen a complete one, except in a photograph. Until now all he had were artists' outline drawings of what pathologists had found beneath the skin. The acid had burned into the flesh enough to destroy surface detail, but with tattoos something always remained below the surface. Only traces, but experts insisted the tattoos were of similar things. Small flowers in the groin.

'Small flowers' was a pathetic misnomer. In its full glory, like this one, it was a miniature work of art tattooed on what had once been a living body. In reality far more breathtaking than he had imagined from the drawings, or the photo taken more than a thousand miles, and two years, away from here.

Twenty-two months, he thought.

Pathologists' findings, reports from crime-scene investigators, background from the Home Office Large Major Enquiry System, HOLMES. Three cases spanning nearly two years and nothing beyond mutilated bodies and artists' incomplete drawings. Hundreds of man hours, tens of thousands of pounds from the budget.

A cold case.

Until today.

Now fate, and the worst storm in decades in the Channel might finally have provided the impetus to warm it up.

Two

The Lake District, England. Two weeks later.

The quarrel cut through the air and rammed into the archery target fifty yards away.

'Shit,' Simon Tabor muttered out loud, shaking his head in disgust. It had struck outside the centre and that was no use to anyone. The breeze wasn't strong but it was steady and he'd been trying for more than an hour to compensate, but every shot drifted either right or left of the bull's eye.

The target was protected by a stand of small trees, and beyond that he could see the wavelets flickering over Wast Water. The trees created variations in the wind direction and strength as it curled around trunks, but he should have been able to cope with that. This was the tenth day of practice in the heart of the Copeland Forest, and so far he hadn't achieved the kind of efficiency with the crossbow that he wanted.

The hills and the lake lay serene in the early afternoon, the pale sun playing over his naked upper body, not enough to burn. Satisfactorily cool.

But, at this moment, something was troubling him.

Breaking his concentration. For the past five minut
silence had been interrupted by the low rumble
engine. At first he thought it was in the distance, ar
Nether Wasdale, but usually such sounds lasted only a few moments then evaporated as the tourists vanished off to their holiday homes or bed and breakfasts. This one stayed like a persistent mosquito, buzzing in his ears, picking at his senses.

It was coming closer.

Of that he was quite certain. He could tell from the sound that it wasn't bogging down or grounding in the ruts, which suggested a professional was driving.

Police? Civil or military? He forced himself not to turn around, but the tension was rising inside him.

He sighted down the crossbow and willed the bolt to follow his eyes, into the centre of the target, squeezing the trigger, but it was wrong again. The bolt slammed into the hard-packed straw of the target, two inches away from where he intended.

This time he turned around angrily, aware the vehicle was stopping, inwardly blaming the noise for his errors as it came to a halt on the more level surface of the pasture.

It was an ordinary black saloon. The driver got out of the car and walked towards him, hunched slightly in an instinctive, involuntary crouch, as if the breeze were stronger than it felt.

Tabor said nothing. The crossbow hung in his hand and he pointedly inserted a new quarrel and stretched the bow ready.

'It looks as if you need more practice,' Landon said as he approached. He was a tall man, a fraction over the six-feet mark, but Tabor stood at least an inch taller. At a distance one might have thought they were brothers, so similar were their height and build, but close up the differences were obvious. Landon was crowding his fifties and it showed;

Tabor had a couple of years to run before he reached thirty and he could have passed for even younger.

The policeman held out his identification. Tabor read it and handed it back.

'That's what I'm getting,' he snapped irritably, finally answering Landon's comment. There was neither warmth nor welcome in his voice. He was blaming this interruption for his inaccuracy.

Landon turned and looked at the house, some two hundred and fifty yards away, not far from the lake.

'Can we go inside?'

'There's nothing to be said inside that can't be said out here. I live alone.'

Landon smiled tolerantly. 'My understanding is you have company from time to time,' he said mildly. 'Trainees in survivalism.'

'This is a National Park,' Tabor hedged. 'You probably need permits for things such as survival courses. You've obviously checked up on me, so you'll know I don't have one.'

'True.'

'Is that what this is about? Since when has the Metropolitan Police CID been interested in acting as park warden?'

'Since I made it my business to be interested.'

Landon stepped back from what was hovering on the edge of confrontation. He needed to get the discussion on to an even footing. He strolled over to a fallen tree trunk and sat down, then pulled an envelope from the inside pocket of his jacket. 'I've got something I'd like you to look at. Something you may want to see.'

'As far as I'm aware I'm not in trouble with you lot.' Tabor stayed where he was, the crossbow clutched in his right hand. 'I'm in no breach of my parole.'

'Whether you're in breach of your parole isn't up to me to

say. These visitors that come here on survivalism courses may be casual friends or they could be paying you to teach them skills. Nothing wrong with the training but there could be a parole breach if you're making a commercial business out of an operation in the park without telling the authorities.'

'Are you threatening me?'

'Don't be stupid,' Landon replied dismissively, patting the space beside him on the tree trunk. 'Blackmail is illegal even for a copper, so come and sit down and look at this. I'm not after you for a parole breach. I want your opinion then maybe your help. Ten minutes is all I need. I won't delay you longer if you turn me down.'

'Policemen from London don't drive to an out-of-the-way place in Cumbria for ten minutes.'

But he strode over, sat down and took the envelope from Landon. He pulled out the photograph of the tattoo. His face blanched, his lips tightened. 'Where did you get this?'

'The body was washed ashore near Burnham-on-Crouch in Essex two weeks ago,' Landon replied quietly. 'Since then, five other bodies have washed up. Four girls, all about the same age as that one, and a male adult. The girls haven't been identified and there's no evidence they were all together on the same boat, but it's highly probable they were.'

'Where were they found?'

'They drifted onshore in Holland and Belgium and had no papers or identification. The man was found close to Whitstable. He was a yachtsman called Tom Winters, quite well known in east-coast yachting circles. One theory is he was out with the other victims on a boat and got caught in a storm. The boat capsized and everyone drowned.'

'All of the girls had tattoos like this?'

'No. Only the one in Burnham.'

'So what's it got to do with me?'

'You *know* what I want,' Landon said patiently. 'You've

seen a tattoo like that in Spain. You want to find out who did the tattooing. So do I. Tell me I'm right and we'll talk more. Tell me I'm wrong and I'll go away and leave you with a couple of forms to apply for a commercial licence to work in the National Park.'

Tabor hesitated briefly. 'Go on.'

'This isn't the only girl we've found dead, bearing a similar tattoo,' Landon said. 'There have been three others. They've never been identified, but they were murdered, killed either in the street or in a city house or apartment block, with an ice axe.'

Tabor studied the photograph then handed it back. 'Why didn't you contact me about the earlier ones?' he demanded. 'What suddenly makes you need me now?'

'The others didn't have an identifiable tattoo,' Landon replied. 'They'd been burned off with acid. This is the first we've seen fully. Only you know if it's the same as the one you saw in Spain. That's why I want you. So what's it to be, Tabor? Do you want to know more or take those forms I mentioned and leave this behind you? Leave Emma behind you?'

Tabor quivered at the mention of the name. Despair and anger flashed momentarily across his face, but just as quickly vanished. He pointed to the car. 'Will you take me to the girl's body?'

Landon nodded and Tabor went over to pick up a gilet he had dropped close to where he had been standing to practise.

'Then let's go.'

He brought up the crossbow and without sighting on the target let fly the bolt. It smacked as if on wire, directly into the centre.

Three

Sevilla, Spain.

Ask an Englishman about Spanish bullfighting and three distinct attitudes emerge.

To one group it is an abomination, to be banned in the way fox hunting was in England, to have tradition discarded like a broken eggshell and good riddance. To another sector the tradition is held sacred, based on a complex inter-reaction between man and beast, the conflict between life and death, wrapped in a theatrical performance beyond description. To the third group it is background noise on a Spanish-bar television set, unheard over the clink of glasses and loud conversation, watched only in case the matador slips and the bull can gore his opponent. The *expectation* of someone dying.

Felix Blake despised all of them.

In the British mind, he understood clearly, bullfighting meant only Spain and only men on foot. Uneducated fools, all of them. Dismissible. The protest groups searched for a cause, and moved from one to another without rhyme or reason; the environment this week, nuclear weapons the week before, bullfighting today and tomorrow. Off with their heads, as the Queen of Hearts demanded. The second group toyed with phrases such as theatre and art, but knew nothing of the reality. If anything those in the third group were more understandable. At least they didn't try to dignify their attitudes with empty thoughts and observations. They wanted the matador to die. The bull was an instrument to do it.

Blake sought purity and perfection.

Purity in the breeding of the bull, perfection in the actions of the *cuadrillo* and in the essence of what was enacted every time a bull and a matador faced one another across the sand.

Each time he hoped to find it. In the bullring, in his orchids, in his work. For a brief moment he thought about *Tatú*, but that was an intrusion.

He switched back mentally to the scene in front of him.

Each time he went to the bullring he hoped to witness the perfect moment. Mostly he came away hollow and unfulfilled, but this time it was different. He sensed it the moment the bull thundered into the ring, tossing his head this way and that, black baleful eyes taking note of the men milling around him, assessing them, *judging* them.

Once in a lifetime there was such a bull, once in a lifetime there was such a matador, and this evening, in the 32-degree heat of La Maestranza in Sevilla, the oldest bullring in Spain, the two had come together.

Thirty metres away from where Blake sat in the shade, Satanas snorted and breathed furiously, his huge chest heaving as he pawed at the ground with his right front hoof. His flanks rippled and sweat rolled off his huge black body. Steam rose from his withers and back in small wisps that drifted into the air then vanished.

More than ten thousand people were packed into the stadium and a thousand or more *abanicos* – the ubiquitous fan used by millions of Spanish women throughout the summer – fluttered from the benches, as they tried to keep cool.

But they were whisper quiet. They too sensed this was different.

From the edge of their seats they watched the matador, a small scarlet-clad figure, standing bareheaded no more than two metres from the bull, waiting.

The bull *knew.* Somehow everyone could tell. Everyone could understand. The tension palpable.

A fighting bull hooks mostly to one particular side, but Satanas was a maverick. He hooked both right and left without favouring either. He learned from the men, rather than blindly reacting to them. Satanas *learned.* He learned from the capes, from the pain inflicted by the *picador*, from the barbs of the *banderillas* planted in his shoulders. Satanas did not play the game according to the traditional, the theatrical rules.

His tail flicked from side to side and there was the fire of anger, pain and hate in his black eyes. As his shoulders flexed, the green and white *banderillas* of Andalucia swayed in response to the motion of the muscles. Blood from the wound at the base of the neck, where the *picador* had sunk his lance, was coagulating over his chest and legs, and streaks of it were splattered over the clothing of the matador facing him.

The vibration of the mobile phone broke Felix Blake's concentration. He pulled it impatiently from his shirt pocket and flicked open the lid.

'Yes?' he snapped.

'We have a problem,' said a soft voice at the other end.

Blake heard the trumpets calling for the start of the third and last *tercio.* The *suerte del muerte.* It was the fourth bull of the evening and the main fight of the *corrida*.

'Half an hour,' he said. 'Call me then. I must watch.'

He snapped the phone shut, cutting off the call, and turned his attention back to the ring.

Four

Chelmsford, England.

'He's a surly sod,' said DCI Ellis bluntly. 'A big bugger too.'

Landon looked at the closed door, beyond which lay the morgue that Tabor had entered fifteen minutes earlier.

'He doesn't like coppers a lot,' answered Landon diffidently. 'Some would say he's got no reason to.'

But the DCI was right. Tabor *was* big and it wasn't merely his height. He was still dressed in the clothes he'd been wearing for the crossbow session, except that he'd pulled on a white T-shirt to accompany the sand-coloured camouflage trousers and carried the gilet in his hand. Beneath the thin shirt, the muscles in his arms and shoulders rippled with every movement.

'He was a captain in the SAS until a couple of years ago,' Landon said. 'His fifteen-year-old sister Emma went missing on a backpacking trip with a friend across Morocco and he applied for compassionate leave to go search for her. It turned out the friend, who was eighteen, had already been found, wandering out of the Atlas Mountains. She'd been raped and abandoned there. Tabor's sister vanished.'

'So he kept looking for her?'

'He asked for extra leave, but it was denied. Tabor was wanted for a mission. So he went AWOL. Three months later he traced the kidnappers to Spain where the girl was being held. He broke down the bedroom door and found a naked man astride her, bashing her around. It was an S&M brothel. He threw the man out of the window. It was four storeys up in an apartment block. The police were called and it took five of them to restrain him. One policeman had a cracked rib, another a broken arm. They only pulled him down by using a Taser.'

'The girl?'

'The man punched her in the nose with his fist. Drove the bone right up into her brain. Killed her instantly. She was Tabor's only family. The police said later the brothel was well known for sado-masochism, either the clients being beaten by the girls, or the girls being beaten by the clients. Tabor's sister got the "being beaten" treatment.'

'The police let him off?'

'They charged him with manslaughter then our government applied pressure, thanks to Tabor's commander at Hereford. The Spanish gave him ten years, without any formal trial and handed him over to us. They were happy to be rid of him. When Tabor got back to Hereford the sentence was reduced to ten years parole, but he was given three months in the glasshouse for going AWOL then dishonourably discharged.'

'So what's he to you?'

'Coincidence.' Landon hesitated before he said it. 'I've seen the documentation sent over from Malaga. Tabor's sister had a tattoo of an exotic flower. I thought if Tabor saw the girl here in the morgue it would ring bells. It might give us a lead on these tattoo murders. It's a long shot, but I've played them before.'

'You don't have anything else to go on?'

'Just the murders and the tattoo.'

'Best of luck,' muttered Ellis. 'Personally I wish he'd wrap it up inside there. It's already nearly nine o'clock and I'd like to get home some time tonight.'

'Go now,' Landon suggested. 'I know you had to be here for protocol's sake, but you don't need to stay.'

'Right.' Ellis sighed with relief. 'What about the body here?'

'The Belgians and Dutch have done autopsies on the girls over there and I've got copies of the reports. All death by drowning. There were no more tattoos. Maybe the girls were from different boats to ours. The Belgians and Dutch don't know and nor do we. I don't need this girl's body now Tabor's seen it. There's no evidence of anything but the yachting accident. As you said, there's been no identification. I'd like them to do a blood test but you can't do much more.'

'She's just a Jane Doe who got too close to the water, poor little sod. What a waste of a young life. I've spoken to the coroner. He's ready when you are, so we'll schedule the inquest tomorrow then have her cremated at public expense. Are you sure you don't want one last look at that tattoo?'

'No thanks.'

'Right then. I'm off,' Ellis said.

It was another ten minutes before Tabor emerged.

'The tattoo?' Landon asked immediately. 'Was it the same as Spain?'

'Similar,' replied Tabor. 'Is this where we talk? Here in the corridor?'

'No,' answered Landon. 'I needed your confirmation first. You had to see the body in the flesh, photographs can lie. I've got to get back to London now, but I want to see you in the morning. We'll talk then.'

‘So find me a place to stay,’ Tabor said curtly.

Landon remembered Ellis’s words. ‘Surly sod,’ he’d said. But it wasn’t surly. It was matter of fact. He’d brought Tabor here but there was no way he could get back to the Lake District tonight. Putting him up in a B&B was the least Landon could do.

‘I’ll find you a place but it won’t be five-star luxury.’

‘I don’t care if it’s a police cell as long as it’s dry, has a bed and a shower,’ Tabor replied. His voice said he didn’t care. His attitude, and the file on him that Landon had read, confirmed it.

‘Send a copy of that photograph of the tattoo to a botanist,’ Tabor said. ‘Or someone else who’s an expert on exotic plants. I want to know exactly what he says before we talk.’

‘I already have. It’s an orchid. A *Masdevallia elephanticeps* to be specific.’

Tabor turned away. ‘You didn’t need my confirmation,’ he said. ‘You only wanted to know how it relates to the one in Spain. I’ll tell you. He’s doing a series.’

Five

Sevilla.

Blake stood up with thousands of others, his heart pounding from the sheer magnificence of the history he was witnessing.

An *estacado recibido.* The kill-or-be-killed movement where neither bull nor matador gives way. They were weighing each other across the narrow divide, each consumed in contemplation of imminent death.

The silence was absolute. The *abanicos* stilled, breath escaping slowly from held-in lungs, no sound passing the ten thousand tightly compressed lips. *The moment!*

Satanas charged.

At the same instant the matador leaped up and dived between the slashing horns, rolling over the bull's head, ramming the blade to the hilt in the cervical vertebrae, deep into the heart. One horn ripped into the red satin of the *trace de luces*, tearing the gold embroidery, carving into the matador's stomach, before he landed on the other side of the bull, his feet placed astride on the ground, holding himself upright, pride and tradition demanding he witness the denouement.

Satanas, the bull who had showed only fire and never fear in his five years of life, stood still for a moment, his head hung low, close to the ground. Drops of blood dribbled through the nostrils. He sank to his knees and then lay down.

Moments later he rolled over and died.

The matador stood for another moment, blood staining his extravagant clothing, then collapsed into the sand, his head gently touching Satanas's still body.

The phone rang again. He had left the bullring as Satanas's carcass was dragged out by the horses and was now standing outside in the road, his mind racing over the splendour of the encounter, but vexed that he had been disturbed at all.

'Is there a problem?' Blake demanded tersely.

'My latest consignment has been lost, including a package that interests you.' The voice was still as soft and sibilant as before. Calm but threatening, the English accent lightly laced with what Blake had once mentally labelled Transylvanian. Blake despised the little man but he was a necessary evil. For the moment at least. 'There may be an investigation that could cause difficulties for you, as well as us.'

'Fix them.'

'I'm flying out tonight to rectify matters. A delivery man has to lose his job. Not a major problem, but you asked me to tell you if anything ever happened again. It has and it's in hand.'

'Good.'

Blake clicked the phone shut irritably. The man was a lackey without redeeming grace, apart from his efficiency at what he did. Soon, Blake thought, he won't be necessary any more.

He looked around for a taxi to take him to San Paulo airport. There were plenty available. There were two more bulls to fight before the crowd began to stream out of the building.

Half an hour later he boarded his private helicopter at the airport and took off, heading across the plain, dropping over the Serrania de Ronda towards his home in the mountains of the Sierra de Las Nieves.

He was looking forward to an hour in the orchid house then some further relaxation.

Perhaps Mahler's 4th.

It was ideal for his mood. It would go down perfectly with a bottle of Louis Roederer Cristal Rosé. The 1999 vintage. Intense. Generous bouquet. Silky elegance.

He thought about it a little more. Perhaps he might even drink two.

Six

London. Early hours.

Sanchez stood in the doorway of the club, smoking a cigarette. It was pungent and acrid, but Spanish cigarettes were what he was used to and there was always a plentiful supply brought over in the trips from the Costa del Sol.

The club was one of dozens in central London where the drinks were overpriced, along with the girls, and the 'dancing' was nothing more than window dressing. The rooms upstairs were let by the half-hour and were rarely empty between midnight and four o'clock.

He leaned against the wall and puffed smoke into the street, watching the rings, amused at the way the light wind disposed of them in seconds. Like the girls upstairs, he thought idly. Totally disposable.

Jorge Sanchez was only a small man but he had a big sexual appetite, and the money to indulge it, which made life pleasant except when things went wrong as they had a couple of weeks ago when the boatload of new girls sank.

They'd been worth £250 each to him, on arrival in London, for his end of the transport arrangements and he'd see none of that money now. It wasn't an unbearable loss but £5,000 paid for a lot of new shirts and ties.

'Passing the time of night, Jorge?'

Sanchez pushed himself away from the wall and stood upright, smiling at the huge man in front of him.

'It's unusual to see you here, Serghei,' he said, reaching up to pat the man on the shoulder. 'I thought your tastes lay elsewhere.'

'You can keep your women,' Serghei Lacatus answered lightly. 'Too much scent and sweat. There's a job for you. We have to take a little walk where no one will see us, but don't worry. I'll be there to protect you.'

Jorge stubbed out his cigarette against the wall and dropped the half-smoked butt into the gutter. He pushed his shoulders back and put a scowl on his face to look tougher. He straightened his tie. It was black, with a gold dragon motif, and stood out vividly against the yellow of his silk shirt.

'Let's go,' he said, leaving the shelter of the club and stepping into the street.

Serghei smiled, put an arm around Jorge's shoulders and led him off into the maze of alleys, heading east, amiably teasing him about Sanchez's gymnastics with the girls in his bed.

It was past three and they kept to side streets where there were few pedestrians around. The bulk of the noise was from the squalling of cats, burrowing in the rubbish bins, knocking off lids and clawing into black bags to reach the food waste tossed out from nearby restaurants.

They had been walking for fifteen minutes when Serghei let the arm slide from around Jorge's shoulders and began to stride out ahead. As they delved deeper into the darkness of the back streets, Jorge began to feel concerned.

'Slow down. I can't keep up.'

They were engulfed in the blackness. Not a crack of light

showed from shuttered or curtained windows. Street lamps had either gone out or been broken. Even the cats seemed to have departed mysteriously, unwilling to be silent witnesses to what was happening.

Something was wrong. Jorge's instincts gnawed at him. These dark alleys, the inkiness of the night, screaming at him that here lurked danger. He broke into a sweat. He kept turning to look behind, stumbling over his feet as he did, but there was nothing to be seen there, while in front the gap with Serghei continued to widen.

'Wait!' Jorge yelled out. 'You said you'd protect me!'

'He lied,' whispered the soft voice from behind him and Jorge staggered to a halt, panting heavily, trying to catch his breath. He sank down, resting his hands on his knees in a half-crouch then looked up. Serghei had stopped about thirty feet away and was standing in the roadway, his legs astride, his arms folded across his stomach.

'Serghei often lies,' the almost lifeless voice continued. 'He was brought up never to tell anyone the truth because in his day it could be dangerous. It still is, Jorge.'

'Costel? Thank God for that.' Jorge sighed in relief. He straightened up and held out his hand.

Potrascu ignored the outstretched hand. 'It's a pity, Jorge,' he said, his voice a sibilant hiss. 'There are times in life when things you've done in the past catch up with you. Serghei knows that. He understands.'

'Is this to do with the police?'

'Police?' Potrascu laughed this time but the voice didn't rise and there was no humour in it. 'In a way, I suppose.'

'I haven't told anyone anything,' said Jorge, suddenly deeply afraid and looking around for an avenue of escape. To the sides were the high walls that barred access to the backs of other houses or shops. No way out past the other two men. 'No one at all!'

'Not even the man you go to meet at the pick-ups on the coast?'

'No one.' Jorge shook his head frantically. 'I kept everything to myself to protect you.'

'Very professional, but stupid. Spreading your knowledge might have made it more difficult for us. Since you told no one, it makes it easier. The loose ends can all be tied up here.'

He came closer and in the faint light of the moon Jorge could finally pick out his features. Sallow and sharp, his head covered in a mass of tight black curls, his neck thick, like that of a bull. But his body was slim and well looked after and he walked lightly, so quietly that Jorge hadn't even heard a footstep until now.

Jorge went to speak but his mouth was dry and no words would come out. He looked to the right, then to the left and behind him towards Serghei who had moved a little closer.

He turned back to Potrascu and saw what he was holding in his hand.

He went cold and his eyes began to bulge. In desperation he threw himself to the right, trying to get out of the way of the man blocking his escape, searching to go somewhere, anywhere away from here as long as he could reach safety. Fear would lend him wings.

But fear did nothing.

As Jorge moved, the ice axe smashed in his left temple, driving the spiked edge into the brain, the steel smashing into the skull and laying it open, killing him instantly. Jorge fell to the ground and Potrascu watched the blood flow out into a puddle spreading around his head.

He moved his polished shoes away, careful not to touch the blood and studied the body for a few moments, as if assuring himself it was all over. Then he leaned down and pulled out the ice axe, took a couple of man-sized tissues from his pocket and wiped the blood from the metal. He tossed the paper into the gutter. It was Jorge's blood and Potrascu was wearing latex surgical gloves. There would be no fingerprints on the tissue. The police would learn nothing from it.

Serghei came up alongside him and looked without expression at the corpse splayed out in the street.

'There are no tattoos to look for,' Potrascu said. His voice sounded heavy with regret. 'But we can't leave it at that, can we?'

Serghei shrugged. It was immaterial to him. 'A man who is dead knows no more pain. He gives no more enjoyment to anyone else.'

'Ah, Serghei, sometimes I despair of you. Unlike our friend in Spain, you have no sense of the artist in you.'

He took a bottle from his pocket, pulled out the glass stopper and poured the clear liquid contents over Jorge's face, watching as it seared into the skin, giving off fumes that stank of roast pork, eating away at the flesh and the eyes deep into the bone.

He carefully replaced the stopper in its bottle. When they reached a suitable location it could be thrown into the river. The bottle first, then the gloves, placed in individual plastic bags and weighted down with bricks so that they would sink.

'He'll be identified anyway,' Potrascu admitted regretfully. 'He's a colourful person and when the police ask around Soho someone will recognise the clothes. But it amuses me and it gives the policemen something to do. Now we can go home.'

They walked away down the alley, vanishing into the darkness.

Jorge Sanchez's faceless body lay on the ground.

The cats began to yowl again.

Monday morning.

The café was full. Around them voices rasped out, higher than might be normal as people tried to talk across the tables.

The air was redolent with the smell of oil from the cooking, the scent of female perfume, the tang of male aftershave.

A sign dangling from a light chain twisted in the breeze each time the entrance door opened or closed. 'PLEASE RETURN YOUR TRAYS HERE.' Hardly anyone did, but Tabor finished the double burger, left the uneaten fries on the tray and took it across to the litter bin to dump.

Once he was comfortable again, Landon plunged in. 'I read the SAS report on you and those from police in Malaga before I went to the Lake District. The flower tattoo on your sister Emma's body? I saw a photograph, but I still don't know what exactly it was.'

'Another orchid. A *Masdevallia veitchiana*. The same genus as on the girl in the morgue. That's why I said the tattooist was doing a series.'

'How do you know so much about orchids?'

'When I was in jail I had access to the Internet. I traced the identity of the orchid tattooed on my sister's body then had a couple of months to look at pictures of other tropical orchids.'

'Why?'

'That should be obvious, even to a copper.'

Landon paused. This had to be played carefully. He needed to keep Tabor hooked.

They were close to a window and he watched as a pigeon landed on the outside windowsill, only inches from the ground. It seemed to be staring inside, looking at the people, its beady eyes watching the food on the tables, waiting for leftovers for the taking. Fat chance, Landon thought.

'I think you still want the people behind Emma's abduction,' he said. Beating about the bush was no way to handle Tabor. 'Killing the man who attacked her wasn't enough. He was sick. You want the people who were sicker, so sick they'd kidnap a child, rape her and force her into prostitution. You want revenge.'

'Revenge is an unfocused emotion,' Tabor said matter-of-factly. 'It's counterproductive. I want justice. I haven't been given it. Why should I help the police?'

'You don't have to, but you may want to help yourself.'

Behind the stony face Landon suspected Tabor was reliving the torment of his sister's killing. The colonel in charge of his unit in Hereford had told him Tabor was an emotional cauldron, usefully channelled for the army's purposes, but always with the capacity to boil over. Tabor was boiling.

'How?' he demanded.

Landon relaxed. Quickly he reiterated the discovery of the girl's body at Burnham and his belief that it, and those of the other girls in Belgium and Holland, along with the sailor, Winters, came from a single vessel. Then he switched to the seemingly unconnected ice-axe murders.

'The link between the girl in the morgue, your sister and the ice-axe murders is a tattoo in the groin. I can link Emma and the Burnham body, thanks to you. In the ice-axe murders there were tattoos but we still don't know exactly what they were. Not enough remained for the pathologists to work on, but they thought it was some kind of intricate flower.'

Tabor sat impassive, listening.

'That's where it stands. There have been three killings in London in the past twenty-two months but we've found no clue as to the murders or reason for them. They're at irregular intervals, the MO always involves the use of the ice axe, prostitutes who are partially stripped, the fact that they can't be identified and the use of acid to burn off their tattoos. More or less that's the sum total of our knowledge.'

The pigeon flew away, his hunger unabated. Other customers came and went from the burger bar but Landon and Tabor stayed, occupying a table, a waitress eyeing them in frustration, as if telling them this was a fast-food place and they weren't being fast enough.

'Now I'll tell you my theory. We've checked on Tom Winters. He came from Burnham-on-Crouch, where the girl was washed ashore. He was known locally as a solid upright worker, but a couple of people we've spoken to think he had smuggling rackets going on the side. A pub manager in Maldon told us Winters occasionally provided cigarettes in bulk, brought across the Channel at cost price. Tourists do it all the time, but it isn't legal to sell the cigarettes. He said Winters would add a little to the cost of the cigarettes "for his trouble". Another man said there might be more to it than cigarettes, but wouldn't amplify other than to suggest "Tom liked the ladies a bit too much".'

He paused, but Tabor did no more than nod to signify he was still listening.

'I think Winters smuggled people from the Continent to England. I believe he was smuggling people that night he drowned and I think they were young prostitutes. There's no proof yet, but I intend to find some. This is where you come in and it's off the record. You're a convicted criminal, on parole and banned from leaving this country. Your passport's been revoked so you can't legally go abroad, but what I want would mean you'd violate that condition and it would land you back in jail if you were caught. I could go to prison too. What I'm asking you to do would force the Met to take action if they found out. They'd have to dismiss me and prosecute me as well. The government doesn't take kindly to CID officers taking matters into their own hands. I can't offer expenses and that's why you only got a B&B last night. I've got you a rail warrant back to Penrith and that's above board. It's the closest I can get you to Wast Water.' He took two envelopes out of his pocket and slid the smaller one across the table. 'There's the warrant and a £50 note for your trouble.'

Tabor left it where it was.

'Where did the £50 come from?'

'Me,' said Landon. 'It won't show on any paperwork.'

'Take it back. If you can't give me officially what I'm entitled to, I don't want anything.'

For a moment they stared at each other, then Landon silently picked up the smaller envelope, took out the banknote, put it into his wallet then handed the envelope back. Tabor left the larger one lying on the table, but scrutinised the warrant before putting it inside his gilet.

'Go on.'

'You don't trust anybody, do you, Tabor?'

'I've got no reason to.'

Landon leaned over the table and his voice dropped a little. 'Like I said, I think Winters was running prostitutes across the Channel. The ice-axe victims were prostitutes and we don't think they were British. The tattoos are clearly linked and you saw the one on Emma in Spain. There's other circumstantial evidence to back up Spain as a focal point, but nothing hard. Nonetheless, I think the chain of prostitution running starts there, perhaps on the Costa del Sol where your sister died. Spanish police haven't been helpful, but, if the girl who died in Burnham was sent here for prostitution, her death, by extension, was murder.'

He stopped and sat back, waiting for Tabor to comment.

'You said you could be prosecuted.' Tabor's face gave away nothing. 'Why take the risk?'

'Personal reasons. You don't need to know what they are, only that they're worth it for me.'

Tabor leaned back, studying the policeman, considering his options. No doubt Landon's reasons would become clear in time. Not that he gave a shit. There were matters to clarify first.

'I want a couple of direct answers,' he said. 'About this operation.'

'Anything I know I'll tell you.'

'The other bodies across the Channel. You said they didn't have tattoos, but what makes you think they were prostitutes?'

'All of the autopsies showed multiple penetration. Some of those kids were barely in their teens. It wasn't a group of girls enjoying a few men's favours in return for a yacht ride. Not unless the girls were rampant nymphomaniacs.'

'Was there anything else abnormal about the girls who were murdered and had their tattoos removed?'

Landon frowned. 'Actually, yes, but it's not straightforward. All had something in their blood the pathologists haven't identified so far. They suspect the girls had taken medicine, or had an injection or other kind of treatment. They were also all in the very early stages of pregnancy. The girls across the Channel weren't pregnant, didn't have tattoos or anything strange in the blood. We don't know about the girl from Burnham yet. I should get her test results later today. The pathologists guessed that the earlier pregnant victims *might* – and they stress might – have developed malformed foetuses. They don't know. They never found an embryo that had gone much past the first-month stage.'

'I need the forensic and pathology reports.'

'Not that fast. First I want something from you. If we have a deal you get the reports.'

Tabor studied him thoughtfully. Then he asked, 'How much do *you* know about orchids?'

'Nothing. You see them around a lot at weddings and that's about my limit.'

'Well, it's not mine,' Tabor said forcefully. 'There were more than eight thousand species at last count and they're finding more every year. Breeders develop new strains all the time. The tattoo on the body in the morgue, *Masdevallia elephanticeps*, is extraordinary. It's not only beautiful, it also has a lip so lightly hinged it can be moved by the slightest touch. There's another *Masdevallia* called *muscosa* that snaps shut when insects land on it. The one tattooed on my sister was also striking. It has a brilliant-orange hue and a shape few laymen would take for being an orchid. That's the thing about *Masdevallias*. They're highly intricate, there are around five hundred varieties and it would take an expert botanist to identify more than a handful. These tattoos haven't been done by a common or garden ink jockey using a transfer from a drawer in a corner parlour. Whoever is doing the *Masdevallia* tattooing is an extraordinary artist.'

Landon was assessing him. Watching the mind work. Neither had relaxed, but for the first time the younger man was almost animated. It was the longest Landon had heard him speak.

'Did you ever speculate why?' Landon asked. *He* had, almost constantly since he saw the first one. He had never found an answer.

'Speculation is a waste of mental effort,' Tabor answered. 'Sufficient proof to act on is all that matters. You said there was other evidence pointing to Spain.'

'I said it wasn't hard evidence, but we've been able to isolate the inks used in the tattoo on the girl at Burnham. A fragment from the skin was enough. That particular shade of yellow comes from dyes only produced by one manufacturer and it's in Spain.'

Tabor's eyebrows rose slightly.

'There's something else. I was late getting here today because I was called to a murder scene in Soho. A man called Sanchez, in his mid-forties. He didn't have a tattoo, but he was killed with an ice axe and his face was burned off with sulphuric acid. Before Sanchez came to London he worked in brothels in Spain, mostly on the Costa del Sol.'

It was almost the only bait he had. If Tabor didn't bite now he possibly never would.

Landon stood up abruptly from the table.

'That's it. Spain, brothels, tattoos. All I know and all I can tell you. There's no point in keeping you any longer.'

'Spell it out,' Tabor growled. 'I want to hear you say it.'

Landon sighed. 'OK,' he said. 'I want you to go to Spain, learn who's doing the tattoos and find a link to the man killing tattooed prostitutes in London. I thought it was clear.'

'Not clear enough. Why should I do this? You're the police.'

'I can't ask anyone on the force. We can't operate in another country unless we're invited,' Landon admitted. It was his last attempt. 'You have the best motivation. You're desperate to find the men behind your sister's abduction and I think the same men are behind the prostitute running to Britain and the ice-axe murders in London. It's the same people and to my way of thinking we would have a mutual purpose in working together.'

Tabor said nothing.

Landon waited a few moments then shrugged. 'Thanks for listening.' He picked up the larger envelope from the table. 'These are documents I brought on the off-chance you'd agree, but since you're not interested I'll take them away. If you change your mind you can call me through the switchboard at New Scotland Yard. Goodbye, Tabor. Sorry I troubled you.'

Tabor followed Landon into the street and took him by the shoulder.

'What's the deal?'

'Not a very good one. You get a free hand as far as I'm concerned, but that won't help you much. You can handle everything however you want,' Landon answered, trying to hide his satisfaction. He held up the large envelope. 'Use your own methods and run your own risks. All I can give you are these, the reports I mentioned.'

Tabor inclined his head slightly, as if in agreement.

'If you discover anything, you tell me,' Landon went on. 'We're talking about the business of running girls from the Costa del Sol to Britain and redistributing them to British brothels. That's organised crime and I want the bastards behind it.'

He paused for a moment. 'I can use my resources to track down anything you want that emerges in Spain. Any paperwork that needs to be chased, background searches on people you think could be involved, even peripherally. There's the caveat I indicated earlier. If you get caught doing anything illegal, being where you shouldn't be, I can't help you. You're a convicted killer who should be in jail as far as the Spanish are concerned. If you find what you want you'll probably do something that will put you in jail for life, but that's your business. It's not much of a deal, but it's the best I can offer.'

'I'll take it,' said Tabor, reaching for the envelope.

'Thank you.' Landon smiled. He hadn't believed it would work. In truth, he was offering Tabor nothing and asking for a great deal.

'What's the rest? You said there'd be more help once I agreed.'

'The documents in that envelope,' Landon answered. 'I told you there's something in the blood of all the victims that can't be identified but that might lead to malformed foetuses, like in the old Thalidomide days.'

'Are you saying that happened to Emma?'

'We don't know because we didn't have her blood. But I'm working on the theory the ice-axe killer is fixated with prostitutes who have a tattoo of orchids in their groin, and that the tattooing is being done in Spain. I think that the girls with the tattoos, along with other prostitutes who aren't tattooed, are being smuggled in small boats across the channel. My hypothesis is that the girls are killed *because* they get pregnant and that it's connected to the possible malformations. So there's another part to this mission. I want you to do what I can't: find the tattooist and the reason behind the orchids, find the people who smuggle the girls to Britain, and give me the names of the people in London who run the handling here. That will give me the ice-axe killer. You get the men behind Emma's abduction and imprisonment in that brothel. I can't do it without you. I don't think you can do it without me and the resources I can use this end.'

Landon took a card from his jacket pocket.

'I've written my mobile number on it,' he said, handing it over. 'And my email address. Don't contact me on any voice phone. You know as well as I do they can be intercepted. Use encrypted email for anything lengthy. Your file says you understand encryption and decryption. For anything very short, four or five words, send me a text message. Send the decryption key the same way. Are you certain you won't take back that £50?'

'Positive. Which station do I need for Penrith?'

'Euston. Fifteen minutes' walk away. There's a train in about an hour. Good luck. You're going to need it.'

Tabor was already turning away when Landon called out to him. 'There's something else,' he said. 'Something you should know.'

'What?'

'I was going to tell you earlier but there was no point

unless you agreed to what I want. I checked with the Spanish police before I went to see you yesterday. The papers were never sent to Hereford so you may not know. Your sister was pregnant, Tabor. Three months. If you hadn't intervened the way you did, sooner or later someone would have used an ice axe on her anyway.'

Seven

Puerto Banus, Costa del Sol.

She was, he thought, quite delicious. From the spacious lounge of the ocean-going yacht, he studied her through the open door of the bathroom, walking from the shower to the other side of the room where the dressing table was surrounded by make-up lights. She was naked.

She walked like a model, back straight, breasts tight and uplifted, her stomach flat. Her hair shone as if it were spun black silk, down to the middle of her back. Her fingers were long and slender like those of a piano player.

You're a lucky man, Iain Duncan reminded himself again. Not that luck had anything to do with it. Money bought its own luck. Money for the girl, money for the yacht on which they were anchored in the harbour in Puerto Banus, money for the crew that tended his every need, including the chef he'd flown in from Paris for the next month. If the guy continued to cook as well as he had up to now, Duncan might take him back to California with him. He was growing irritated by his Italian chef at the house in La Jolla, whose dishes, at first definitive, now seemed tired and repetitive. French cuisine might be a change for the better.

Duncan reached over to the glass-topped coffee table close to the settee where he was lounging, picked up the half-empty bottle of champagne and filled his flute. Champagne was not his alcohol of first choice. He preferred liquor with a stronger kick, but the girl liked it and he liked the girl.

The television set was switched on, but the sound was muted and he wasn't watching. He'd spent much of the early afternoon talking by satellite phone to his number two, Jerry Ferdetta in San Diego, keeping him in touch with developments at Duncan's personally owned corporation Cytek.

But the time for business was over. At the moment he was much more interested in the moving patterns cast by the girl on the mirrored walls around the bathroom, reflecting her nakedness in a dozen or more different ways.

She had put her wet hair up in a towel, and wrapped another around her body leaving her arms and shoulders clear. She came out carrying a hairdryer.

He stared at the band-aid on her arm.

'The bruise is ugly,' he murmured.

'I always get one,' she said hesitantly. 'After . . .'

'I know.' He touched the dressing lightly and caressed her shoulder. 'Not much longer.'

'I don't mind,' she flashed, panic written instantly across her face. 'It doesn't hurt. Not really.'

'Don't stress yourself out,' he said soothingly. 'You tense up every time you go there. They don't hurt you, do they?'

'They . . .' She let the words hang there, her head low, choking back the tears. Tears wouldn't help. He hated tears.

He took the towel from her hair, running his finger through the wet strands, then took the hairdryer from her and plugged it in, using the nozzle to direct it over her head and the hair hanging down the back, teasing the strands so that they dried.

The hot air tickled her back and she shivered involuntarily. When it was dry he switched it off and laid the dryer aside.

'Would you like some more champagne?'

She shook her head, making the hair drift around her face and back.

'Are we going out?' She had a voice like a mountain stream, rippling and clear. Her Eastern European accent was delicate and inviting.

'Whatever you want.' Duncan was an accommodating man.

'Choose for me,' she said quietly.

'Dinner? A run offshore and a midnight swim?'

'We could do both. Go out a few miles then the chef can cook.'

'He could,' Duncan agreed mildly. 'But he's not much of a sailor and if there's any kind of swell out there he might not be up to his best.'

'But the boat is stabilised. It does not roll at all.'

'Tell that to the chef.'

'You are the boss. You tell him what to do and he does it.'

'I can.' Duncan laughed lightly. 'But you don't know a lot about chefs of this quality. If I tell him to do something he doesn't want to do, he'll down knives and walk off. He can get a new post faster than I can find a new chef.'

'I don't understand,' she answered, puzzled. 'In Bucharest people do what their bosses tell them.'

He was going to say something when the phone on the table rang.

He picked it up and listened. 'Fine,' he said, and hung up. He sank the champagne in the flute, and stood up.

'Change of plan,' he said as he came up behind her, and

unfastened the towel, allowing it to drop to the floor. 'We're going to the casino.'

'Wonderful,' she said, her face breaking into a strained smile. She'd been there four nights earlier, the first time he took her out, and played roulette with a thousand dollars of his money while he talked business with friends. She came back with four thousand dollars, which he promptly told her to keep. She had never seen four thousand dollars in her life before. She'd never seen four hundred. All she'd managed to save until now was thirteen euros and she'd been in Spain for the past eight months.

Duncan stared at what he perceived to be delight on her face. Still a child. She had a right to show her emotions. The thing that mattered was she looked older and in public carried herself with the poise of a twenty-one-year-old.

He put his hand over her naked groin, tracing the tattoo there, and leaned over to kiss her on the left nipple.

'No hurry,' he said softly in her ear. 'We've got a couple of hours to while away yet.'

Eight

New Scotland Yard, London.

Landon was by the window, watching the pedestrians filing by like parading ants. He often stood there, staring at the activity below as if in some way it could act as a stimulant to his thoughts. Sometimes it did. Often, as now, it was a waste of time.

Right now, he thought, Tabor was on his way back to the Lake District and his life was about to lurch in a new direction. If he could, he would have left Tabor well alone. His life had been turbulent enough already, but there *was* no alternative. Landon had used emotional blackmail, he had lied, and now he had placed Tabor in extreme jeopardy.

But he had no choice.

The ice-axe killings had hit a brick wall. No evidence, no witnesses. The key lay in Spain and, as far as Landon was concerned, the Spanish were not being helpful. There were no grounds for a British policeman to investigate Spanish infringements to their laws. Madrid had a unit dedicated to the trafficking of illegal aliens, and merely said they would contact Scotland Yard if they had any evidence of illegal transport of children from Spain to Britain. They hadn't, and Landon had been waiting eighteen months. He had asked for permission to go to Spain without invitation and that had been flatly rejected. He had nowhere to move.

That was why he turned to Tabor.

He thought of the SAS files on the killing of Tabor's sister, and his heart ached for her. Once again he wondered if he was doing this for the right reasons. Personal, he had told Tabor. Perhaps too personal. His mind switched to his wife, Helen, sitting in her bedroom at home, looking out of her window as he was looking down from this one in his office. Would she approve of what he was doing? A rhetorical question and he would never ask her.

He shook his thoughts free, left the window and the human ants and picked up the file from his desk.

The first murdered girl had been found in an alleyway in Whitechapel. Her upper clothing was intact, but the other garments were nowhere to be found. Her blouse and bra had been laundered so many times that nothing of use was found in their examination. A task force was assembled, houses canvassed, informers questioned. By the second day, they had learned she was a prostitute, but no one would narrow it down to any specific streets she worked. The people they spoke to were vague to the point of evasion, but not to the extent that any could be charged with failure to disclose evidence. The media picked up on the ice-axe method of killing and speculated about a psychopath and a possible new wave of Ripper murders, but news is ephemeral. It needs fresh material to fuel the fires of interest and after a couple of weeks it died down. After three months of investigation the task force was stood down and the case left with Landon's unit.

Four months later the second girl was found on the landing of a flight of stairs in an apartment block in West Ham.

The circumstances were identical apart from the location. The lower items of clothing had again been torn off, but there was no other injury to the girl except for the blow with the ice axe and the damage done by the acid. Normally in such killings there were bruises and scratches to indicate violent assault. Not with these two cases. The CSI and forensic experts compared notes to the first attack and decided the girls were killed elsewhere and moved to where they were found. Once again a team gathered to canvass everyone in the block and those nearby. No one admitted seeing anything.

They used the HOLMES relational database to compare the murders to any others that might show a pattern. Again nothing.

Often in such cases someone felt a need to contact the police, to taunt them for their inadequacies if for no other reason. This time no one made contact.

Local prostitutes were interviewed. None admitted anything.

It was nearly another year before the third case, in Maida Vale. This time the body was dumped on a main street in the middle of the night and found by a police patrol car.

The media raised the Ripper theory again and once more a trickle of information came in and was analysed, but nothing led any further. With no more killings media focus again faded. There had been no mention of the prostitute murders in the newspapers or on television for months now. Landon preferred to keep it that way. Some CID officers thought publicity sparked valuable information. Landon's opinion was that sensationalism generated by killings such as this was usually counterproductive. From the start he insisted that no mention of the tattoos be leaked. It sometimes seemed to him that half of the young girls in the country had tattoos nowadays. Disclosure of that could lead to copycats and add to the police confusion.

At the heart of the puzzle were the reasons for the destruction of the tattoos, and why all of those killed had them in the same place. Now he could reasonably assume they were all a particular species of orchid that had first been seen in a brothel in Spain.

He accepted the killings were the work of a psychopath, but experience told him that to ascribe everything to that was simplistic. It appeared to him this killer was working to order: eliminating only prostitutes with orchid tattoos and erasing them, as part of a wider plan.

The reason had to lie in the changes in the girls' blood that pathologists couldn't identify. But their theory that it may have led eventually to malformed foetuses couldn't be substantiated because the pregnancies hadn't developed sufficient for further examination.

The file now in his hand was that on the girl from Burnham. Minutes earlier he had added the report on her blood test. The girl was pregnant, but only by a few weeks. Insufficient to show anything more, but her death had opened the door that Landon had now, thanks to Tabor, walked through. That door linked the ice-axe killer to Emma and Spain.

As he had said to Tabor, there was no proof the killer was anything more than someone with a fixation on ice axes, acid and prostitutes with an orchid tattoo in their groin. No proof that anyone was running prostitutes from Spain to England. If there were such a chain, there was no proof that it had any connection with the ice-axe killer. Circle incomplete.

All he had was the vision in his mind of the girl on the mud bank, the photo once seen of Emma on the bed in the brothel, and Tabor, a man he had possibly sent to end up in a Spanish jail. Or dead.

A knock on the door aroused Landon from his reverie.

Detective Inspector Ruth Hartley had just passed thirty.

Slim, without paying particular attention to staying that way, eating and drinking what she wanted. Sensible, some people would say. Fortunate, she admitted to herself. Her hair was naturally blonde and stylishly cut around a face that owed nothing to additional make-up. Her eyes were like sloes, her gaze always watchful.

She dressed well if not expensively. Right now she was wearing a dark-blue trouser suit, with a white blouse showing discreetly underneath, the cut of the clothes silhouetting her body. At five foot ten she was one of the tallest women in the Met, but that had its disadvantages in personal terms.

He had heard other officers talking about her behind her back. Legs up to her chin, snotty and aloof, up herself or even a dyke. All tales spread by colleagues she'd held at arm's length. To others, who had no interest in her body, or those that worked with her closely like the other two men on Landon's team, she was a highly competent police officer who put in long hours, and got results.

It helped that she gave credit to them when things went right, carried her share of the blame when things went wrong. The way Landon had taught her.

As far as he was concerned, she was incomparable.

She sat down and opened the file she laid on the desk in front of him, but he waved it shut.

Hartley looked puzzled. 'I thought you wanted an update on the Soho murder?'

She could see Landon was tired. His brow was furrowed and the lines around his eyes showed lack of sleep.

'I already know what it says,' he answered. His voice sounded weary, she thought. 'I read the midday edition of the *Standard*. Another mystery killing, but at least they didn't know about the ice axe. You'll tell me the pathologists confirmed our suspicion about the weapon but there are no other clues. You've got a couple of extra people working on his old haunts and known associates, but nobody is saying anything. Right?'

'Right.' Landon hadn't called her in for a social chat and he wasn't a man to beat around the bush.

In the main office, photographs of the three ice-axe victims were displayed on the chalkboard, white lines leading to a central question mark at the bottom. It was standard practice and normally there would be a tentative theory written there. So far there was none. Landon had left it blank because, until this past two weeks and the girl washed up at Burnham, no one had come up with anything plausible. In truth, no one had looked at the board for weeks. Now Hartley would add a picture of Sanchez if Landon thought it necessary, and replace the question mark with a theory. If he had one that he was ready to talk about yet.

'I've brought the file on the prostitutes too,' she said. 'If you recall, the profiler says the killer is a male psychopath, probably mid- to late thirties, with a hatred of women or at least a dismissive attitude to them. When I talked off the record to him after the last one in Maida Vale he said the killer seemed to regard women as cockroaches to be stepped on if they cross his path. That doesn't square with the Soho male this morning.'

She closed the file and sat waiting for his comments. Landon didn't go off into wild speculation and waste time and energy as some of the other CID team leaders did. He was focused and usually ahead of the game. But she could see that right now he had something on his mind. Was that to do with the murders? Why was he so tired?

He was staring back at her, as if weighing her in the balance.

He leaned forward. 'Drop everything else and pick up on the tattoos again,' he said.

Hartley frowned quizzically.

'You take charge,' Landon continued. 'Get a photo of the girl from Burnham and put that on the wall too. I'll be in the background from now on. I can't let you have any extra men, you'll have to rely on DS Field or DC Rogers and only bring in others if there's anything specific. Field's a good man and authority's what he needs at this stage. The same with Rogers.'

'Are you going to tell me why, sir?'

Landon sat back and smiled weakly at her. 'The Soho killing may or may not be linked but I'm certain the tattoo on the girl in Burnham is, even though there's no evidence. But you want to know why I'm stepping aside. Two reasons. Both of them stay in this room. The first is that my wife is dying.'

He held up his hand to silence her as she went to comment.

'Don't bother. We've known it was coming for some time. Two days ago they confirmed the cancer had spread and said she can't live more than a few weeks longer. We're prepared and you know our marriage hasn't exactly been a bed of roses.'

Hartley had heard the gossip that Landon and his wife hadn't slept in the same bed for years. They were never seen out together and they attended as few police social functions as politically possible. Most of the CID staff had never seen her.

'The Super told me to take all the time I need so that's what I'm doing. I won't lie to you. There won't be a lot of wailing and weeping when Helen dies. We've done all we need to of that in the past, but she *is* dying and I've got a responsibility to make it as easy as I can for her over the next few weeks. So I won't be in the office much of the time and you have to take over on the tattoos. Put everything else aside until I get back. From here on it's your only case. If I didn't think you could handle it I'd tell you so and bring in someone else. As far as I'm concerned you're the best there is.'

'Thank you, sir.' Hartley felt a flush of uncomfortable pride that he felt so highly of her. She quashed it. 'But I still don't understand why the sudden urgency. Why not wait until you feel you can take over again? There are other things we can do.'

'This is the most important thing there is, Ruth, and right now, after two years of getting nowhere, you can make headway. It's not only because of Helen that I'm stepping back. I've done something I have no right to do and it could compromise the investigation if it gets out.'

'Then undo it. Why wreck your career on an impulse when you've spent your whole life sticking by the rules?'

'Maybe I haven't been as saintly as you think,' he said heavily. 'But that's not what I mean. I've told you before that I think there's some kind of organised operation involving these murders and the tattoos and they're not confined to Britain.'

'I saw the requests you sent out for help from the authorities in Madrid. You asked for details of people who control brothels on the Costa del Sol and anything they have on prostitute smuggling between here and Spain, as well as clinics that may be performing illegal medical activities in the area. You never did say why you wanted that kind of information.'

'They gave us nothing anyway, but the authorities in Spain have their ways of handling things.' He shoved back his chair, stood up and paced to the window.

'I've chosen a different method to get the information, without the hierarchy knowing. I've asked to go over there to investigate and been turned down. It's illegal to hire a civilian to do it for me, even without payment, but I'm doing it anyway. So, as of this moment, I'm on compassionate leave, but unofficially I'm staying in touch in an advisory capacity.' He turned to face her. 'From time to time I may have snippets of information from one special source, but I'll be the only contact and if it comes to nothing no one else will ever know. I don't want you to tell anyone else, not even Field and Rogers. I don't want you to put my theory on the chalkboard either. Not yet. If anything blows up it has to be my face it explodes in, not yours.'

'How does this source tie into the tattoo on the girl in Burnham? And why Spain?'

'He saw a similar tattoo when he was in a brothel in Spain two years ago. He thinks there's a possible link. So do I. It's the first break we've had, but the boss would turn it down flat if I suggested it. The man's banned from returning to Spain.' He hesitated a moment. 'You shouldn't know too much. It could compromise you if things go wrong, but you should know the man killed someone, that's why he can't go back. He's on parole and his passport has been withdrawn.'

'If anyone finds out, your career is gone.'

'I accept that.'

'Why?'

'Personal reasons.' He knew he was on thin ice. Anyone other than Hartley would report it instantly. He had to trust her. 'Professional ones too. We're getting nowhere with this case and we need a break. My source could help create it.'

He stood there for a moment, rocking slightly on the balls of his feet.

'That's it, Ruth,' he said finally. 'It's your ball. Pick it up and run with it.'

It was her dismissal. Hartley took her file and stood up. She hesitated for a moment more.

'Sir,' she said quietly, 'I *am* sorry. About your wife.'

'No need to be,' he said. 'She's the one dying, not me. She says it will be a relief to escape from a wasted life. That was to make me feel guilty. Well, I do. You don't have to feel bad for anyone.'

'Only you,' she answered levelly.

She turned and left the room.

Nine

Cumbria. Early afternoon.

Cities, towns and villages sped by through the south, past the Midlands, heading steadily towards the north. It was a pleasant day and Tabor had little to do except watch the changing scenery unfold, pages in a book, each new chapter telling its own story about the variety of England. The train took hours to reach Penrith, allowing him plenty of time to mull over the meeting with Landon.

He was concerned that Landon had found him. It was feasible that the army told the police where he was or he'd discovered the location through the parole system, but Tabor doubted the SAS would have passed on anything. He'd been dishonourably discharged, but the men and officers of the company wrapped themselves around each other and kept their secrets, and Tabor's parole records didn't mention the cottage at Wast Water. He reported to the parole office in Lancaster and his address on their records was that of an old friend in Ambleside, but Landon hadn't mentioned that at all. Why?

A mystery. Tabor switched off. Some twisted mysteries need time to unravel.

North of the Midlands he stood up and stretched to ease the stiffness of sitting so long, then made his way down the coach to the toilet. He locked the door, unbuttoned his trousers and reached for the hidden pocket sewn in the waistband. Forethought. Always have an emergency exit. Money was one of the most valuable. He pulled out two £50 notes, a £20 and a £10, and put them into his gilet pocket. He refastened the trousers and flushed the toilet for effect before unlocking the door and returning along the rolling carriageway to his seat.

Tabor learned years earlier that cash or important documents such as passports or driving licences should never be put into an easily accessible pocket. The best pickpockets could even steal from someone trained to detect their touch. Inside the trousers no one could get at them.

He got off the train at Kendal and waited outside the station for fifteen minutes to see if he was being followed. A couple of other men left the train at the same time, but soon friends or colleagues arrived to pick them up and he was alone in the slight breeze blowing across the National Park.

In town he found a taxi. Half an hour later he was in Windermere.

It was a roundabout route and Landon had ticketed him to Penrith, but it could be under surveillance. Although he was out of the SAS now, terrorists have long memories and solid grudges they harbour forever. Being 'recruited' the way he had, so illegally, signalled caution to him. He needed to be aware of everything and everybody again, as he had been before they threw him out of the Unit. Some would say it was paranoia, based on his years of covert operations, but it was too late to change his way of life now. And Landon *had* found him in Cumbria. The policeman might be telling the truth about the prostitute-smuggling ring, but equally he might have an ulterior motive that hadn't been disclosed. If he did, then having someone follow Tabor would be a natural course of action, no matter what Landon might say to his face.

Safety demanded trusting no one. Tabor had chosen Kendal because it was small enough for anyone checking on arriving passengers to stand out.

Nevertheless, he walked around Windermere for ten minutes before he was satisfied he was clear. He went into a pub and ordered a half of lager, handed over the £10 note and waited for the change then crossed to a public phone in the corner and dialled a number. He spoke quickly, finished his drink and left then strolled to the boat pier on the edge of the lake and sat waiting on a bollard.

The late evening was dropping over the hills and he could see a pale wedge of moon fighting to take shape against the dying rays of the sun. Wavelets danced over the water and lapped at the hulls of moored boats. Birds swooped low over the lake, picking up the last insects of the day. Leaves on the trees along the shore waved in lethargic motion. Soon it would be autumn and the leaves would turn red and gold and yellow and the surrealism of nature would be freely visible to all. This was the place. These lakes, these hills, these fresh fields and moors dotted with their ancient monuments and clean shallow rivers. This was his only real home. This was where he felt at peace. Waiting, watching, staring at its beauty made time immaterial.

Until now he'd had plenty of it.

Half an hour later the small motorboat landed him at Ambleside and Tabor waited while the owner tied up the vessel and came across to him. He handed over a set of car keys.

'Next time try to come back at a reasonable time,' he growled.

'Thanks, Davey,' said Tabor, smiling at him. 'I'll bring her back tomorrow morning.'

'I know you will,' David Reed said grumpily. 'Or I'll have your guts for garters.'

Tabor laughed lightly. It was an old joke but Reed was an old man, a grandfatherly figure he'd known all his life.

'Can I drop you off on the way?' Tabor asked as they strolled up to the rusty Vauxhall Astra that Reed had owned for at least the last fifteen years. It was past MOT stage when he bought it.

'Like where? You know where I'm going and if I have too many the landlord will bring me back. Take care of my car but be careful with her. You drive like a bloody maniac. I ought to know better than to let you touch her.'

'I'll treat her as if she were your mother.'

'I'd rather you treat her like she was your own,' Reed flashed back, but the look of dismay that shot across his face was instantaneous. He went to say something but Tabor reached out and touched him on the shoulder.

'So would I, Davey,' he said softly. 'But we'll make do with your mother anyway.'

Ten

Sierra de Las Nieves, Andalucia. Early evening.

It was the hot section of the orchid houses and the humidity was high. Blake sweated as he bent a little closer to the golden lip of the plant in front of him.

Phalaenopsis Golden Sands was a most remarkable hybrid, shown off to perfection by the long sprays of arching waxy flowers. In very few species of the *Phalaenopsi*s was any yellow colouring found and only in the *leuddmanniana* group. Breeding traces of true yellow had proven impossible until the 1960s, despite decades of attempts by the finest orchid experts. Then along came *Golden Sands.* It had a definite orange-yellow lip and mottling of the same colour on the remainder of the plant. It was also meristemmed. In layman's terms it was cloned, and used in the commercial world to mass-produce orchids for the general market, but mostly the *Phalaenopsis* genus had defied meristemming. *Golden Sands* was an exception and a definite requirement in any orchid collection, despite its expense.

His eyes roved once more over it then he stood up and straightened his back. The hot section was the one he loved most because of the incredible beauty of some of the plants, but it wasn't a place to remain for hours on end. Already he'd been in the orchid rooms for the past two hours, working mostly in the cool or intermediate sections where he did the bulk of his breeding of new hybrids. It was exacting and time-consuming work, involving flask culture, but with orchids no two hybrids were alike and the varieties had proven endless. That made them interesting, but for Blake it was also a frustration.

What he wanted was perfection.

Anything that did not breed true, animal or plant, must by definition be imperfect.

Blake was determined that one day he would develop a hybrid that would breed true by seed culture, not by cloning. It was at the heart of his life's work.

That and *Tatú*.

The thought of *Tatú* brought him out of the serene contemplation of his orchids. He glanced at the clock. It was time to get changed for the meeting. It was yet another intrusion on one of his passions, but it was necessary and time was limited.

In a couple of weeks the fighting season in Spain would be over and he would go to Mexico to follow the bulls and look for more orchids on the illicit collector network.

In the meantime, there was the other work. *Tatú* called. *Tatú* was the culmination of everything. *Tatú* was everything.

Tatú would change the world.

A little patience, but soon.

Very, very soon.

Eleven

The Lake District, Cumbria.

The road from Ambleside led to Skelwith Bridge and turned off on a moorland road towards Hard Knott Pass. In winter such roads were occasionally impassable, but at this time of year there was no problem. Tabor reached Nether Wasdale before ten o'clock, but dowsed the lights more than half a mile away from his home and parked. He locked the door before walking over the fields towards the cottage, pausing from time to time to listen to the sounds of the night or anything that shouldn't be there. As he passed through the glade where he'd been training with the crossbow, he picked up the fallen weapon and quarrels and fitted one before he moved off again.

He walked carefully, stopping frequently, until he came within yards of the building. Then he skirted his home, checking it from all angles.

No one was there.

Moments later he was inside, locking the door behind him and closing the internal shutters before he switched on the light.

He went across the room and rolled back a large carpet that covered the floor almost wall to wall, unlocked the trapdoor, lifted it and went down into the darkness of the cellar. Only after he'd closed the trapdoor did he switch on the cellar lights.

Tabor had made no external changes to the property after he bought it, but there were alterations beneath the house where, for nearly two centuries, the cellar was used as a refuge when storms ripped away the roof. This cellar was now unlike any refuge anyone had ever seen. Around the walls were locked armaments of every kind. Automatic rifles of old as well as most modern military makes, shotguns, normal sporting and pump action, a variety of pistols, revolvers and automatics, three sniper's rifles and four grenade launchers. In the harsh glare of the fluorescent lighting overhead, the metal parts flashed like blue steel. The wooden stocks shone with oil and the fibreglass parts were clean and polished.

There were a number of crossbows and three fibreglass target bows, together with knives of all kinds. In the epicentre of the armament mosaic was a long blowpipe, twenty barbs hanging delicately from a rack beneath it.

Most of the weapons were used to train two- or three-man teams of mercenaries, mostly for operations in Africa and South America. Others would have trained the men if Tabor hadn't and he was better skilled than most of them, which meant that with his reputation he could charge more. He had no moral scruples about that, but it *was* illegal and that was another reason he was so wary of Landon.

The small arms had no ammunition and Tabor sold no guns: that was up to the clients after they left him at Wast Water. There were enough people ready and willing to supply them with the arms they would need. The variety of weapons was there partly because Tabor liked guns, much as other men liked fast cars, but also because he wanted anyone who left his courses to be conversant with everything from antique Springfields of the American Civil War through to modern weapons from NATO and the former Warsaw Pact.

He crossed to the heavy iron safe in the corner. It wouldn't have defeated a safebreaker but the combined value of the arms in this room was far more than anything the safe contained.

He dialled the combination, opened the safe, took out the small stack of banknotes and put them on one side. It included sterling, US notes of various denominations and at least 2,000 in euros, paid by cash-only clients for services rendered. In six months he'd earned more than £50,000, all tax-free. Had he been able to go abroad officially and work for a security firm, or on loan to a multinational conglomerate training bodyguards, he could have earned four times that amount in a year, but until his parole concluded he couldn't sign up for anything like that. In any case, he didn't want to. For the moment the illegal sideline provided money enough. The future would look after itself.

He took out a tin box that had once held shortbread biscuits, and lifted the lid. The authorities had taken his passport from him, but there were many ways to get others. Inside the box were half a dozen envelopes containing British passports in different names. The Passport Office had legitimately issued all of them, with official forms. Only the identification documents supplied to the Passport Office with the forms were fake. Tabor took out one in the name of Ransome. Other documents he might need in the same name, such as a driving licence and NHS card, were in the same envelope.

He climbed back up the steps, switching off the cellar light as he did, locked the trapdoor and rolled back the carpet to hide any trace of the hidden access.

He put the banknotes and the passport on to a sideboard then went into the kitchen and made a mug of coffee.

He was thinking about his mother and Emma.

The two commanding forces in his life and both of them dead in ways he nowadays never spoke about, not even to Davey.

In particular he was remembering the first time he ran away, the day his mother told him she was having another baby. He ran off on to the moors that now surrounded him in this house, and shivered away the night, ignoring the calls of search teams trying to find him but imagining he was going to die. The way he eventually struggled home and cried to his mother that he didn't want to die like that, and she hugged him and told him he wouldn't because he was a survivor.

And he remembered the scrawny little baby his mother never saw. Numbly he tried to wipe the memories from his mind. They did no good.

Thoughts were destructive. Action was the only thing that mattered.

He went into the bedroom, pulled a holdall from under the bed and started packing. Finally he went into the bathroom and showered under cold water, hoping it would drive his thoughts away. He towelled himself dry, returned to the bedroom and lay on top of the blankets. He closed his eyes but couldn't sleep. The memories were too stubborn. Too close. Too raw. He stared at the ceiling until his eyes grew weary and, eventually, he drifted into a disturbed and fitful sleep.

Twelve

Marbella, Costa del Sol. Night.

He ushered her into the casino and saw men's eyes swivel to stare at her.

She was wearing a full-length white silk sheath dress, accentuating her figure to perfection. It was clear from the lack of ridges that she was wearing no underwear. The dress shimmered as she glided across the floor and the contrast with the black, lustrous hair hanging down her back was stunning. Every eye followed her and every man glanced enviously at Duncan. It was worth every cent he'd paid for the dress. This was his first chance to show her off wearing it and he revelled in it.

He had sent her to a beautician to have her make-up applied, and at the same time they had used concealer to hide the bruise from any casual glance.

He held her arm possessively and ushered her inside, nodding to three or four people as he passed, but not stopping to speak or introduce her to anyone. Duncan was carrying a large box, wrapped in plain white paper, neatly taped all around. Guards at the door would have demanded other people leave the box with them until departure but for Duncan it was not an issue.

He went over to the bar, put the box on a stool beside him and ordered a bottle of champagne. He sat there with her while she sipped at the golden liquid bubbling in the flute, her face aglow. Such a child, he thought. Such a beautiful, sensuous child.

He felt the tap on his shoulder and turned around.

'Hi, Felix,' he said, holding out his hand and smiling.

Blake accepted the hand with his own limp fingers then stared pointedly at the girl.

'She's going off to play the wheel, I guess,' Duncan said affably. 'We'll go to a table to talk. Costel will be here soon. Meanwhile, I've got a present for you.'

He handed Blake the box from the stool then turned to the girl and refilled her glass. He leaned over and whispered in her ear. 'Go play. I put a thousand bucks in your purse before we left the boat. Have a good time. I'll be back in an hour or so.'

She watched them thread their way to a table at the far end of the room and sit down. She knew Blake, disliked him intensely and preferred him not to be close to her, but it was when the other man walked in, caught sight of Duncan and started to cross towards him that the colour drained slowly from her face. She started to shiver. Panic churned in her stomach and she had to choke back the bile rising in her throat.

She picked up her glass but her hand was shaking. She couldn't hold it still. The champagne spilled on to the dress and soaked into her thigh.

She could feel the terror and knew it must be showing on her face. She got up from the bar stool, her evening bag clutched tightly in her hand, and walked as quickly as she could, trying to maintain some semblance of decorum, desperate to reach the safety of the powder room.

Once inside she went into a cubicle and sat down on the seat, shivering and shaking, with tears of desperation welling up into her eyes. She grabbed some tissues and dabbed her eyes but they kept running. She fought back the tears and breathed in, trying to quench her panic, squeezing her eyes shut to black out the memories of that room.

The stainless-steel instruments in the tray glistened under the powerful surgery lights. They were laid out with military precision: scalpels, scissors, forceps, clamps, retractors, dilators and injection needles with an array of tips and tubes.

Light flashes bounced from them, as if inviting further inspection but serving only to increase her terror.

The bed felt hard beneath her shoulder blades; the light burned into her eyes. She wanted to scream, wanted them to stop what they were going to do, but no words came and the fear kept growing inside her, so much she felt she would explode.

She sensed rather than saw the nurse bending over her, the needle in her hand, flicking it professionally with a finger to ensure there was no air and then it was coming towards her and the scream erupted from her mouth.

The needle touched her arm. She was unconscious even before the anaesthetic worked into her.

Slowly she pulled herself together.

Duncan was right. While she remembered the surgery so vividly, she also recalled there was no physical pain, and she was asleep for several hours afterwards. Each time she left there was another layer of shadowing, or colour to add to the tattoo in her groin. The flower that would always be there to display her shame.

If she lived for very much longer.

After a time she felt composed enough to look at her hands. They were steady.

She stood up, hoping she wouldn't faint, opened the toilet door and went to look at herself in the mirror. Her eyes were red from where she had rubbed them and beneath them the skin was swollen. She bathed her face in cold water and waited, breathing deeply.

Half an hour later she walked back on to the floor of the casino. It had filled out and there were crowds around the gaming tables. Waitresses flitted about carrying trays of drinks, slipping between the players with an enviable and assured dexterity, the product of long training.

Duncan was still with the other two men, his hands moving as he emphasised point after point. He was doing most of the talking. Blake was saying nothing and only from time to time did the third man, the one called Costel Potrascu, interject with brief comments.

From this distance she could see Duncan had a glass of bourbon on the table, while Blake had nothing, not even a glass of water. Potrascu was drinking what looked like straight vodka, but that was not his normal drink. What he drank could not be found in the casino, only in his home. Potrascu liked *palinca*, distilled to maximum strength, and rarely found outside its homeland. It was very special, brought over from the Apuseni Mountains of Romania in his home village outside Rogojel.

She too came from the village, in the days of her innocence.

She had to calm her nerves again as she thought about it, thought about everything. Then she edged as steadily as she could manage to the roulette table, took out her thousand dollars in hundred-dollar bills and changed them for chips.

Mechanically, unnerved by the presence of Potrascu in the corner, she watched the roulette wheel spin.

Three-quarters of an hour later Duncan came across, put his hands on her shoulders and leaned down to kiss her on the ear. She shook her head, as if the kiss had been a fly landing on her.

'Are you winning?' he asked softly, holding on to her shoulders, kneading his fingers gently into her flesh.

'I lost it all,' she said in a hollow voice.

'So quickly? Last time you won handsomely.'

'I only played once. I lost it all in the first go. I had nowhere else to go so I sat here waiting for you.'

Duncan frowned. 'Everything? You lost everything on the first roll of the wheel? Why?'

'I was afraid,' she said, turning to him and burying her face in his shirt. Now she was truly crying. She looked up at him with the tears flowing down her face. 'I'll do anything,' she sobbed in a whisper. 'Please God don't let him send me back again. I don't want to die.'

Thirteen

Blackhall, Edinburgh, Scotland. Tuesday, early hours.

Silence hung in the air as the three cars turned into a lane, some miles from central Edinburgh. A few hundred yards further on, they parked in the gateway of a field. On the other side of the road were the high walls of a Georgian house, spreading on three sides. At the end the grounds were blocked by three separate layers of chain-link fencing, each with coils of razor wire. On top of the brick walls was strung a single length of wire with the telltale ceramic connections visible by the light of the moon. The fence was electrified.

But the twelve men who got out of the cars had come prepared. Using an extendable ladder, one man climbed up on to the wall and used by-pass wire to make a new connection, cutting out a twelve-foot section of the electrification.

According to their information, there were no acoustic devices on the inside of the wall, but nevertheless he threw a heavy rucksack on to the grass just in case.

Nothing happened. No alarm bells rang, no floodlights illuminated.

In a few minutes all of the men were over the wall taking

weapons from the rucksack – automatic pistols, small military machine rifles and a number of knives.

They were dressed in dark clothing, with black ski masks hiding most of their faces. Within seconds they melded into the darkness. Behind them, in the gateway of the field, a driver sat with each vehicle watching the now empty wall.

The house stood in the middle of spacious grounds, with a copse to one side and lawns most of the way to the building, which was surrounded by luxuriant flowerbeds. They moved swiftly through the trees, before coming to a halt close to the house, but short of the alarm visible high on the wall.

One went ahead alone, crawled over the grass and climbed the stout trunks of ivy to snip the wire connected to the central alarm system.

Back on the ground he beckoned to the men and they fanned out, two to each side of the main doorway and three to the French windows at the back, leaving the others to cover the remaining windows. Then he raised his rifle and shattered the glass in one window with the butt. The alarm inside the house clammered, but the floodlights stayed off.

As the front door was flung open and three men ran out, those on either side opened fire. Bullets traced a pattern from one side to the other, tearing into them, spinning them around, knocking them back into the doorway. The rifles were fitted with silencers and the sound they made wouldn't carry beyond the grounds. No one had a chance to shout out or scream.

Instantly the four men ran up to the door, jumping over fallen bodies, heading for rooms on either side of the hallway and the staircase that rose above.

From the back, two other men smashed the French windows and again the guns began to stutter. In only a few minutes everything went silent.

*

An hour later all twelve were back in their vehicles, the ladders left behind, the alarm bypasses abandoned where they were.

One car returned to Manchester. The others went further north in Scotland. All drove like model British citizens.

Amid a clump of five yew trees more than forty yards away from the house, Dmitri Cerdachescu stood as if rooted to the soil like the trees that hid and sheltered him.

He had been three-quarters asleep, sitting under one of the trees, and the first thing he heard was the choked bark of guns fitted with high-quality silencers. He knew the sound; he heard it nightly on the DVD or television movies that were his constant companions. Dmitri threw himself under the shelter of dense, low branches and tried to burrow into the ground. He stayed there, unflinching, for twenty minutes after he heard the men leave and vanish in the darkness towards the eastern wall.

He was trembling with fear and his brain told him to stay where he was, to burrow like a mole under the ground. Dmitri was only thirteen and his father had given him strict instructions not to go out of the house after dark, but like any thirteen-year-old he wanted to show his independence. He wanted to defy his father. He wanted to be grown up. He wanted to scale the wall to the main road, climb over and find a girl, any girl except the ones his father and his men had in the house. Those girls he didn't want. He wanted a real girl, a Scottish girl, untainted by anyone else, but he couldn't climb the wall because of the alarms and, in reality, he knew he didn't attempt to leave because deep in his heart he was afraid to go and look for such a girl. He could fantasise about them, but he was afraid to do more. He might be rejected. He couldn't speak their language and they couldn't understand his. That was why he came out here, at this hour in the morning, when there would be no girls outside anyway. To fantasise where no one could see him or hear him. No one to ridicule him. No one to hurt him.

But these men could hurt him in a different way. Better burrow away where no one else could see him.

Gradually he realised they were not returning. He'd heard cars go past the front gate but was too afraid to lift up his head and try to see them. Now everything was quiet.

Tentatively, ready to fall flat at any moment, he raised himself on to his knees. He crawled out of the shelter of the trees, then, trying not to attract attention, he stood up.

He stayed motionless for another few minutes before he tiptoed towards the door, up the marble steps and walked inside. There was no one to be seen. He crossed the hall and stared up the staircase. No one was there. He looked around, through to the open door of the rear sitting room. No lights were on and he could see nothing.

He retreated to the main entrance and tried to focus more clearly. With the light of the stars, and his eyes adjusted to the darkness, he realised that only one door, leading off the hallway, was closed.

He edged across to it, treading as silently as he could, pulled down the handle and pushed the door open, switching on the light as he did.

Dmitri stumbled down the steps, his eyes wild with fear, clutching at his gagging throat, lurching and falling, then getting up again and running towards the shrubbery more than two hundred yards away, beside the western wall. He collapsed into it and on to the ground beneath the shelter of the shrubs and flowers then began to vomit violently and incessantly until there was nothing left inside him but ache, terror and incredible loneliness.

In time he picked himself up and used fallen leaves to

wipe the vomit from his chin and the front of his shirt. When he felt steady enough he walked alongside the wall, keeping his hand in touch with it. Two yards from the gate a switch was cleverly concealed inside the wall, mostly covered by ivy. He didn't know if the electric fencing was still live or not but he couldn't take any chances. Instead he reached inside the ivy and opened the cover of the switch then stabbed the buttons on the panel there, entering the pass code.

The gates swung open silently. He shot through them and began to run.

The gates waited one minute then started to close again.

Dmitri ran along the road until he passed the edge of the wall. He kept running until he came to the neighbouring house, but still raced on. He ran until his breath left him and he couldn't stagger forward another step.

Then he fell to the ground on his knees and began to cry.

Fourteen

Edinburgh. Wednesday, early afternoon.

'Wholesale slaughter,' Detective Superintendent Euan Murchie from Borders and Lothian police said, indicating the bodies piled in the centre of the room. 'There are some bloody sick bastards in the world. They dragged the bodies from the bedrooms and from outside on the front steps, to put them like that, sitting upright.'

'They were sending a message,' Hartley said. She'd flown up from London immediately word was passed back from Edinburgh. The notification to all forces, in place for around eighteen months, said, in the event of cases involving prostitutes murdered in bizarre ways anywhere in Britain, Landon should be informed. Months later he sent a follow-up request that anyone finding a dead prostitute with a tattoo of a flower in her groin contact him immediately, no matter how she came to die.

Murchie's call that morning was to Landon and to say all of those elements might be there, but not together.

There *was* a bizarre murder, and there *had* been a tattoo, but not at the same time.

When he was told Landon was not available, Murchie said brusquely someone should come to Edinburgh anyway. It was possible that what had happened there was connected to the London cases and he wanted on-the-spot advice. Hartley elected herself.

'They wanted this to get out as a warning,' she said.

'Aye, that's what we thought.' Murchie looked away. 'I've seen some nasty killings over the years and the gangs often do stuff to send messages. I never understand what the bastards are trying to tell us or what the message is they're trying to get out.'

'All of the prostitutes here were Romanian?'

'All the ones we found. The Romanians run a lot of the organised brothels on this side of the coast, right up to Aberdeen. They leave the west coast alone. They don't want to tangle with the mobs from Glasgow.'

'Which means it's not a local turf war,' said Hartley thoughtfully, thinking about the way the bodies had been arranged. There were three neat circles, men back-to-back in the centre of the carpet, then half a dozen naked women stuck between their legs and more men in an outer ring. All had been shot except the one who was perched in a chair at one end of the carpet.

His throat was cut from side to side. Tiebacks from the drapes were used to hold the top part of his body upright and another one restrained his head. Blood from the slashed neck had oozed out over his naked body and run down into the seat, but that wasn't what had sickened the superintendent.

It was the eyes.

They'd been gouged out of his skull and placed between his legs, peering out at the others huddled together on the carpet.

Murchie traced Hartley's gaze. 'Any ideas?'

'Nothing immediately linked to the ice-axe murders so far

as I can tell. The MO is different. In London only one prostitute at a time died and it looks like the work of a serial killer. This is more like a gangland slaying. Both point to demented minds at work, but as I see it the only link is to prostitution. We can't tell if there's a tattoo until we can see the women properly.'

'It won't be long. See the rest while you're waiting.'

They left the room and walked up the stairs to the bedrooms. Expensive fittings were everywhere, but blood had splashed over several of the walls and soaked into the covers where some of the men and women were shot while they were in bed. That was probably why the girls were naked. Apart from the blood the house smelled only of money. Lots of it.

Hartley commented on it.

'This is Blackhall,' Murchie said as they inspected the rooms. 'North of the city in Millionaires' Row. There was a survey a few years back that showed there were more millionaires in this area than anywhere else in Scotland. Over two hundred and sixty then and there have been a lot more since. There was a three-bedroom flat in Blackhall advertised by one of the estate agents in Edinburgh a few months ago worth £1 million on its own.'

Hartley stayed silent. The vision of wealth inspired no emotion in her. She'd never had it and was never likely to. Why envy what you can never get?

'Who owns it?' she asked instead.

'The one without the eyes, Bogdan Cerdachescu,' the superintendent replied. 'He's been operating here for about three years. He came out of nowhere with loads of money and bought a couple of big houses to set up the girls, then expanded. We haven't been able to pin anything on him, but he's known as the head of the brothels in Edinburgh and he's making inroads into the drugs trade. Or at least he *was*. Now he's making his peace with the Devil.'

'Who found them?'

'Local policemen. The gardener came and the gates were closed. He comes every Tuesday and Friday. No one answered the bell on the gateway. It was only eight in the morning but he likes to start then. He said folks who lived in the house often got drunk and slept in but they always had the gates open by eight. So he hung around and kept trying the bell until ten when he called the police. They used a ladder to get over the gate and told the gardener later there was nothing wrong, but the owner wouldn't be around for a couple of days and didn't need him to be here until later.'

'So you kept it quiet.' Hartley nodded with approval. 'Good.'

'Massacres don't make us look good in the newspapers. Especially not ones like this. We've had unmarked vans brought in to take the bodies out. We should be able to keep a lid on it.'

It was sound thinking. The less publicity this had the better. The more time it could be kept quiet, the more time the police had to find out who was behind it.

They started back down the staircase. 'Well, sir,' Hartley said, 'on the face of it there's no connection to our enquiries in London. When you called you mentioned another tattoo. What's that about, sir?'

Murchie shifted uncomfortably, but went ahead, talking over his shoulder, avoiding the question. 'Why isn't your DCI here? Landon.'

'Personal problems.' It was Hartley's turn to be evasive. 'He's having a few official days off.'

He shrugged. They *all* had personal problems.

'Have there been attacks like this elsewhere locally?' Hartley asked as they neared the hallway. She wanted to ask again about the other tattoo but you don't push a superintendent with a problem on his mind. 'Glasgow for example?'

'Glasgow's the murder capital of Britain, but, no, nothing quite like this. I've not known anything similar since the ice-cream murders,' Murchie said with an air of indifference. 'The Weegies tend to go for straightforward kills – knives, axes, burning people alive inside their homes. You name it, they do it, but they don't try to make it an artistic statement. We've liaised with them and they haven't heard of any turf problems over the brothels or of any murdered prostitutes with tattoos either, but I said there's a connection and I'm getting to it, Inspector.'

Behind Hartley, the bodies were being removed, ready to go to the morgue. Mostly the wounds spoke for themselves. Someone would shout for her to check for tattoos on the girls when they cleared the men.

Murchie went out of the house, opened the back door of the nearest car and pulled out an envelope. 'This is what I told you on the phone.'

It's also why you're nervous, she thought. She could read it in his fidgeting.

'It slipped through the system.'

So that was it! Slipped through the system meant the local police had ballsed up!

'It happened more than a couple of years back, long before your DCI notified us to be on the lookout for anything connected to prostitutes with a flower tattoo,' Murchie said stiffly. He didn't like being forced to admit to failure. 'This reminded one of my DIs of an old case. A suicide on Waverley Station. That's the point – it was a suicide, nothing more. The only link is that our suicide was a prostitute who had a flower tattoo. Whatever else you make of it is up to you.'

Hartley pulled out the photographs. Any caustic comment she might have made was instantly wiped away.

The girl's body had been ripped to pieces, the head torn

from the neck, the torso severed around the stomach. Arms were crushed. From the little she could tell of the face the girl had been young and pretty, with long dark hair. In another photograph was a picture of the groin area. There was the tattoo of a flower.

She looked across at him.

'Aye, right,' Murchie muttered. 'She threw herself under a train as it was coming into the station. She'd stripped naked running down from the Old Town. Most of the tourists thought she was drunk. A couple of men tried to help her but she was blethering about rape and sex and so on. None of it making any sense. Someone called a policeman.'

'*Was* she drunk?'

'Not a trace of alcohol in her. The autopsy showed no alcohol and no hallucinogenic drugs. We think she'd gone crazy.'

'Was there any reason to suppose that?'

'She was four months pregnant. The foetus was horribly deformed. The pathologist said it was as if males and females were mixed together in the same body, including two heads.'

The first van had been filled up. A plain-clothes driver and another detective got in and drove away. There were still more vans to load, mostly the women. The tyres crunched on the gravel as the van sped past, through the open gates where two other men were standing guard.

'One head was male and the other female,' Murchie added. 'The pathologist said it was impossible, but it was there. Siamese are usually same sex. Our theory is that the girl found out about the deformities, probably from an illegal doctor, and went off her head. That's why she killed herself.'

'Have you any idea why the incident wasn't picked up through our database search or HOLMES, sir?'

'It wasn't in there,' said Murchie with a look of exasperation on his face. 'It should have been but it wasn't. We're looking into it.'

There it was again. The evasion because of guilt. 'Looking into it' carried a variety of implications.

'There's no connection to that girl and what happened here?' she asked, letting the chance to point-score slip by again.

'Well, nothing concrete. It's in the notes. We had Bogdan Cerdachescu – the one without the eyes – in for questioning over her death but got nothing out of him. If there are any more tattoos on the girls inside, you'll get a connection.'

'Then we'd better have a look at the girls now, sir. If we find tattoos we've got a link. Otherwise, we all have to think again.'

There were no tattoos.

Hartley caught the next flight back and was in her office by eight p.m. It was empty. At her desk she took out the envelope and studied the photograph of the tattoo, reading again the notes that Borders and Lothian police had given her about the incident two years earlier.

The girl had never been traced but a street prostitute told them she thought the body was a Romanian called Nadia. That was the only identification there was. Cerdachescu had been pulled in because he was Romanian and involved in prostitution, although nothing was ever proven. When he was interviewed he demanded his lawyer present then denied all knowledge of the girl, or of prostitution. He'd stuck with his story that he had an import-export business between Romania and Scotland with legal papers confirming his residency and his business. He'd been allowed to go after no more than an hour.

Hartley sat back and thought about it. The discovery of

the tattoo on the girl at Waverley Station was puzzling, but there was no direct connection to the ice-axe murders in London. It *was* a tattoo and it *did* look similar to the ones on the photograph of the girl washed up in Burnham but in itself that wasn't strong enough to make any connection to what had happened at Blackhall.

However, the deformities in the embryo could arguably be linked to pathologists' theories on the ice-axe victims in London. The problem was, as Murchie had been forced again to admit, there were no photographs of the deformities to be found any more, no data of any kind either printed or on the computer databanks. All he had were the photographs of the girl and the data from police interviews. He had interviewed the pathologist again, and she obviously had clear memories of the incident, but there were no records. They had vanished.

'Either we've been hacked, or there's been some data corruption on the servers,' Murchie had said. 'We're investigating, but don't expect an answer tomorrow. This could take weeks to sort out.'

That left increased suspicion, but nothing more. Suspicion, intuition – those were Landon's specialities. She decided to run it by him when they had further contact.

She slipped the photographs into her desk drawer. For the moment they wouldn't join the display on the crime wall. She would wait for the Eureka moment when it would all become clear.

She tidied up her desk and left for home.

Fifteen

Costa del Sol. Thursday.

It was more than two years since he'd last been in this place and he expected the weather to be much the same as it had been last time, hot and sunny. He hadn't packed for rain but soon after ten o'clock banks of black cloud zeroed in over Benalmadena and it was now pouring in a solid sheet, a waterfall of Niagara proportions that had magically appeared over the Costa del Sol and chosen this moment to unload itself.

Tourists retreated, sodden, from the beaches, women and children yelling and shouting, running into the shelter of bars whose owners relished the prospect the rain might stay for hours and keep their unexpected clients inside.

Tabor was caught in the rain like the others, but he had a destination in mind and searched for it until he stood inside the shop, the proprietor eyeing his wet clothes, smiling sympathetically.

Since flying to Malaga on Tuesday and checking into a cheap hotel near the castle, he had spent all his time searching in brothels and tattoo parlours.

First he returned to the apartment block where he had found Emma and studied it, sitting outside a nearby café for a couple of hours, reliving what had happened, inspecting men going in, watching them stay for a while then leave. It was clearly still a brothel. Some men going in were obvious tourists, others were probably Spaniards with businesses in the town. Some seemed furtive, others open about what was happening behind the main doors. Outside them two bouncers stood with arms folded, ready for anything.

In his mind he reconstructed the interior of the building. Other than the discreet bronze plaque on the wall announcing it was 'Club Apuseni', externally it appeared to be a normal apartment block. But inside it was radically changed. On the ground floor, instead of apartments, there was a large reception area and a long lounge bar fitted with comfortable armchairs and tables. Some of those who used the place went not for sex, but merely for plusher surroundings than the beachfront bars offered. It was somewhat reminiscent of an old-fashioned English gentleman's club, with girls. On the second and third floors the apartments were rebuilt to provide dual bedrooms on either side of each entrance door, allowing those who wanted it to easily swap girls throughout the night. The fourth floor had been turned into single rooms for specific purposes. That was where he found Emma.

There was one more floor, but he hadn't needed to get up there. It had no staircase and its entrance had to be from a lift, somewhere hidden away privately on the ground floor. He could only guess that it was the heart of the brothel administration.

After watching the block for two hours, he was filled with hatred, anger, revenge, call it what anyone might. He wanted those who had taken Emma and put her into that brothel. He wanted them with a fever that had never left him from the time he lay alongside her, her hands and feet still bound by the bondage straps. For two years, all but imprisoned in Britain, he had thought about it every day. Landon had provided the conduit, the excuse, which had brought him back again. He harboured no illusions. He wasn't doing this for Landon or the police or the British government. He was doing it for Emma. *Wrong.* He was doing it for himself, because, while the men who had done this lived, the hatred would always burn inside him. When they were dead he would have to live with the memories, but perhaps some little part of him would feel avenged. *Perhaps.*

That evening he went looking for other prostitutes with tattoos. The tattoo was his only lead, slim as it was. He started in Fuengirola, never staying more than half an hour, ordering a beer but not drinking any. He followed the same pattern along the ribbon development of the Costa to Benalmadena then Torremolinos but it was a hopeless short-term task. Anywhere there was a sign, usually in fluorescent lighting flashing 'Club', the probability was that it was another brothel, and there were dozens to try. The brothels ran twenty-four hours a day. When he went to bed in the early hours of Wednesday, he was exhausted, his head was spinning and he had learned nothing.

After three hours' sleep he started again and, changing tactics, decided to stop going into individual brothels but concentrate on bars at night, asking about prostitutes. During the day he visited tattoo parlours trying to find the person who had drawn the orchids. He used the cover of a freelance journalist researching tattooing on the Costa del Sol for one of the glossy magazines because it meant he could go in and talk to the tattooists – or artists as most insisted they should be called – without having any tattoo inflicted. The idea of having one's name and photograph in a magazine was irresistible to most people and Tabor found everyone willing to talk, but when he produced a photograph of the tattoo most remarks had been aimed at pubic, rather than public, comments and he'd come away with nothing.

That night he moved from one tourist bar to another in Fuengirola, waiting for touts to ask if he wanted a woman before showing the photograph and asking if anyone had seen any women similarly marked. He got the by-now standard roars of smutty laughter and was offered everything from children through to sixty-five-year-old grandmothers, but no one admitted seeing such a tattoo. Several times Tabor sensed abnormal interest in his questioning but no one carried it further.

Today he'd started back at tattoo parlours here in Benalmadena. In this one something seemed slightly different.

Most tattoo parlours merited the name. They were small, unlicensed affairs, often huddled in an old shop in a back street, with large posters of tattooed men and women overlying the peeling paint on the walls. The posters were cheaper to move from place to place when the authorities came to call, than repaint a room in a house every few months.

But this shop was on the sea front and the plate-glass window was sparkling clean on the inside, though the rain was streaming down the outside. There were only two posters on the wall and a certificate from what he supposed was a professional organisation.

The owner saw Tabor looking at it.

'It doesn't mean much,' he admitted. 'But it helps inspire confidence in some people who worry about things like hygiene and infection. Most tattooists don't belong to an organisation. There's no law says they have to.'

Tabor continued to look around.

The tattooing implements were prominent. Electric machines that inserted ink under the skin through a group of needles in an oscillating bar. Most of them were fitted with a five-needle set-up, but he'd been told the number of needles depended on the size of the tattoo and the depth of shading wanted. Such machines repeatedly drove the needles in and out of the skin at up to 150 times a second.

He continued his inspection of the glass shelves and cupboard tops ranged either side of a stainless-steel sink. Pigments of various kinds stared back at him, along with containers for old needles, packs of fresh needles tightly sealed and an autoclave for sterilising tools. In a glass-fronted drawer he saw packs of disposable latex gloves and a litterbin in one corner contained a solitary pair of used ones.

'I use a fresh pair for every client,' the owner said quietly. His voice had an accent Tabor couldn't place. The English was excellent but there were Gallic overtones in it. 'As you can see, business isn't exactly booming.' He paused, looking at Tabor. 'Something tells me you're not here for a tattoo either.'

'What makes you think that?'

The man smiled. 'People are my business. You learn to identify them quickly. They have tattoos for all kinds of reasons. Decoration, identification, cosmetic surgery. You don't seem the type to want any of those.'

'What type am I supposed to be?'

He looked thoughtful. 'Some cultures have tattoos to signify rites of passage, others define their status or rank. You don't fit that mould either. I've been asked in the past for symbols associated with fertility, love pledges, talismans and one from a man who wanted to be tattooed with swastikas on his face. I turned him down. No doubt he went elsewhere and got what he asked for.'

'Do you turn down many clients?'

'I won't tattoo minors without their parents' consent,' he replied, as if by rote. 'Or anyone drunk or under the influence of drugs or alcohol. No one with a skin condition that could be dangerous and no mentally incapacitated people. There are other reasons I make up from time to time when I see what the client is asking for.'

'What about something like this?' Tabor handed over the colour photograph of the tattoo on the groin.

The man studied it for a minute or so and Tabor saw him frown, but, unlike so many of the others he'd spoken to, he didn't snigger or make lewd comments. Instead, he sat down, laying the photograph on the shelf beside him and asked very quietly, so softly Tabor had difficulty hearing him, 'Who are you? What do you want with me?'

Tabor sat in another chair the man indicated, then Tabor used his journalist ploy. The man picked up the photograph again and stared at it anew, then laid it back beside him.

'My name is Meerschaert,' he said. 'François. I'm Belgian. You have asked about these tattoos in other parlours?'

'Yes.'

'Then there's something you must understand. I am not what you might call a cowboy. To the best of my ability I do things in a professional way, in accordance with the wishes of each individual client. I ensure all transfers I have in stock are shown to the client first, so that he or she can approve them. Then I press them again to make certain they want to go ahead. Some people regret it instantly the tattoo is done and it's too late then.'

'Commendable,' said Tabor shortly. 'What about tattoos like that one in the photograph?'

The rain was cascading down outside and Meerschaert could see there was no possibility of another client until the downpour stopped.

He switched his attention back to Tabor. 'I have a whole

book of tattoos. Everything from criminal identities to Chinese characters and Maori designs. The bulk of people who want flowers ask for roses, tulips, irises or lotus blossoms. Those that are easily recognisable or recall memories from the past.'

'What about free-form tattoos?'

'It's easy with simple designs. There are graduates of Fine Arts schools who have gone into tattooing. They have gallery exhibitions of photographs of their art, but I've been tattooing for more than thirty years and nothing remotely similar to that photograph has crossed my path. If I were asked for it, and had a design, I wouldn't do it.'

'Why not?'

Meerschaert looked out of the window again. Something about the man disturbed him. Irritated him. He was too abrupt in his questioning. Too terse. Almost curt. Abrasive. Meerschaert had been interviewed by journalists before in a variety of languages, but usually they laughed and joked and tried to elicit colourful tales and take him out for a drink. Not this one.

'Several years back I was asked to tattoo a man's penis,' he said. He noted the questioning look that came into Tabor's eyes. 'There's a large gay population here in Benalmadena. There are gay bars and gay clubs. Does this bore or offend you?'

Tabor shook his head.

Meerschaert waited a moment for comment. When none came he went on: 'A Harris Poll some years ago showed thirty-one per cent of people asking for tattoos were gay, lesbian or bisexual, so Benalmadena is a good place for a tattooist. I don't have any sexual hang-ups and tattooing gays isn't my reason for rejecting that particular request. Nor did I have any reservations about the organ involved.'

He paused but Tabor nodded, indicating he should go on.

'I refused because I felt I shouldn't do it without a qualified doctor at my side, and perhaps a general anaesthetic and I have no competence in that, or the range of equipment that could be needed. It's been known for a patient to go into anaphylactic shock as an allergic reaction to tattoo pigments. In some jurisdictions that would be construed as involuntary manslaughter. The photograph you've shown me comes into that category. As far as I'm concerned, the tattoo is too close to the vagina to be done without access to a hospital. Even a local anaesthetic could frighten a susceptible person to death – I have known people faint at the sight of a needle – and it would require numerous treatments to get a flower of such complexity right.'

'Why would anyone have a tattoo like that, in such a place if it was going to involve them in pain?' Tabor asked. The whole subject had turned out to be fascinating to him. 'Some inverted masochism?'

'There may be something of that in it,' Meerschaert answered. 'But vanity is often enough. You must understand, most people feel nothing more than a buzzing on the skin because of the rapidity of the punctures, and for those who enjoy that sensation there is no problem. Then there are people who will endure anything, even discomfort in a sensitive region, to look different. Some feel the pain, but invite it because it gives them a sense of personal accomplishment.'

'Masochism,' Tabor grunted.

'Not at all,' Meerschaert answered. 'You can get that in the brothels here but in some races tattooing under the most primitive conditions is a necessary rite of passage to manhood. As recently as the past century Maoris underwent what may have been agonising pain, having the tattoo punched into their skin with fine spears of wood and colouring them with injection of homemade dyes that could turn a wound septic. They did not do it for sensual enjoyment but because the tattoos were a symbol of their strength of resolve, their ability to defeat pain. Some of the most intricate work on a Maori's body was on the face, one of the most delicate parts of the body where a slip on the part of the tattooist could drive a splint into a man's eyes, or even into his brain through delicate areas where the skin covers cavities such as the temples. I'm sorry – I don't suppose you came in here for a lecture.'

'Not at all,' Tabor said. 'I'm grateful. Lectures come with the business. I ask questions, someone provides answers and it's up to me to cut out the stuff no one wants to read. Besides, you've begun to make tattooing more fascinating than anywhere I've been so far. Like the tattoo in the photograph I showed you. That must have taken lots of sessions, and perhaps a lot of pain. What happens to someone who undergoes all of that, but doesn't want a tattoo when they see it finished? What do they do then?'

Meerschaert smiled patiently and pointed to the photograph. 'That is the tattoo of a maestro,' he said, 'and I for one am astonished at its complexity. But you're right, sometimes people do not appreciate such things when they finally see it revealed. The green ink in the flower there is intense. Green shading into almost black. Green-based inks are the most difficult to remove. Sometimes people want a tattoo removed and with black inks they can be. Trained surgeons can use lasers to break black ink down so the body absorbs it, but it means repeated treatment with the lasers over a period of weeks and there is permanent scarring. There are other methods and much research work is going on into tattoo removal, but most solutions so far result in scarring and there's always tattoo damage below the skin layer.'

Tabor remembered what Landon had said about the tattoos in London being removed with acid. 'Are you saying if the person carrying this tattoo wanted it removed, beyond all trace, no one could do it?'

'That's exactly what I am saying.' He pushed the photograph back towards Tabor. The rain was slowing. Very soon it would stop. 'There's a possibility of a paying client when the rain comes to an end. I'd like to be free to handle him, if that is all you want to know?'

'Other than the name of the tattooist, yes. You've been helpful. Thank you.' There was no point in pushing Meerschaert further.

He stood up to shake the man's hand, but momentarily Meerschaert held on to his grip. 'The photograph,' he said softly. 'That tattoo. Can you tell me what the flower is?'

'An orchid. Why?'

'I've never seen anything like it, nothing quite as intricate and detailed in my life. I'm sorry I can't tell you the name of the artist, but I've heard of someone who would know the flower instantly and might be able to recognise the work. An orchid expert.'

'Here in Spain?'

'Here in Andalucia,' Meerschaert answered. 'I've never met him, but he's known as one of the foremost orchid experts in the world. Dr Felix Blake. He lives in a mansion about fifty kilometres away in a little place called Jorox, in the Sierra de Las Nieves. If anyone can advise you, it's Dr Blake.'

'Does he tattoo as well?'

'Hardly.' Meerschaert chuckled. 'This man is a millionaire several times over. Why would he need to tattoo? But he does have one other attribute that might interest you as a journalist. Throughout Spain he's known as an aficionado in the art of *tauromaquia*. Better known perhaps as bullfighting. His reputation for that is as great as it is for his orchids.'

Sixteen

Sierra de Las Nieves.

Blake unwrapped the white paper, taking care to cut the tape with a clean knife then remove the wrapping, folding it out of the way and placing it on one side in a space he had pre-prepared away from his work surface.

He had already waited too long but it was imperative to finish his other work in the laboratory before he could unwrap the parcel that Duncan had given him in the casino. Duncan said there was no urgency. 'A week or two makes no difference,' were his actual words. But with Duncan words came easily and not always in strict adherence to the truth. Nevertheless, he always had something interesting when he gave presents and this time Blake had been given no clue as to what it might be.

He opened the box, quivering with excitement and anticipation. For a moment he stood stock still, overawed at what he found. Almost reverently he lifted the package, caressing it as if it were a delicate newborn baby. He'd twice seen similar ones in private collections and he'd briefly watched a movie featuring one, but the film was Hollywood trivia and irrelevant to Blake.

The flower was everything.

It was beauty personified.

Not that a layman would have thought of it that way, especially in its dormant state.

It was an exceptional monocot, lacking a stem and the leaves were reduced to scales. Only the cord-like roots trailed down, like strands of dried green cotton.

Hardly able to drag his eyes away from it as it lay there on the table, he gradually edged into a corner where he had a number of short lengths of old tree branches placed ready for cultivation in the medium of choice for such orchids.

He carried one over and placed it on the work surface. It was an epiphyte and, in its natural habitat in Florida or the Bahamas or Cuba, it would be anchored in a large tangled mass in a tree, in moist and swampy forests.

It was out of flowering season and no trace of its blossoms was visible but it excited him almost to the edge of orgiastic ecstasy.

The orchid was *very* rare. Some claimed it was the rarest in the world but he couldn't accept that. The rarest orchid in the world was simply one that hadn't yet been found, but it *was* so rare that any reaching the private market sold for extremely high prices. Blake could afford it many hundreds of times over, but it was out of the price range of most people and the opportunity to acquire it was offered to very few.

Yet, as important for Blake was the knowledge that cultivation of this orchid had proven unsuccessful outside its normal habitat.

It was an endangered species, protected in the United States, but that meant nothing to him. What mattered was that he now had the chance to successfully propagate such an orchid in unnatural conditions, thousands of miles from where it belonged. It would be a crowning achievement in a lifetime of endeavour and one no others would know about unless he chose to tell the select few who also experimented in such fields. They would be jealous beyond compare if he could successfully do what the rest of the world had been unable to do.

Come next June, if all went well, it would open with as many as ten fragrant flowers at a time. They would be white, about two inches wide and four or five inches long, spearing out from the root network. The lower lip of the white orchid would have two long petals that twisted slightly downwards. Some claimed the petals resembled the legs of a jumping frog.

Every plant would be different to others, giving each an individual personality. The roots would blend so well with the branch he was now preparing that only the blossom, floating as it were in space unattached to the world at large, would be seen.

That was what had given it its name. That was what sent shivers of excitement down him at this very moment.

Dendrophylax Lindenii, once know as *Polyrhizal Lindenii.*

In recent years it had been found only in the Fakahatchee Strand Nature Reserve, near Naples in South Florida, and was guarded there by the Florida National Park rangers and the police, as well as dedicated conservationists.

The rarest orchid in the world?

No, but it was arguably the closest pretender at this time.

The Ghost Orchid.

Iain Duncan, he thought as his long fingers played delicately with the moss he was bedding around the branch, was a commercial Neanderthal with no trace of taste or sense of beauty other than the women he took to bed and who interested Blake not in the least. However, he had his uses.

Obtaining orchids such as this, while others could not was one of the talents that made him most useful of all. Providing the millions of dollars necessary to finance the *Tatú* project was another. *Tatú* would change history and the lives of billions of people.

It was a pity Duncan had to have any part in it all, but, while history is made by visionaries, reality is the underpinning that comes with cash.

When *this* history was written, the genius would be that of Felix Blake.

Duncan would be no more than a commercial by-product.

Seventeen

New Scotland Yard. Lunchtime.

The police report from Chelmsford quoted a cleaner in Burnham-on-Crouch saying someone was missing. An Edward Beech, who lived in the town most weekends, especially during the yachting season. Written across the bottom Ellis had scribbled: 'Beech and Winters sailed together.'

There was no other comment, but buried in some of the original papers was a note that Beech owned a yacht called *Pesadilla*, which Tom Winters, the dead man washed ashore at Whitstable, skippered.

Hartley called DCI Ellis.

'Apparently Beech and Winters were close friends, as well as owner and employee,' he told her. 'Winters skippered the yacht, did Beech's work on it, handled the rigging and the off-season clean-ups, liaised with the sail-makers. In fact, he did everything except put down the cash that Beech outlays on the boat, but he had no restrictions on when he took it out, or where, or who with. He often went out on it alone.'

'Who is this cleaner, sir?' she asked.

'She works for a businesswoman in Burnham called

McGlynn. Kelly McGlynn. One of the locals from Maldon contacted her and I gather she's not happy about the cleaner saying anything. McGlynn runs a variety of services in the town, targeting yachties. She's got a team of cleaners who go to owners' houses and do them out once a week. The cleaner for Beech says he's never been away for this long before without prior warning. McGlynn's been told to make herself available if you need to go down there. She's got an office in the main street and she's still got the keys to Beech's house.'

'Why didn't this McGlynn call in the missing person? Why the cleaner?'

'We asked that. McGlynn's not exactly a "one of the girls" type. A cleaner's a cleaner in her books and she dismissed the cleaner's worry about Beech. The cleaner bypassed her to make the report. Wouldn't be surprised if it's an ex-cleaner when the fuss has died down.'

'What about Beech's family?'

'He doesn't have any. He's a bachelor, no parents or other family as far as we know. He's got another place near Guildford that he uses most of the time.'

Hartley put the phone back on the handset, looking thoughtfully at DS Field who was hovering nearby.

Jack Field was not what anyone would call an impressive man. He didn't fit the visual stereotype of a hard-boiled detective. He was no more than five foot eight inches tall, he had a droopy moustache that had turned white, even though he was only in his forties. He made no attempt to hide the paunch that seemed to get a little more noticeable every few months, but no one passing him in the street would give him a second glance. That was what Landon liked about him. Jack Field was anonymous in a business where anonymity was often an asset, but he was mentally very astute, disinclined to physically hang around, preferring to be on the move in the streets, not shuffling papers in the office. Landon respected him.

'Get your coat, Jack,' she said. 'I think we'll go for a trip to the seaside.'

Kelly McGlynn met them at Edward Beech's house. She was in her mid-thirties and looked more like a catalogue model than a woman who ran a small-time cleaning and yachting-services business. Her shoulder-length auburn hair shone with health and the cut was impeccable.

Hartley imagined the woman probably crewed on the boats throughout the summer or sat back in the sun and lounged on the deck, with a glass of wine in one hand and the other draped around a well-financed yacht owner in the Marlboro-man mould.

Beech's house stood in its own grounds, with three large horse-chestnut trees shading it behind the walls that surrounded the building. It could be late Victorian, she guessed, as they walked up the three steps into the porch and McGlynn unlocked the door.

Hartley nodded to Field who went off, checking rooms on either side of the large hall.

'He's a wealthy man,' McGlynn said. Her voice was deep and rich, with the clipped tone and accent of a private-school education. It echoed her taste in clothes. Top drawer and expensive.

'So I can see,' Hartley answered.

The walls were lined with original oil paintings, none of which she knew offhand, but all impressive and pre-dating the 20th century. Not that she was an expert. The carpets were deep, Oriental and large, laid atop highly polished boards. Because the house had been cleaned only the day before there wasn't a speck of dust to be seen. Probably no clues either, Hartley thought, if indeed there were any crime to be investigating.

A number of envelopes sat in a letter rack on a long

sideboard. Hartley rifled through them. Mostly bills or flyers according to the logos on the envelopes.

She looked for indicators of anything untoward. There was no sign of damage, no telltale removal of paintings from the walls, no marks on the doorjamb to indicate anyone had attempted to open it forcibly.

'What makes you so certain he's missing?'

McGlynn tossed her silky hair and the strands glowed in the sunlight passing through the window. 'I never said he was.' For a moment her voice was hard and curt. DCI Ellis was right. She didn't like Beech's absence being reported. Why? Hartley wondered. Wouldn't it be normal for someone like her to be concerned if one of her clients was absent without explanation?

'My cleaner seems to think so. I don't,' McGlynn said. The voice was still cool but quickly becoming more professional. 'She's over-protective sometimes. She thinks of her houses as if they're her own, and the owners as children who need to be looked after at all times. He goes away frequently, especially when there's an important race overseas.'

'Are there any races on now, or were there any recently that he could have been involved in?'

McGlynn shook her head. Her voice changed and became concerned. Professional concern? Hartley couldn't tell. 'I'd have known if there were any big races anywhere in Europe. I would probably have been there with some of the yachtsmen, urging them on. The last one was in St Tropez a week ago and he didn't go. I had friends on one crew that went and they would have told me.'

'Wouldn't he have let you know if he was going away for a while? In case of emergencies?'

'Of course.' McGlynn paused for a moment. When she spoke again, she sounded puzzled and more supportive of her staff. She's like a chameleon, Hartley thought. Adapt to the conditions. 'I told you the cleaner is over-protective, but in retrospect perhaps she was right, and I over-reacted. He *would* normally tell me if he was going away for more than a week, or call in so that I could make any other necessary arrangements. He probably will in a day or so. Storm in a tea cup, Inspector.'

Hartley changed her approach. 'Do you know if Mr Beech was on his yacht with Tom Winters a couple of weeks back?'

'If you're going to ask me about the night before Winters was found, Mr Beech wasn't in Burnham then.'

'Have you any idea where he is?'

'None at all. He doesn't appear to be at his home in Guildford. I called today and there was no answer. I've tried a couple of times, but not made contact.'

'Could he be away sailing on another boat?'

'Other than the *Pesadilla*? I suppose it's possible. He hasn't gone off on the *Pesadilla*. She's right where she should be,' McGlynn answered. 'Moored in the middle of the river.'

Hartley looked up. On the way here, after being told that Beech was missing and Winters was his skipper, she'd automatically assumed Winters must have been on Beech's boat when he drowned. But McGlynn seemed to assume Beech was alive, yet his boat hadn't been moved. So where was the one Winters was sailing when he died?

'Is the *Pesadilla* Mr Beech's only yacht?' she asked as Field joined them in the hall after finding nothing in the bedrooms.

'It's the only one he owns,' McGlynn answered. 'He's crewed on other boats, including a few transatlantic crossings. He also likes to ferry new boats from Europe for other owners. He'll fly over there then bring a boat back. Yachtsmen do it all the time.'

She saw Hartley's frown. 'Of course, he doesn't have to,' McGlynn said swiftly. 'He does it because he loves boats and likes to try out as many as he can. Whenever he gets the chance, he ferries boats for friends who haven't got as much time to spare. It's not a business thing. He doesn't get paid, he likes doing it. Any distance. He ferried one from South Africa to Boston once.'

Nice work if you can get it, thought Hartley.

'Is there anyone, or any other boat, he might have gone off with this time?'

'I wouldn't necessarily know that. He's a business client, not a confidante.'

'You said earlier he tells you everything.'

'I actually said he would *normally* tell me. I also admitted I over-reacted in showing no concern this time. I suppose what I'm saying now may seem contradictory but I put things badly. He doesn't confide in me in specific business terms, but, as I said, he *does* usually tell me if he's going to be away as long as this. This time he didn't.'

'A business client only then – but you have been out socially with him?'

'Of course. This is Burnham,' she retorted as if it explained everything.

Well, perhaps it did. She was a good-looking woman, he was a wealthy bachelor.

'Do you know which bank he used for his account with you?' Field asked. He'd sorted through the unopened letters too. No bank statements.

'Not offhand,' McGlynn answered. 'I could dig it out for you, but is it necessary? Mr Beech would be furious if he thought someone was to trying to nose into his business.'

'No one is trying to do that, Ms McGlynn. The cleaner reported Mr Beech missing and we're responding to it. We'll keep the matter in mind and, if you hear of anything, please contact us.'

She looked relieved.

'We'll make more enquiries and see what we come up with,' Hartley said. 'Leave it in our hands. If Mr Beech contacts you, we need to speak with him.'

She fell in alongside Field as they walked towards the door. McGlynn stayed where she was in the middle of the hallway.

As they were about to leave, Field stopped and looked back.

'By the way,' he said, 'the name of the boat – *Pesadilla* – what does it mean?'

McGlynn laughed. A strange laugh, Field thought. 'It's actually *Pesadilla V*,' she answered. 'He's had four previous ones and each one becomes bigger and more of a nightmare to handle than the one before. That's what it means. *Pesadilla* means "Nightmare" in Spanish.'

While they'd been inside the wind had blown up and grey skies settled over the whole of the east coast. It had begun to drizzle.

'What do you think?' Hartley asked, as they sheltered in the doorway of an estate agent's office.

'She was evasive over the boat ferrying. He's probably gone off with some female who looks better than she does,' Field replied. 'Winters obviously wasn't lost off the *Pesadilla* and there's no evidence to suggest Beech was with him on any other vessel. Winters must have been on one we don't know about. As for Beech, no one seems alarmed except McGlynn's cleaner. How about you?'

'She was contradictory at first. Started off saying one thing, changed it when she thought we weren't buying her hard line.'

'It often happens,' Field muttered. 'Look, it's way past lunchtime, it's raining and I'm hungry. There's a place called the White Hart on the quay where we should be able to get something to eat and a pint in the dry.'

The drizzle was continuous and neither of them was wearing a raincoat. The car was parked half a mile away outside McGlynn's office. Hartley sighed agreement. She would have preferred to get on with it, but Field liked his afternoon sandwich and drink. 'OK, we'll do that, then go and see Winters's widow. I'll call Ellis in Chelmsford and get her address.'

'No need,' Field said, as they stepped out into the rain and headed towards the quay. 'I looked it up in the file on the way down. There's not much on her from Chelmsford Police so I had a feeling you'd want to cover that too. Another reason for being here.'

Mary Winters came to the door in her dressing gown, although it was mid-afternoon. Her hair was uncombed, her eyes listless and her face pale. She stared at them with resentment when they said who they were.

'I already talked to the police,' she grumbled. 'They said they wouldn't be bothering me any more.'

But Field's gentle handling won her around.

'They've never found any wreckage,' she said sadly. 'But they don't seem to be in any doubt Tom took the boat out and the storm came up and it sank.'

Then she revealed the boat was Winters's own sloop. According to her, he used it to go out beyond the estuary to catch fish or sail down the coast to places such as Deal.

With Beech, she said, they would go over to France and stay, but always on the *Pesadilla*. He was often away for a week or more at a time.

When Hartley hesitated, appearing unsure how to ask the question on her mind, Mary Winters blurted out she knew what they were thinking.

'You're going to ask if he went out with other women when he was away,' she flared, her voice rising.

Field nodded and smiled kindly at her. 'We've heard Mr Beech likes to go out for a sail with girls on board. As his skipper, Tom would have known about it, wouldn't he? He'd probably have told you?'

That opened the floodgate. At first Mary Winters called Beech 'an attractive man with lots of money and women, especially the young ones, who threw themselves at him', but she insisted Tom didn't have anything to do with that kind of thing. 'He wouldn't go out with Mr Beech and women on a sex orgy, he wasn't that kind of a man. All he lived for was the boat. That was what he loved, not me. Not women.'

It was only as they were leaving that she suddenly said Beech liked foreign women most of all. According to her, he went everywhere looking for them. He'd go across the Channel and moor, then fly from there to places such as Spain, Italy and Germany.

Several times Tom brought back Romanian cigarettes, but no one would buy them and he had to throw them into the rubbish. Her main tirade was against Beech who, she said, wouldn't travel direct from England like anyone else.

'He wanted to keep it a secret but *I* knew. I overheard Tom talking to him on the phone. Beech took out several women at a time on that yacht and, while Tom did the sailing, Beech went down to the cabin. That was why he was away for days at a time. When Beech went away to get foreign girls, Tom had to stay in port and wait for him.

'Beech was a bastard,' she said savagely. 'I haven't told the police but I'm sure Beech went out with Tom that night, whoring again, but the storm caught them and they died. I hope he rots in Hell and the fish spit the taste of him out their mouths. Beech was a twenty-four-carat pig and he killed my Tom as surely as if he'd stuck a knife in his guts. Beech was rotten to the core. If he *is* dead, it's the only decent thing he ever did in his life. Good riddance.'

Then she cupped her hands around her head and began to weep.

Burnham receded into the distance, allowing the drizzle to wrap comfortably around it again, but as they reached the junction with the A12 outside Chelmsford a weak sun broke through.

'Comments?' Hartley asked. Until then she'd been focusing on the road, thinking about the half-hour they'd spent with Mary Winters in her 1930s semi-detached house on Station Road, close to the rarely manned police station.

'She's lost, the poor bugger,' Field answered. London-bound traffic bowled past him, overtaking beyond the speed limit, ignoring the wet and slippery road surface. 'Winters was a bastard who never gave her much of a life and spent all of his time on Beech's boat with his big buddy. She doesn't like Beech a lot and she's certain he died with her husband. It's interesting that Winters had his own boat, though. The *Gilbert Merrick*. Old-time Birmingham City footballer. McGlynn didn't tell us that.'

'She didn't tell us what Mary Winters said about Beech's whoring parties on board his boat, either, or Beech and Winters's trips to the Continent to look for women.'

'A woman scorned? Mary Winters changed her tune mid-stream, don't forget. At first she was all pie-eyed about Beech then she switched at the last minute into hate mode. That spells envy, or something like it, to me. She thinks her husband liked Beech more than he liked her. Did you notice there wasn't a single photograph of her among the collection of yacht pictures on the walls and the sideboard? They were all of Winters, his mates and his trophies.'

Hartley sank back into contemplation with Field keeping silent company beside her.

Lots of words, she thought. Lots of envy, lots of hate, lots of money and power, all in a tiny end-of-the-world powder keg called Burnham-on-Crouch.

Suddenly she was tired. She needed to be home, in bed, in uncomplicated surroundings. Tomorrow she could think about it again.

Eighteen

Fuengirola. Almost midnight.

According to the hotel receptionist, there was a bar in the tiny hamlet of Jorox where he could ask about Blake.

'You probably won't find anyone there who speaks English,' she said. 'Very few locals in villages in the Sierras do. You should find someone here in Fuengirola who can translate for you, then take a hire car.'

'Thanks,' said Tabor, but he had to leave it at that. There was no way he could ask anyone else.

He sat in a bar close to the sea front, toying with an untouched beer. Days of questioning had brought him no return. He was no closer to finding anyone who knew of a similar tattoo to the one on Emma. He had thought that frequenting tourist bars asking about tattooed prostitutes would attract attention. He *wanted* someone to be concerned enough about his pointed questioning to confront him. Tabor wasn't an investigator, he was a soldier who did the things that had to be done after he'd been told where and when. He couldn't go into brothels and inspect every girl, nor could he ask about the people who controlled the girls. The brothel owners would call the police if he started making trouble and that he couldn't afford.

All he could do was keep asking and wait for someone to react. He didn't like waiting. He didn't like inaction. A few times he'd wondered what he was actually doing. Emma was dead. Even if he found the people who forced her into prostitution it wouldn't bring her back. Logic told him to forget it and get on with life.

In the peace and quiet of Wast Water he'd thought he was getting there. He'd contained his anger and ignored his troubled dreams. He'd kept out of the way of others, except those who came to him for training. Then along came Landon.

He was thinking about it, twirling the glass, staring through the liquid rather than at it, when someone sat down on the stool next to him.

Tabor glanced across at him. Nondescript. No tan, which meant he was either a recently arrived tourist or a local who kept out of the sun. He was in his mid-twenties at a guess, but his hair was already receding. He'd tried to compensate for it with a small moustache. To Tabor it merely looked stupid. He was wearing a khaki singlet over flowery patterned shorts and the omnipresent sandals, feet resting on the bottom rung of the bar stool. He ordered a Mai Tai. Tourist or tout. Tabor looked away.

'You never drink,' the man said suddenly. He didn't look at Tabor but the words were obviously meant for him.

'What makes you say that?' answered Tabor, swivelling a little on the stool to inspect the man more fully.

'I've seen you in several places. You go into bars and buy a beer, but you never drink, you ask questions.'

'Clever you.' Suddenly Tabor was alert. The approach, the way the man looked at the bottles behind the bar rather than at Tabor's face. It was the reaction he'd been seeking, but almost given up hope of getting.

'You want a prostitute.' The man picked up his drink and held it against the light as if it were wine he was inspecting. The only way to tell anything about a cocktail was to try it. The man was doing nothing more than letting time slide by while he assessed Tabor.

'If I do, I can go get one,' Tabor growled, turning back to his beer.

'Why do you buy beer and not drink it? Why do you talk about prostitutes, but never have one?'

'None of your business. It's a free world so everybody tells me.'

The man shrugged his shoulders. 'It doesn't matter to me, mate. You can be a teetotal queer for all I care.'

'Then piss off and stop bugging me.'

'If I did, it would be your loss.'

'What does that mean?'

'It means you don't want any prostitute for a one-off bonk. You want a particular shag for something she can offer and no one else can, one with a flower where only a bloke staring at a naked pro would see it.'

'And I suppose you know one.'

'I'm in trade. I trade information.'

'For money, of course.'

'Everybody's got to make a living somehow. It'll cost you two hundred. Then I'll take you where you want to go.'

He downed his cocktail and held out his hand for the money.

Tabor laughed at him.

The man withdrew his hand and shrugged again as if it were of no consequence. 'Please yourself. I can take you to where she is right now. You might ask around for another six months and find the one you've been looking for, but by then she could have been passed on, up the coast. They like to shuffle the shags. Regular clients don't like poking the same dead fire all the time.'

'Who is "they"?' Tabor asked, picking up his beer for the first time.

The man watched him drink deeply then put the glass down three-quarters empty. Tabor shrugged and took out his wallet, pulled out a note and stuffed it into the top pocket of his shirt before shoving his wallet back into his trousers. The note could clearly be seen through the shirt's thin cotton.

'That kind of information's worth more than a measly hundred euros,' the man answered after a second's pause. 'I wouldn't talk about it in here anyway.'

'Take me to the girl first,' Tabor said. 'Then we'll talk and finally I'll give you this hundred euros. If the conversation covers what I want then maybe I'll give you another. The girl, the conversation, and last of all the pay-off.'

The man slid off his stool and smiled. 'Sounds fair enough to me. I like a man who knows when to be careful.'

Tabor followed him to the sea front heading in the direction of the castle more than a mile distant. After about ten minutes he turned into another street and Tabor followed, pulling a little closer to him. Around him were blocks of apartments, most of them no more than five storeys high, but there were fewer shops and bars and the street lamps were less frequent.

A hundred yards further on, the man turned into an alleyway and Tabor followed, five or six feet behind him. There had been no other conversation but Tabor could sense they were getting to the end. The alley was dark and buildings rose up either side, with rubbish bins parked at intervals outside what looked like basement doors. The man walked purposefully ahead.

Tabor was expecting something to happen, but the speed at which the man suddenly reached out and turned a door handle, opened it and shot inside took him by surprise. Tabor lunged for the door, but as he grabbed the handle he heard the lock click shut. The door was metal and impossible to break down with his hands.

Tabor backed off into the alley, sensing rather than seeing another man who came from behind one of the large rubbish bins. He was tossing a baseball bat between his hands. Tabor looked over his shoulder. About thirty yards away three men stood at the far end of the alley. Even in the gloom he could tell they were people he'd seen sitting close to him earlier in the bar where the pimp picked him up.

Four of them.

He turned to the one with the baseball bat and, without pausing, jumped at him, his left leg held rigid, high in the air. The heel of the shoe ripped into the face of the man approaching him. He screamed and dropped the bat, reaching for his smashed nose as the blood poured through his nostrils and his mouth from teeth that had been broken. Tabor didn't pause. As he landed on both hands and feet, he twisted around and lunged again, this time with the right foot, pulling the man's legs from beneath him. He reeled backwards and crashed on to the concrete of the alley floor, his head banging heavily against it. He didn't move and Tabor didn't stop to check whether he was alive or dead.

The other three would be coming for him. They would prefer to take him alive for questioning, and they wouldn't want gunfire if they could help it. That meant knives or something blunt, such as a length of iron or lead pipe. He picked up the fallen baseball bat and whirled around.

The leading man was only a few yards away, a knife in one hand and a length of bicycle chain in the other, but he'd seen what Tabor could do and came to a halt, waiting.

Tabor threw the baseball bat, striking him across the cheek and splitting it open. The man dropped the chain, yelling at the pain and put his hand to his cheek, then turned back to face Tabor, his teeth bared like an angry wolf, spitting and shouting in a language Tabor didn't understand. He jerked forward with the knife, pointing it at Tabor's chest.

Tabor let him get close and when the knife was only a foot away he twisted to one side, feeling the blade slice into his shirt and cut into the flesh. But he was running on adrenalin and pain meant nothing. His left hand shot out, gripping the wrist like a vice, pulling it down, while simultaneously he turned with his back into the man, his right hand coming up to grip the upper and lower parts of the arm and used both hands to press in opposite directions, breaking the arm at the elbow. The knife dropped to the ground and the man staggered back, screaming and trying to hold the shattered limb but Tabor slammed his fist into the man's body three times until he fell against the wall of the building and slid to the ground, gagging and almost choking on the vomit rising inside him.

It had taken only seconds but time was already running out. Tabor picked up the knife and turned to meet the other two, now on top of him. He plunged the knife into one man's shoulder then turned to the other, but it was one man too many and this one, so far unscathed, was chopping down at him with a length of chain, whipping it across his shoulders then his windpipe.

Tabor staggered back and bumped into one of the rubbish bins. He could feel himself going faint and beginning to fall. He tried to get out of the way, but his legs turned to rubber and he slipped down between the rubbish bin and the wall, waiting for the blows to come.

That was when he heard the shot.

Tabor tried to sit upright. He was having trouble breathing. Who was shooting? Why hadn't they tried to finish him off? He pushed himself up the wall, forcing his legs to stay apart and steady, pain lancing through his neck and shoulders and his stomach where the blood was coming out and staining his shirt a dark red.

He grabbed hold of the rubbish bin for support, looking for the men who had attacked him.

They had gone.

He tried to focus on the figure near him but his eyes were half-glazed from the pain and the only thing he could see was a gun pointed at his middle. He held on to the bin until his eyes cleared.

She waited, pointing the pistol.

He tried to stand erect, but he was in no condition to tackle anyone holding a gun, even a woman. It was obvious she knew about weapons. She'd stayed far enough away for him not to be able to reach her before she could fire, but close enough to hit him. Such a small bullet might not kill him, but it would stop him long enough for her to try again in a more vulnerable place. Between the eyes.

Then he recognised her. She too had been at the bar less than twenty minutes earlier. He breathed in deeply, fighting off the waves of pain in his shoulder and throat. She was in control. It was her move. Then he watched in astonishment as she calmly opened her handbag and put the gun inside.

'They've gone,' she said in English. 'I fired over the head of the last one. Two of the others hobbled away, but they'll need hospital treatment. The one still standing carried the unconscious one off. I couldn't prevent them on my own.'

Tabor narrowed his eyes in puzzlement. 'I thought you were going to kill me,' he breathed hoarsely. His head was spinning and very soon he might pass out. His hand was across his stomach, but the blood was coming through his fingers and dripping slowly to the ground.

'I was. I changed my mind. I think I'd better get you somewhere safe before you die anyway. That gunfire could have been reported to the police.'

Tabor tried to smile his thanks. Instead, he crumpled to the floor.

Nineteen

London. Friday, early hours.

Pavel Potrascu missed Romania. The mountains and valleys beyond Rogojel were beautiful and he loved his youth there, but they were poor until Costel organised the sale and distribution of the local *palinca*. Then he had no more time for the mountains and the rural village where they lived, and his home and money moved into the city. Where Costel went, Pavel followed like a shadow pinned to his coat tails.

Costel wouldn't feel the same way, Pavel thought. Costel had no poetry in his soul. He wouldn't waste his time thinking about the mountains. He would rather buy and exploit them. He was a hard man, infinitely harder than Pavel, which was why Costel took care of everything difficult, although it meant flying here every few weeks. His older brother actually made the money. Pavel wasn't an empire builder. His power came from Costel's reputation.

He sighed a little at this mental confession and turned away from the window. The clock on the wall showed it was time to go home. Pavel picked up his coat from the rack beside the white painted steel door, and one of his men stepped out in front, checking up and down the corridor. It was routine. They were on the third storey and no one could come up here unannounced or uninvited. The ground floor was for clients, the second floor for the girls and up here was the control centre.

There were six brothels in various parts of central London and eight more in the suburbs, aimed at the lower-class market. Many of the girls who ended up there were Africans from places such as Mali, Chad, the Ivory Coast and Senegal. Some sailed around the Atlantic and were picked up on the southern Spanish coast near Cadiz; others were trekked across the Sahara and sailed in ramshackle ships from Libya towards Italy. More than two-thirds of those who tried to make the trip died before they reached Europe: if the Saharan heat and emptiness did not kill them, the Atlantic and Mediterranean mostly did. Those who survived were picked up when they landed, and the girls inspected. Around a hundred a year, from those who would appeal most to the London market, were picked out and ferried through Europe to various points close to Britain, and carried in small sailboats or motorboats to isolated spots on the British coast. Once in the hands of Potrascu's minders, they spent their lives trapped in his brothels, rather than going on for the great times they'd dreamed of in Madrid, Paris or Rome.

In the brothels in the city centre the girls were mostly Eastern European, with a smattering of Orientals and a couple of Swedish girls who weren't forced into the business. They liked what they did, especially for the wealthy, and financially considerate, Japanese businessmen.

During the evening Pavel visited the various locations, making certain everything functioned properly, picking up money accrued at that time. He always came here around one in the morning and handled anything else that had arisen, either from overseas or locally.

Now he'd had enough for the day.

The man in front went down the corridor to the private lift, waiting for it to arrive and be inspected before Pavel moved out of the safety of his office. Two other men took station behind him. Pavel wrapped the coat loosely over his shoulders, not bothering to slip his arms into it. He merely had to go to the basement and get into the car with his protectors. The only time he would come into contact with the weather would be walking from the car into his house near Hampstead Heath.

He waited for the doors to open in the basement and the first bodyguard to get out and switch on the light and look around, before he followed.

None of them knew what hit them.

Half a dozen men emerged from the shadows, two from beneath the window level of the car on the hidden side from the elevator. They were carrying silenced automatics and for a full half minute the shots coughed out, riddling the four men with bullets, sending them twitching and jerking until their bodies fell in pools of blood on to the garage floor.

Pavel saw the men emerge from hiding, but his reactions were too slow. He wasn't a physically violent man and that was why the bodyguards were always with him, but he realised as the bullets began to slam into his body that they had become accustomed to the safety of this place, with the big steel shutter that only opened to allow the car to pass in and out. No one but his own three men knew anything about it. At least he had thought not. But they were wrong. Someone else knew.

It was the last thought he had as the blackness overwhelmed him and he fell to the ground.

The guns went silent.

Then, quite casually, knowing there was no hurry, one of the attackers strolled across to the bodies and rolled them over to stare at their faces. When he came to Pavel he smiled, then casually emptied the remainder of the clip of bullets into Pavel's face.

It cut it to pieces, smashing blood and bone and brain across the floor, spilling it over the coat that had jerked from Pavel's shoulders. When the police found him, they would have to check Pavel's fingerprints to find out who he was.

He bent down and pulled out the thick wad of notes, one from each inside pocket of the coat, then turned to the others, and nodded. No one needed to speak. They knew what they had to do.

They hid their rifles under long coats and left by the side exit, punching in the code to have the door open electronically.

They got into three separate cars, parked in different streets and drove away. One car took the M1 north to Manchester, the others drove up the A1 to Scotland. Once again they kept carefully to the speed limits.

Twenty

Fuengirola, Costa del Sol. Friday morning.

The sphere light on the ceiling stared at him like a full moon glaring from a white sky. His head throbbed and his throat felt as if it had been hit with a hammer. Stabs of pain carved through his stomach the moment he tried to move.

She was studying him from a chair at the side of the bed. He looked around the room, saying nothing. It was big enough for the double bed on which he was lying, a bedside table and a dressing table, but little else. In a corner he could see louvre doors that he supposed must be cupboards. Curtains were drawn across a narrow window.

He turned back to face her.

'You're in our flat,' she said. Tabor hadn't noticed when she spoke in the alley but he could hear an accent in her voice, although her English was excellent. 'My brother and I rent it together.'

He frowned but said nothing.

'I phoned him and he came with the car. We brought you here.'

He raised his head a little and looked down at his body. A

strip of bandage and plaster covered the area where the pain was hurting.

'The cut wasn't deep,' she said. 'I used tape to hold it together without stitches. It's been cleaned and covered and should be fine in a week or so. I can't do anything about the neck or shoulders. The bruising is already showing.'

'How long have I been here?' he asked wearily, the pain in his throat making him wince as he spoke.

'About six hours. It's slightly after nine in the morning.' She handed him a glass of water. 'It will help ease your throat if you drink it straight down. Sipping is of no use.'

He took the glass. The water was cold and he swallowed it in one gulp as she'd suggested, and appreciated it. He tried to remember what had happened, but there was nothing after he fainted. It was his own fault. He'd deliberately walked into the trap, even invited it. It was what he'd been wanting, but he hadn't anticipated four big men in a tight space. It showed he was losing his edge. That or childish arrogance. He'd believed he could take them on, even four at a time, and two years ago they wouldn't have been able to walk away. They would have been carried away dead. But courses were not the same thing as SAS constant training, and he had grown mentally and physically less able. He tried to tell himself he hadn't wanted these men dead, that he'd wanted at least one of them kept alive long enough to question him about the tattooing of Emma and her kidnapping, but reality told him he hadn't been up to it and he was back to square one, no leads to anything. Inwardly he groaned.

'Why did you go to that place?'

'My business,' Tabor said, holding his head as if to ease the ache. 'Thanks for bringing me back and fixing me up, but I'm not in the mood for answering questions.'

'I don't care about your mood. I can kill you, as I originally intended.'

'Then why didn't you?'

'Because of what you did to those men. They were your enemies and, as they say, the enemy of my enemy is my friend. That's why you're alive, Mr Ransome, but it can change if I think I made a mistake about you.'

Ransome? Then he remembered. That was the name on his driving licence and passport.

'You went through my clothes?'

'There wasn't much to go through. A clever idea, the passport, driving licence and so much money in a hidden pocket. That made me wonder about you. It made me think you're not what I originally believed you were.'

'What was that?' His eyes were drifting around the room, but he was trying to concentrate on what she wanted and how he could escape.

'You were asking about a prostitute with a tattoo.' The voice remained unemotional. 'I'm also interested in such a girl. I've been watching you in various bars. You always ask about a prostitute with a flower. I thought you'd lead me to her.'

'What's she to you?'

'My sister,' she said in a matter-of-fact tone. 'If you'd been looking for her to force yourself on her or do anything else, like so many of the men who want girls such as her, I would have killed you, as I said. After I found her. Now I have you, but still not my sister. Unless you tell me where to find her, I may have to kill you all the same.'

Twenty-one

Puerto Banus, Costa del Sol.

Sitting on the settee in the lounge of the yacht at Puerto Banus, Duncan concentrated on what Jerry Ferdetta was saying, nodding silently without initially make any comment.

Ferdetta was speaking from home, but Duncan knew exactly where he would be. In the office of his house overlooking the sea, with the terraces and decks facing the ocean, imported palm trees swaying almost perpetually in the breeze around the large swimming pool.

Ferdetta didn't own the mansion. It was allocated to him free of charge as senior vice president, and lieutenant of Duncan's group of companies. Iain Duncan was the man who made the money, paid what were among the highest salaries found in the bioengineering world, and who therefore called the shots.

Many had called La Jolla the 'jewel of the sea'. A suburb of San Diego where the mansions came with an initial price tag of $10 million and spiralled over the $20 million level.

Not far away was the University of California. There were

major medical research and bioengineering facilities located near the University and the state-of-the-art companies that had sprung up to support them.

Among those was Duncan's company, Cytek. Its scientists were developing products that would eventually change the world.

Ferdetta had called him on a routine update of business matters, but seemed to be edgy. There was nothing to be concerned about and plans were well advanced, but he was fretting again about the quarterly accounts.

'It's the *Tatú* project,' Ferdetta repeated. 'I'm still not happy about the expense.'

'Happiness is a moment, Jerry,' said Duncan. 'Enjoy it for that.'

'Moments I can. Two years of expenses I can't. I have to face the IRS if there's a query.'

Duncan laughed. 'Don't anticipate trouble. Life's too short to be worried all the time.'

That was how it ended, but Duncan knew it wouldn't go away. Ferdetta was like a pit bull.

But pit bulls could be controlled, with a bullet in the head if necessary.

The girl climbed up the ladder to the yacht. She wanted a shower to wash off the salt and she could see Duncan in the lounge using the phone.

One of the crew had been showing her how to manipulate a jet ski, but as she left the crewman to haul the skis aboard she knew what Duncan would want: a drink, a shower together and after that whatever he decided.

Already she was beginning to shiver with fear.

The money, the lifestyle, the carefree ease on board the yacht were only distractions and always the reality remained. She was a captive, set amid luxury and beauty. She was there to be decorative and to be used, but increasingly she was becoming terrified of what would happen once her usefulness was over. It had already been longer than she expected. Days of what amounted to heaven contrasted to the hell she'd suffered since she was picked up months ago, with promises of a modelling assignment in Barcelona, but which ended in Andalucia in the brothel at Fuengirola.

Duncan had taken her from that and she was grateful, but she'd heard tales of what happened to other girls once he finished with them. She didn't want that to happen to her. What she wanted was to be set free, with her passport so that she could go home and try to forget Spain. She needed to keep him interested in her. She needed him to keep her alive.

He'd told her half a dozen times everything would be fine, and he was certainly considerate of her every need. He bought her whatever she wanted and he took her to fine restaurants and places such as the casino.

But he had never promised her eternity.

While she was enjoying herself with Duncan's paid-for toys, she could forget some things, but the time might come for the toys to be put aside. Perhaps permanently. She was only young, but she could smell finality in the air. Two weeks, three weeks, a month. Who could tell? She was shaking again with the very thought of it.

Please God, she prayed silently, don't let them kill me. Don't let me die.

Twenty-two

London. Nearly midnight.

She was staring at the crime wall when he came up and stood behind her.

'Isn't it a bit late?' Landon chided quietly. 'It's almost midnight.'

She turned around. 'I'm sorry, sir,' Hartley replied. 'I didn't expect anyone to be here at this time. It's easier with no one around. It gives me a chance to think.'

'I got your material about Edward Beech,' he said.

Each night she left a report on his desk and most mornings it was put away before she arrived. He was obviously coming in for an hour or two when the office was normally empty, then going back to look after his wife.

'Don't eliminate him,' Landon said carefully. 'I don't like wealthy men vanishing coincidentally when one of his best friends gets drowned.'

'Winters was only an employee.'

'Yacht owners are a different breed. They'd show up for their skipper's funeral if nothing else. It's like an old boys' club, the yachting fraternity.'

'That doesn't mean anything is wrong though, sir.'

'It doesn't mean it's right either.' He switched subjects. 'What do you make of what happened in Edinburgh?'

'I still can't find any connection to our ice-axe murders.'

'Maybe not, but run the details of our prostitutes down here by the pathologists again. There won't be any blood samples left over from our murdered girls but look at the test results. They may firm up our surmise that the local killings are connected to possible malformations in the foetus. Compare them to what they found with the four-month-old foetus in Edinburgh. If they match, it could be a strong motive for the girls down here to have been killed. What about Sanchez, the man in Soho?'

'We haven't found anything useful,' she said. 'We're trying to make a connection between our prostitutes and Sanchez, but so far it's not there. Do you have anything more from your source?'

'Early days, Ruth,' he said, shaking his head. 'I'm off. You should go home too and get some sleep. I'll be in touch if I get anything.'

Hartley watched him leave. He was clearly preoccupied with his wife. Whether it was a happy marriage or not, it had lasted more than thirty years and that wasn't lightly dismissed. She sighed and opened the drawer, pulled out the envelope with the photographs of the room in Edinburgh and the figures heaped in a circle.

She stared at them, trying to see what they could tell her. *Nothing.* It would have to wait for the criminal psychologist to get back to her. She locked them away, stood up and put on her coat.

Landon was right. A night's sleep would be useful. If she could sleep at all.

Landon sat in his car in the car park and watched her leave. He knew he should go directly home, but he procrastinated.

There was nothing for him to go home for. Nothing pleasant anyway.

Sometimes it was easier to sit in the car, or in the world he'd always known here at New Scotland Yard, and do nothing. Not even think. Not about his own dilemmas, his own failures.

Procrastination covered many areas.

But he thought about Hartley and he concerned himself about her. She was one of the younger DIs in the Yard when she joined him four years earlier. Young but bright, and skilled. Well ordered in her mind and, it seemed to him, not burdened by the kind of personal emotional problems he was facing now.

Ruth Hartley had ambition, without being ruthless about it. She would succeed because she was good. She was *very* good, but she also didn't cut corners the way he did, and she didn't allow outside life to interfere.

Again, he thought, the way I did.

Hartley was young for the pressure he'd laid on her over the tattoo murders. Young to have to control a much older and more experienced man like Field, and a sometimes flighty DC like Paul Rogers, but capable of handling them both so admirably that they didn't resent her or her rise in the force.

It was a rare gift. Landon had taken her on to his team because he recognised it, and it had paid off.

Sometimes he wondered why she had no partner. She was a strikingly good-looking woman, accomplished in her field, but she seemed to think only of her work.

And worry about him, he admitted inwardly.

Perhaps if things had been different?

He dismissed the thought, switched on the ignition and eased back into the central London night.

He had to go home to Helen, like it or not.

Twenty-three

Fuengirola. Saturday.

His throat and shoulders ached as he slid to the end of the bed and looked into the mirror on the dressing table. Blue-black bruises had turned his tanned neck into a Technicolor mass. He hadn't shaved for more than a day and the beard was more than elementary stubble.

There was deep discoloration under Tabor's eyes, across his shoulders and back where the chain had struck. All in all, he admitted, not exactly a sight to excite pretty eyes.

He got up quietly, walked across to the curtains and slid them aside. The windows were open. It was light outside but like most Spanish windows it was covered with a *reja* – a grille bolted into the concrete of the wall. No means of escape there. He could hear movement in another room, but not talking. He went to the door and tried the handle. It turned easily and was unlocked.

Next he checked the other door in the corner of the room. As he suspected it was a built-in wardrobe. Not many clothes. Few shoes. The wardrobe of someone who either had little money or had only recently moved there with hardly more than one small suitcase. But she had a gun and that smacked of something more than a tourist enjoying the dying days of the Andalucian summer.

Tabor reached for the clothing on the chair near to him and dressed. There was no shirt to be found. He took a deep breath, opened the door and walked into the room beyond.

She was standing at a sink cutting vegetables on a chopping board.

His eyes inspected the room swiftly. There was an exit door immediately facing him and another close to the kitchen. That would probably be the bathroom. The kitchen-living area was functional. A holiday let. It had barely more comforts than his hotel room. There was no sign of anything that could be converted into a weapon except the kitchen knife she was using for her vegetables.

She turned away from the chopping board, facing him with the knife clutched firmly in her hand. He thought he'd made no noise, but she'd either heard him or sensed his presence.

She studied his chest. The dressing remained clean and the blood hadn't seeped through. Satisfactory, her look seemed to be saying.

She indicated the table. 'I went out last night and bought you a new shirt. The other was covered in blood and unusable. I took some of your money to pay for it and the change is on the packet.'

Tabor glanced at the shirt. Plain white, short sleeves, polyester that would get hot, but cheaper than cotton.

He nodded his thanks and slipped the change into his trouser pocket. He put the shirt to one side. It was too hot to wear indoors.

'You drugged me?'

'Something to make you sleep.' She had her back to him again, continuing with her cooking preparations. The gun was nowhere to be seen. 'It was in the glass of water I gave you,' she said over her shoulder. 'Colourless and odourless but it works very quickly.'

'Some expertise!'

'Enough.' She finished chopping the vegetables and scooped them into a saucepan already filled with water, put it on top of the hob and lit the gas ring beneath, then turned back to him. 'I'm making soup. Quite thick but not so bulky you won't be able to swallow. It will take an hour or so.'

'For what?'

'For the soup to be ready and for you to tell me what I want to know.'

Tabor hadn't moved from the side of the table. He could easily have reached out and grabbed her but she seemed unafraid.

He sat down on one of the chairs. 'Why should I tell you anything?'

'Because I saved your life. For the moment anyway. You'll tell me some of the truth because you feel you're under an obligation. You're probably the kind of man who would want to repay his debts.'

'Don't count on it.'

'Then I'll kill you, as I said I would.'

She wiped down the chopping board and washed the knife. Ants and cockroaches were prevalent in such climates. No one would leave dishes or cooking utensils dirty here. When she was satisfied, she left the kitchen area and sat on the settee about a yard or more away from him. He turned in his seat to watch her.

She moved with a sensuous ease, the walk of someone used to treading lightly and acting quickly. Someone very similar to himself. Dangerous. But she was an attractive woman. Not beautiful in any classical sense but there was a certain magnetism about her. The hair was cut short, sculpted around a tanned face and eyes so dark they seemed to vanish in their own depth. In a simple outfit of store-bought jeans and a thin top, she looked well dressed. She had the natural ability to carry clothes shared by many Latin races.

'What are you?' Tabor demanded. There was no point in asking *who* she was. She wouldn't tell him, not at this stage. What intrigued him was the woman herself. Her air of authority, her unyielding manner and her competence with the gun.

'Someone who asks the questions rather than answering them. Why are you trying to find my sister?'

Tabor breathed in deeply. *The truth, the whole truth and nothing but the truth?* Hardly. But something told him despite her tone she wasn't particularly hostile to him, at this moment. Everything could change in an instant. *Where was the gun?* The handbag was nowhere to be seen. There were no bulges in her jeans pockets. Yet the gun had vanished from sight. *The cupboard drawers?*

'Do you speak Spanish?'

'Yes, but you don't. You were asking only in the English bars rather than talking to local Spaniards who know as much about prostitution as any of the touts. They've seen it all before. I repeat, why are you trying to find my sister?'

Tabor hesitated. Was there anything to lose?

'I'm not,' he said. 'I haven't got a clue who your sister is and I'd never seen you before until I noticed you in the bar last night.'

'You weren't looking for anyone keeping a check on you,' she said, shrugging. 'I've been in at least a dozen bars over the past few days, waiting for you to find what you were searching for. Why were you looking for a tattooed girl if you weren't trying to find my sister?'

He was listening for an indication of another presence,

hidden away perhaps in the bathroom, or anyone approaching the door. All was silent except for the popping of the water bubbling away on the gas stove.

'Why do you think your sister has a tattoo like the one I've been showing around?'

'Because she told me so. Or rather she wrote a letter telling me. She described the tattoo and said it had been put there while she was unconscious in hospital. She also said the tattoo wasn't finished and she had been to the hospital recently. The letter was postmarked Malaga. She was being forced to work in a brothel in Fuengirola but she says it wasn't for sex. In her words, "they made me do things". I'm guessing that means something such as S&M. She added that she's allowed out occasionally, as long as someone is with her. I've checked with hospitals within two hundred kilometres and they've never heard of her. The police have nothing on record. That was a couple of weeks ago. I've been here since the day after.'

'Trying to get her back?'

'Of course. Why are you looking for someone with the same tattoo?'

'Not the same. Similar. My sister had a tattoo in the same place.'

'Had?'

'She's dead,' Tabor said bluntly. 'A brothel client killed her.'

For a moment her eyes opened in surprise, then she half-smiled in understanding. 'Did you deal with him the way you dealt with those men in the alleyway?'

'No. I threw him out of a window. He broke his neck.'

'Murder?'

'They said manslaughter,' answered Tabor. 'I called it doing what any brother would do.'

'Or any sister,' she said, the smile broadening. She stood

up and walked over the couple of steps to him and held out her hand.

'My name is Anca. Anca Aron. I'm Romanian, as were those men who tried to kill you in the alleyway. My sister is called Dorina. We seem to be looking for the same thing. Perhaps we should join forces. Be partners.'

'Give me the gun and we'll talk about it,' Tabor answered, staring unblinking into her eyes.

She chuckled softly, then turned and reached over to one of the drawers, pulled the gun out and laid it on the cupboard top where he could see it.

'I could like you, Mr Ransome,' she said. 'You trust nobody and believe nothing. That's an excellent way to stay alive.'

Twenty-four

Fuengirola.

Dani was little more than a boy, probably no older than seventeen, slightly built and thin, but wiry. His face was open, but his blue eyes were cold and untrusting. He spoke no English and, as far as Tabor could tell, very little Spanish. He had to assume they spoke in Romanian. There was only Anca's word that she was Romanian and he hadn't asked for proof. Anca had said the men who tackled him in the alley were Romanians, but that also remained to be verified. *Trust nobody and believe nothing.* There was much more to Anca Aron than met the eye.

For a while they sat in a café in El Faro, a few kilometres west of Fuengirola, tossing small talk backwards and forwards across the table. Having eaten the soup earlier, Tabor and Anca were no longer hungry but Dani ordered *tapas* for himself. Cheap and, when supplemented by the bread, quite filling.

It was over half an hour later when she turned to Tabor and asked, 'Where did you learn your martial arts? The routines aren't standard Asian *kata*.'

'Why should you care?' he said, sipping the cola he'd ordered while the boy had a beer. 'You have a gun. I don't.'

'I have a gun because I'm in the police. I'm on leave for a month and I've already used up two weeks. That's why I need a partner. You have an incentive, you're not afraid of anyone, you're competent with your hands. But you're not a policeman because you go about things in the wrong way. I think you're in the army. Am I right?'

'And you're really with the police?'

'A section that deals with vice and in particular with criminal gangs and the export of Romanian girls for prostitution in other parts of Europe. I didn't know until the other week I was personally involved.'

'Him?' Tabor indicated Dani, sitting opposite and clearly understanding nothing.

She spoke quickly to him and he answered angrily. She turned back to Tabor. 'He doesn't trust you. He's not with the police or our armed forces. Dani is here because he loves his sister. He loves both of his sisters and he thinks it's a man's job to protect the women of his family.'

'He's a liability,' Tabor said bluntly, sitting back in his seat and staring at the boy. 'Look at him. He wouldn't last five minutes if trouble started. He'd be in the way. He doesn't have his sister's gene pool.'

'He doesn't have to. Dani has other attributes you don't.'

'Such as?'

'Such as being able to go into a brothel and ask for a girl. You can't any more because you're well known around the brothels of Fuengirola now. The reality, Mr Ransome, is that in some respects *you* are the liability and Dani knows that. He is an expert on computers. He's been using them since he was six or seven. I'm told he's a hero in some hacking circles. Is that one of your accomplishments?'

'Why should I need it?'

'Dani can tap into most systems in Europe. He looked up your records earlier today. There was nothing except the normal passport details. I find that odd. You hide your passport and money like a professional, you fight like a soldier, but your records say you're snowy white.'

Tabor looked at her. She was staring at him, waiting for an answer.

'My real name is Tabor,' he said. 'Simon Tabor.'

'Thank you.' She showed no surprise. 'Tomorrow Dani will run that name. If you have something on record, he'll find it. He's also tapped in the past into the French DGSE and the French Intelligence Service, the DCRI; along with the main German intelligence services, the BND and German Military Intelligence, the MAD. He can access the files of the National Intelligence Centre in Madrid and those of the SRI in Romania and, of course, Interpol. He can find anything you want to know that's on official record about the gangs who run the prostitution rings. I think that's enough to show he can do anything that is on record that you will need.'

'But he can't tell you where his sister is.' Tabor was dismissive.

'No, because such details are never recorded, either on paper or in electronic data, but I can tell you what I know and what he's confirmed in the past week accessing various systems.'

'Can he tell me who kidnapped my sister and forced her into prostitution?'

'No. I said there are no personal records.'

'Then what use are you to me? Why should I saddle myself with a partner? Or worse, with two partners.'

'Because I *can* tell you who runs the Romanian brothels here on the Costa del Sol.'

'Who?'

'Are we partners?'

Tabor went quiet. Show time. Put up, or shut up. It wasn't enough for him to think he should simply learn what he could from this woman then go away to do his own thing. A promise wasn't to be broken lightly. He might have few scruples and fewer friends but the enemies he had could never say honestly that he'd fallen down on a promise. And he promised Emma in his thoughts every night that she would find justice.

But it was too sudden and he knew too little.

'Your sister,' he said, without answering her question. 'How long has she been missing?'

'I don't know for certain. About eight months.'

'You don't know?'

'My sister comes from a small village in the mountains outside Rogojel. She lived there with our mother and grandmother. I was in Bucharest and Dani was working on a building site in a seaside area on the Black Sea. I was busy with my career and my mother didn't have a telephone so we only had contact by letter, and she didn't write well so it was sporadic.'

Tabor said nothing but his expression was enough.

'We all have things in our life we should have done, but didn't, Mr Tabor. I should have made certain I kept in touch, but I was too busy forging a career. I hardly gave a thought to my sister.' Her face was stiff. 'When I finally drove over to see her, my mother told me she hadn't heard from Dorina since she ran away one day. She had a fight with a boy in the village and my mother interfered, sending the boy away. In small villages like ours, young people often run away because their parents interfere, usually because the girl is pregnant. Their parents don't want to know. They think if they don't know about it perhaps it won't have happened so they never tell. My mother and grandmother didn't until I went there and asked. My sister ran away taking a small case of clothes with her. She hadn't contacted anyone since.'

'And?'

'I went to the police in Rogojel and later tried to find out through Bucharest, but there was nothing. Any trail there had been was cold. Then two weeks ago my mother went to the police with a letter, asking them to contact me immediately. That was the letter posted in Malaga.'

Tabor thought about it. Eight months. Emma had been missing for hardly more than three but by the time he found her it was too late. Her spirit was already broken. And she was pregnant. Would she still have been alive if he had handled things differently in that room? Would she have ever left for Morocco if he had given her brotherly love and watched over her in her infancy, instead of abrogating his responsibilities, transferring his personal obligations to the supervision of a school, concerning himself with his own life rather than that of his sister?

He pushed the thoughts aside and tried to focus on the girl sitting opposite him.

She had information Tabor wanted about the people who had abducted Emma. If she had a similar interest in finding someone missing, did Tabor have anything to lose?

'*Is* your sister pregnant?' He winced inwardly as he said it, thinking again of Emma.

'She didn't say so in her letter. I doubt she would have been taken into a brothel if she had been.'

'Maybe, maybe not,' he hedged. What could he say? *My sister was pregnant and they killed her.* That was the hard truth and normally he would have said it without a second thought. But this woman might be the first lead he'd had. Could he afford to ignore it with a throwaway line? 'I'll try to help you,' he said. The delay while he thought was almost imperceptible. 'Now tell me who's running the brothels.'

'A man called Costel Potrascu,' she answered immediately.

Next to her Dani flinched. He might not understand the English but he knew that name.

'What did your brother find out about this man?'

But she shook her head. 'Later.'

She spoke rapidly to Dani then turned back to Tabor.

'You said you would help. Now I have to ask you to trust me.' She drew in a deep breath, a signal of things that had to be said but were difficult for some reason. 'I think you should leave your hotel. I have been watching you and so have they. They know where you're staying and after the fight in the alley they *will* come for you. I think you should come to stay at my place, at least for the next few days.'

She turned and translated to Dani. Tabor watched his face. He didn't like what he was being told and he glared across the table at Tabor. Tabor stared back, not allowing any reaction to show on his face.

Anca switched back to him, ignoring Dani who had retreated into what could have been an angry sulk.

'We're leaving now. I want you to stay an hour or so and then go to the taxi rank on the other side of the road. Return to your hotel. Dani has been on the streets and he thinks they've been looking for you all over Fuengirola, but they have kept one guard permanently watching your hotel. There was no reason to tell you earlier but since we're now partners it's imperative you know.'

'How do you know your place is safer than the hotel?'

'No one had any reason to look for our place until I intervened in the alley,' she answered. 'Now they'll be looking but it will be half-hearted because they are lazy people. They jump when Costel is close, sleep when he's not.' She paused reflectively. 'Do I need to tell you how to evade the people who are watching outside your hotel when you get there? Or is evasion one of your other skills?'

'I'll get by,' Tabor said enigmatically.

'You will need our address.' She pulled a notepad from her handbag, wrote on it with a cheap ballpoint pen and handed the slip of torn-out paper to him. 'You'll have to bunk with Dani.'

She paused for a moment. 'Thank you, Tabor. Partners, but we both have to work at it.'

Tabor packed his bags. He could feel the excitement and apprehension rising in him the way it always had on a mission. When he finished he pulled out his phone and tapped a message to Landon's mobile number.

'Romanian,' it said tersely. Landon would have to do what he could with that for the moment.

He put the phone in a pocket of the jacket hanging ready on a doorknob, switched out the light and tried to doze, but no sleep came. In time he picked up his bag and left.

Two hours later, he was in Anca's living room with a wide-awake Dani staring at him with hostility from atop the unfolded sofa bed.

Tabor locked the door behind him and pushed the flimsy bolts shut. It wouldn't hold anyone determined to get through, but it was the only entrance and easily watched. In daylight he would find a gun. There were always places to buy one if the price was right. He sat down on the chair by the table, ignoring the bed and closed his eyes but remained awake. Anca was wrong.

There *were* watchers outside the hotel but they *weren't* lazy. One was inside the lobby, waiting patiently with a drink on a small table beside the armchair, two others were outside in a car. Instead of taking a taxi, he'd headed into the morass of streets along the sea front, but it had taken a long time before he was satisfied he'd lost them and then walked back to Anca's place.

He didn't need the address.

The minute he left the place last evening he'd memorised its location, right down to the number on the door. But he didn't need to tell her that.

Partners they might be. Bosom buddies they were not.

And there was another reason he stayed awake.

He was good at evasion and escape techniques, but only a fool would think he was unbeatable.

Tabor didn't like to think of himself as a fool.

Someone could know where Anca lived. Someone could have followed him and know where he was now. They could come calling any time they wanted.

Tabor waited.

Twenty-five

Edinburgh.

The house was close to the Firth, enclosed in its own grounds. It was quiet, and, while the neighbours were uneasy about what happened there, no one made an official complaint. They minded their own business.

The two cars drove through the gateway and pulled up outside the forecourt, joining four other vehicles. The men from one car went inside, wearing heavy coats, not unusual for this time of year. Girls glanced at them, but other clients paid no attention.

Two of the newcomers parked themselves on stools, one at either end of the bar and two others went up to the smiling barman.

'What can I get you, gentlemen?' he asked in a pleasant voice that had a tinge of something foreign, but no ancestry based in Scotland.

'Dmitri would be a start,' said the taller of the two men. Unlike the barman he had a broad brogue, one that smacked of the Highlands.

'I don't know any Dmitri,' the barman said nervously, glancing behind him at the mirror.

'Sure, you do,' said the Scotsman. 'Dmitri may not be behind yon mirror but the man who's staring at us will know where he is. Won't he, Wadim?'

Beyond the wall of mirrors, Wadim Tepes looked up, startled at the sound of his name. The two-way system was installed to allow him to check on possible troublemakers, but it hadn't been needed since they'd been here. There was no CCTV here, although they had them at other city brothels.

He stared at the man grinning at him unseen on the other side of the bar, but he was puzzled. It was no one he knew.

'Come on, Wadim,' said the man a little more loudly. 'Dmitri's here, or if he isn'ae you can tell me where to find him.'

Tepes went up to the mirror wall to peer more closely. He stared into ice-blue eyes. Cold and without emotion.

'Och, well,' said the Scotsman, his voice lowering again. 'Dinnae say I didn'ae ask politely.'

Tepes was moving towards the telephone on the desk and the shotgun propped against it, but as he reached it the mirror shattered into fragments. The barman crashed through, bounced on the floor and slammed his head against the side of the desk. He lay motionless as shards of broken mirror rained down on him.

Tepes screamed as pieces of glass attacked him like a horde of angry hornets, nicking into his flesh, scouring his face, cutting his arms and hands, ripping through his hair. One earlobe was sliced off as he went down in a pool of blood, falling across the unconscious barman.

On the other side of the wall, the two men took pistols from under their coats. Through the doorway ran four men from the second car, carrying automatic rifles. Within seconds the Scotsman and his colleague broke into the room behind the mirror.

The Scotsman went over to Tepes lying bleeding on the ground and knelt beside him. 'Where's Dmitri?' he whispered in Tepes's ear. 'One chance. Tell me and I'll let you live.'

'Fuck off!' Tepes shouted.

The Scotsman shot him through the head. The bullet entered as a small hole smashed through the brain and carried on into the unconscious body of the barman. The barman jerked and the Scotsman turned to look at him. His eyes were open and the pain was crying out from them.

'I don't suppose you'll tell me politely either,' the Scotsman said. 'That's what comes of keeping bad company.'

He shot him between the eyes and the pain went out.

Upstairs he could hear the guns coughing. He stood up and spoke to his colleague who had so far done nothing.

'Leave the calling card. If they haven'ae found the brat by now, it means he's gone to ground somewhere else. We've got to find him. Give the girls time to get out. Dinnae kill all o' them if ye dinnae have to but gi' them fair warnin' and maybe waste a couple so they understand not to talk. If you find the boy, dinnae hurt him. We want him alive.'

Minutes later the guns went silent and his men came out, stowing their weapons inside the cars or in their waistbands.

The one with the ice-blue eyes came up to him.

'It's done,' he said. 'The kid wasn't there. Better luck at the next place.'

Stockbridge. Early hours.

The brothel was of similar size and proportions, and equal seclusion, but this time they made no attempt at subterfuge. There was now the possibility someone had phoned after the others were killed and they could take no chances.

They walked through the door and raised their guns. One client stood up and started towards them as if to protest and the Scotsman shot him in the left knee. As he went down, screaming in agony, the Scotsman put a bullet in the other knee. The man was writhing and crying and yelling and the girls were hysterical.

The Scotsman went over to him. 'We put sick animals out of their misery, as an act of kindness,' he said softly. Then he knelt down, opened the man's mouth, shoved the pistol in and shot through the roof of his mouth, blowing the back of his skull to pieces.

He stood up. 'The Irish do it better,' he admitted, turning and smiling at the others. 'But we Scots dinnae have time for finesse.'

He turned back to the one with the blue eyes. 'Lock the girls in a room so no one sees the rest o' the lads. Tell them what we'll do if they give our descriptions to the polis. They're Romanian. They know what happens to ones who squeal. Get on with it, man. Bring me the boy.'

From the top floor, Dmitri heard the screaming and knew they had caught up with him. He'd known from the moment he fled through the gate that they would come. They wanted to kill him the way they had his father because they thought he'd seen them. They would kill him for what they thought he knew and they wouldn't believe him if he said he had seen nothing. He had to run! Fear had driven him to this house, which his father owned, and for days he'd been hiding here, reliving every moment of the horror, afraid to leave the room.

They were coming.

He scrambled into his trousers and put on his shoes without bothering to find socks. He grabbed his shirt, fiddling to find the buttons, but his fingers wouldn't function properly. The sickness was rising inside him and fright was crowding his brain. He needed to go to the toilet, but he didn't want to be killed in there with his trousers down. Oddly at such a moment he thought of the indignity of that.

Panic lent him momentary decision. He opened the window and climbed out. The wall was covered in thick ivy, decades old, and he swung himself into it, reaching for the fattest and safest strands and clambered down the way he'd scrambled down trees as a child in the woods, back home. There were large trees close to the wall. He raced over to the nearest and climbed to a branch that overhung the pavement. He edged along it, feeling it droop with his weight as he neared the thin end.

It snapped.

Dmitri let out a scream as it broke beneath him, then he was falling through space, his hands reaching desperately up to the sky but grasping nothing.

The Scotsman heard the scream and looked up in time to see the branch breaking and the boy falling. 'The brat's outside,' he shouted. 'He got over the wall.'

He headed down the driveway, his heavy boots thundering on the gravel as he skidded through the open gate and turned to the right.

Dmitri landed on his back and pain shot through him, but it was only bruising. He said thanks to God that nothing had broken, then struggled upright. His back was aching and his knee was throbbing. He straightened up and began to run.

He raced through the parkland on to another deserted road and saw railings ahead of him, enclosing the blackness of more heavily treed territory that promised sanctuary. He scaled a four-feet-high ornamental cast-iron railing and fell on to the mown grass of a playing field. He could hear the boots on the road and the squeal of car tyres heading in his general direction.

They hadn't fired, he thought, as he went past the fields and fell down the hill to crash through some shrubbery. Why hadn't they shot at him?

He burst out on to a wide gravelled area. Directly in front were the monstrous towers of some huge Gothic building. It could have been translocated from Transylvania, clawing the memory from drawings he'd seen in books about Vlad the Impaler.

The darkness of the building rose up, spires sweeping into the sky and black blank windows staring sightlessly from above. No movement. No one around. Nothing to be seen. No one to see.

He slipped around the imposing façade of the building, down the massive series of wide steps in front of it towards ornate gates in the distance, but well before he reached them he saw two cars come to a halt outside. He turned right into a tunnel of tall old trees, hearing men behind him. Dmitri was panting, finding it hard to draw breath and he could feel fresh blood running down his arm, but he kept moving, his heart pounding, his legs pumping. He darted past a tennis court and saw a house directly ahead, with a driveway, only wide enough for a single car off to the left.

He stumbled along it to a gate, about six feet high. He hauled himself up and dropped over the top, ignoring the ornamental spear tops. He felt the fabric tearing, shreds hanging on to the points, then he fell on to the pavement.

He didn't stop. He couldn't stop. He picked himself up, but he was blinded by the headlights of a car that pulled up beside him. Dmitri slammed into the side, went up and over the bonnet and dropped down the other side on to the road-way.

The car doors began to open, but Dmitri was up and run-ning again, avoiding another vehicle travelling fast towards him, feeling the wind of its passage as it clipped him on the backside and twisted him around and around. He tottered towards the kerbside, but stayed upright. Ahead he could see a large building with many windows lit up inside. It was too high for him to climb the fence, but the lights meant there was someone in there. There was shelter. There was refuge.

An opening loomed up and he turned into it. No gates. He was running down the asphalt, his arms held out wide as if trying to fly, as he lunged through the doorway of the building and collapsed, sobbing into a foyer.

Twenty-six

London. Sunday morning.

A sullen September had fallen over London. The cloud layer was thick, the streets grey and the light was unable to cast shadows. A day with no emotion in the air. People went about their businesses in automatic mode. Leaves on trees were turning in anticipation of autumn, but not the colours Hartley remembered from the Worcestershire countryside of her childhood. Down-at-heel trees on a down-at-heel day.

Edinburgh police had called. There had been developments.

Fresh footprints had been found in the newly dug shrubbery and they appeared to be the size of a child. They believed it was the thirteen-year-old son of Cerdachescu who had moved from Romania after his mother died.

It appeared that whoever killed Cerdachescu knew the boy had escaped, and had gone after him to two other brothels.

They had killed people in both brothels, but all the indications were that the boy had escaped them again and fled through the grounds of Fettes College into the headquarters of Borders and Lothian police.

'He what?'

'He escaped from there too,' Hartley said. 'It would be funny if it weren't so serious.'

As Murchie explained it, not exactly happily, it had been a horrendous night.

They'd managed to keep news of what had happened in Blackhall out of the media, but there was no way the latest killings could be covered up. In total, eight male clients were dead in the two brothels, plus three male staff and five girls caught up in the shooting.

'They didn't lay them out the way they did in Blackhall, but the manager of one of the brothels, a Romanian called Wadim Tepes, had his eyes gouged out and placed on his chest. In my book that means it's the same mob,' Murchie said. 'Some of the girls must have seen who did the killing, but they're too terrified to describe anyone. What they did say was they wanted the boy more than anything. He may be the only witness to these massacres. We have to find him, before they do.'

Field shook his head in disbelief.

'Talk about a comedy of errors,' he said. 'The boy *really* ran into the police headquarters?'

'He obviously didn't know what it was. He probably saw lights inside and headed there for safety. He collapsed through the doors and two duty policemen went to see what was wrong. He was unconscious for a few minutes, but when he came to he took one look at the policemen's uniforms and tried to run. They brought in a DI, but the lad spoke no English. All he could do was scribble the word "Romania" on a piece of paper, so they put him in a side room and went to find an interpreter. The kid climbed through the window. By the time they got back he'd vanished. There's an all-points out, but he's gone to ground.'

Field's face saddened. He stroked his moustache reflectively. It was too long and needed cutting, but he rarely got around to doing it until it hung over his lips. Until then, as now, he used it as an aid to contemplation, the way some people subconsciously twiddle pencils.

'Poor kid,' he said softly. 'No parents, the only people he knew shot in front of him. No English, no knowledge of Edinburgh. The lad must be going out of his mind knowing the police are after him as well. He's obviously terrified of them. He's got nowhere to turn. I take it there's no picture of him?'

Hartley shook her head. 'Nothing,' she said. 'Murchie's team has drawn up a list of places where they think Romanians have brothels and they're staking them out in case the boy went to one of those. Murchie's hoping that there may be some info from the media. He thinks a London gang may be trying to muscle in on the Romanian operation up in Scotland.'

'You don't agree?'

'I don't know. We haven't heard a word about anything like that.'

She thought about the boy. Field was right. Somewhere out there, in weather colder and damper than London, a boy was in hiding, not knowing where to go or who to turn to. Even if he knew the other brothels his father had owned, the lad might be too scared to go near them.

'You're thinking about the lad?' Field asked.

She nodded. 'It's Edinburgh's case, but I hope the poor kid makes it through this alive.'

'If he does he'll get thrown into an orphanage.'

'I don't think it will come to that,' Hartley said, but her

voice lacked conviction. What happened later was for other people to decide. 'Right now some of Cerdachescu's henchmen have had contact with their Romanian colleague,' she guessed, thinking aloud. 'Someone will fly out to take over and they're going to want to find the boy first and then eliminate the people who did this to him and the others.' She stopped and looked at Field. 'I don't like it, Jack. I don't like it at all.'

Twenty-seven

Sierra de Las Nieves. Monday.

Someone wrote that, once someone has been touched by the astonishing beauty of an orchid, he will remain besotted with them all his life, allowing everything but his attention to his love to fall by the wayside. More than a love. More than a passion. A consummation.

Blake leaned over the bench and peered more closely at the splendid branches of the *Odontonia Debutante* '*Oxbow*'. He whispered gently into its olive and brown flowers, charming it with his hushed syllables, sensing it preen with pride at the flattery bestowed on it as he stepped back to inspect, for the thousandth time, the yellow tip of the flower. So unusual. *Oxbow* was different to most other orchids, created by an unusual kind of breeding in the late 1950s – a bigeneric between an *Odontoglossum* and *Miltonia*. Even in the 21st century it remained a wonder.

He passed through the *Odontoglossum* section, stopping from time to time to inspect a plant, although the species was one of the best known in the cut-flower world, along with the *Cymbidiums* that were the stock-in-trade of the corsage business.

Their exploitation by the commercial world was, he declaimed at every opportunity, to be deplored, but the beauty of the flowers defied their debasement.

He crossed into the hot house to examine a *Trichglottis*, a striking orchid that mixed dark shades of maroon, pink and orange and white. Blake had planted his on a piece of Australian tree fern and there it flourished happily.

He stood back from the plant with a sigh. Not of dismay but of admiration and unbridled respect. Blake had heard even reputable orchid breeders describe some plants as 'ugly' or 'curious'. It was not an attitude or a description he would accept. Tropical orchids demanded not merely respect but unquestioning adoration.

The ringing of the phone violated his thoughts.

Blake didn't appreciate interruptions and allowed no one to enter the orchid houses without his permission. His staff had to communicate with him by mobile phone while he was locked away inside them. It wasn't only his innate dislike of other company, or a concern to guard his privacy, but also the damage unknowing outsiders could do if they left doors open, or carried outside pests such as red spiders, whitefly and springtails on their clothes. There had been one occasion when, after he unwisely allowed a fellow enthusiast to enter without the necessary precautions, he'd been forced to treat the whole of the medium-heat orchid house with aerosols. The task took him an entire day. Each plant had to be inspected separately and no insecticide could be permitted to hit the buds or flower spikes.

So angry was Blake at the work it caused and the potential damage to his plants that the man was banned from the orchid houses forever, along with Blake's own staff. The phone was now the only way he could be contacted while he was in them.

He opened the phone and snapped, 'Yes?'

It was the gardener. He was standing beside the main gate, talking to a man and woman who wanted to speak to the doctor about orchids.

'Send them away,' ordered Blake, cutting the call and shuddering. The last thing he wanted was to talk to boring tourists.

But a moment later the phone went again and he opened it angrily. 'Can't you understand? I don't want to be disturbed,' he shouted.

At the other end of the phone the gardener quivered. He didn't want to be fired, but there were some things Blake insisted on being told about. This could be one of them.

The man at the gate spoke no Spanish, the gardener said in an apologetic voice, but the girl explained that he was an English journalist who wanted an interview.

'Give him the usual answer,' Blake barked, and cut the call again. He scowled at the telephone. The gardener was correct, but the call was a nuisance.

Blake didn't turn down media interviews out of hand, but he disliked talking to journalists and only did so if it could advance him in some way. That meant 'the standard response'. It also meant he hadn't spoken to any journalist for several years.

'Dr Blake's rules are that you must submit a request on the letterhead of your newspaper or company, giving your reasons for wanting an interview,' the gardener explained, speaking to Anca through the tall wrought-iron gates. 'It should be brought here personally. When the doctor has called your company's office, he'll decide whether to speak to you or not.'

'That could take days,' Tabor said in exasperation, as Anca translated. 'Tell him I'm only in the region for a short time.'

Anca reported exactly and the gardener shrugged.

'The doctor works to his own timetable,' he said. 'But if you get the letter back here quickly he may be more inclined to see you. There's another bullfight coming up and he won't miss that to speak with you. For the doctor bullfights and orchids take precedence.'

Anca translated, then added, 'That's it then. A wasted trip.'

But this time Tabor smiled, a rare smile that showed he had some kind of trick up his sleeve. 'Tell him I'll be back with a signed letter on headed paper.'

A short exchange of words followed, then Anca turned back to Tabor. 'He says to make it nine o'clock. He says the doctor is precise. He has his breakfast at seven thirty, then retires until eight forty-five. He wouldn't welcome us being early. Or late.'

In the hot house the phone rang again and Blake dropped the pipette of pollen he had so painstakingly gathered. He swore vehemently as he picked up the mobile, but not the one issued to the gardener. This one had only two contacts and neither would call him unless it was vital.

'Have you watched the television news?' Costel Potrascu asked in his soft voice, as Blake answered.

'I rarely watch television,' said Blake testily. 'And I never watch the news. It's inevitably inaccurate, skewed by the emphasis on pictures the hoi polloi seem to find so fascinating.'

Potrascu sniffed. He had little time for Blake's idiosyncrasies.

'This time there's no room for misunderstanding or misquoting. It was confirmed by the police.'

'Police?'

'There has been an attack on friends in Edinburgh. My colleagues tell me there was another that hasn't been officially revealed. My cousin, Bogdan Cerdachescu. They massacred him and his main people. Some of the girls too.'

'The girls!' Blake was instantly concerned.

'None of yours and it's not your responsibility, but it *was* my cousin. The other two attacks were at houses owned by Bogdan's business concerns. Our informers in Edinburgh tell us police are saying it's a gang war and the killers may have come from London.'

'London?'

'If you stop repeating everything I say we'll get done faster. It's worse. My brother is also missing.'

Potrascu had been holding himself back. Normally he spoke in a soft voice, but at times his true self showed through. Then his voice became hard and tense with an edge of madness to it. It was moving towards that now. He brought himself under control.

'I'm flying to London,' he said. 'This has to be sorted out.'

'Do what you have to,' said Blake with calculated indifference. 'I've got no interest in your brother. You know what must be safeguarded.'

'You may have no interest in Pavel, but I do, and it has to do with you if the police trace our operation and link it to our joint activity. That said, there's no reason there should be any problems. Your concerns are side issues. We're not bound together in steel ropes. I wouldn't bother to tell you at all except there's something else. Someone is looking for you. Someone who is interested in tattoos.'

Blake flinched. 'Why?'

'He's interested in prostitutes too. Put two and two together, you're the genius. There's one more thing. He's just been to your gate.'

'Here!' Blake almost dropped the phone in his instant of panic. The journalist? 'How do you know?'

'The same reason I know he's looking for you.' There was satisfaction in Potrascu's voice. Business was business, but the doctor wasn't a likeable person and Potrascu felt it was fun to make him squirm. He would have liked to keep doing it, but time was running out. He needed to catch the plane.

'The man has been asking all over the Costa about tattoos and prostitutes. I sent four of my men to bring him in some days ago. He disabled some of them then a woman turned up with a gun. My people left, but since then I've had a tail on him. Do you want me to handle it?'

Blake didn't hesitate. 'Immediately,' he said. 'Is that all?'

'Someone will be in touch,' Potrascu answered. 'You have strange friends, Dr Blake. Violent ones who may not like you very much. I can understand that, though. Can't you?'

He put the phone down, laughing.

Tabor strolled back to the car chuckling inwardly. As the Boy Scouts motto said, be prepared. There would be no problem getting the letterhead of a newspaper or magazine. It was easy to download the logos of whichever newspaper he chose, add the relevant addresses, then use photo-editing to print out a version that would pass scrutiny by anyone who didn't know the actual newspaper stationery from experience.

In the cottage at Wast Water he also had a number of self-made press badges with his photograph and names matching his passports and he'd brought with him the one with the name of Ransome. There was someone on the *Sunday Times* magazine who would vouch for him under that name. Tabor had done him favours in the past, as he had done with other journalists who could be useful. It was one of the tools of the trade. Scratch my back and I'll scratch yours.

All he had to do was phone London and ensure the real journalist would answer the kind of questions Dr Blake might ask. Verify his existence and his intentions. Dani could handle the faking of the letterhead.

Anca slid in behind the steering wheel of the twenty-year-old battered red Ford Fiesta outside Blake's home.

She'd bought it when she and Dani first arrived in Fuengirola. It belched oil, the bearings rattled and the exhaust would probably only last a couple of months but that was more time than she had anyway. Numerous cars overtook her and that gave Tabor more concern than the reliability of Anca's car. In the Sierra de Las Nieves one side of the narrow road was defended by stout steel guard rails, preventing cars going over the edge, while on the other were open concrete culverts half a metre deep, designed to carry away winter rains.

But the Spanish would happily overtake when a truck or bus was coming up fast in front. His concern was that Anca's vehicle would be forced by one of those into the culvert.

Anca retraced the route she had taken on the way up, driving downhill five or six kilometres, towards a bridge over the Rio Grande. Here the road was a little wider, in some stretches clear for overtaking, and by the time they were closing on the river only one vehicle remained behind, a black BMW. It was creeping closer, but there was no way to overtake before the bridge. Tabor turned around and stared at it a couple of times, but the windows were of black privacy glass. He could see nothing of the driver as they rounded a bend that ran the last forty yards to the bridge.

A concrete-mixing truck was coming in the opposite direction and Tabor relaxed, returning his attention to the road. There was room on the bridge for the concrete mixer and the Ford to pass comfortably. He began to speak to Anca, as she checked in the rear-view mirror, and he saw sudden alarm in her eyes.

He tried to swivel around in his seat to see what was happening. There came the roar of a high-powered engine shrieking as the driver changed down a gear and began to howl past the Ford. The air horns of the concrete mixer were blaring, but already the mixer was on the bridge and there was no way it could stop in time. Anca braked hard, but the linings were worn and unable to bring her to a halt quickly. Tabor knew they were going to crash.

The BMW streaked past the Ford, cutting in front of them, squeezing into the space alongside the concrete mixer. Anca swung the wheel violently to the right and the Ford slammed into the culvert before the edge of the bridge. Its front end crumbled, but its motion was such that it continued up on to the top of the ditch, ripping away the sump and spewing oil over the road.

The tyres on the concrete mixer screeched as it continued to brake, bearing down at over 60kph on the rear end of the now useless Ford, straddled on top of the culvert with the caved-in front swaying over the edge, wobbling towards the Rio Grande flowing below.

For a moment Tabor thought they would make it, but the mixer was slewing across the road. The driver fought to bring it to a halt, but the front wheels hit the oil slick spewing from the shattered Ford's sump. The mixer began to broadside across the end of the bridge. It whipped around in an almost 360-degree turn and as it slammed against the steel guards the rear end shunted the boot of the Ford, hanging like a see-saw over the concrete rim of the culvert, and threw it over the top.

Anca was shouting out and Tabor was aware of the Ford falling, the front end crumpling as it began rolling over and over down the bank towards the rippling water.

Instinctively he slammed his hand on the seatbelt release. It came free but it was too late. The passenger door ripped off, windows shattered and the front end crumpled against the windscreen. It smashed through the stands of bamboo that lined the river, hit the water and rolled again, burying Tabor's side into the rocky pebbles of the riverbed. Anca's head slammed against the wheel and knocked her unconscious.

Water poured in. Tabor tried to lean over to open her door, but, although he was technically free, she had fallen hard against him. Her seatbelt was still fastened and he couldn't reach under to release her. He tried to shove her up, but without sufficient leverage she was a dead weight and he was half-buried already in the riverbed. There was no way he could get out. The pebbles were large and he couldn't squeeze under the edge of the car.

Water was shooting like a torrent through the smashed windows. The river was normally shallow, but now it was swollen to a depth of nearly a metre by the recent rains and the water rose up in his mouth, closing over him. He was like a trapped animal fighting to save himself and the girl, but there *was* no escape. Only inevitability. The water level was settling below the roof of the car. Too far. He couldn't push himself up to reach the air. His brain was starting to reel as the oxygen he gulped in his last moment escaped in small bubbles from the side of his mouth. In his mind flashed a picture of Emma, dead on the bed where the bastard had raped and killed her. Emma, an unborn baby inside her. There were things he needed to do before he made his peace for her, and with her. Now he never would. All of his adult life he'd been a man who did things, who got them done any way he could, but now he could do nothing. He was impotent. Trapped inside a rusty old car while the cold river buried him.

His lungs ached for air but there was none coming. They were ready to burst, but the moment he opened his mouth to breathe he would drink down pint after pint of the river water and he would suffocate, unable to fend it off.

Through the water he could hear Anca spluttering and her head attempting to move, but she was too weak and dazed and it was too late. His vision was blurring. He was sinking into an abyss. With one last gargantuan effort he pushed his left arm upwards, grabbing the bottom of the steering wheel, lifting her head through the smashed windscreen into the air above the water, clenching his fingers and willing them to go rigid and never let go, hoping he could support her long enough to clear her head, relax the seatbelt and allow her to escape from this coffin.

Blackness.

It seemed like night.

Eternal night.

From the depths of his mind he could hear his mother.

'You'll live, Simon,' she told him quietly. *'You'll live because you're a survivor.'*

Twenty-eight

San Diego, California.

Out of sight of the lawns the single-storey building sat like a strip of shimmering mirrors in a semi-circle half-enclosing a small lake at the rear, where fountains played, shooting dancing sprays up to twelve feet into the air. At night the fountains were linked to lights so that the water could dance in a multitude of colours, a rainbow of changing effects that spoke to the world of money and success.

The roof was a solid layer of solar panels that gathered the Californian sun by day, powering hot-water systems throughout the building and simultaneously charging a range of large hidden batteries that supplied power for some functions at night. As with other things owned by Iain Duncan, Cytek Corporation exhibited its abilities as if they were wares in a biotechnology supermarket. They shouted out their own achievements.

The biggest of all was its trademark, the statue of a golden giant armadillo that stood atop the building, over the wide front entrance, like a triumphant soldier signifying victory.

More than six hundred people worked at Cytek, developing state-of-the-art advances in artificial limbs and implants for human body functions. Cytek researchers worked on biomedical computation, imaging, cell and molecular engineering, and regenerative medicine. They were inventing novel biomaterials and reverse engineering biological systems. They studied micro-fabrication, micro-sensors of clinical and research applications, and biomimetics – the mechanophysiology of swimming, walking, undulating and flying. They helped create new standards in human engineering and the companies that manufactured the actual products paid annual fees. Cytek never released its patents and that had turned it into a billion-dollar company.

Jerry Ferdetta sat in his opulent office, overlooking the back of the building, directly opposite the dancing fountains where half a dozen peacocks strutted and screamed over the lawns.

He was behind his glass-topped desk, reading departmental reports, but his mind was no longer on them. The quarterly accounts were due and once again he was about to sign off on *Tatú* millions that had been hidden in other projects.

He had spent another sleepless night thinking about them and all the Advil in the world wasn't helping his headache.

With a heavy sigh he pulled over the slimline phone on his desk. It looked the same as any other hi-tech landline, but it had only one target recipient who was now sitting on his yacht in some goddam Spanish harbour, tickling up some stray pussy.

The phone bypassed all normal commercial surface or satellite based lines, and had been developed as a spin-off from an earlier Cytek project. It was one that the NSA couldn't intercept. The government undoubtedly had others, as did the Japanese, Chinese, Russians and Brits, but Cytek's was unique. If its technology were ever copied and the codes broken, Cytek would change to something else.

Duncan picked up the receiver. The phone was linked to cameras so that each could see the other, and Duncan could tell immediately that Ferdetta had had another sleepless night.

'Out on the town too late, Jerry?' he asked with a chuckle. Ferdetta was single, asexual, had no steady partner and rarely frequented the multiple high-class clubs of San Diego. He had no vices and lived almost uniquely for his work, which was making money, at the moment for Duncan, but maybe not for too much longer.

Ferdetta had serious ambition, which meant that, in turn, he also had serious concerns.

He didn't mind financial deception – that was taken for granted in business. What he didn't fancy were fifteen years in jail.

'You know why I'm calling,' he said wearily.

'Sure I do. The quarterly figures are late, but nothing out of the normal, with only the official edits to clean up and print out, but we're up to scratch on the projections. Right?'

'Smart ass,' Ferdetta growled.

Duncan laughed. 'What are we hitting, around 160?'

'Just over $150 million, a little down on last quarter. Close enough.'

Cytek was a private company and didn't have to worry about the vagaries of the stock market, but Duncan didn't appreciate falling down on the projections. Nor did Ferdetta.

'So it's something else?'

'You know goddam well it is,' Ferdetta snapped. 'Look, I accept that you're passionate about the *Tatú* project. Your in-joke. Who the hell else in the world but Argentineans knows *Tatú* is their word for armadillo. But forget the linguistics, Iain. You seem to be working with an unlimited budget. No one spends this kind of money without crunching the figures to see what the possible returns will be.'

'They'll be gigantic, Jerry,' Duncan said in a soothing voice. 'Think of the potential. This could rock the world and you know it.'

'What I know is I've done more thinking about this than about anything in my life, and I'm worried. It's not only illegal, but I'm starting to realise how great the reaction to it will be. Half the world will say it's immoral, the Vatican will be up in arms along with most western governments and medical authorities. Holy shit, Iain, you know how they react to anything that interferes with sexual reproduction, and right now I'm starting to think that maybe your experiments have gone beyond the pale. I'm a Catholic, Iain, and it's never bothered me until recently, but it sure is now. This latest stuff is terrifying me.'

'You don't have to concern yourself about ethics, friend. I do that.'

'I've got to,' Ferdetta insisted stubbornly. 'Not only ethics in the moral sense – financial ethics. We're pouring money down a black hole. With this quarter's load of bills we've sunk over $200 million into *Tatú* and there's not a dime in sight to show for it.'

'It's close, Jerry. Very close. Where have you hidden the *Tatú* funding this quarter?'

'Genetic morphing.'

'That's OK. That's a great place to hide it. Genetic scanners cost the earth but they'll change the world. Soon we'll be able to sequence genetic code in a matter of hours instead of months or years, maybe even seconds. Then all we do is develop software in-house and bring the whole genetic code its biggest ever breakthrough. It will be a river of gold to our business, no matter how much we invest in it. *Tatú* is easily hidden in that. We're not talking a paltry $200 million here, Jerry.'

'I had an argument with one of the research guys about our genetic scanning programme this week. He wanted to know how long it'll be before we're working on genetic design of kids. He said that's what Josef Mengele was doing. Guess what, Iain? He was too close for comfort. *My* comfort.'

'And you know the counter-argument.' Duncan held back his temper. Argument didn't help and Ferdetta was a brilliant man who could also be dangerous if he started to talk about the secrets he knew, or guessed he knew. 'Tell him we're talking about technology to detect and prevent illnesses in genetically related individuals, we're talking about the kinds of crops that could save the Third World from starvation.'

'You know that's crap,' said Ferdetta bluntly. '*Tatú* isn't about genetically engineered crops. I've gone along with it, but the longer this goes on, the more frightened I get about what you're doing.'

'What *we're* doing, Jerry.'

'I know it. I'm just wishing I didn't. The guy I spoke about – he said genetic scanning was a potential evil. What *Tatú* is about could be ten times worse.'

'And provide ten times the financial return. What half the world sees as evil, the other half sees as a blessing. Do we have to go through this over and over again?'

'Maybe not. I've been thinking about a change. I've had offers.'

'I know you have, Jerry, but I need you. Look, I think I'm very, very close to it over here now. Give me six more months and I'll hand Cytek to you. I'll set up another company for *Tatú*, and unload the remainder. I'll *give* you the remainder.'

'*Give?* You mean Cytek, lock, stock and barrel? No cash or stock transfer, no options for you, and without that albatross around my neck?'

'That's what I mean. I've got enough money, anyway.'

'Make it three months and it's a deal.'

'I'll get the papers drawn up.' Duncan sighed. 'But I tell you, fella, you're going to be the financial loser.'

'Like *you* said, I'll have enough money anyway and at least I'll get to sleep at night.'

Twenty-nine

Sierra de Las Nieves.

He could hear the voice but it wasn't his mother. Davey? *How did you come into my dying mind, Davey? It's good to hear you again. I'm sorry it didn't work out. That's the way things go.*

Music was ringing in his ears and he could see the vague outline of a woman bending over him. She had a beautiful face. *Emma? Is that you, Emma? Have you forgiven me now?*

He was shivering and he didn't know why. The dead shouldn't shiver. Perhaps he was in limbo, waiting for someone to make a decision with others about his fate. That would be a short conference. Thirty seconds' debate, unanimous decision and they'd send him down to where he would never shiver again.

I'm rambling. I don't believe in God. I told Him that when I first started doing the things I had to do. God and me can't be perfect partners. But maybe when you're dead what some people say is true. God forgives and everyone becomes a believer.

A voice was shouting. The woman's voice, in a language he didn't immediately recognise. *Spanish.* She was shouting in Spanish!

He was being struck, time and time again and he wanted to scream, tell them to stop and let him go to hell in his own way, but the hammering wouldn't end. Then he realised he wasn't actually being struck. His chest was being pressed down repeatedly and it hurt because his lungs were fighting it, his stomach was protesting and suddenly he was heaving and the water was pouring out of his throat. The pressure eased, but he was retching; water spurting from his mouth, soaking into the soil around his face.

She was kneeling beside him and he could hear the voice. 'Simon,' she was saying in English in his ear. 'Pull yourself out of it. Simon! Listen to me! Breathe in. Fill your lungs! Don't let go!'

Tabor retched again, a violent torrent of water and bile spewing from his throat. He could hear music, see the ground and feel the water trickling over his feet.

He groaned and tried to push himself up.

'Hold on,' she said. 'The driver will help you.'

Strong arms lifted him, almost as if he were a baby, and carried him up the bank on to the roadway where a small bar had the radio playing on the terrace. The strong man carried Tabor inside the terrace and sat him at a table.

Tabor opened his eyes. The man standing over him, smiling with satisfaction, was a giant. Huge arms, as thick as tree trunks, were folded across a chest built like a battle tank. His face was as craggy and weathered as an old olive tree and had the colour of macadamia nuts. He knelt in front of Tabor and held out a hand. Tabor recoiled, not from the extended hand, but from the smell. The giant must have eaten a couple of dozen heads of garlic before he crashed. One could probably smell it back in Malaga.

'He wants you to shake hands,' Anca said. 'He saved your life but *he* wants to thank *you*!'

'For what?' muttered Tabor weakly, holding out his hand

as he'd been ordered. The hand that took it could have crushed him but the pressure was gentle.

'For not dying. He blames himself for the final smash by his concrete mixer that knocked the car into the river.'

Tabor looked up at her. Her clothes were soaked and her hair hung lank and wet, clinging to her face but her eyes were full of concern. Oddly it made him happy.

'The concrete-mixer driver pulled me out?'

'He was partially knocked out by the crash. His head hit the windscreen and it was a minute or so before he came to. Then he saw the car in the river and scrambled down to us. He pulled me out first. You'd kept my head above water with your arm. I was able to walk out of the river then he pulled you out as well, but he thought you were dead.'

'I thought I was,' Tabor muttered. 'I still think I might be.'

She smiled at him. 'You're alive, no thanks to that madman in the BMW. He didn't stop and I didn't get his licence number.'

Tabor's mind was spinning as he tried to grasp what had happened. He remembered the BMW overtaking and the car going into the culvert. He could hear the grinding of the metal and screeching of the brakes, and picture the concrete mixer as it broadsided over the road, but after that there was nothing except the inner terror as the water rose over his head and he tried to hold his breath, afraid of the river reaching up through his nostrils, trying to tear out his soul.

'Why was he hitting me?' He couldn't think properly. It was a fair enough question.

The giant said something rapidly to Anca and she smiled agreement. The handful of people who were in the bar when it happened had run out to try to help but the giant waved them off. Too many people trying to wade into the river could get in the way and make it worse. They returned to the terrace and were standing around him now, talking animatedly. A barman appeared at Tabor's side, put a glass of something on the table in front of him and tapped him on the shoulder.

Tabor looked at him. The barman was pointing at the drink.

Long and malt coloured. Full of ice. A cola? Tabor picked it up and drank it down in one long gulp then came upright instantly, spluttering and gasping, and staggered from the table to get to the low wall surrounding the terrace. He vomited over the side, into the roadway.

He could hear people laughing and, when he straightened up, his face flushed with colour and his mouth and throat burning, they clustered around him, patting him on the back, shouting to him and nodding excitedly.

'Brandy?' he croaked, as Anca came over.

She was laughing with the others too. 'Whisky. They serve drinks in large quantities in Spain and the barman gave you extra because he said you needed to get everything out of your lungs and stomach.'

'He was right.' Tabor groaned. His voice was getting stronger and his vision was clearing. His chest hurt not only from the pounding the concrete-mixer driver had given him but also from the bruising that was still there from the beating on the Costa.

'He didn't know the first thing about lifesaving,' Anca said when she led him back to the table and sat him down again. 'I was shaken so I told him what to do. Push until the water you'd swallowed came out. He may have been lacking in technique, but he got the job done.'

Tabor looked up. He could almost taste the smell from the driver, hovering near him, smiling at him.

Tabor shook his head and turned back to Anca.

'All I can say is thank God he didn't give me mouth to mouth.'

Thirty

Edinburgh.

He'd stayed awake much of the night and it was only when he heard the sound of numerous vehicles passing that he shoved aside the boxes in the alley at the back of the shop where he had hidden, and stood up. In the streets, in the traffic and in the daylight he might be safe for a time.

But he was dirty from the alley, his clothes were torn and his shoes had rubbed his feet because he had no socks on. It was cold and drizzling with a fine rain. His hands hurt from where he had torn away some of his skin climbing the tree. They had scabbed over but nevertheless the fingers pained him when he flexed them.

For a time he huddled in a doorway, getting strange looks from passers-by, and he knew he had to move. Sooner or later someone would call a policeman. He'd seen police cars going by, easily recognisable, although he couldn't read English. Unless he did something the next one might stop to see what he was up to.

Dmitri began to walk, keeping under the lee of the

rooftops, dropping into doorways to shelter from time to time, heading he knew not where.

He was shivering both with the fright and cold. He thought about going to other houses he'd been to with his father, but he was so lost in this maze of streets that he had no idea where he was, and by now the police would also be watching them. He'd run away from the police station, but they would know about the killings in the house because he'd written it down for them. Romania. It was as good as a pointer directly to him. The police would know Romanians ran the house and they would put two and two together. Even in Romania the police weren't stupid enough to ignore that connection.

He put his hand in his pocket and felt the banknotes. Money he'd saved originally to impress a girl. Now they were his only lifeline. There would be no girls for Dmitri unless he found warmth, shelter and food and waited for someone to come to find him.

They had killed his father. Someone would come to take revenge.

But in the meantime people stared at him and he had to get out of sight.

For a time he hid in a park, standing shivering in the drizzle under some trees, but there was no one else out because of the weather. It was wet, it was miserable, but it was safe.

That night he found another shop with boxes and crept under those again and when he woke next morning the weather had cleared.

His clothes were even more crumpled and dirty, but he had thought about it a lot as he shivered under the boxes and he knew what he had to do.

He found a shop with army clothing in a window, along with sturdy boots, whistles and the kind of cooking utensils one used when camping. He fondled the banknotes then went inside.

He emerged twenty minutes later with a small knapsack packed with two shirts, a khaki pullover, a canister of Camping Gaz and a small stove, along with one saucepan. He bought a pair of boots and three pairs of socks. He pulled a warm ski jacket over the torn shirt, and had camouflage army trousers in a plastic bag.

He had wanted a knife but the man shook his head and said something Dmitri didn't understand. The gesture was a clear 'No'.

Dmitri had no way to argue so he hesitantly held out one banknote, not knowing how much it was worth. The man shook his head, spoke again and tapped the note. Whatever the words, they were clearly negative. Dmitri handed over a second note of the same denomination and the man shoved the items across the counter, gave him back another note in a different colour and some coins, and spoke to him kindly. Dmitri nodded sheepishly and left the shop.

As soon as he could, he found a secluded spot where he slipped out of his trousers and put on the army ones. He shoved the other trousers into his knapsack. He took off his shoes and put on a new pair of socks and the boots and put the old shoes in his pack as well. He was transformed. No passing policeman would recognise him like this. They would be looking for him dressed as he was when he ran from the police station.

He walked until dusk settled and the darkness was becoming absolute. The street lamps were few and far between, many of them long since broken and never repaired.

But, although he was tired and frightened and his feet ached from the heavy boots and the walking, he was alive and warm. What he needed now was shelter.

In an area where everything was deserted he came to a warehouse with a faded sign above it. He picked out the letters. They were in the Roman alphabet, like his own language, not in the Russian Cyrillic that he hated but had been taught in school.

Half aloud he spelled out the words. 'Carter & Son. Ships Chandlers. Leith.' He had no idea what the words meant. It wasn't of particular interest. He tried the door, but it was locked so he walked around the corner and there he found a wall he could climb. He scrambled over and dropped down on the other side.

The yard was strewn with old débris. Things that had been dragged out of the warehouse when the yard closed down, other bits and pieces people had flung over the wall rather than take to the tip. All kinds of discarded or broken electronic items, including two smashed television sets and an old gas cooking stove. There, propped upright against the inside of the wall, was a mattress stained with urine, probably from a child's bed.

Dmitri touched it. It was wet from the rain, but it could be useful. He scouted around and found another door that opened to the turn of the handle. Inside it was dark, but empty. He smiled to himself. He put down his pack then returned to the yard and dragged the mattress inside. In a day or so it would dry out. Until then he would make do with the floor.

He set up his cooking stove then realised he had neither food nor water.

Once again fear and misery overwhelmed him but he fought back his tears and tried to calm himself. He was safe, he was hidden away, he was warm and he had the money he'd transferred into his new camouflage trouser pocket. Tomorrow he would find food and water.

Tonight, once again, he would stay alive.

Thirty-one

Fuengirola.

In the darkness of her room Anca Aron sat staring at the ceiling as if something were written there, hidden by the blackness, waiting for light to dawn so that it could be read. She'd drawn the curtains once Tabor and Dani left, cutting off the glare that shone in from the street lamps.

She locked and bolted the door, took the pistol out of her handbag and carried it into the bathroom while she showered for the second time that evening then wrapped herself in a thin bathrobe, picked up the gun and returned to the main room to wait for the two men to return.

It would be an early night, once they were back. Tabor wanted to start no later than seven thirty next morning and she needed to sleep and shake off the memories of the crash.

As she'd expected, the Guardia Civil Trafico at the accident scene had no interest in what had actually happened. No one was dead. Traffic accidents happened by the hundred every day in Malaga province alone. One took statements, checked their passports and insurance documents and told them they'd be in touch if the owner of the

BMW were found. Then he turned his attention to sorting out the mess on the bridge where traffic stretched back two kilometres in both directions.

Only when it cleared could Anca call a taxi to take them to Fuengirola.

There they showered, changed clothes and almost immediately went out to hire a car.

She thought about the accident. Another reckless driver? It was possible, maybe even probable, but she couldn't get over the blacked-out windows of the car and the fact that someone had already tried once to kill Tabor. Logic said she should be suspicious, but she had other things on her mind as well. Her thoughts were mostly on her sister and on Tabor.

There had been no sign of Dorina despite spending days walking the streets, hoping to catch a glimpse. She'd asked in the Guardia station in Fuengirola and again in the provincial headquarters in Malaga, offering her police identification from Bucharest, but was told, as she had been when she telephoned Madrid before leaving Romania, that there was no evidence the girl was in Spain.

But Romania was a focal point of human trafficking and there were Eastern European girls everywhere in this country. Her research showed there were an estimated 85,000 prostitutes in Andalucia, only about a thousand of them on the streets. The remainder were in brothels and ninety per cent, the statistics said, were foreigners. No one, the Spanish police insisted, had complained about girls being held against their will, but every European police force knew why. There were no laws in Spain to protect prostitutes who denounced brothel owners. If a woman complained, most probably the brothel owner would pay off the police, but assuredly the woman would be thrown in jail as an illegal immigrant and deported, then imprisoned again in her home country.

She had turned up nothing on her own.

Tabor's line of enquiry held some promise. Her sister had mentioned the tattoo, but given no indication of who put it there, or why. Nor had Dorina identified where she was being held. The question Anca kept asking herself was why she had been allowed outside, able to post a letter, but hadn't taken the opportunity to run away? *Perhaps she didn't want to any more.* Anca's brain rebelled at the thought, but any police officer would point out that it was a plausible explanation for her disappearance. She could be making far more money in a brothel here than in a tiny rural village in Romania, and money talked.

She had noted the comment in the letter about the tattoo and filed the information away in her mind. Then Tabor started asking about the same kind of tattoo. The attack in the alley showed the tattoo was of such importance that people were prepared to kill because of it. Why?

That was when she decided to follow Tabor's lead.

There was a vague chance the orchid-loving doctor could give them a pointer, with luck the name of the tattooist. She and Tabor could take it from there.

But Tabor was also on her mind for other reasons.

The man had a strength and clear emotional depth that shone through and bypassed his terse, sometimes taciturn conversation. She knew nothing about him. Dani had offered to run his background after he had given this other name, but she had told him not to. For the moment, she said, Tabor was an ally and entitled to his privacy. Should she have reason to change her mind Dani could check up on Tabor – if that indeed were his real name – but somehow she thought even Dani would not get far beyond the passport and education details. She could only make guesses and everything told her Tabor was as much a killer as the people in the alley, but in a different way. Tabor, she felt, killed not for fun or profit but for something almost akin to duty, and that was why she'd come to the conclusion he was in the military, probably in some special forces unit. Soldiers she could understand.

Tabor wasn't what some would call a handsome man. Not in the way people spoke of film stars and sportsmen, but he had a rugged, attractive face, a strong body and an inner presence that made her feel confident being with him. More than mere confidence, he made her feel necessary to him. *Essential.* And not solely because of her command of Spanish and his lack of it. She wouldn't forget that, although he thought *he* was dying in the river, he'd forced her head up above the surface so that *she* could stay alive. That was the action of more than an ordinarily brave man. It was one of total selflessness.

She recalled her emptiness as the concrete-mixer driver pulled him, seemingly dead, from the river, and the tears she had to fight back. She relived the relief when she realised his heart was beating, even if barely, and he could be revived. The moment he began to gush water from his mouth was sheer joy.

And that troubled her more.

There had been only two relationships in her life and both lasted almost a year.

Her first love grew resentful of her dedication to police work, and the way it interfered with his personal requirements.

He was at the university where she learned Spanish, but by then she was in her first year at the Vasile Lascar Police Agents School. He was studying physics and their approaches to their disciplines were so different both felt being opposites was an attraction. It wasn't. The liaison collapsed.

The second was in her third year in the police force,

newly transferred to the capital. She was captivated by one of the senior officers notorious for his sexual affairs. At one stage she thought they loved each other and he would divorce his wife to marry her, but when she finally made the suggestion he not only raged in her face but tried to get her moved to Craiova, near the Macedonian and Bulgarian borders.

She survived because her lover's affairs were becoming an embarrassment to the hierarchy in Bucharest. Instead of moving Anca, his superior transferred her lover and they had never met, spoken or written to each other since. Anca buried herself in her work, keeping out of serious entanglements.

The concentration on work had its own rewards. She was a senior inspector with a facility for languages. She could handle weapons, she was trained in police storming tactics and she'd been taught self-defence skills. She was learning to fly a helicopter, but that took time because flying was an expensive hobby and a police officer's pay was meagre. Her lessons were given free by a police pilot angling for a place in her bed, but he hadn't managed to get inside her apartment, let alone the bedroom. He was frustrated, but had plenty of other girlfriends and seemed content to take it slowly with Anca. Which, in turn, meant she had become quite settled.

Tabor was making her feel unsettled again.

He pulled up a seat alongside Dani, beaming with satisfaction at the letterhead the boy had created for him. Now he needed to move to stage two.

Through Anca, he had explained that, while he could write a simple algorithm to put into an email, Dani would be faster. It took half an hour. When it was done he wrote down the decryption key.

The key to any encryption is a code, a series of letters or

numbers, single or mixed, that sets the decryption process into play. Dani's code key was eight characters long.

The message was equally short. It said simply: 'Dr Felix Blake. Orchids and bulls. Jorox, 45 kilometres from Malaga. Speaks English, Nationality unknown.' Landon would understand it was an instruction to check out the name as thoroughly as possible. Why it was needed was Tabor's affair for the moment. Landon would have to wait and chafe. Encrypting it might be considered overly cautious, but emails were as unsafe as phones if someone knew how to intercept them. Encryption provided a modicum of protection against cyber-browsing and he saw no reason why someone else should start wondering why Blake was of any interest to others. He sent it to Landon immediately.

He stood up and tapped Dani on the shoulder. It was time to go home

Home? Tabor realised he had only known the place for a couple of days!

Thirty-two

London. Tuesday.

Costel Potrascu was cold. Not from the temperature, but from the chill that came over him when his men in London called to say his brother Pavel and three of his bodyguards were missing. They'd failed to return from their early hours pick-up of the money at the various brothels and his lieutenant, Marku Simeonescu, waited three days before reporting it to Spain. That was unforgivable.

He'd done nothing but think about it since the phone call. Pavel was dead. There could be no other answer. The money he was carrying would probably have run to several thousand pounds but Pavel had over three million in his personal account. He had no need to run away and hide with company money and certainly not with his brother's share.

He got out of the taxi in Soho following Serghei, handed over the fare without a word and stood on the pavement for a few moments, watching the vehicle drive away.

On the plane he'd worried about Simeonescu. Waiting three days to warn that his brother had vanished could mean several things. It could be Simeonescu was searching

London, trying to pick up a whisper of Pavel's whereabouts. It could be he was afraid of what Potrascu would do when he found out about his younger brother or – and this was foremost in his mind – it could be Simeonescu was being paid by someone else, other powerful figures in the world of London prostitution. Even trying to take over the operation himself.

If that were so, Potrascu would be walking into a trap and they would be waiting for him.

On the way from the airport he called at a store owned by a Romanian and picked up four automatic pistols and an ice axe he kept hidden there, and a small bag of groceries as camouflage for the sake of the cab driver. The storeowner had a legitimate mini-market business, but no one in the Romanian community wanted to disobey Potrascu or stand in his way.

He fondled the pistol in the right-hand pocket of his raincoat. It was early evening, but still light and he watched tourists pass by. This was Soho. Most people were looking in windows, eyeing girls, reading the come-on signs alongside and above various shop doorways.

After a few minutes Potrascu and Serghei walked off together, towards Piccadilly, Serghei self-consciously carrying the groceries. It took them half an hour to get to the building but Potrascu didn't phone ahead. If what he suspected was true, there was no point in forewarning anyone.

Instead they walked up the steps into the house, through the heavy oak-faced front door and the hallway into the main room. It was too early for clients and the girls were upstairs, but the barman was standing there, polishing glasses and Simeonescu was sitting in an armchair with a drink on the table in front of him.

He turned and saw them and immediately stood up. 'You should have told me you were arriving. I would have picked you up at the airport,' he blustered, showing surprise as he crossed over to take Potrascu's coat.

Potrascu shook the hand away. 'Have you searched the other houses?' he asked in a voice as cold and hard as an iceberg. His pale eyes showed no emotion and Simeonescu looked puzzled.

'Searched?' he replied, with a frown etched on his forehead. 'What's to search? We've been to his home and he's not there, nor is his car. No one has seen him or the other three men he had with him.'

'Where was he last seen alive?'

'The house in Cricklewood. Pavel collected the night's takings and left. No one saw him after that.'

'Which one was the next collection point on his list, after Cricklewood.'

'He didn't have a routine, Costel. He liked variables, you know that. It was a safety thing. No one ever knew where he would start or end, or which route he'd take.'

'How many collections were there left to make?'

Simeonescu didn't like this questioning or the stony look on Potrascu's rigid face. 'He'd been to four of the black houses and three of the others. We've picked up the money from all of them and I've been doing the run myself every night since. The takings are in the safe here, waiting for you.'

'What did they say at the Richmond house?'

'The same as the others. They hadn't seen him or been in contact until I went around. They were wondering where he was.'

'We'll check each of the houses again. Leave Richmond to last. Go with Serghei for the car. I'll check the money here.'

Serghei smiled innocently as he discarded the bag of groceries on the chair where Simeonescu had been sitting. He understood what his boss was thinking.

The house at Richmond was large and stood in wooded

grounds, hidden from public view. It was the most profitable of the London houses, but had a secret never shared with Simeonescu.

It had a private entrance and exit that bypassed the staff. There Pavel kept documents and information that few were privy to, other than his own closest bodyguards and they came from the same village as the Potrascus. All would be loyal to the point of dying for either of them.

Serghei, like Potrascu, was thinking they already had.

Thirty-three

Edinburgh. Tuesday.

For the first time in his life, Dmitri was truly alone. He'd known long periods when he'd wandered through the hills and the forests on his own, and times when he'd sought out quiet corners to think and dream, undisturbed by other people or other pressures. But never totally alone. Always there was his mother until she died, or his teachers, or someone around to console him when he was unhappy, be happy with when he was having fun, feel proud with when he did well and cheer him up when he did badly. But in the space of weeks his world had crashed, his mother dead, the father he barely knew also dead and not even his father's colleagues able to contact him. His only family were his father's cousins, Costel, whom he'd last seen in Spain, and Pavel, who lived somewhere in London. He knew nothing about London. He didn't even really know where it was.

For a long time Dmitri hovered on the edge of tears but slowly as the day drew on, hidden away inside the old warehouse, he'd pulled himself together.

There was no hint of rain in the air so he dragged the

mattress out and leaned it against the wall, close to the doorway. It might dry out there more quickly.

He pulled the banknotes from his pocket and counted them. There were twenty. He had no idea of their value but, apart from the one note he was given in exchange for the clothing in the store the day before, all carried the number '50'. More or less he had 1,000 of whatever the values represented here. A little experimentation would soon show what he could get for each unit of currency.

He left his belongings behind, carrying only the knapsack, and climbed the wall into the deserted street. Ten minutes later he reached an area where there were many shops of all kinds but he was looking in particular for a bank.

It took only minutes to find one with a sign above it. It was similar to the Romanian word 'banc' and he peered inside. The place was almost empty. With a lot of smiles and a ballpoint pen to write the number '10' five times he got five notes for one of the 50s.

Buying a length of smoked sausage that didn't have to be cooked, some cheese and a loaf of bread, cans of soft drink, fruit and bars of chocolate, and finally potatoes to boil in his saucepan, a carton of milk and some bottled water, cost him less than a 10 from the nearest mini market.

He pocketed the handful of coins the checkout assistant gave him back, stowed his purchases in the knapsack and left, pleased with himself. Without knowing a word of English, he was starting to understand this currency. He knew approximately what a £50 note and a £10 note would buy. That meant he had plenty of money in his pocket and could survive on it for some time.

Language was only one means of communication. There were many others if one tried.

He returned to the warehouse, following the landmarks he'd identified on his way in, using quiet back streets to make certain no one was following, before he tossed the knapsack over the wall and clambered into the yard.

An hour later, he cooked the potatoes and chewed some of the sausage, swilled it down with one of the cans of soft drink and sat with his back against the wall, thinking.

Someone would come for him, of that he was certain.

He didn't know how they would find him but God had provided in the past and would do so again. All he had to do was stay out of the way of the police and the people who had killed his father and tried to seize him.

They wanted Dmitri. They wanted him badly. Whether to kill him or for some other reason he didn't know but they wouldn't give up trying.

Survival was the only thing that mattered. He could buy food, he had a place to rest once the mattress dried properly. He had money to buy more clothes.

Time would provide the answer to everything else.

Thirty-four

London. Wednesday.

Potrascu stood rigid, only his eyes moving from one body to another.

It had only been three days, but already there was a stench in the Richmond garage.

They had checked every other house in Potrascu's brothel empire, questioning the girls one by one and harshly interrogating the administrative staff. Potrascu scrutinised records, watched videotapes where they existed, but at each stop had drawn nothing.

In Richmond they found Pavel.

The door was steel and in the underground, fully enclosed garage, it got hot. It wasn't air conditioned because Pavel only used it for an hour or so at night. In the garage the bodies were putrefying.

Potrascu walked forward three steps and knelt by Pavel's shattered body, trying to remember his once child-like face. Ants crawled in and around the blown-out brains and facial matter and the blood had congealed over his clothing. Flies swarmed around him, settling in the mouth and ears and the holes where the bullets had entered.

Potrascu reached out and touched him. Rigor mortis had worn off.

He picked up his brother's coat, almost like cardboard because of the dried blood, and laid it over what was left of Pavel's face. He stood up and crossed to the former body-guards, remembering his childhood with them in the mountains. Silently he prayed for them.

Then he turned to Simeonescu with a look of naked hate.

'The ones who killed my cousin, Bogdan,' he said, his voice taut with hidden anger, 'did they do this?'

'How would I know, Costel?' Simeonescu glanced around him, but the garage door was down and the entrance had closed electronically. Serghei stayed where he was, saying and doing nothing, an easy arm's length away from where Simeonescu stood, shaking and uncertain. 'The police in Scotland haven't admitted he's been killed.'

'His men told you he had. I want to know who did it.'

'Police say it's a gang war.' Simeonescu shifted restlessly on his feet. Potrascu was making him nervous. His voice was sibilant, like a hissing snake. He'd heard it before, usually when he was about to kill somebody.

'Who, Marku?' demanded Potrascu, moving slowly towards him. His voice was so soft it was barely audible.

'I don't know. Believe me I don't know. I saw the television news about the Stockbridge attacks. They said it could have been the work of someone from London.'

'Someone you know about? Someone you've spoken to?'

'No,' said Simeonescu in a panic. 'The British haven't touched our operation. They don't like to organise in brothels. They run the women on the street. The gangs prefer the drugs and strip joints.'

'You expect me to believe you?'

'For mercy's sake, Costel, of course I do! I haven't heard anything from anybody. I thought Pavel had run away with the money.'

'What were you planning to do then, Marku?' Potrascu whispered. He was moving forward slightly, his hand in his pocket.

'Nothing! I told you and waited for you to come and sort things out. If Pavel's vanished with company money, you'll want to handle it yourself, that's what I thought. Please, Costel, I've only done what you and Pavel told me to do!'

'And if I don't believe you?'

They were so close that Potrascu was inches from Simeonescu's eyes, searching his face, investigating his thoughts. He could see panic in the man's eyes and his fear spoke of lies and betrayal. Simeonescu edged back, looking around, trying to find something to defend himself with or, better still, an exit. The blood drained from his face and he was quaking.

He sank to his knees and began to cry, holding his hands together, reaching out to Potrascu.

'You've got to believe me, Costel,' he pleaded. 'I've done nothing! You've got to trust me!'

Potrascu drew himself up to his full height. 'I don't.'

From his pocket he took the shiny steel ice axe. Simeonescu started to scream but the underground garage was soundproof and no one would hear him. He was holding his hands up in supplication, but Potrascu could hardly see him.

Grief stricken and in a red-eyed fury, Potrascu lifted the ice axe over his head. It stayed there for a moment, glistening in the light from the overhead fluorescent strips, then smashed down, brushing aside Simeonescu's uplifted hands, crashing through the skull and Simeonescu's screaming suddenly stopped. For one moment he knelt there, his eyes wide open, staring at Potrascu but not seeing him. Then he slumped forward on to the concrete floor, his arms outstretched, almost touching the foot of Pavel's body.

Potrascu kicked the arms aside. He didn't want the scum anywhere near his brother.

'There's a small garden shed outside. It has spades to dig with and the soil should be soft. We'll take Pavel and our friends into the grounds at the far end and bury them there. No one will hear us from that distance.'

Serghei understood. There was no way the police could be called, but nor could Pavel's body be left where it might be found. It was dark outside and the nighttime trade rarely started before midnight. In that time they could handle the burials.

'I'll get the tools.' Potrascu's voice had a hint of torment in it. 'You carry the bodies out to the trees and I'll start digging.'

Serghei pointed to the motionless corpse of Simeonescu. 'Him?'

Potrascu looked at the body then leaned down and pulled out the ice axe. He wiped it on Simeonescu's jacket and put it back into his raincoat pocket.

He took out a knife that was also in there and tossed it over to Serghei. 'Take out his eyes. We'll keep them to return to those who killed my brother. I hear from Edinburgh that's what they did to Bogdan and the other manager. There's been a police informer on Bogdan's payroll for more than two years, and he said it was meant as some kind of calling card. I've talked to our people up there and they think that whoever killed Pavel came from Edinburgh and it must have been people who knew the operation here. They knew the houses we run, and how to bypass the alarms and the remote-control gate to this garage. I've always thought it was Simeonescu.'

Serghei said nothing. It didn't matter what anyone

thought. Potrascu did what he felt was necessary or pleasurable.

'There's one other thing, my friend. My cousin's son, Dmitri. We have to find him before they get to the boy. He's the last male heir left in our family.'

'Shall I leave *him* behind?' Serghei was looking without emotion at Simeonescu.

'I'd like to but he'll start to stink more in death than he did in life. The staff upstairs would have to do something because of the complaints.'

Serghei shrugged. Whatever Potrascu wanted. It was all the same to him.

'I'd like to throw the lump of shit on to a rubbish dump,' Potrascu snarled. 'Or toss him in the river and let the fish swim inside his skull, but it would be found quickly and that might alert the people who killed Pavel before I'm ready. I need more time. First we bury Pavel and our friends. They deserve a proper funeral, unlike that piece of shit there.'

He kicked Simeonescu's inert body and a smile broke across his face for the first time all day. 'I know,' he said. 'There's a pig farm only a short drive away. Pavel took me that way once when we came to this house. We'll throw the scum into a pigsty. By the time the pigs have finished there'll be nothing left to identify. They'll eat him, bones and all, by morning.'

Thirty-five

London, Friday.

Field and Hartley came out of the morgue at Richmond, each wrapped in their own thoughts.

Hartley had witnessed death in various forms in the years she'd been on the force but never had she come across anyone who'd been eaten by pigs. Her flesh crawled at the thought.

Field stared at her pale face. 'Are you all right?'

'I don't think I'll ever be able to look a pork chop in the face again. Not as long as I live.'

'Nothing in this world is unique.' Field put a hand on her arm and led her to a bench seat to sit down for a moment. He stood hovering over her. 'You're too young to remember it. So would I be, except it's gone down in Met history. The first pig-eating I'd ever heard about.'

She looked up at him. 'It's happened before?'

'It's probably happened dozens of times, but one stands out because of the people involved. When Rupert Murdoch was trying to turn the *Sun* into a profitable newspaper, the wife of his managing director was kidnapped and held for ransom. Eventually the men involved were caught and tried, but the woman was never found. The belief was they killed her and fed her to the pigs on their farm. There wasn't a trace of her left.'

Hartley shuddered.

'There's no outward evidence at the farm,' Field said, sitting down next to her, 'but my guess is they killed our John Doe first then threw him into the pigs. There's no sign of a rope, which suggests he wasn't tied up, and if he'd been alive and able to get up he'd have run like hell before the pigs got to him. We're lucky the farmer came out before daylight to take some of the pigs to the slaughterhouse.'

When the farmer turned on the floodlights to organise the cull, it took him only minutes to find the remains of the body, driven into the mud. The face and body was stripped of flesh but parts of the legs and feet survived, along with the hands.

The fingerprints taken from one hand provided no identification and there was no DNA match in the databanks. For the moment they had a total unknown on their hands.

Almost.

They couldn't identify the body, but the method of execution seemed clear. The skull had been pierced by something sharp and heavy. There were dozens of possible explanations, but the way the man had died and been thrown into the pigsties spoke of a psychopath who enjoyed not only the killing, but also everything associated with it. One who had killed that way before and intended to continue in the same fashion.

The pathologist was examining the skull and would report in due course, but in Hartley's mind there was no doubt what he would say. Field thought the same thing.

This was the ice-axe killer.

Whether or not the victim had been tattooed was another question.

There wasn't enough flesh left in the groin area for anyone to tell.

Hartley sat at the desk in their office with Field and Rogers.

'Right,' she said. 'On first glance the pathologist confirms the skull injury could be an ice axe or similar sharp instrument. He found nothing else obvious that could relate to the murder, except some scoring around the eye sockets.'

'The eyeballs again?' Field asked.

'I think so. The pathologist won't be certain without further scrutiny. On visual examination he admits it's possible the eyes were removed with a knife, nothing more. We can have him check the socket bone scarring against those in the eyeballs taken out in Scotland.'

That was what Landon had asked when he'd spoken to her in his office earlier. He'd come in with a message from his source saying that he wanted the background of an orchid fancier called Dr Felix Blake checked out. She had briefed him on the find at the pig farm.

Landon was having a bad morning. He had been from the time he went into his wife's room and saw Helen staring at him sullenly from her bed. She had the look that showed unspoken resentment as well as pain. It would be another day when they would be silent with each other. The news of another possible ice-axe killing did nothing to ease his mood.

He passed on the message from Spain then returned home to his wife. The day might not get better, but he had to stay with her. She had weeks at the most, he had a lifetime left. A lifetime of self-recrimination, probably.

'The eyeballs were in Edinburgh, the ice axe down here. There's no connection until this latest one where there's both the ice axe and possible missing eyes,' Field said.

'And perhaps a tattoo.'

'Perhaps.' Field sounded sceptical.

'There may be now.' Hartley glanced at some notes she'd scribbled on a pad. 'The criminal psychologist says there's a long history of eyeball removal, back to Samson in the Bible. In recent times most of them have been racially motivated and there was one in Glasgow in 2004. He says race doesn't always mean colour so there could be a connection with a conflict in Edinburgh between locals and Romanians they see as aliens. If the killer is the ice-axe murderer he could have cut out the eyeballs as retaliation for what happened in Edinburgh.'

'What about the way the bodies were laid out there?'

'Criminal psychology isn't an exact science but he thinks they wanted to make it mysterious, hoping the media would find out and any other gangs thinking of taking a piece of the brothel cake would be warned off. The eyeball removal was for horror effect. He called it the tabloid-headline syndrome.'

Field toyed with his moustache. Someone had cut it for him and his lips showed clearly for the first time in a few weeks.

'We all want this killer, Ruth, but it has to be based on reality. What we have are two separate crime investigations, hundreds of miles apart and one inconclusive connecting feature – someone who may have removed eyeballs and used an ice axe. It wouldn't get past the DCI here, let alone to court. Start again. What do we have that could point to both London and Edinburgh?'

Hartley thought for a moment and picked up on it. 'Romania,' she said. 'There's no confirmation that the girl washed up at Burnham was Romanian, but the DCI thinks she was and so were the girls killed with the ice axes. If Romanian girls are being used in Edinburgh, how did they get there? Landon thinks they landed somewhere along the east coast, such as Burnham-on-Crouch. Lonely. Isolated. Trucks to take them anywhere in Britain. I think he's right, so *we* need to find out who's doing the cross-channel running. Start with the missing Edward Beech.'

Field smiled approval, but he had to point out other facts. 'Rogers checked out the Beech house in Guildford. There was nothing. We don't even really know he's dead. West Surrey Divisional HQ says he's potentially missing, believed dead along with Winters,' he said bluntly.

Hartley sat back in her seat, toying with a pencil. She realised that was what Landon often did and quickly put it down again. 'There's another lead,' she said. 'It's been a busy morning. Twenty minutes ago Mary Winters phoned. She still believes Beech is dead, but now says there could have been another boat, not the sloop *Gilbert Merrick* that supposedly went down with her old man.'

'I ran a check on both Winters and Beech through the Register of yachts,' Field objected. 'There was nothing. Beech had *Pesadilla V* at anchor in the river at Burnham. Winters only had the sloop.'

'True, but we didn't run a check on Kelly McGlynn.'

'She's not a sailor.' Field was sitting forward with a puzzled look on his face. 'She liked men who sailed, Beech among them, but she didn't say she could sail.'

'We didn't ask her, did we? We assumed she was in it for the good times, the champagne and caviar on the big boats, sunning herself in the ocean, getting an all-over suntan.' Hartley let her stare flick over the other two, encompassing them, dragging them into the conversation.

'Mrs Winters says McGlynn *does* have a boat and she's a competent sailor. Winters doesn't know what the boat is called or where it's moored, but she insists there *is* one, so we go back, and find the missing boat. It could be the link to the illegal girl trafficking.'

She turned to Rogers. 'Paul, you've got another angle to chase. A Dr Felix Blake. He's an orchid lover and a bullfight fan who lives in a place called Jorox near the Costa del Sol. Blake speaks English. My source is reliable and wouldn't waste our time if this wasn't considered important.'

'Is this a medical doctor we're looking for?' Rogers asked quickly.

'I haven't got a clue so start with the orchid side of it. He could be a member of the Royal Horticultural Society or have links to orchid growers around the world.' She stood up. 'Jack, have a go at tracing McGlynn's yacht.'

'And you?' Field asked.

'Me?' She grinned. 'I'm going to the canteen for a cup of tea and a doughnut. That little chore shouldn't take you more than twenty minutes.'

It didn't.

Half an hour later when Hartley came back from her breakfast break, Field was waiting for her.

'It's a 32-footer called *Wanton Lady*. Talk about typecasting,' he said. 'Normally it's moored at Maldon, a few miles up the coast from Burnham. I take it we're going?'

'I'll get my raincoat,' Hartley answered. 'I found out last time it gets damn cold and wet over there.'

Thirty-six

Burnham-on-Crouch.

The rain swept along the high street, driven by the steady breeze rolling in from the North Sea, and under the shelter of her umbrella Hartley felt it soaking into the lower half of her skirt. Field had pulled on a raincoat and was striding out, but he stopped at the doorway and waited for her to catch up. He caught the look of exasperation on her face as the wet skirt clung to her long legs.

He was grinning as he opened the door and allowed her to pass in front of him.

Kelly McGlynn looked at them. 'Inspector? Sergeant?' She stood up, astonished. 'Have you found Mr Beech?'

Hartley waved her to sit down and nodded to Field to take a chair in front of the desk. Hartley stayed where she was. She was better standing and hoping the skirt would dry out a little, but somehow she didn't think there would be time enough for that.

'No,' she said when McGlynn was settled again. 'I suppose that means he hasn't contacted you either?'

'Nothing.'

'None of his friends has been in touch with you?'

'No one. He usually met them here at weekends. It's end of the season and not everyone bothers to come. As you can see, the weather isn't exactly what one gets on the Côte d'Azur.'

'How about the Costa del Sol?'

She was puzzled and looked up at Field as if asking him for an explanation. Field returned the look, saying nothing. She turned back to Hartley. 'Meaning what?' she asked hesitantly.

Hartley waved a hand. 'A policeman's quip. It didn't mean anything in particular. Why didn't you tell us you had a boat of your own and went out on it with Mr Beech?'

McGlynn's eyes narrowed and she sat up in her seat. 'I suppose Mary Winters told you that?'

'Who told us doesn't matter. I'd like to know why *you* didn't tell us about it.'

She shrugged. 'Everyone here has something to sail in. It's a sailing town. Everything from dinghies to ocean-going racers. I had one because it's something the other yacht owners understand and I felt it would be a business asset, but I'm established enough now not to need it as a gesture. I can't see that it's any of your business, but I didn't mention it because I don't have the *Wanton Lady* any more. I sold her more than two months ago and I haven't bought a replacement.'

'Sold?' Field looked puzzled. 'The boat is registered to you.'

'She may be,' answered McGlynn, a smile hovering on her lips. 'Yachties aren't always the most prompt people in the world, and I sold her to Lithuanians. A couple that I've met over the past few years who come to Burnham every summer took a liking to my boat. They asked several times if she was for sale and eventually I agreed. They offered me a good price and came back later with the money. They sailed her away the next day.'

'I don't suppose you could show us the receipts?'

'Sorry, I bought her for cash and I sold her the same way. I made a slight profit and it cost a lot to keep her. Yachts aren't cheap to run.'

'Don't you have to notify anyone about sales like that?' Field had a bland expression on his face, registering neither interest nor suspicion.

'I told you, yachties aren't prompt. Frankly, I forgot all about it.'

'And, of course, you don't have an address for these people in Lithuania?'

'No, they were regular summer visitors, not clients. I had no need to contact them. Is there a reason for this interrogation?'

'We don't need a reason, Ms McGlynn,' Hartley said. Her face too lacked expression. 'Why didn't you tell us about your sailing skills when you spoke readily about how competent Mr Beech and Mr Winters were?'

McGlynn shrugged her shoulders. 'I'm not very good. Not like them. I leave serious sailing to those who can handle it. I'm a fairweather sailor and I don't much like getting my clothes wet.' She glanced pityingly at Hartley.

Hartley bristled. She knew how she must look. McGlynn was groomed and dry, while Hartley exemplified a drowned rat.

She curtly nodded at Field, who stood up.

'I'm not too sure about how the boat transfer system works,' he said to McGlynn, as Hartley stalked towards the door. 'But if you should have told anyone officially I suggest you do it as quickly as possible. It might be illegal.'

McGlynn watched them hurry away down the road, the rain whipping around them.

Then she picked up the phone and called overseas.

Maldon was only about ten miles from Burnham, but driving along the narrow, winding lanes it took them half an hour to find the town, then another fifteen minutes to ask around and locate the multitude of moorings in the River Blackwater.

The slate-grey water rippled with the wind, and the rain drove into their eyes as they walked along the water's edge, examining the line of yachts, looking for the *Wanton Lady*. As Field had said, old-fashioned police work. McGlynn could be lying about the boat being sold. The only way to be certain was to check personally. Even in the rain.

'It's taking too long like this,' Hartley said eventually. They had seen no one. This part of town appeared deserted. 'You go right and I'll go left. If you find anyone who might know where she kept the boat, come and fetch me. I'll do the same.'

The river was long and, at Maldon, was an estuary far wider than the Crouch at Burnham and still, after another 30 minutes, she had found nothing. She walked disconsolately, rechecking the names on yachts. The rain was steady and miserable. She was shivering with the wetness and the cold. So much for the joys of CID work, she muttered to herself as she turned and retraced her steps towards where she could see Field standing in the distance, looking at the boats, doing what she was. Getting wet.

Another waste of time.

He didn't move as she approached. His clothing was as wet as hers, she thought a little guiltily. She'd been thinking only of herself. Through the raincoat he could be sodden.

'No sign of her, I suppose?'

He shook his head. The moustache splashed small beads of water off it. 'The *Wanton Lady* seems to have gone, as McGlynn said it had.' Then he lifted his hand and pointed to the small boat rolling in the choppy water only a few yards out from him. 'But that one hasn't.'

Hartley followed his hand and saw the vessel, its mast swaying as the wind buffeted it around on its mooring.

She peered at the name on the hull.

There, tied firmly to its mooring rope, was Winters's sloop the *Gilbert Merrick*, the boat that had supposedly sunk.

Thirty-seven

London.

Rogers was waiting when Hartley and Field got back to the office, both still wet from the rain. He grinned as they walked in, Hartley glowering at his amusement.

'What have you got?' she demanded curtly.

'Blake,' he answered. 'I traced him through the Royal Horticultural Society Orchid Committee. He's rated one of the top men in orchid breeding in the world. He's also rich, which is why he spends half of his life visiting places like Central and South America, looking for orchids that no one else has.'

'What about Asia? No trips there?'

'His orchid study covers Asian plants too but he's also an aficionado of bullfighting so that's why he goes to Latin America – he combines orchid hunting with visiting bull-rings over there.'

'Nothing to do with smuggling girls from Spain to here?' She was clutching at straws, trying to determine if, by any remote chance, Blake could be linked to the brothel trade.

'Not that I can see. Nor with tattoos. He seems to be

eccentric. One orchid fancier who told me Blake's fanatical about orchids actually used the word "demented".'

'Where does his money come from?'

'That's the interesting part,' he said as Field listened, occasionally running his fingers through his wet hair. He needed to find a towel, but Hartley hadn't given him a chance. 'Blake isn't a medical doctor. The title is a PhD as you suggested it might be. He's also big in the biochemical business. He's made a fortune in the development of drugs for the pharmaceutical industry. There was a time when Blake was considered a Nobel Prize candidate.'

'What went wrong?' Hartley was suddenly very attentive.

'Officially, nothing. Unofficially, the rumours were that his drug work was getting close to the knuckle. He had connections to a Korean who was named in an investigation into research on human cloning. That's not Blake's field. He's strictly a pill or vaccine developer but his relationship with the Korean seems to have thrown a shadow over Blake's career. Human cloning is illegal, experiments could end with horrific results, and no one in his right mind would be associated with it. Mention of possible Nobel Prizes stopped about three years ago and Blake vanished from sight.'

'Who does he work for now?' Field interrupted for the first time.

'No one. Blake disappeared. He's a recluse. He doesn't like people or anything much, other than his work. He's so secretive people in the medical field didn't know he was a renowned orchid expert, while the orchid growers didn't realise he's an exalted chemist. There's been nothing on him in the medical or garden magazines for years.'

'Biochemical engineer,' Hartley murmured. She tossed the idea around. Landon's source had to have a strong reason to ask about Blake. Landon wouldn't waste time on a trifle. But where did Blake fit into this investigation?

'Is Blake a sailor?'

'Not that anyone has told us,' Rogers replied. 'I didn't ask specifically. I'll check it out if you want.'

Hartley shook her head. 'Later,' she said, reaching for the sheet of paper Rogers had typed for her. It seemed to be a thorough check on Blake's career, but lacked human background. There had obviously been no time for that. She put it on one side to study later. 'I've got another job for you.'

She brought Rogers up to date on their meeting with McGlynn and the visit to Maldon.

'Beech is still missing. There must be pictures of him in the trade magazines or yacht clubs. I think both Beech and Winters went out in the *Wanton Lady* to ferry girls from Spanish brothels to England and that's the yacht that capsized and left Winters and the others dead. McGlynn was lying about selling the yacht. She knows us, but she's never seen you, so it's your job. Get Beech's photograph for the crime wall, then round up more people. Pick up a picture of Winters from somewhere too. Dawn tomorrow hike your backsides to Burnham-on-Crouch. Follow McGlynn wherever she goes. She's to be watched at all times, 24/7 if necessary. Divide shifts any way you want. Report to me whenever you can.'

Thirty-eight

Puerto Banus. Friday.

Beyond the hot walls of the harbour, the Mediterranean water danced gently in the breeze, tiny waves twinkling like fireflies, reminding him of the lanes in Virginia in the spring when the miraculous insects flitted and twisted, then settled and glowed with seeming passion amid the white and pink flowers of the dogwood in the hedges.

One day, he thought to himself as he sat in the lounge on the yacht, I'll buy a place in Virginia. An old plantation with a clapboard front and white painted columns that soar from the terraces until they touch the eaves. A place where oak trees line the driveways, deer roam over the lawns and surrounding woods and horsemen in red livery follow the baying of the hounds. So different from his house in San Diego. That was new, expensive and sterile.

He had no real idea why Virginia had come into mind. Perhaps he was thinking about change. If *Tatú* succeeded, Duncan would have no need to chase more success. He'd long had more money than he needed, but he wanted to change the world. He wanted to be able to play God, in a simple form.

Blake could deliver it for him.

Blake was a genius, Duncan acknowledged. An arrogant iceberg, untouched by emotion except for his adoration of his precious orchids and his rapturous endorsement of the bull-ring. A contradiction even in his own pleasures, revelling in the beauty of his flowers on the one hand and the savagery of the bullring on the other. Not that Duncan cared about either, but he *was* concerned that Blake insisted matters proceed at his personal pace, according to his timetable and his meticulous attention to detail. Duncan provided the money. Blake should have provided results. The project should have been completed by now, but was on hold waiting for what Blake called his 'remaining possibilities' to prove his experiments.

The delay was causing problems, and Ferdetta wouldn't stop complaining about the ethics of the project.

And Blake was pestering him because a journalist was at the gates, with a verified request from the head of a prestigious colour magazine, asking about orchid tattoos.

Potrascu had promised the day before that the journalist would be dealt with, but had then flown to London, ignoring Blake's orders.

Now Blake was demanding that Duncan fly up immediately and handle the matter. I don't have to do anything for the prick, Duncan thought, allowing his irritation with Blake to rankle, but if this journalist had anything specific on the tattooing it could be dangerous.

He kissed the girl on her ear.

'I've got to go get the helicopter ready,' he said. 'You need a trip. We'll go to Sotogrande for a change of scenery, a quiet restaurant. You don't seem to be eating well and you're looking a little pale, under that beautiful tan. A change from the chef's cooking might bring a smile back to your lips.'

Panic flared in her eyes. 'You're not taking me there?' she pleaded. 'Please, don't take me there.'

‘No need to worry.’ Duncan stroked her hair. ‘When I get back we’ll go down the coast.’

She looked up at him, her eyes serious, no smile to be seen. ‘Will you take me with you when you leave this place?’ she asked, in little more than a whisper. A child’s whisper.

‘Why talk about leaving? Relax, have fun. Try fishing. Who knows, you might catch a Great White. Take one of the crew and go out with those new electronic e-jet skis. I haven’t even tried them myself yet.’

He was at the door without waiting for an answer.

‘I don’t want a jet ski,’ she whispered again. ‘I don’t want to go fishing.’

She put her hands together close to her lips. ‘Please God,’ she prayed. ‘I don’t want to go back *there* again.’

The motor roared into life above her then came the clatter of the rotors and the thump of the blades as they sliced the air and she felt the slight lift as it took off from the helipad.

She listened to it chattering over the sea then whirling inland. Gradually the sound vanished and she returned to the silence of the cabin.

There was a mixture of panic and relief. Here on the boat she felt safe, but every time he took her up in the helicopter he could be returning her.

Before Duncan was the nightmare. Never-ending days in the hospital, drugs pumped into her arm and her stomach with hypodermic needles; gleaming probes inside her while she was still conscious.

And the bottles.

The bottles displayed in the hospital with *things* floating in them. Tiny bundles that she could never reach to see and wouldn’t have wanted to anyway because they looked so *terrifying.*

The pain.

Pain that burned in her stomach while they were using those probes on her. Pain that continued after the nurse sterilised the instruments, after he took away material from inside with the tube they shoved up inside her.

She had seen him drop it into a tray, and take it out of sight.

Ten days, she counted. Ten days while they stuck things into her flesh, and up inside her, while they probed and fed her awful mixtures, forcing her to drink.

Now it was worse than ever.

Now the pain was in her heart and in her mind.

Her last period had failed to come.

It happened the week before Duncan brought her here, seducing her with this comparative Paradise, but she remembered how it had been.

How they forced her to do things that she had never even heard of before.

The sweat, the groaning, the sperm that sometimes ejaculated all over her.

But no one had ever entered her. Not before Duncan, of that she was sure, and Duncan always used protection.

But the pain was in her mind again.

It could not be. God, please help me and say it's not.

But it was saying it in her groin.

It was saying it from the beautiful flower they had finished on the tenth day of that treatment, the day they sent her back to the Romanian and the brothel.

It was whispering in her mind, day and night, night and day.

You're pregnant, it was saying. *You're going to have a baby!*

God, please say it's not true.

She didn't want a baby. She didn't want Duncan to learn about it, and discard her because of it. She didn't want to die. She was only fifteen.

Thirty-nine

Sierra de Las Nieves.

They looked up as they saw the helicopter swinging in like a huge black dragonfly, growing steadily bigger as it swept over the valley, heading towards Jorox. It roared over Blake's property and set down out of Tabor's sight, on the other side of the mansion.

They'd been waiting for half an hour, but the gardener had, after all, warned them it could take time. Tabor was prepared to stay until Dr Blake made up his mind.

It had been an uneasy few days for him.

He had no doubt that the crash at the bridge was deliberate. The simplest explanation was often the right one in his experience and his training told him always to expect and believe the worst. To his mind the attack in the alley and the BMW were explained if one accepted they were ordered by the same person who wanted him dead.

He hadn't managed to get around to buying a gun for himself, so asked Anca to bring her pistol. To his surprise she handed him another, a Tokarev, a gun first made in the Soviet Union in the 1930s, but produced for decades and still in service with security forces in some of the former Warsaw Pact countries. He checked it. Eight bullets in the clip.

'Good things come in twos,' she said, without commenting on how she'd brought the guns through Customs in so many countries. He remembered that first night he'd asked if she and Dani had flown to Spain from Bucharest, but she shook her head. 'By road,' she murmured, but again there was no further explanation.

Now he asked if she had additional clips. She handed him five. She was a walking arsenal.

But with the gun inside the waistband of his trouser belt, hidden by the jacket, he felt more confident. He was physically weakened, both from the attack in the alley and the near drowning in the river, but nothing he couldn't cope with.

Anca, he thought as he drove up the mountain road with her sitting beside him, staring out of the window and saying very little, was a beautiful and complex woman. He knew nothing about her, yet in some ways he trusted her more than he'd trusted most other people in his life. Apart from Davey Reed, he'd known few true friends. The closest he'd come was the Tabors and Emma, and the other 'family' he gathered in the shape of his men in the SAS. Now there was only Reed and his wife, and Tabor was content to keep it like that.

Yet he felt at ease with this woman at his side. She had demonstrated her competence and bravery. In return all he'd given her so far was trouble.

Blake might help them change that.

Anca wanted her sister back and he would help her if he could. *He* wanted the people who had forced his sister into the brothel and he would handle that himself. Anca shouldn't complicate her life by having his actions on her conscience.

The drive from the coast was uneventful and now they

were sitting together on the bonnet of the hire car, waiting for Blake. The gardener was on the other side of the gates, but when the phone finally rang he answered briefly, then came towards them smiling.

He pushed a remote-control button and the gates swung silently open, giving them a full minute to walk through before it automatically closed again.

They had breached the citadel. Metaphorically anyway.

For some reason Tabor took an instant dislike to Blake. The man was gaunt, above five foot ten tall and with his hair long since gone. With his sunken eyes – a shade of pale grey – and the black patches of the sockets around them, his cheeks devoid of surplus flesh, his face gave the impression of being little more than a piece of old yellow papyrus stretched over a skull. The remainder of his body matched the head. The frame was slight and the hands – the only other part of the flesh that showed – had skin stretched taut, tapering to fingers so long and thin they reminded Tabor of Alaskan snow crab legs.

He stood there, his back erect as they walked in.

'I don't normally see people in my home,' he said, without introducing himself. Blake had no interest in manners. 'However, I found the approach of your editor faintly interesting and I can spare half an hour. Then I shall see if there's any point in our continuing.'

He crossed the hallway to a room on one side and threw open the double doors. There was no verbal invitation, but it was clear they were expected to follow.

The room was huge, dominated by a marble fireplace that could have come straight from Regency England. Over it, where one might expect a gilded mirror, was a large unframed canvas of a fringed green orchid, so pale it was almost white, set on a dark-green background with its leaves nestling around it.

Tabor's eyes wandered everywhere quickly. Two settees, two armchairs, an ornate desk, a large floor-to-ceiling bookcase on one wall, all in expensive woods and fabrics. Oriental carpets topped a polished wooden floor that could be made of imported oak. But what stunned him most were the paintings. At least twenty of them, unframed, all of them orchids of several species.

'Quite an art show,' said the man standing up from the armchair in front of the fireplace. He was shorter than Tabor, medium height, around the five-foot-nine mark, but well built. He had an easy smile and an open face that was the very opposite to Blake. His hair was wavy and sandy and his dark-brown eyes seemed penetrating. 'I'm Iain Duncan, a friend of the doctor's.'

He took Anca's hand, then Tabor's. The grip was firm. The man looked after himself, Tabor thought.

'You should excuse Dr Blake,' he said. His voice was pleasant and amiable. 'He doesn't have much social conversation, but he's an excellent artist. What he fails to communicate with words, he does with his brush.'

'These are your paintings?' Anca looked at Blake in something approaching admiration.

'Only a person who can speak with his soul to orchids can paint them,' Blake replied. There was neither enthusiasm nor boast in his voice. 'No human can actually capture that, but one can strive for such perfection.'

Anca studied the canvas over the mantelpiece. 'What kind of orchid is it?'

'A *Ryncholaelia*,' Tabor said before Blake could answer. Blake's eyes narrowed a little and Tabor noted it. 'A *digbyana*, if my guess is correct.'

Blake inclined his head in what passed for a nod of agreement.

'It comes from Central America. Honduras, I think. The

fringe is unique, not found on any other plant within its own sub-tribe,' Tabor said calmly, looking at Duncan. Then he smiled. 'I got the impression the doctor doubts I know anything about orchids and this is a waste of time. A demonstration sometimes works wonders.'

Duncan laughed. 'Brilliant. It's the first time I've ever seen Felix dumbstruck. Would you like a drink? And you, Miss . . .?'

'Aron,' said Anca. 'A soft drink of some kind would be welcome.'

'Aron?' Duncan looked quizzical. He took in the black hair and the olive complexion. 'Israeli?'

'It seems you're as perceptive as my colleague,' Anca lied sweetly.

'What about you, Mr Ransome?'

Tabor shook his head. 'If the doctor's satisfied with my credentials I'd like to get on with it.'

Blake stared at Tabor with hostility. 'You're collaborating with the Earthwatch Institute in New York, I see from the letter.'

'Buffalo, New York State,' Tabor conceded. 'It's an international project – Staffordshire University, Alterra in the Netherlands, Complutense in Madrid, the University of Basel and others.'

Blake was testing him. Suggesting the Earthwatch Institute was in New York City was deliberate, trying to see if Tabor would bite. Naïve. Tabor had researched it the night before, just as for months in jail he'd researched tropical orchids to the point where he had a better knowledge of them than some experts.

He switched attention to Duncan. 'Perhaps Dr Blake can show me around and Anca can stay with you? She doesn't have to suffer a lecture about orchids.'

'Delighted,' Duncan replied. 'Felix has a thing about his

orchids. He normally doesn't allow anyone to go inside the orchid houses. I persuaded him your magazine was too important to be stubborn and this time should be an exception, so he'll take you down there, but I have to admit I find them boring too, at times.' He pointed to an armchair. 'Take a seat and I'll get your drink. Then we'll find something more interesting to talk about.'

In the grounds Blake pointed out the stubby growth of some *Ophrys*, a bee orchid and an early spider orchid, but it wasn't the flowering season and they looked like any other green-leafed plant, similar to the shoot of a dormant hyacinth. Blake wasn't interested in them anyway.

It wasn't until they got into the tropical orchid house that he began to display emotion. Then he spoke animatedly about orchids and breeding techniques, but reacted angrily when Tabor suggested Blake was trying to take the Ugly Ducklings of the orchid world and turn them into Swans.

'What I do is create perfection,' Blake snapped. 'Anything less is pointless.'

He dropped the subject and turned back to talking about other plants until suddenly he realised Tabor was no longer tagging along patiently behind. He was in a far corner of the orchid house staring at the Ghost Orchid.

Blake went over quickly. 'That's delicate,' he said in an agitated voice. 'Please step away from it. There are other places that are environmentally safer to the flowers than here.'

'It's a Ghost Orchid,' Tabor said in awe. 'It's not in flower but I recognise the roots. I didn't think they could be bred in captivity.'

'Anything can be done by those who have the knowledge and the skill, Mr Ransome. Please come with me. We've been too long in here, contaminating the atmosphere.'

Tabor stayed where he was, a strange look on his face. 'They're protected. It's illegal to pick or export them.'

'I've already told you. The Ghost Orchid can be bred if you have the knowledge.' Blake was getting angrier. All a journalist ever wanted was a sensational story and now this man had one. It was most unfortunate. 'I think you should leave,' he said, pointing towards the orchid-house door. 'The interview is over.'

Tabor stared at the Ghost Orchid again then back into Blake's grey eyes.

'Do you know anyone who can do tattoos?'

Blake was startled. 'Tattoos? Why should I?'

He'd been expecting this journalist to mention the tattoos at some stage but it shook him when it came out as bluntly as that. The man was dangerous. He asked too many unwanted questions. And he'd seen the Ghost Orchid.

'Someone told me about a tattooist on the coast who can do beautiful orchid designs on a person's skin.' Tabor studied Blake closely, noting the change in his face when he asked about the tattoo. Perhaps he did know something after all. 'I was hoping to find out who it is.'

'I have no idea.' But Blake's eyes were darting around and there was a hint of anger in his voice. Or was it fear? 'Tattoos are uncouth and unclean. They're useful for nothing except the identification of animals.'

'Are you certain you have no idea about orchid tattoos, Dr Blake?'

'There's probably no such thing. An orchid is highly intricate and tattooing is a rigorous and lengthy technical process. Far too lengthy, I suspect, for a street-corner tattooist.'

From his inside pocket Tabor pulled out the sheet of paper.

It was taken from the photograph of the girl washed up in Burnham, but Dani had scanned it into the computer and worked on it with a photo-manipulating package to eliminate everything except the flower itself, so that no one could have any idea where the drawing had been placed on the person's skin. It was almost anonymous, except for the detail work of the drawing, which was that of a master.

He handed it to Blake. 'That's the tattoo. I want to find the person who did it. It's far more interesting to the public than any real orchid, no matter how sexy I try to make it. If I can find the tattooist I won't need to mention you, Dr Blake. Your illegal Ghost Orchid can stay your secret for ever.'

The hire car ran smoothly and they dropped back across the Rio Grande where they had nearly died and this time carried on towards the coast.

Tabor kept a regular eye on traffic behind. He told himself it wasn't paranoia, merely necessary caution, so drove steadily, but not too quickly, studying each vehicle that came up behind him. He saw nothing untoward.

He wanted to send another email. There was more to Felix Blake than he'd thought. The fact that the man had an illegal orchid on his property was, on the surface, partly to be expected of someone who had such an avid love of the plants, but there was something else about Blake that didn't ring true.

He had to find out what Landon had learned about Blake's background. He had told Anca about the orchid, explained its illegality and seen her eyes arch in surprise, but beyond that she made no comment, watching as Tabor handled the curves on the mountain road, her thoughts kept to herself.

It was after he passed the Rio Grande that he spoke.

'What did you find out about Duncan?' he asked, keeping his eyes on the road, still wary of oncoming traffic or anything behind him.

“He’s rich. Very rich.’

Tabor laughed. ‘You don’t fly your own helicopter without money. As you know yourself.’ She had told him about her flying lessons. ‘What’s he doing in Spain?’

‘He’s got a chain of clinics on the Mediterranean coast. They do cosmetic surgery.’

‘That’s big business in Europe,’ mused Tabor, thinking about it. On television in his hotel room he’d seen advertisements for such clinics, new and fitted with expensive equipment. Being kept beautiful cost lots of money.

‘He waved it aside. He said it was a sideline to his real business in the United States. San Diego. He apparently has a major bioengineering organisation.’

‘Replacement parts for hearts and knees and that kind of thing?’

‘He didn’t try to explain. He said the business has become boring for him.’

‘So presumably the cosmetic surgery is an extension of that?’

‘He didn’t say. He talked mostly about food, and me.’

‘You?’

‘I think he likes women.’ Anca smiled. ‘He was quite charming, and very attentive.’

‘Is he married?’

‘He’d be unlikely to say so if he was hitting on me, wouldn’t he?’

‘Was he?’

He half-caught the turn of her head, the flounce of her hair and the deep grin etched on her face. He felt himself blushing because she’d understood what he was thinking.

‘He’s invited me to the casino,’ she said, waiting for his reaction. He held everything in. She reached out and touched his hand on the steering wheel. ‘You too, of course. He suggested next Thursday around ten o’clock. Are you interested?’

'I don't have clothes for a classy casino,' he dodged, trying to think of some way out of it.

But she was ahead of him. 'There are hire shops. You have enough money for that. And besides . . .'

'Besides what?'

'He says he'll bring his own date, who apparently is very beautiful. Does that make you feel any better?'

Forty

Edinburgh. Saturday.

Potrascu checked into the Sheraton Grand Hotel in Festival Square with Serghei in the room next to him on the fourth floor.

Edinburgh Castle dominated the skyline no more than a third of a mile from his room, Princes Street was only a few minutes' stroll away and the brochures on his table told him Holyrood Palace was two miles distant, but Potrascu wasn't in this city for tourist attractions. He ignored the hotel phone and used his mobile.

Fifteen minutes later he and Serghei got into the hire car they had picked up at the airport and drove off in the direction of the Forth road bridge. They knew where they were going. The instructions came from Simeonescu's next-in-line, who'd had a map of all the properties printed out.

Serghei noted the police car parked a hundred yards away. The information in London was that police had some of Bogdan's houses staked out, but the police couldn't storm in without a warrant in this country and, in any case, the day after the killings all of the brothels had temporarily ceased operations and the girls transferred to other locations. The police would find no evidence of prostitution if they raided the place. To all intents and purposes, it was now an unconventional large home.

Grigori Amanar showed them into his office on the top floor. He was the manager and the room was comfortable without being ostentatious. Bogdan had kept extravagance to a minimum in the houses used by clients.

Amanar offered them whisky but Potrascu waved it away.

'I'm here for the boy,' he said sharply. 'And to find out who killed my cousin and why.'

'The police . . .' Amanar started to say, as he poured himself a large measure of malt into a tumbler.

'I know what the police think. I want to know what *you* say.'

Amanar sat down. Potrascu's reputation was earned before he left Romania. Amanar might be innocent of everything, but that wouldn't necessarily be the way Potrascu would see it. His hand shook a little as he gulped his drink.

'The boy has vanished,' he said, avoiding Potrascu's eyes and staring into his glass. 'The police are searching for him because they think he saw what happened at Bogdan's place. They think he'll try to come here, or one of the other houses.'

Potrascu stared at him coldly. The man in front of him was from Bucharest. He had no loyalty to Costel's village. Perhaps not to Bogdan either.

'Who killed my cousin? Don't tell me the police think it was someone from London. I've already been told that.'

Amanar shivered a little despite the warmth in the house and the malt.

His eyes lowered. 'We don't know. No one knows where the cars went after they hit the house and none of our contacts has learned anything.'

'Why is this happening?'

Amanar saw Serghei staring at him impassively and his fears rose up inside him. Serghei was another one with a reputation. He had no interest in life or death. It made him more dangerous in some ways than Potrascu. Serghei would do what Potrascu told him, whether it was right or not. At the cost of his own life if necessary.

'I've had people asking around,' was all Amanar could say, hesitating as he did. 'Everyone is afraid. No one knows anything. It's a dead end whichever direction we turn.'

Serghei watched Amanar's eyes. He read dismay in them.

Finally Potrascu spoke. 'The operation is now mine. You will stay here to run the Edinburgh side of things.'

Amanar didn't want the job, but there was no point in arguing. No *future* in arguing.

'These people will return,' Potrascu said. 'The attacks were professional and I think they intend to eliminate or take over the Cerdachescu empire here. They'll return in force when the police go. Perhaps sooner. Meanwhile, they want to find Dmitri and execute him. He's now my responsibility and I'm not as easy-going as Bogdan. I don't tolerate failure. Dead ends in my book are really dead. Remember that, Amanar.'

Amanar stayed silent.

'Find the boy. I want the names of all Romanian storeowners in Edinburgh within walking distance of the police station where Dmitri disappeared. Every store and anyone else of influence. You have twenty-four hours. I'll come back tomorrow at this time. No telephones.'

He stood up and Serghei followed suit, smiling at Amanar sitting in his chair.

Serghei leaned over. 'Sit there for a time,' he said. 'Then get your fat backside into gear. There's already one minute wasted of the twenty-four hours you have left.'

Forty-one

London. Sunday.

Hartley picked up the phone.

'Bingo!' said Rogers excitedly from the other end of the line.

'Are we into cryptic crosswords now or are you trying to tell me something?' she snapped.

Rogers pulled himself back into official police mode. 'Sorry. I thought I should call you immediately. DC Robieson is watching McGlynn's office. DC Hedgecock's on rest and I'm keeping an eye on the Beech house. He's just gone in there.'

'Beech?'

'I recognised him from the photograph. McGlynn is in her office and he let himself into his house with his own key.'

'How long ago?'

'Two, three minutes. I called Robieson to make certain McGlynn is still there, then phoned you. He . . . hold on a minute, Inspector. Robieson's coming through on the other phone.'

She looked at Field standing beside her at her desk. 'Beech,' she said. 'He's not dead. He's . . . yes?'

Rogers had come back to her.

She listened for a minute. 'Watch the house,' she said. 'If he goes out, stop him. We're leaving now.'

She replaced the phone.

'McGlynn has already gone to Beech's house.'

Field stood up with her. It might be Sunday but there were no weekends off when work pressured. 'So it's back to balmy Burnham. I hope to Christ the rain has finally stopped.'

It had. It was five o'clock and the town was all but deserted. Lunchtime drinkers had gone home to eat and sleep off the morning's beer. Puffs of smoke blew from the chimney tops of several homes. It felt like winter.

This time Hartley drove through the gateway and pulled up in front of the steps. She parked alongside a large new silver Aston Martin DB9 that obviously belonged to Beech.

Before they were out of the car Beech was waiting at his front door, McGlynn visible behind him.

He was a medium-sized man, tanned and well built. His eyes held a constant smile. He was dressed in casual clothes, without a jacket.

Hartley nodded to Rogers standing near the entrance to the property, the nod telling him to stay there. He huddled into his raincoat against the shelter of the wall.

Beech beckoned them out of the wind. 'It's warmer inside,' he said. 'The central heating's on and I've started a fire.'

Logs were roaring in the hearth in the lounge. Beech was right about the warmth.

He showed Hartley to an armchair and indicated Field should take another, but he remained standing. Beech shrugged and sat down on the settee, with McGlynn next to him.

'Can I offer you tea or coffee, or something stronger?'

Hartley shook her head. 'No thank you, Mr Beech. Why didn't you phone me when you got back to England?'

'I've never been away. Well, perhaps being politically and geographically incorrect I haven't. I have a shoot up in Scotland, near a place called Loch Scye. I've been there for the last three weeks. I needed the relaxation and the seclusion. Then yesterday I phoned Kelly,' he said, half-turning to acknowledge her. 'She said the police had been to see me because the cleaner was worried because I hadn't said anything about being away. I gather Kelly told you the cleaner is over-protective, but she does an excellent job and I find the way she worries about me rather comforting. In any case, Kelly suggested I come down and make myself available for you, in case there are any problems. So here I am.'

He spread his hands palms up, the kind of gesture that says 'what else could I do?'

Hartley turned to McGlynn. 'You didn't tell me he had a house in Scotland?'

'I didn't know.'

'A pity. We could have contacted him there and it would have been settled much more easily and rapidly.' She turned back to Beech. 'I take it you can prove where you've been, Mr Beech?'

'If I have to. It's a large house up there and I have some live-in staff. A manager for the land, a gillie and so on. The phone records will show I called regularly from there to various business contacts. Is there any need for that?'

'Why didn't you go to Mr Winters's funeral?' she demanded, ignoring his question. *She* would decide what there was a need for. From her point of view Beech had wasted the time and the energy of a lot of people.

'I didn't know about it,' he answered sadly. 'It's the far north of Scotland, Inspector. Miles from a newspaper delivery and I doubt if Tom's death would have been reported in Scotland anyway. I wouldn't have thought his demise would warrant more than an East Anglian news mention.' He paused, and retracted immediately. 'I'm sorry. Demise is such a cold word. Tom was a great friend and a brilliant skipper. I'll miss him enormously, but I only found out about it when I phoned Kelly yesterday.'

'I take it you've called Mrs Winters?'

'No. Frankly, Inspector, Mary doesn't like me very much. She thinks I spent too much time with Tom on the *Pesadilla*. I was intending to go round there today until your men stopped me at the gate and told me to wait for you to arrive. I'll go when we've finished here.'

'When did you go to Scotland, Mr Beech?'

'As I said, maybe three weeks ago. I can't remember the exact date. I drove up in my Jeep. It's quite rough country up there. A cross-country vehicle is vital. I flew back here and had the Aston meet me at Stansted.'

'I take it you went to Scotland before Mr Winters died?'

'Yes.' The responses came immediately and without hesitation.

Field listened impassively. Beech was a man very much in control of himself, Field thought. He could have rehearsed this and it would still sound genuine.

'There were no more races scheduled and I told Tom to have a rest. He had things to do as well, so we left it at that. Now I think about it, I talked to Tom on the phone and right after was when I decided to go up to the estate. I was at my place in Guildford at the time but left then and drove overnight. I like doing that. It's easier north of the border in the dark with far less traffic. I don't know when Tom died, but he could have gone off doing whatever he wanted right away.'

McGlynn leaned forward, as if reinforcing what Beech

was saying. 'Tom went off regularly,' she said. 'Rumour has it he had his own business activities. Mostly illegal cigarettes, so the story goes.'

'You didn't tell me that when I spoke to you,' Hartley said sharply.

'The man is dead,' McGlynn replied evenly. 'Why sully his reputation after the event?'

Hartley looked away. It was a fair enough comment, but she didn't like the ease with which it had been said. Why mention it at all? She glanced at Field.

He knew what she was asking silently. Should she mention the *Gilbert Merrick* being moored at Maldon? He shook his head. There was no need. Not at this stage.

Hartley switched back to Beech. 'Do you ever go out on other yachts, Mr Beech?'

'I told you that,' McGlynn interjected.

'And now I'm asking Mr Beech to tell me. *Without* your help, Ms McGlynn.'

Beech grinned. 'Hey, let's not get into a scrap, ladies.' His voice had a slight twang, Hartley thought, but nothing she could place. 'As it happens, I go out on other yachts regularly. I can spare the time, I enjoy trying different vessels and helping friends is what yachting's about.'

Field spoke up for the first time. 'What *is* your business, Mr Beech, seeing it allows you so much time off to do what you like?'

Again Beech smiled. The question had been anticipated, Field thought.

'In the old days they'd call it wheeling and dealing,' he replied. 'Or maybe being a fixer. I arrange things between people who have a need to buy or a need to sell and I take a commission. How much commission depends on the size of the deal. I also play the stock market. I'll give you my broker's name if you want. It's a bit like being an old-time riverboat gambler except much more sophisticated and with bigger bets to win or lose.'

'And you don't lose?'

'Not if I can help it. I had a bit of a downturn during the financial crisis, the markets weren't good, but things are fine now.'

Hartley stirred. Beech seemed above board but warranted more investigation.

'Are you intending to stay in Burnham long?'

'Only overnight. Tomorrow I'll go to Guildford.'

'And if I need to contact you?'

He indicated McGlynn. 'I move around a lot,' he said. 'It's part of the job description, but I'll let Kelly know if I'm going any place where I'll be out of touch for more than a day and give her a contact number. There's no point in giving you a phone number of my own. I use several mobiles, depending on which part of the world I'm in. Not all of them work with British networks. Kelly will handle it. Is that sufficient, Inspector?'

'I'd prefer *all* of your numbers,' Hartley insisted.

'I explained. It's not practical. Not unless you intend to force me to stay in one place and that could cost me a lot of money. My lawyer wouldn't like it.'

'Is that a threat, Mr Beech?'

'What's there to be threatening about?' But he looked apologetic then pulled a business card from his wallet. He took out a Cross fountain pen and wrote on the back. 'Those are all of them. The one on the front of the card is my direct phone in Guildford. I'll stay there a couple of days. That should be long enough for you to check on me, but I have an appointment I can't break later this week.'

Hartley took it, examined the numbers and slipped the card into her coat.

'It's a long way for you to come for such little information.'

Beech smiled. 'I'm sorry I caused you so much trouble. I could have phoned you from Scotland, but Kelly kind of suggested she thought you'd want to see me face to face.'

'She was right,' Hartley said shortly. 'We've wasted a lot of time on this, Mr Beech.'

'What can I say? If I'd known about Tom, I'd have been back right away. As it was, not knowing meant I had no special reason to be here. I didn't know the police wanted me.'

'Perhaps not, but make certain we know where you're going to be for the next few days. Winters's death may have been accidental, but there's still an investigation into how and where he died. We may need to talk to you again, face to face, as you said.' She turned to McGlynn. 'Without intermediaries,' she added.

Forty-two

London. Monday.

On and off through the night she lay awake, thinking about Beech. He had given a perfectly reasonable explanation for his absence, but Beech had the money to run a Scottish estate, a valuable yacht and house in Essex, a big Surrey home *and* ultra-expensive cars. A little largesse would easily sort out any qualms a servant might have about a minor lie.

Jack Field was checking Beech's alibi but common sense told Hartley that he would find nothing. Beech wouldn't have mentioned his estate or his 'wheeler dealing' if there was nothing to substantiate it.

In fact, the more she thought about it, the more she was forced to accept there was no hole in Beech's story. So why did she fret about it?

She tossed and turned, with intermittent snatches of sleep, until around dawn she got up, showered, drank a cup of coffee and an hour later went to the office.

Landon was already there, sitting at her desk. No one else had yet arrived.

He looked up in surprise. 'Problems?'

'Questions I can't put words to,' she answered. She didn't ask why Landon was in so early. Or rather, why he was in at all. Her guess was that there'd been another bad night with his wife. 'Our missing sailor, Beech, has turned up. He says he's been in the north of Scotland and didn't know Winters was dead.'

'Do you believe him?'

'His alibi will be strong. Beech is the kind of man who organises ahead and knows his game plan down to the last detail.'

She went over to the photographs on the wall and studied them. She'd rearranged them and the lines leading to the circle in the middle had gone. She preferred ordered rows of photographs so that she could skim them without distraction. Those of the ice-axe victims were now lined up in rows to the left; in the centre were the pictures of the girl washed up at Burnham and the one killed under a train in Edinburgh. Next to that was a photograph of Tom Winters and Edward Beech together, jointly holding on to a trophy from some sailing event. Off a little way to the far right was a solitary picture of Felix Blake.

She had drawn a circle in white chalk around it and added a simple question mark.

Landon joined her at the crime wall, stopping to pick up the sheet of paper he was in the process of committing to print when she came in. He held it in his hand as he looked first at the picture of Blake, then at the other photographs and finally directly at her.

'Why the question mark?'

'Because I don't understand. We've checked out that name. Blake seems to be a bit weird, but there's nothing to connect him to any of the murders, except that the tattoos are the work of an expert and he's an orchid guru. As far as I can see, your source is accepting expert advice from his Dr

Blake, nothing more. Can you tell me anything more about this source, sir? Anything at all?'

'No, Ruth. I can see it's an irritation to you, but you'll have to ignore that. I read the report on Blake. Biochemist. As you say, no link to the murders or the tattoo.' He handed her the sheet of paper. 'This will only compound your confusion about my source. It's another name to check out. A man called Iain Duncan. American. He has a big business in San Diego and cosmetic-surgery clinics in Spain. Probably lots of other things too. The thing is, his business is supposedly bioengineering. Biochemist? Bioengineer? A possible connection?'

'We don't have any information suggesting Blake was employed.' Hartley was frowning as she read the information Landon had typed for her, almost word for word the contents of the encrypted email Tabor had sent to Landon the evening before.

'Maybe he isn't. My source doesn't suggest Blake does anything except breed orchids and go to bullfights. Oh, and trade in illegal plants.'

Hartley looked up from the note. 'Ghost Orchid?'

'Supposed to be the rarest orchid in the world. It's illegal for anyone to remove it from its native habitat in the Everglades.'

She was thinking rapidly. 'This Duncan? American. Everglades. Could he be supplying Blake with illegal orchids? Why? What would he gain from that? A big businessman wouldn't risk being tainted with trafficking in stolen plants. The Green Lobby would have him by the balls.'

Landon smiled. 'That's exactly what I was asking myself. What's in it for this Duncan? Then it struck me that if he traffics illegal orchids maybe he traffics illegal humans as well?'

She arched her eyebrows.

'I know, you're going to ask me where's the evidence?' Landon countered, seeing her expression. 'There are a couple of questions that come to mind, though. If Duncan is sending Blake rare orchids, how does he do it? I guess he wouldn't send it by Federal Express or carry it in baggage that has to go through a Customs check. So how? And what do Duncan and Blake have in common apart from the strained possibility of the bioengineering business? Anyway, that's it. I came in early to leave that on your desk. This way is better.'

He studied her face. 'You're tired,' he said gruffly. 'Try to get more sleep. Let Field and Rogers carry more of the load.'

'Would *you*?' she answered. Then added quietly, 'Sir.'

Landon didn't reply. He had trained her and she followed his methods. He turned away from the crime wall and returned to her desk, picked up a pencil and scribbled a name and number on a piece of paper.

'It's someone I know at the FBI in Washington,' he said. 'You might be able to bypass the system. He may have to be told Blake has a Ghost Orchid, but hold it back if you don't need to say. I always like to have an ace up my sleeve when I'm working on something difficult.'

'Such as your mysterious source?'

He smiled. 'Exactly,' he said. 'My Ace of Clubs.'

He walked out half chuckling at his personal joke. Hartley would know nothing about the connection between Spanish 'Clubs' and brothels.

But it was the first time Hartley had heard anything approaching humour coming from him since he told her his wife was dying.

Forty-three

Edinburgh.

Over the weekend Dmitri had organised his priorities.

He knew his cousins would come for him, but they had no way of knowing where he was. He didn't even know himself. Somehow his presence had to be made known to them, while at the same time kept hidden from the police and those who had killed his father.

It would mean exposing himself but he felt there was no alternative.

He restocked on food and liquid and bought a blanket and more clothing.

He glanced now at the new black plastic watch on his wrist. It was a few minutes after nine a.m.

He'd bought the watch using his new-found knowledge of British money and he was very pleased.

He spent a reasonably comfortable night under the blanket he'd folded double, but unless someone found him soon he'd need to buy another, or perhaps a sleeping bag.

He hadn't been able to get a Romanian-English dictionary

but in one street he'd seen numerous people walking into a building carrying books in their hands. It was a library and there he found a commercial telephone directory that listed shops. He went through it, picking out Romanian names and noting the addresses. He also found a guide to Edinburgh, including street plans. He chose Leith because that was the name painted above the warehouse and logic told him it must be the locality where he was hiding.

Now he had a list of seven names and addresses in the Leith area and a map he drew himself from the book. By following street signs he would be able to find them.

It would take time, a lot of time, but it had to be done.

When he was ready he headed off to the town centre, to the first name on his list.

His feet were aching when he saw a sign he recognised. McDonald's. He'd eaten in one in Marbella months earlier and knew what he liked, so he went inside, pointed to one of the pictures. The woman asked him something, but he shook his head to indicate he didn't understand, so she shrugged and went to the showcase, took out a burger wrapped in paper and a box of fries, poured the drink, placed them on a tray and handed it to him, along with his change.

Dmitri took everything to a corner table and sat down to eat, out of view of the nearest window.

He had been to all seven shops. In three of them no one spoke Romanian and he left without any further attempt at communication. In the others he told them the minimum; his name was Dmitri and someone would be looking for him. If they were men called Costel or Pavel Potrascu, who were friends of Bogdan Cerdachescu, they were to say he would be back. He saw the looks on the faces of the shopkeepers when he mentioned his father. None of the Romanian community would defy him.

Now all he could do was let time pass by, make the rounds of the shops each day, and wait until his cousins found him.

Forty-four

London.

Landon took a cup of tea up to his wife in the bedroom. She was sitting in an armchair, close to a bay window, staring at the leaves drifting past in the wind.

Increasingly over the past week she'd stayed in her room all day, wrapping a dressing gown around her, sitting in the chair, doing nothing except watch the street outside. She spoke to him occasionally, but there was no meaningful conversation. There never had been much, not after that first flush of romance, but there had been an acceptance of realities at first, until it turned into resentment. Now even that had vanished.

She wanted to die and have it behind her.

She showed no bitterness now and that hurt him more than normal. He deserved hurt. He wanted her to shout at him again the way she had in the past. He wanted her to show anger, and emotion. He wanted his sackcloth and ashes, but she denied him even that. All she did was stare through the window at leaves already dead, wishing she could drift away with them.

He put down the tea on the table beside her, but she didn't look at him. The stare stayed fixed on what lay beyond the glass.

He went away without speaking, closing the bedroom door. He would make dinner for her, but he doubted she would eat. These past few days the food was cold when he went to retrieve the plate. Almost nothing was touched except for the sweet tea and an occasional biscuit.

The doctor had told him that morning, when he called by, there might be only days left. She wanted to spend them in her own way, inside herself.

He sat in front of the gas fire, flames playing over the simulated coals, and tried to remember the brief months when their marriage had been good, but nothing would come. She was dying and all he could think of was work. All he had ever thought of was work.

Now, from time to time, he thought about Tabor.

What would Tabor have said about Helen? he wondered.

They had never spoken to each other before the meeting at Nether Wasdale, but Landon *knew* him. He knew what Tabor would be thinking, in the very same way he knew what he was thinking himself. Like minds. Like spirits.

Tabor would not have allowed her to wallow in her introspection, but nor would he have told her to snap out of it and make the best of whatever life she had left. He would have said life is a journey with a beginning and an end, and everything between is only filling in time, lurching from one meaningless happening to another, until that ending came.

Perhaps he should have told Ruth Hartley more about Tabor. Landon gave so little of himself to other people, and hid so much. But, as Tabor would say, in life there are things that only emerge in their own good time.

He sighed at his own inadequacies, pulled out the last email Tabor had sent him from the file lying on the table and re-read it. There was nothing more in it than he had told Hartley, but it was the reason for Tabor's request that intrigued him.

What did Blake and Duncan have that made Tabor think he should pursue them?

That had never been said.

He now had Tabor's number from the brief messages he'd sent. For a moment he was tempted to call direct but it would be unwise. He'd told Tabor he couldn't get involved personally and removed himself from the case because that was the sensible thing to do.

It still was.

Forty-five

San Diego.

Ferdetta typed the latest expenditure figures for *Tatú* into his personal database.

He admired Duncan, the man was a business genius, but he had never trusted him.

Least of all did he trust him now with his offer to hand over Cytek 'lock, stock and barrel' without the slightest financial remuneration.

They might be friends but Ferdetta knew that Duncan would stiff him if he got the chance. He might even kill him. Ferdetta had every reason to think Duncan had done it before, and would have no hesitation in doing it again.

His only real defence was this database.

He had pulled out of the old accounts details of all of the equipment bought for *Tatú* but which he had buried in the projects designated for other uses.

Most of it was for use in various branches of bioengineering, but there were a number of items solely used in the chemical division.

Anyone with bioengineering understanding would recognise it was for genetic experimentation with some kind of chemical twist.

The FBI would understand it too. That was the main thing.

This information, which he updated and printed out whenever he had more *Tatú* material to incorporate, was put into a large envelope and buried inside his legal papers, every time he left the office. If he died an 'accidental death' or if Duncan cheated him over this new deal, the papers would go to the lawyer and then to the FBI.

Ferdetta knew that the FBI could charge him too, but if he lived he would be able to use the papers to plea bargain. Even if he did eighteen months in jail, it might be worth it to bring down Duncan and his whole Cytek empire.

But then again, if Duncan were true to his word, that was one big empire for Ferdetta to inherit.

Forty-six

Edinburgh.

Grigori Amanar was alone in the house.

Twenty-four hours earlier he'd handed Potrascu a list of names and addresses, mostly Romanian shopkeepers or small businessmen. With Serghei in charge, they divided the manpower they had at the remaining brothels into small teams and sent them to knock on doors, leaving only Amanar to guard the property.

Edinburgh might not be a big city by international standards, but it was large enough and had a sizeable community of Romanians trying to climb the financial ladder. The radius Potrascu had dictated encompassed a large territory, and there were almost two hundred people to be visited.

Last night two of his men called by Amanar's place to say they'd had no luck, but the teams would start again this morning. It was now late evening and still there had been no response.

Amanar went over to the bar, poured himself a whisky and returned to his chair, bringing the bottle with him. He sat down, contemplating what he feared would happen if the search failed. There was no point in running. Potrascu would track him, wherever he went. Silently he said a prayer that the boy would be found.

He was a nice lad anyway but even if he'd been a brat Amanar would have wanted him found, for his own sake, not the boy's.

He closed his eyes and tried to visualise the boy's face, bringing up mental images of the teams going into shops, interrogating owners, not always gently if they proved awkward as some might.

The glass of whisky shot in the air, the liquid went over his face and shirt as Amanar jumped up out of the chair at the touch on his shoulder.

'What . . .?' He dropped the whisky to the carpet and stepped back, but someone else was behind him and Amanar felt strong arms clasp his shoulders. His tongue went dry and the colour faded from his face.

'What do you want?' he demanded thickly when he gathered his wits. He licked his lips to moisten them. There were only the two men, but that was enough.

The Scotsman smiled. 'You know what we want, Grigori.'

'How did you get in here?'

'Questions, questions,' the man sighed. 'Why do you people always ask so many questions and want so many answers? Have you no learned by now that we Scots prefer to ask our own questions? And we like the ones we ask to be answered politely. Besides, you've seen us before. You know who we are.'

Amanar knew. They'd both been clients several times in the past few weeks. They'd tried the girls and drunk the whisky and seemed to have money to burn.

'You're the people who killed Bogdan and his men?' he asked nervously.

'Aye,' the Scotsman replied. 'They were surplus to requirements.'

'I don't understand?'

'You weren't supposed to, but it can do nae harm. You see, Grigor,' he said, dropping the full name as if trying to be more familiar, 'you're out of business. You, and Bogdan and the whole fucking lot of you aliens. We don't like you, Grigor. We don't like you fucking up our fair city. We gave you your marching orders when we taught Bogdan a lesson but none of ye' could take the hint. Did you no hear we took his eyes out?'

The Scotsman was enjoying himself.

He picked up the whisky bottle and took a large slug of the liquid, wiped his lips with the back of his hand and handed the bottle to his colleague. Amanar stared at him with stark fear. The Scotsman was tall and built as though he tossed cabers for fun. Despite the cold, he wasn't wearing a coat. His tartan shirt had the sleeves rolled up and prominent on one arm was a tattoo. It had a horseshoe-shaped pair of what appeared to be feathers or wings, sweeping upwards from the handle of a dagger. A wavy band with a motto was printed across it touching the bottom of the wings. Amanar had seen this man and made it his business to find out what it was.

The Special Air Service. The SAS.

The Scotsman noticed Amanar's stare. He grinned and pointed to the tattoo. 'Fifteen years. If you know what it is, Grigor, you'll know better than to fuck wi' us. My mate there served wi' me too.'

Amanar turned and the other man looked down at him, a laugh on his face and a twinkle in his icy eyes.

'O' course, he's no Scottish,' the Scotsman said, 'so he'll maybe be rougher wi' you than I am. He's an Ulsterman. Treacherous bastards. Too damn devious. Can't let them out of your sight.'

'Who are you? How did you get in here?' Amanar asked again weakly. There was no point in trying to get away. Either of the men would have caught him in one stride.

'Through the upstairs window,' the Ulsterman behind him answered. 'People always leave upstairs windows unfastened. They seem to think because they're twenty feet up no one can get to them. Bad mistake.'

'The police?'

'You mean the napkin brigade out there in yon car?' said the Scotsman with a slight chuckle. 'They're too busy with their tea and doughnuts to notice anyone coming o'er the back wall. You've no need to worry, Grigor. The polis'll nae harm you.'

'Who are you working for?'

The Scotsman's chuckle vanished and a scowl was suddenly drawn like a curtain across his face.

'Too many fucking questions, Grigor. We're no working for piss-ants like you, that's fer sure. We're professionals, little man, and we're working for a professional too. We're putting an end to your little nastiness, Grigor. The brothel business in Edinburgh is under new management, as they say. No fucking imported Romanian managers. Just the girls. We'll do the managing. Now it's time for answers.'

'I don't know what you want.' Amanar's eyes were pleading.

'Yes you do, you fucking liar. We want the boy.'

'I don't know where he is.' Amanar looked from one man to the other, half-turning to take in the Ulsterman. His face was impassive. Amanar twisted back to the Scotsman. 'Why is he so important? Please! No one knows where he is. We have people looking for him.'

'Aye, right, and if you find him nae doubt you'll gi' me a telephone call to let us know where he is?'

'You know I can't do that!'

'At last, some fucking truth,' the Scotsman said, shaking

his head. 'It takes you lot a long time to get around to the truth, but nae matter. I'll gi' you one last chance to tell me where he is. If you willnae tell me I'll have to take a look around. There may be something in the books in your office, when we go through it. A pity the office won't look pretty when we've finished. Or you either.'

'Costel is searching for him!'

'And who the fuck is Costel?'

'Costel Potrascu. He owns the business. He's Bogdan's cousin. He runs the operation in Spain and organises the girls to come here.'

'Ah, *that* fucking Costel!' The Scotsman nodded as if it meant something. In fact, it was only information to be relayed back. He glanced at the Ulsterman as if with regret. 'He's no going to tell us a thing, I'm afraid. It's a pity. He's such a *wee* man, yon cock-a-drule. I'd like to encourage him but I dinnae think there's any point.'

He turned back to Amanar. 'I cannae say it was a fruitful discussion,' he said staring into Amanar's eyes. 'And I cannae promise you'll remember it for ever. Somehow I dinnae think there'll be much remembering left in Hell.'

He turned to the Ulsterman. 'Leave a reminder, Sean. For anyone who finds him.'

He picked up the bottle and finished the malt while Sean Flynn did what he'd been waiting to do.

When they climbed out through the upstairs window half an hour later, they left the reminder sitting by the empty bottle.

Not that the eyes could see it any more.

Forty-seven

Edinburgh.

Dmitri made his daily trek around the shops in the late afternoon.

He'd decided to leave it until that kind of hour, reasoning that the less time he spent on the streets the better. He was safer inside the warehouse. Until now he'd taken two hours each day to visit the shops and in none had there been anything said about the Potrascus. He reminded the shopkeepers that he would return.

It was almost dark by seven o'clock in the evening and he wanted to make his rounds and get back before night closed in. It was the last shop and as he entered he saw the man's eyes light up in recognition.

The shopkeeper came scurrying over, leaving two customers waiting at the counter unattended.

He took the boy by the arm and leaned closer to his ear so that no one could overhear.

'Two men came in an hour ago,' he whispered. 'They said they were looking for Dmitri Cerdachescu. I didn't tell them I'd seen you. It's better to tell no one anything, but they left a telephone number.' He reached into his trouser pocket and came out with a slip of paper. 'Do you have a telephone?'

Dmitri shook his head. The only one he had was in his room at the mansion. The room he couldn't bear to go back to.

The man pulled a phone from another pocket. He punched in the number written on the slip of paper and pushed the phone into Dmitri's hand.

'Go somewhere quiet,' he said. 'Listen to whoever answers. If you know who it is, then talk if you want to. If you're not sure, say nothing. It's very dangerous for everyone at this moment. Only speak to someone if you're certain who it is and that they're friends. You can keep the phone. If the people who came here today are not the ones you need, you must continue to wait but remember, someone wants to find you. There's no way I can be certain if those looking for you are friends or enemies. You have to make the choice.'

Then he pointed to a button on the phone. 'When you're ready to make your call, press that button. It will ring out.' He patted the boy on the shoulder. 'Go,' he said. 'And good luck.'

He straightened up and held out his hand to shake Dmitri's. Then he turned and went back to his customers, a professional smile on his face.

Dmitri left.

In the warehouse yard he checked the phone. The number was staring back at him and he took the precaution of writing it down on his notepad.

Then he took a deep breath, closed his eyes and pushed the green call button.

For a few moments he listened to the call tone ringing then a voice answered.

Dmitri felt weak and his knees were close to collapse.

He wiped his eyes with the back of his hand, knowing he was crying.

Then he sobbed into the phone. 'Costel! Please come and get me. Please, cousin. Now!'

Potrascu ushered the boy into the bathroom and made certain he was composed before he closed the door. Dmitri looked terrible, he thought. His big wide eyes were glazed with horror at everything he'd seen and experienced. They'd talked only briefly in the warehouse when he and Serghei arrived, following the map to the street sign that Dmitri spelled out for him.

Inside the building Potrascu looked in disgust at the way the boy had been living; the urine-stained mattress, the uncombed hair, the discarded clothes he'd been unable to wash, the solitary blanket carefully folded over the mattress. Dmitri had put empty cans into a carrier bag along with the finished boxes of milk and the plastic water bottles. There was so little. And he had the smell that came from days without washing, from fear and sweat. He needed soap and water and much, much else.

He put his arm around Dmitri and nodded to Serghei, indicating the old clothing.

Serghei picked up everything except the mattress, took it back over the wall and threw it into the boot of the hire car. The police were unlikely to come in here and if they did there were plenty of homeless people around to account for the mattress, but Potrascu liked to sew up potential loose ends. The debris from Dmitri's stay could go in the rubbish bins later.

In the car Dmitri told him what he'd seen, while Serghei concentrated on driving back to the hotel. They'd been treated to strange looks as they walked through the lobby, Potrascu shepherding the boy in his camouflage trousers and army store clothing ahead of him. First thing in the morning they would buy clean clothes then discard the army surplus material along with everything in the boot.

Immediately after they would fly back to Spain.

He heard the shower start. Once the boy was clean, Potrascu would order room service for the lad to have decent warm food, then put him into bed. Potrascu would lie on the settee and Serghei would bring in blankets and sleep on the floor.

He called Amanar, but there was still no answer. Amanar would have to wait. Wherever he was he would be found and his disappearance remedied. No one else needed to be contacted for the moment. It was safer that way.

He couldn't ignore the reality that someone had told the killers where Bogdan was to be found. Nor did he forget Pavel and his belief that his brother was betrayed by one of his employees. There were probably the same leaks inside the operation in Edinburgh. In particular, he no longer trusted Amanar. Amanar who wasn't answering his phone tonight.

Potrascu sat on the end of the bed waiting for Dmitri, thinking about what the boy had told him. Dmitri had only heard a few of the words shouted in the second brothel and had no idea what they meant. He didn't know the differences in dialects between England and Scotland. The lad would be of no help, but somehow Potrascu had to find out who was behind these attacks and put the matter straight. Something had to be done quickly.

The boy wouldn't need to visit a grave to pay his respects to his father's memory. Bogdan would have accepted that. The boy would too.

He heard the shower switch off and the clatter of a toothbrush on the bathroom shelf. Then came the sound of the handle turning and he stood up to check on Dmitri.

The boy came out of the bathroom naked, using both hands to towel his hair dry and turned to Potrascu with a weak smile, which changed instantly to puzzlement.

Potrascu's eyes were wide with shock.

For a moment he stared at the boy, his body crawling with horror.

Dmitri dropped the towel in amazement, feeling it collapse in a crumpled heap over his feet.

Potrascu was staring at the boy's penis and Dmitri felt suddenly uncomfortable, although nudity had never bothered him before.

'What is it?' he asked, the frown furrowing his brow.

Potrascu pointed at Dmitri and he looked down. A smile crept across the boy's face. It wasn't his penis that was causing the problem.

He looked up at Potrascu. 'Isn't it beautiful,' he said. 'I've never seen anything more beautiful. While you were away for that first month after my mother died and I stayed in Spain I had to go for medical treatment. That's when they did it. I love it. Lots of people have them but I've never heard of anything like mine.'

Potrascu was dumbstruck.

His eyes began to glaze over and tears were pricking at his eyeballs.

Dmitri may never have seen anything like it but Potrascu had.

It was a flower.

An orchid.

Tattooed expertly into the boy's groin.

Forty-eight

Fuengirola. Thursday.

Tabor fastened the bow tie and left the bedroom mirror for her to take over.

He didn't like dress clothes. They felt tight and unnaturally strained, no matter how loose they were, and they were archaic. Something that belonged to the 19th or early 20th centuries when people wanted to be seen to be different to the working man.

But he wore them because she asked him to and because he wanted to talk more with Iain Duncan. Landon had replied to his queries. It came as a surprise that Blake was a biochemist. Duncan was in bioengineering, a related field, and the probability was that he and Blake were engaged in business activities that involved an occasional gift such as the Ghost Orchid. For services rendered. It had nothing to do with tattoos or prostitution as far as he could tell.

For the past few days, he'd kept a low profile, off the streets where he could be picked up. His only trip outside the flat had been to the hire shop in Marbella.

Anca hired an outfit from the same place. She tried on

several items, but finally committed to a crepe-satin two-piece, overlaid with chiffon. Shoestring straps fitted the bodice and the skirt was a soft satin A-line. It was in burgundy, and shimmered with matching sequins. The outfit was bare around the arms, shoulders and back, but the skirt ended some six inches from the ground, making it easy for her to walk without it catching the floor. She had no jewellery with her, other than a pair of costume earrings and she discarded her cheap wristwatch knowing it would mar the effect of the outfit. As it was, the deep burgundy of the dress against the duskiness of her skin was perfect.

Dani spent most of his time chasing information about Blake and the cosmetic-surgery clinics Duncan owned. Tabor wanted to know if Blake worked in them, but the doctor wasn't mentioned on any of the websites. Dani hacked into several company databases, but found no mention of Blake on their staff or consultancy lists.

And Tabor was no further forward in finding the people behind his sister's abduction. Dani gave him a printout from police files in Bucharest about Costel Potrascu, but other than confirming he was a much-feared psychopath, who controlled gangs in Romania and Spain, there was nothing.

He had made up his mind in the last couple of hours.

Tonight he would socialise with Duncan, but tomorrow he would take the plunge. He would break into the brothel where he'd found his sister and either confront Potrascu or try to find written evidence of the connection. But he doubted such evidence existed. Tabor would have to use other methods on the Romanian.

So be it.

He heard the door open and looked around.

She was framed in the bedroom doorway, looking radiant. The dress sparkled in the light of the central lamp, tiny stars scattering from spangles with every minor move of her body.

Duncan could think what he liked about his own escort. As far as Tabor was concerned, at this very moment Anca Aron was the most beautiful woman in the world.

They left the car a short distance away from the hotel casino. It had valet parking, but Tabor preferred to know where his lifeline to escape was at any given time. Stuck in a car park, reliant on a valet, didn't fit with his operational background.

The night was warm and they parked a couple of hundred yards away.

Dani had looked up details about Marbella on the 'Net and found that, among other things, it was the home of dozens of famous people, including the Saudi royal family who were actually in residence at this moment.

The closer Anca and Tabor got to the casino, the more armed guards were visible. Police cars were conspicuously parked on both sides of the main highway and in a side road he noted a van filled with an armed response team.

The Saudi royal family, he thought. That was the reason for the full-scale turnout.

They passed the palms and the tall stands of Bird of Paradise trees in front of the casino and were approaching the entrance when Anca suddenly froze.

Tabor halted with her.

She was staring as if transfixed. Tabor followed her eyes.

Walking up the steps to the casino was Iain Duncan. The parking valet was already inside the vehicle, closing the door to drive away. On Duncan's arm was a poised, slender woman, dressed revealingly in a backless black dress, the slit in the skirt almost up to the top of her thighs. Her hair was dark and long and straight, and floated around her face as she moved, almost gliding, towards the entrance.

In the brilliant glow of the entrance lights he could clearly see the girl's features. Young, perhaps nineteen or so, her cheekbones high, her head held up, eyes facing directly ahead, walking with the stance of a model.

It was instantly obvious why Duncan had spoken about the girl being beautiful. Had Tabor not seen Anca as she was tonight, he might have felt the same way.

Tabor suddenly winced. She was clutching his arm and her long nails were digging into his flesh. There was disbelief in her eyes and her jaw had dropped slightly open. He could feel her swaying as she stood there and he put his arm around to hold her steady. He could see she was on the edge of collapse: the colour had ebbed from her face, her lips were trying to move, but no sound emerged.

'Anca,' he said urgently. 'What's wrong? What is it?'

But for moments she seemed to be unable to speak. Then she turned to him, her eyes brimming with stifled tears. 'Duncan,' she said in a tight voice. She looked up into Tabor's eyes and he read pain and anguish there.

'What about him?' Tabor asked anxiously.

'Not him,' she whispered. 'The girl with him. That's Dorina. Dorina, my sister.'

Forty-nine

London.

Earlier in the evening Jack Field phoned.

'He checks out,' Field said. 'The house in Scotland is miles from the nearest town and it's not the kind of place to go in this weather. Thurso Police say they've already had snow and there's no surfaced road to the house. I looked on the map and it seems rather remote to me, but they gave me a phone number for the estate manager, a man called Brodie. He's pretty abrupt. Doesn't seem to like people much, but he confirms Beech was there. Beech's finances look sound as well. Paul went through the Inland Revenue. Everything appears above board. He pays his taxes and National Insurance contributions for more than a dozen people on the payroll. Most of them are in Scotland, but there's a couple in Manchester. He's got several stockbrokers and they're hazy about what Beech actually does, but the last one I spoke to confirmed he makes a lot on the Stock Exchange. Even in the credit crunch. He quoted client confidentiality to dodge most of the questions.'

'As he would,' Hartley murmured, only half aloud, but he heard her.

'I'm with you,' Field said. 'I don't like the man, but I don't know why, and there's still something wrong about that boat.'

'I spoke to McGlynn this afternoon. She called to say Beech was going away for a few days. I asked again for the name of the Lithuanian couple that bought the boat and she gave me a surname but no location, no address and no home port. I'll dig deeper into it. Are you off now?'

'Darts match at the pub. I'll imagine Beech is the treble twenty and break my personal record.'

Hartley laughed quietly. 'Have a good night,' she said.

She put down the phone and sat back in the chair, staring at the crime wall of photographs. It gave her no inspiration.

Now it was dark and she had to go home. Home to cook, shower and go to bed.

Not the most exciting time of life for a thirty-year-old woman, but there were no men on her romantic horizon and she didn't see the point in casual relationships. One day someone would come along. Someone she could grow old with.

She thought of Alan Landon and felt unaccountably sad.

Fifty

Sierra de Las Nieves.

He needed very little. It was, after all, only a short stay.

Normally he would have the pilot fly him to the *corrida* on Saturday and make him wait around at the airport, but Blake was uneasy and a couple of nights out in Sevilla might settle him.

The pilot could return for him on Sunday.

It was the last fight of the season and he had to be there for it. He needed to feel the energy of the bulls, the power of the matadors, witness the cape work. He wanted to engulf himself in it, and in two or three weeks he would leave Andalucia for a few months, finding new enthusiasms in Mexico and Central America.

But he also wanted to get away, for a time at least, from Duncan.

He was finding the man irksome. He demanded too much, always impatient over things that should not, *could* not be hurried. This was the critical phase of the operation. The results involved a continual process of refinement, eliminating rejects in pursuit of the perfection that was imperative.

Duncan didn't see it that way. He didn't understand the difficulties of breeding. He *pried* too much.

The thought sent him off at a tangent and he left the packing to go to the top floor of the mansion, an area guarded by a sophisticated combination lock incorporating a retina scan and a panelled door that appeared to be oak but was only veneer over two inches of heavy steel. Fireproof, lock proof and, short of using explosives, entry proof.

Blake opened the box concealed in the wall behind a painting of a trigeneric hybrid *Brassolaeliocattleya* and, when the retina scan was confirmed, he flicked his long fingers over the keypad to punch in the combination.

He opened the door and went in. It closed and locked automatically behind him.

The floor was divided into three rooms. One was an office, with a computer on a desk, filing cabinets, research books in a large bookcase against one wall and three comfortable chairs.

Another room was a laboratory. It was in miniature because his experiments were aimed at a limited target, but it was more than adequate for his purposes. The cupboard tops had a small column of sterilised Petri-dishes in sealed plastic bags ready for use and, in one corner, what resembled a catering-size electric mixer. A fully automatic pill-making machine was at the side of one wall. On the strong shelves were ten 12 × 14 inch bell jars, in which floated tiny embryos that had never reached beyond the three-month stage of development.

Blake hardly spared them a glance. The earliest had been there over four years, the most recent were two years old, all of them from before he decided to use only virgins in his work. He had kept them originally for comparison purposes and several others had been dissected and examined as part of the experiments, the remains disposed of in the sea. A number of times he had intended to have them all taken out and fed to the fishes, but in a way they were the only remaining visible reminders of his long struggle to bring his work to perfection. They were *not* trophies as a layman might call them. They were stages of evolution.

The other room was the surgery. It had a hospital bed plus the trappings of an Intensive Care Unit. The trays of sterilised instruments were out of sight, as were the other basic requirements of his work – rolls of cotton wool, rubber sheets, surgical gloves, facemasks and disposable gowns.

There was no operation on the horizon. When necessary he would order other bulky supplies such as oxygen cylinders, but for the moment all he needed was here. The instruments and equipment in this room alone had cost more than $20 million, but money was only a means to an end, and in this case the end would be world shaking.

In one corner was a piece of equipment oddly out of place. A 10-needle tattooing machine. In a cupboard to the side were the inks, the packages of sterile needles and medical equipment needed for after-care or possible allergic reaction.

Blake inspected everything, confirmed nothing was out of place, then checked the windows and fussed with the locks, ensuring they were secure. His personal records were in a filing cabinet and securely locked. Finally satisfied, he returned downstairs.

The only person, other than Blake and Duncan, who went into the room, was a nurse, who was paid extravagantly to assist when an operation was under way, and deal with post-operative care. She was also the anaesthetist. At the very start of her employment she was introduced to Costel Potrascu as an incentive for her to say nothing.

The nurse was originally from Romania. Potrascu's reputation was legendary among the Romanians on the coast and she had never breathed a word to anyone.

But it wasn't Potrascu who worried Blake. The Romanian was a peasant, a necessary evil.

It was Duncan.

For some days Duncan had seemed overly intense about the experiments. Several times he'd asked for copies of Blake's data so that Cytek experts could evaluate them. From the moment Blake went to Duncan to discuss his ideas, the American had been an enthusiastic backer and supporter. Now he appeared to be wavering, wanting ever more detail. Blake refused. It was *his* work, *his* research and *his* project, not to be shared with anyone until he was certain it was right. Then the world could know and be overwhelmed by his brilliance. The world could be changed. Until then he would share nothing with those other so-called experts at Cytek.

But Duncan was not accustomed to rejection, and Blake could sense a controlled anger inside the man. That was his problem, Blake thought. Duncan had multiple personal flaws.

In that respect, Blake was particularly concerned about Duncan's 'arm candy' as he called them. It hadn't mattered with other girls Potrascu supplied, but the one Duncan now had in tow was a different matter. He normally had his 'little dalliances' disposed of by Potrascu in the Mediterranean after he'd tired of them, but that couldn't be allowed to happen with this girl.

Then there was the reporter. Duncan assured him the man was no problem and would be taken care of, but Potrascu had failed to do that once already.

Things were becoming complicated. Sevilla and the bullfight was the balm to ease his mind.

It was late evening. He rang the pilot in the Jorox bar where he usually was midweek and told him to be ready for an early flight. By ten a.m. tomorrow, traffic permitting, Blake would be in the Alfonso XIII.

Fifty-one

Marbella. Costa del Sol.

Tabor strolled confidently into the casino, his icy calm countering the anger burning in his stomach. His first intention had been to confront Duncan then take the girl and have her flown immediately with Anca to Bucharest.

Anca was initially distraught. The shock of seeing her sister stunned her. She was expecting something, but it was as if her mind couldn't accept the reality of seeing her sister, dressed as she was, on Duncan's arm walking into the casino.

Her worst nightmares were realised. Dorina was alive, looking radiantly well and Anca should be happy, but her emotions insisted that what she was seeing was *wrong*. Dorina had written that she was being kept captive. If she had since been freed and able to leave, she would have let her family know.

Duncan was holding her. That was the only answer, and Anca knew it the moment she caught sight of them together. After an instant there had been no excitement and joy at seeing her sister, rather fear and anger for what had been done to her and loathing for the man she *knew* was holding her against her wishes. Anca was on an emotional roller-coaster. First amazement, then despair, followed by rage then impotence in snaps that flashed by like panels in a comic strip. That was when she almost fainted, only Tabor's strong and steady arms holding her up.

Moments later she asked to go. She didn't want Dorina to recognise her here. There was more to this than her sister's initial disappearance, but she had already begun to reassess the situation. She needed to step back and look at other possibilities, the way she would have done were she on normal police duties, not affected by external personal emotional impediments. Tabor had to rein in his explosive anger and do nothing precipitous. In the quietness of the car reason prevailed.

As she said on reflection, there was a possibility Duncan was innocent of anything except having a prostitute supplied to him and perhaps he didn't know what she was being forced to do. Clearly she wasn't being ill treated. Her clothing and jewellery, from the distance Anca witnessed, appeared expensive and Dorina looked exquisitely beautiful.

But if Duncan *were* involved, a confrontation between him and Tabor in the most public place on the Costa del Sol, with armed security guards everywhere, could lead to disaster. Tabor was in Spain illegally. He would be arrested and at best deported to England. At worst they might incarcerate him in the top-security jail at Alhaurin el Torre, to spend the ten years they'd given him on the manslaughter charge and more for the illegal return.

It was the police officer in her speaking.

Ten minutes later, Tabor agreed to go to the casino while she returned to the flat and changed into different clothes. She would come back in two hours to pick him up. In the meantime he would restrain his temper and ask, in a circumspect way, about Dorina and the operation that had ensnared her.

His emotions told him to strangle Duncan there and then. Anca's was the sensible route.

Duncan was waiting in the foyer and the girl was alongside him, looking enchanting.

Tabor took in the dark skin, the high cheekbones, the taut shape of her body and the resemblance to Anca was clear. Hopefully Duncan hadn't noticed it and without the two women side by side he probably wouldn't.

Duncan was frowning. 'Your interpreter isn't with you?' he asked as he held out his hand to greet Tabor. The girl beside him smiled slightly, but said nothing.

'She got dressed, but then came over nauseous,' Tabor half lied. 'Headache, stomach pains, the whole catastrophe. She sends her apologies. I'm afraid you'll have to put up with me.'

'That's no hardship,' Duncan replied, beaming at him, white teeth flashing. He had the most natural of manners. It would be easy to be taken in by such a man. 'But it *is* a slight problem. You don't speak any Spanish at all?'

'*Cerveza*, *por favor* and *gracias*. That's my limit. It wouldn't take me far. That's why I hired her.'

'It can't be helped.' Duncan's frown had vanished and the perma-smile was back. 'Unfortunately Teré doesn't speak any English and I was rather hoping she and your colleague could get along in Spanish while you and I had a look at the tables, or a drink or whatever.'

'Nice name. So she's Spanish?'

'No, but she speaks Spanish. Enough to get by anyway.'

'You too?'

'Hey, I live in Southern California. You don't go far without Spanish in San Diego. That's border country. Every labourer, gardener, maid, cook or cleaner is from Mexico or another part of Latin America. Spanish speakers run the infrastructure of California and a couple of other states besides. My Spanish comes with Mexican words but Teré and I get along fine.'

The girl was uneasily looking at both men, trying to understand what they were saying and failing. She was tense, Tabor thought.

Duncan caught it too. 'Excuse me a minute,' he said, taking hold of her arm, leaning closer to her ear and whispering. He put his hand in his inside pocket, pulled out a thin wad of banknotes and handed it to her. She turned to Tabor and smiled politely. Her eyes looked tired and afraid. Or maybe Tabor was imagining that. She said something to Duncan then walked away into the interior of the casino, the eyes of most men following her.

'She likes to play roulette,' Duncan said, switching back to Tabor. He enjoyed the other men watching her. Tabor was doing the same. 'I thought she may as well try to make herself some money while we kill time over a drink. Are you staying to eat?'

'Sorry,' Tabor said, as the girl vanished into the gaming area. 'I have to get back and check with Anca in a couple of hours. I'm not much of a drinker, but I'd be glad of conversation. It gets tiring having it coming to you third-hand through an interpreter most of the time.'

Duncan took him by the arm. 'This bar's good enough,' he said, guiding Tabor towards it with practised ease. 'If you're strictly teetotal, there's the regular stuff and alcohol-free cocktails. Otherwise, whatever you fancy. Is this general conversation you're after or are you still chasing our good doctor and his orchids? He told me about the Ghost Orchid, by the way. I confess right now I gave it to him. Let's have a drink and I'll tell you why it's nothing to worry about.'

They sat at a table, some distance from the bar where the noise was less. Tabor took a small beer and Duncan had a large straight malt Scotch, without ice. Interesting, Tabor thought. In his experience, most Americans drank their whisky with something, even if it was only water.

'You gave Blake a helluva scare over the orchid,' Duncan said as he settled into the chair. 'He thinks you're going to denounce him to the US authorities and that will get him in trouble on the international orchid-breeding circuit.'

'Ghost Orchids are illegal. He shouldn't have them and he's got reason to be scared, but he doesn't have to concern himself on my behalf. It's too late to do anything except punish him and that's none of my business. I'd rather he gave me information but he seems reluctant to do that.'

Duncan twirled his glass and looked through the smoky liquid at the light.

'The Ghost Orchid,' he said. 'It's not from the Everglades where you might think. It's from Cuba. They grow there too. I've got a yacht and from time to time some Cuban friends of mine get together down there, not far from Varadero. It's frowned on by Washington, but business makes the world go around and they know that. Blake is also a friend and I knew what he'd think about a Ghost Orchid so while I was down there last time I mentioned it. When I came over here, I brought one with me. A local orchid expert had it packed sufficient for the trip and I got it in with some of the medical supplies for my clinics. Illegal, but not exactly a matter for the electric chair. Blake didn't know he was getting it. It was a gift from me to him. I'm sorry if it upset you, but it wasn't his fault. If you want to blame anyone, blame me.'

'I wouldn't have thought you and Dr Blake had a lot in common?'

Duncan smiled. 'Friends come in strange packages,' he said. 'He's also a business contact. He does some consulting work for me from time to time.'

'In your clinics?'

'Got it.' Duncan nodded agreement. 'That's why I'd appreciate your not letting anyone know about the orchid. It was my fault, as I said.'

'I won't be telling anybody.'

'Thanks.' Duncan smiled. 'Blake says you were pushing him about tattoos.'

Tabor blinked, saying nothing.

'I think he knows who the artist is,' Duncan said. He saw the surprise show. 'He's not saying anything because he's almost pissing in his pants worrying himself about the orchid. Give it a few days and I'll go back to see him and tell him there's nothing to get concerned about. I think he'll open up for me.'

'I don't have a few days. Hanging around in Spain isn't producing words. No words, no money and I don't have your resources.'

'Hold out until next week. I'm leaving for home soon, but before I go I'll get back to Felix and see what I can do. Do you have a phone number?'

Tabor shook his head. 'I don't like using phones. You get a lot more out of talking to people face to face. Where can I find you tomorrow?'

'Out at sea. I own a yacht, remember? It's in harbour at Puerto Banus but I don't keep it to have it sit by the quay and be inspected by tourists. I use it to go up and down the coast to my clinics. That's where I'll be tomorrow and over the weekend.'

He paused, as if thinking about it.

'What say you come down to Puerto Banus on Monday? I was going to take Teré out for a romantic run anyway. The crew need time off so they'll be away. I can handle it single-handed in calm weather. Come to the yacht and we'll do some fishing. Stay overnight. Your interpreter should be over her problems by then hopefully and it's a good chance for you both to see my boat. She's quite something. The name's *Blancanieves.* You see, I told you San Diego is half Spanish. *Blancanieves* is what you'd call Snow White in England.'

'Snow White?' Tabor smiled, sipping at his beer. It would be expensive here, he thought, but Duncan could afford it. 'Not exactly the way you'd describe your girlfriend!'

'Yeah. Hardly an ice maiden,' Duncan agreed. 'But she's not my girl. I don't have time for commitments.'

'How did you meet her then?'

'Escort agency. You're a journalist, you know the way it works. I've got a top-class agency on the coast and when I'm here they provide a woman who comes up to my standards. When I leave, she goes back to escorting. No tears, no trials, no problems, no alimony or paternity suits. In the meantime, I pay the girls well and they treat me the same way.' He looked at his malt. The glass was empty. 'Now,' he said, nodding to the waiter hovering not far away, 'I'm having another. How about you?'

'Plausible,' said Tabor, as they drove back through the crowded main street of Marbella, running parallel to the sea towards Fuengirola. 'He volunteered information about the Ghost Orchid and promised Blake would give me the name of the tattooist. Then he told me about Dorina, although he called her Teré. My guess is it's escort-agency convention. No woman in that kind of business would give her own name. There'd always be a nom de plume. He sounds above board.'

'I don't believe it,' Anca said. Her initial concerns had come flooding back. 'A lot of escorts are prostitutes, but they'd be able to wander around freely anywhere, any time they like. It doesn't ring true. Dorina said she's being held with limited freedom and that doesn't sound like an escort agency to me.'

Her anger was bubbling up again and she couldn't understand why Tabor was being so patronising. If he'd thought Duncan was holding *his* sister, would he have been so understanding? She bit back the words before she spoke them. She was the one who urged reason in the first place. Attacking him now would be unfair and unwise, and the last thing she wanted to do was hurt him.

'Did he mention Potrascu?' she asked, sitting back to watch the road ahead.

'No,' he said. 'But tomorrow Dani can see if there are any Romanian links to escort agencies, although don't hold your breath. If Potrascu *is* involved, he's doing it through his brothels, not through any agency you'd find in the equivalent of Yellow Pages. I could hardly ask Duncan to give me the name. He'd know I couldn't afford that kind of woman.'

'He didn't say anything about me?'

'After I told him you were ill, no. Why?'

'I began to think perhaps he'd mentioned my name to Dorina and she'd picked up on it. Duncan might know who I am.'

'He didn't give any indication of anything like that. If she'd said you were her sister, he'd have dumped her right away and vanished without telling anyone anything. He wouldn't want to get in that kind of trouble with the Spanish police. They're lenient about prostitution, but might not be lax about paedophiles.'

'Reasonable.'

'He'll know on Monday anyway. You hate the idea of her being with him for a couple more days, but we should give him a chance to tell his side of the story. I'm sorry, Anca. If we were going to do anything, we should have done it right away. You persuaded me not to and you were right.'

They were driving past El Faro. The lighthouse was on the cliff edge above the road, the sea on the other side with only the width of the road between them. The lights of Fuengirola were a few kilometres in the distance.

He glanced at Anca. She was staring ahead, through the window, her face without expression.

'Give it until Monday. As you say, I can't afford a confrontation with the police. They'd probably throw Dorina in jail too, saying she was living off the proceeds of prostitution. Monday we'll go to Puerto Banus. One way or another your sister will come back with us. She's only fifteen, no matter how much older she looks. Duncan won't hold on to her once we tell him. He'll want to be out of Spanish waters as fast as he can pull his crew back. Three more days, Anca. Give it three more days.'

'Doing what?'

'Dani will work the Internet. I'll get Costel Potrascu and find out about Emma. You guard my back.'

Fifty-two

London. Friday.

Ruth Hartley put down the phone. 'It's happened again,' she said. 'That was Edinburgh. Someone got into another brothel and killed the manager. They took his eyes out.'

'What were the police doing?' Field asked bluntly.

'Outside watching, but they were the wrong side of the house. A cleaner found the dead man, someone called Amanar, another Romanian. He'd been dead for about two days. The office was ransacked. They were probably looking for paperwork about Cerdachescu's operation. Forensics says they climbed the wall at the back. The police car was parked on the road a hundred yards away from the front of the house.'

'How's Murchie taking it?'

'Spitting bricks. The men on duty outside the house have been suspended and there's an internal investigation going on. He thinks someone on the force is on the Romanian payroll. That would account for the way records on the Waverley girl were eliminated, and how the gang knew all the details on the brothels hit so far.'

Field heard the sound of the fax machine whirring and glanced over at it.

'That's probably Edinburgh,' Hartley said. 'The manager of the brothel had turned on the video surveillance cameras. Two men broke in through an upstairs window then came down and caught him in the bar area. It was all recorded. They obviously thought the surveillance system had been switched off because the brothel wasn't operating for the time being. It supports Murchie's idea about a leak.'

'So we've got pictures of them?'

'Any angle you want as long as it's from above. The bad news is they've already run the pictures and can't find anything. Strathclyde Police don't recognise the men either. They're sending the pictures here in case we can identify some of our locals.'

'Voice as well as video?'

'No. Not that a voice would help necessarily, but it could have identified an accent for us. Run the pictures, Jack. We have to get a lucky break one day.'

There were half a dozen photographs showing two men walking along a corridor. The features were quite clear. Other shots showed them standing over a smaller man, who must have been Amanar.

The last was one of the men cutting the small man's throat with a knife.

'We'll do enlargements on the knife, but you can see they were wearing surgical gloves. There won't be any fingerprints,' Field said.

'I'm getting Edinburgh to transmit a copy of the video. Maybe it will tell us something from the gestures. Edinburgh called in a lip reader, but the cameras were overhead so their lips couldn't be seen. Murchie thinks the rest of Amanar's men are scouring the city for the boy. I keep wondering why one lot of the girls was killed earlier yet the others were herded outside.'

'Conservation of resources,' Field said. 'Other than killing some to make a statement, why shoot them when you can make them work for you? They're eliminating all the Romanians except for the prostitutes, and recycling those. They want to take over going concerns.'

'Makes sense,' Hartley muttered. 'Take over the gangs, eliminate the leaders, absorb the foot soldiers.' Wearily she shoved the photographs across to Field. 'Work with Rogers and check the files. Put a copy of the best mug shots on the crime wall.'

Fifty-three

Sierra de Las Nieves. Saturday.

The valley of the Guardalhorce was layered with mist as the two Mitsubishi four-wheel-drives climbed over the mountains fringing the coast and headed inland.

In the lead car Serghei was driving, Costel in the passenger seat beside him, and another man sitting behind. In the second car were five of Potrascu's most trusted men, all of them from his home village.

Dmitri was back in Marbella, in Potrascu's mansion on the edge of the sea, where he could be guarded, night and day. Now Potrascu's priority was Blake. Blake and the tattoo.

But the doctor was no longer at Jorox.

He had gone to Sevilla for the bullfight, the terrified gardener said. He was staying at the Alfonso overnight.

Potrascu followed.

Sevilla. That afternoon.

Blake stepped out of the hotel. There was still time before the *corrida* began and at this moment he wanted air to cleanse the smell of people from his nose. People *en masse*, except in the bullring, were an intrusion he resented. He marched briskly across the Plaza de España and headed into the narrow alleyways of the old Jewish ghetto. Its cramped streets were packed with flower-bedecked balconies and richly decorated façades boasted their glories to passers-by, but he saw little of those either. His thoughts were concentrated on Duncan. He had not been in contact to report on his meeting with the journalist, and it was playing on Blake's mind. Duncan was being distant because he was angry over Blake's refusal to rush the experiments. But they were so near to success and it would be madness to hurry. Duncan must understand that. He would have to be told and *made* to understand. Next week, after the bullfight and before he left for Mexico.

He came out of the narrow streets on to wider roads and strolled aimlessly until he came to the Guadalquiver River. He'd walked too far, but he knew Sevilla well enough to find his way back to the hotel and there was no hurry.

He was heading past the bullring when a black four-wheel-drive pulled abruptly up on to the pavement in front of him, so suddenly that Blake was almost struck. Another vehicle pulled in behind. Blake's anger flared and he went to raise a fist at the driver of the leading car when the door opened and Potrascu stepped out. Blake's intended remonstration was halted in mid-word.

He felt momentary panic. Potrascu could have hit him, so sharply had he cut in front of him.

'What . . .?' he started to demand, but Potrascu's look silenced him. He took Blake by the arm and shoved him into the back, forcing him into the middle of the seat, and clambered in beside him. Moments later both cars were heading out of Sevilla towards Jerez. Serghei knew where he was going.

The Route of the Bulls.

*

They'd been driving for ages, spending well over an hour at a small farm where Serghei bargained for the things Potrascu wanted. In Andalucia such things couldn't be hurried. Then they travelled for some time over narrow, dirt-covered country roads where Serghei drove quite slowly. By the time they pulled to a halt there had been no sign of houses for almost an hour. In the light of the early moon, Blake could see olive trees beyond a solid wooden fence and beneath them the fighting bulls, their horns wide, showing up as stocky shapes, distinctive even at a distance.

He could hear them snorting, and there was the scuffling of hooves in the dry soil around the trees. He could almost imagine the steam coming out of their wet, black nostrils.

'Why have you brought me here? What's going on?'

He had been asking the same questions over and over again from the moment he was picked up near the Maestranza, but no one had answered.

Now Potrascu turned to him and put his mouth close to Blake's face. 'Why?' he hissed.

'Why what?'

'The boy. Why did you do it?'

Blake moved his face away. Potrascu's breath smelled of cheap alcohol. The Romanian peasant spirit he liked so much.

'I don't know what you mean,' he snapped. At first he'd been angry at being so unceremoniously picked up and bundled into the vehicle, but, as they drove on and no one else spoke, he became first concerned, then afraid. Now, with the vehicle at a standstill, his normal arrogance was attempting to reassert itself.

He tried to reach the door handle, but Potrascu grabbed him by his shirt and pulled him back.

'*You* know.' His voice was strange. It was rising. Hysteria, thought Blake. Potrascu had always been unstable. 'The tattoo. Like the one you also put on my girls. Why?'

Blake shifted uneasily in his seat. Potrascu was unpredictable. Blake had heard rumours. The fear was back.

'I don't know what you're talking about,' he said, hesitating, trying to maintain some composure. It was a losing battle. Potrascu wasn't merely unstable. He was insane.

'I've seen it, Blake.' Potrascu was barely audible, his voice like the hiss of a snake reaching towards a victim. It sent shivers through Blake's body.

Blake looked to the man to the left of him. He was staring impassively ahead, but his hand was firmly on the door handle. There was no possibility of pushing past. He turned back to Potrascu. The eyes were aflame with hatred.

'We needed a white boy,' Blake answered, his voice shaking. 'The Moroccans and blacks were unsuitable. I won't mix the races. Your cousin fitted the requirements. It was urgent and you were away. Duncan authorised it.'

'And who authorised Duncan? I didn't!'

'It was urgent,' Blake repeated. It was hot inside the car and he was sweating. He could smell the body odour of those close to him and the huge man behind the steering wheel, the one they called Serghei. He too was staring at the indistinct shapes of the bulls in the near distance. He was impassive. Only Potrascu showed any animation and it was the kind Blake preferred not to experience.

'And what happens to the boy? Will his children be like the others? You want me to take an ice axe to my own blood? Is that what you want?' Suddenly Potrascu's voice was shrill and he was almost shouting into Blake's ear. He grabbed Blake by his clothing and dragged him close, then spat in his eyes.

Blake screamed, throwing himself away in horror, trying to lift his arm to wipe the spittle from his face but Potrascu was shaking him, like a terrier shakes a captured rabbit. Blake could feel the back of his head hammering against the shoulder of the man on the other side of him, but still neither he nor Serghei budged.

'The boy will be all right,' Blake gasped. Tears formed in his eyes. 'The others went wrong.'

'Wrong! I saw photographs of the one in Scotland. Two heads! It was an abomination! The work of the Devil, Blake!'

'No! No!' Blake pleaded. 'That was why we needed the experiments. I had to get things right. I'll succeed with the boy and Duncan's woman. I promise you. You must believe me. Duncan knows! He's known about *all* of the experiments. He knows why those things are happening in Edinburgh.'

'Liar!' Potrascu roared. He was half standing up in the car and his arm lashed out, smashing Blake across the face with his fist.

Blake felt the pain searing through him and this time the tears came pouring out, the salt stinging in the wound that Potrascu's gold ring cut in the cheekbone. He could feel blood trickling down his face. He tried to raise his arms, but the blows kept raining across his face and head, in his ears and into his throat. He felt himself going dizzy and tried to plead for the Romanian to stop.

'Wait, Costel,' said the voice from the front. Dimly Blake recognised it was the driver, Serghei. 'He spoke about the problems in Edinburgh. Perhaps there's something he can tell us.'

Potrascu was breathing hard and his fingers were around Blake's throat when he stopped. The fingers loosened and Blake fought to catch his breath, wheezing as he drew down air into his lungs.

Serghei's huge hand stretched out and tapped Blake softly on the cheek. A comforting touch. Blake felt oddly grateful. He tried to edge away from Potrascu, but there was nowhere to go.

‘What do you know about what is happening in Edinburgh?’ Serghei asked. His voice was steady.

Blake sought refuge in Serghei’s calmness. ‘It’s nothing to do with me! It’s Duncan. He told me someone is taking over control of the girls in London and Edinburgh.’ He looked with a shiver of fear at Potrascu, biting back whatever else he was about to say.

‘Duncan knows this?’

‘He told me the other night.’

‘Did he also tell you *who* is going to take over?’

Blake’s breath was back and his terror was subsiding. Potrascu was saying nothing, doing nothing. Blake could talk his way out of this. ‘The man who runs the girls across the English Channel. He’s taking over the whole operation, Duncan said.’

‘Did he say anything about Bogdan?’

‘I don’t know Bogdan. Now, may I go? I’ve answered your questions. You can ask Duncan the rest.’

‘Oh, I will.’ Potrascu broke in again, his voice now almost a purr.

‘There’s nothing more you can tell us?’ Serghei was still watching him from the front seat, smiling good-naturedly.

Blake shook his head. ‘That’s it,’ he said. ‘Duncan made the arrangements. I don’t know the other man’s name, but Duncan said that with the boy and the girl almost ready all that remains is monitoring and that can be done in Britain.’

‘Leaving us surplus to requirements.’

‘Oh, no.’ Blake shook his head. He didn’t want Serghei to lose interest. Potrascu was still next to him. ‘It won’t be constant, but there’s work to do here. All of the equipment is here.’

‘And our girls, and our operation in Britain is there with someone else trying to take it over.’ Potrascu’s hands lashed out and hit Blake across the face again. Blood began to seep from his nose. Potrascu reached to grab him by the throat but Serghei's hand held him back.

'Leave him,' he urged. 'He needs to be alive.'

Potrascu sat back and suddenly he was smiling. He had pushed the problem of Edinburgh to the back of his mind. There were other matters to be addressed. Edinburgh, Bogdan, Pavel, all would still be there when tonight was over. These things were not dismissed, they were in suspension. For the moment, as Serghei had reminded him, he needed to keep Blake alive so that they could all enjoy what would soon be happening.

'You're right, Serghei.' He chuckled. 'It will be much more fun helping the doctor to experience what a bull feels in the bullring.'

Blake coughed and felt spittle swelling into his mouth. His nose was probably broken and he choked on his own blood as he breathed.

Potrascu leaned closer to him again and Blake shrank away, but this time there was no attempt to grab him or hit him. Instead the Romanian began to giggle.

'They say you love bulls, Blake,' he said in the soft, flat voice. 'I have heard you say bullfighting is facing death at a level that no one else can understand. I have decided to help you understand. No, I *insist* on helping you find your inner self.'

Now Blake could hear Serghei whistling softly in the front seat. *Carmen*. 'The Toreador Song'. Potrascu was staring at him with insanity in his eyes.

'I don't know what you mean,' Blake wheedled, breathing in between the words.

'I feared you would say that. Tell me, are you afraid at this moment, Blake? Is the matador afraid when he is facing the rogue bull? Do you think the matador believes in the majesty of the animal when he's inches away from its horns?

Have you ever experienced the slightest part of it, except vicariously?'

'What are you going to do?'

'It's a surprise,' Potrascu answered.

Blake averted his eyes, not wanting to look at the insane man beside him. He peered past Potrascu at the dim shapes of the bulls. He no longer had the appearance of a vulture waiting to pounce on carrion or live prey. Blake looked like the prey itself.

'No,' said Potrascu, shaking his head. 'Not the bulls. Not yet. You know a great deal about bullfighting, Doctor, but have you ever been truly close to a fighting bull? Have you run with the bulls in Pamplona or San Sebastian? I think not. Of course not. How could you? You're too old. Too old and too frightened. It takes a brave or foolhardy young man to run with the bulls and you are neither. In any case, I don't think it would help you *understand* the bulls. It wouldn't help you to get inside their psyche. You need something else. Something special. Something I can give you. My special gift, like your special gift to Dmitri. Do you remember Dmitri, Doctor? Did you ever stare into his face as he lay on the table, anaesthetised while you worked on him? Or did you only think of how beautiful you felt your own work was? Did you ever think of Dmitri as a living being? Or did you look on him as entertainment for your twisted mind? You have degraded my cousin's son, Blake. You experimented with him, altered him, tainted him for all time. My own flesh and blood! You have to pay, but you also have to understand why. You don't understand *people*, Blake. You understand flowers and you think you understand bulls, but I don't believe that. I don't think you understand anything.'

Potrascu put his hand on the door handle.

'You need to *know* the bulls. Teaching you about the bulls will be part of your reward for what you did to the boy.

Think of it as the chance to fulfil an obligation to the truths you claim to be exploring.'

In the front Serghei was smiling. This would be the best one ever.

Potrascu tittered. An odd sound after the earlier fury and anger. This wasn't anger any more. It was *expectation*.

'You need an *embolado*.' He sniggered. 'Your personal *embolado*. Your very own!'

Through the mirror Serghei watched and listened.

Serghei knew Potrascu was out of control. He was not thinking clearly. All of his attention was focused on what had happened to the boy and Potrascu's need, his thirst, for revenge, but it was blind revenge. Blake was the scientist. He was the one who might be able to reverse the effects of what he had done to Dmitri, but Potrascu could not see beyond the red rage in his head. To Serghei's mind, killing Blake would be sentencing Dmitri to a life of something terrible, although he had no exact idea what that might be. Dmitri had the tattoo and Potrascu had killed prostitutes with such tattoos because Blake ordered it, saying they were impure. But Serghei didn't think about it very hard. If Blake had a remedy for the deformity, his terror would have made him speak about it now. Serghei knew that Potrascu would not spare the doctor anyway. Potrascu despised the doctor. He regarded killing him as a pleasure.

And Serghei grinned inwardly, thinking of the satisfaction he would get too.

Fifty-four

The Route of the Bulls.

He was tied to the fence posts by ropes from his arms and legs, holding him close to the wood. Blake was staring at Potrascu and his head was shaking, but Serghei had put duct tape over his mouth and no sound emerged to disturb the bulls, fretting in the fields beyond.

One of Potrascu's men had taken a box from the second vehicle and brought it over, while Serghei and the others dragged Blake from the car and pulled him through the dust to the fence. Blake's legs had gone and he had urinated in his trousers but he had neither the strength nor the courage to struggle. His eyes pleaded but no one bothered to look.

Serghei paused for a moment then reached inside Blake's jacket and took out his wallet. He searched the clothes for anything that would identify him and put them in his own shirt pocket. Then he pulled the gold ring from Blake's finger and put that away too. Satisfied there was nothing else, he nodded at Potrascu.

Potrascu removed the contents of the box and held it out to him. 'You should appreciate it,' he said, waving it in front of Blake's eyes. 'It was made by a fine craftsman, one who does leather work for *cuadrillas* who fight in the bullring.' He tapped it with one hand. 'Excellent. Of course, the man who did it didn't know what it was to be used for.'

Serghei smiled. It was from a leather shop near Sevilla, where they had stopped before finding Blake. Serghei told the tanner it was a present, needed immediately and he would pay extra for fast service.

The leatherwork took more than two hours.

'I told him it was a practice bull,' said Serghei, as if the explanation would help him understand. 'I've seen people in the street doing something similar, using bulls' horns strapped to an old cart, with one boy running the cart towards another playing the matador. The children fight the make-believe bull with their capes. It's street fun, Dr Blake. In Romania street boys play with footballs and improve their craft that way. Some become famous. It's the same with bulls. Young boys dreaming of becoming matadors have to learn the way.'

He took the object from Potrascu's hands and showed Blake how the horns of the bull were fitted with leather into the cap beneath. Straps with buckles hung down from it. The leather was intricately stitched and the horns were attached so firmly to the rigid leather cap that no amount of shaking would remove them.

Serghei put the cap with the horns on Blake's head, buckled the straps tight under Blake's chin and stood back to admire the effect. Blake was on the verge of collapse.

'I see you've witnessed an *embolado* after all. A pity in a way,' Potrascu said, studying Blake carefully. 'A surprise would have been better, but we can enjoy watching first hand. I hope I get it right. I've only ever seen it on television. I wonder what it's like for the bull? Do you think he goes insane? Do you think the bull lives the rest of his life with his brains burned out? Or does some butcher get bored once the fun is over and kill it so the townspeople who watch can eat him as part of the fiesta? It happens all over Spain in various forms, but the one I saw was in the Basque Country, in Viscaya. The Basques have some peculiar ways. Some think nature makes them genetically cruel. Do you believe that? You know about genetics and bull breeding too. Could you breed a bull with humanlike emotions or does it already have them? Did you ever wonder about that?'

Suddenly Potrascu tired of it. Blake was now struggling weakly against the ropes, but they were too firm. It was as useless for Blake as it would be for the bull in a genuine *embolado*, tied to the post while the humans wiped thick wet clay over his entire head, leaving only the eyes and ears and the nostrils free. All of the senses left so that the bull could react to them.

Potrascu beckoned and one of the bodyguards handed two buckets to him. They were from the farm they went to after leaving Sevilla.

'You'll have to bear with me if I display no expertise,' he said softly, as he stared at the contents. 'As I told you, I've only seen it on television but it should be right. More or less.'

He took dry grass and rushes from one of the buckets then tied them around the horns of the simulated bull. Two men, one on each side stopped Blake shaking his head or turning away. Potrascu made a thick mat of the grass and small twigs, and from the other bucket took thin tar and coal oil and daubed it over the grass, allowing it to soak through to the horns.

He carefully wiped any surplus oil from Blake's face and ensured the cap was strapped tight.

'Cut the ropes, turn him around and bind his hands behind his back,' he snapped. 'Then lift him over the fence and hold him steady.'

They were ready instantly and before Blake could begin to urinate again it was done. He was in the bull paddock, his arms held by the bodyguards close against the fence.

Potrascu stepped up to him. 'Meet your destiny, Blake,' he said. The softness had gone. The rage had vanished from his face. There was neither menace nor anger. Only the hard voice of unremitting intent.

He took a cigarette lighter from his pocket, flicked it alight and lit the oil-soaked grass. Flames roared into the sky, dancing around Blake's head. Potrascu ripped the tape from Blake's mouth and heard the screams for the first time.

Then he pushed Blake away, staggering around, the fire sizzling over his face and head, the skin blistering and the heat burning his eyes. With his hands bound behind his back he could do nothing to remove the cap. He shook his head trying to release it, but it was immovable. Drops of burning oil and grass dripped on to his clothing and set his shirt and trousers alight and he fell to the ground, trying to douse the flames on his clothes and around his head.

Under the olive trees the bulls began to move. The flames angered them and the screaming of the man disturbed them. They pawed the dirt, bringing up plumes of dust, and moved slowly towards the package writhing on the ground.

Potrascu and the others watched in silence. For him it wasn't lasting long enough. It should take longer. He wanted Blake to suffer the way Dmitri would one day suffer. The wrong done to the boy could never be righted. Revenge was only an emotional discharge.

Blake was already blind. The flames seared his retinas and left blackness where only minutes earlier there had been the brightest lights he had ever seen in his life. The pain was unbearable. His lips were blistered and he couldn't lick them. His voice was one continual scream of agony but no coherent words could form. He couldn't hear them any more. His eardrums were burned out and all that was left was the memory of screaming in his brain.

He heard himself singing in his mind. Nursery rhymes, dirty ditties, things that made no sense. He saw images of beautiful flowers, with monsters crawling over them, snakes sliding in and out of rustling leaves. He felt as if he were dancing but something, something distant asked him what dancing was because he didn't know and he didn't understand how he could think of it if he didn't know.

He could feel something hard beneath him, but how did he know it was hard? There was hard and there was soft, but which was which and why had he thought of that? What were thoughts?

What was agony? What was pain? What were love and hate?

What was emotion?

He thought someone had asked him about emotion.

But he didn't know what it was.

Potrascu watched the flames fade, snuffed out by the dust, but Blake was still alive and his body was twitching, writhing in the soil not far from the fence, silent because his voice box had burned out.

He waited.

He had no interest in bullfights, but he knew a little about them.

Not as much as the great and soon-to-be-late doctor, but he'd read that a fighting bull never faces a man on foot until the moment he enters the bullring. In that way the bull is not afraid. Only angry. That was why the bull charged men on foot. Until then fighting bulls stayed in their pastures, approached only by men on horseback.

There was no horse for Blake.

It took another two minutes before the nearest bull, a huge mottled brown and white beast weighing more than four hundred kilos was angry enough. He pawed at the dirt and snorted. The flames on the man were out and he was trying to stand up and the bull was aware of him, assessing him and this intrusion into his life.

He charged.

Hooves hammered into the soil like the roll of a drumbeat on a battleground.

The bull's forehead took Blake in the stomach and he fell back to the ground, trying to scream but with no noise issuing from his burned throat.

The bull spun in his own length.

The horns went down and he hooked to the left, the horn going into Blake's body at thigh level. He lifted Blake into the air and threw him over his back. As Blake landed in the field again, the bull charged anew, spearing him in the chest, rolling him over and over, further away from the fence.

Another bull moved in, lashing with his horns, then twisting around and stomping him in the ribs with his hooves.

Blake was picked up on the horns again and tossed high into the air.

It twisted as it spun and the body was limp, reacting to nothing.

It fell into the soil and the two bulls played with it in turn, throwing it around like a stuffed toy until finally, bored because there was nothing left to amuse or annoy, they trotted away to return to disturbed slumber.

Blood from Blake's gored and crushed body soaked into the soil.

Potrascu spat in the dust.

'Was it enough?' Serghei asked.

'No,' Potrascu snapped. 'It would have been better if we could have had Blake barbecued and fed to the women in the nearest village. Then he might have understood.'

He laughed. 'Posthumously of course.'

Fifty-five

Sierra de Las Nieves.

A direct return trip would have been faster, but Serghei insisted there were matters to clear up and necessary detours to be made, despite Potrascu's impatience.

One of the men jumped over the fence once the bulls retreated and took away what remained of the helmet. They threw it from a bridge twenty kilometres away. Blake's body was doused with petrol and set on fire. The bulls angrily moved away from the olive trees to the far distance, out of sight of the flames.

Meanwhile, Potrascu phoned the house in Marbella and sent a man to check that Duncan's yacht was in Puerto Banus harbour. Less than half an hour later he called back. The yacht was gone. According to the harbour master, it was not expected to return before Monday evening.

Potrascu swore softly to himself. There were questions to ask of Duncan and Monday was a long time away.

Shortly before midnight, they were approaching the gates to Blake's mansion again. Serghei was driving. There had been no discussion. It wasn't necessary. The gates would be rammed.

But as he drove up, with the other vehicle following close behind, he could see a figure on the driveway. The helicopter pilot leaving the grounds, the gates wide open.

He looked up as Serghei approached, the headlights almost blinding him. He waved his hands, shouting words Serghei couldn't hear but the gestures were clear. He was trying to say they couldn't go in. Serghei pulled the car to a halt, pushed the button and the window in the driver's door slid silently down. As the pilot came over, Serghei shot him between the eyes.

From the back seat one of the other men got out, crossed to the pilot's car and reversed it to the house, with Serghei and the other vehicle following. No one as much as glanced at the body of the dead pilot, crumpled on the roadside by the gate.

At the front door Potrascu used a rifle to blow off the lock and enter. Behind him the bodyguards followed into the hallway, one of them clutching an RPG launcher in one hand.

'Check every room,' Potrascu ordered. 'I want the papers. We'll start at the top, then work our way down until we find Blake's records. We'll think about Duncan later.'

But at the top the door was firmly locked and he could see nowhere for a key. He stared for a moment at the door then fired a burst of bullets into it but they bounced back. Steel inserts, he thought. He stepped aside and nodded to the man with the RPG.

The grenade smacked into the door from only two metres distant and the noise ricocheted around the house. When the smoke cleared the door was scorched, the veneer burned away, but it was intact.

Potrascu pointed to the wall on the left. 'Hit there. It won't be as strong as the door.'

Two grenades later there was a hole wide enough for him to squeeze through.

He stepped over the rubble of brick and plaster into the room, holding a hand over his mouth against the dust. He had never seen anything like it before. It was a hospital! Now he understood. He'd taken it for granted that Blake used one of Duncan's clinics for his experiments. Now it was clear this was where it happened.

He thought for a moment about Blake's insistence that Duncan ordered the experiments on Dmitri and knew about the attacks in Edinburgh. Perhaps that was a lie? Blake had been terrified. He would have said anything to save his life. Blake's soul was already doomed, but Potrascu had always liked Duncan. Blake was a toad, slime that had come up from the depths. He couldn't be believed any more than he'd been trusted.

Perhaps Duncan wasn't involved after all? He tossed the thought around while the dust cleared. Duncan could wait until Potrascu was certain.

First he wanted Dmitri's records. He needed to know exactly what Blake had done to the boy so that someone, somewhere could remedy it. He would pay whatever was needed, but first he had to find the records.

Then, whether or not Duncan was involved, he must finish the business in Britain. The man who ferried the girls to England Blake had said. That was the priority. Find the man.

Serghei searched the surgery and the laboratory.

He stared for several minutes at the creatures in the bell jars.

They looked a little like tiny babies, some no more than six inches long. There were ones with multiple heads and, when he peered closer at the glass, others with a combination of deformities around the genitals. Serghei was almost never physically sick, but the queasiness in his stomach suggested that at this moment he was close to it.

He debated with himself whether or not to draw Costel's attention to them, and decided to wait. There were times with Potrascu when waiting was the best policy.

Instead, he focused on the drawers in the laboratory and then in the surgery.

He found notes in one drawer and pulled those out, putting them into a plastic bin liner. Potrascu would examine the papers later. He was the one who needed to know.

Serghei took the bin liner to the office. Potrascu was sitting at the desk with the contents of files strewn over it. He was leafing through them, looking bewildered.

'I don't understand,' he said with a puzzled frown on his face. 'There are no names, only photographs of flowers like the tattoo on Dmitri's body. Blake refused to tell me anything about the tattoos on the girls.'

He sorted through the files again, staring at the pictures and trying to remember what the tattoos on the girls had looked like.

He began to growl, low and ominous, but it grew into a crescendo and a roar of fury as he swept everything from the desk, slamming a computer screen to the floor, shattering the glass. He turned over a filing cabinet, picked up one of the seats and flung it against the wall.

He careered around the room, turning over furniture, pulling down shelves, kicking books and papers as they lay on the floor.

Sanity returned.

He was panting with his rage, but when he finally spoke his voice was rational and soft.

'Pack the files and papers,' he said. 'All of them. Everything you can find.'

'You know what the pictures mean?'

'I know,' said Potrascu shortly. Then he pulled himself together completely. 'The files are full of words I don't understand. Technical terms in Blake's own handwriting. Most of them I can't read, but there are lots with a combination of letters and figures and they're chemical symbols, Serghei.'

'Could they be drugs Blake was using?'

'How would I know? There's nothing in plain language. We'll take them all.'

'The pictures on the files, Costel?'

'They're not pictures. They're brands. Like those they burn into cattle. Blake was branding the girls and the tattoos on their bodies correspond to those in these files. These files tell what the fucking son of a whore did to every one of them! What he did to Dmitri!'

Serghei stared hard at Costel. He knew him when he went quiet like this. The storm was only moments away. Not storm, cyclone.

'We need someone to tell us how to decipher the notes,' he said, delaying the moment. 'Shall I find Duncan and bring him to Fuengirola?'

Potrascu thought about it then shook his head. 'Just bring everything. Take the hard drive from the computer and any DVD disks you can find. Then we'll settle the British problem. We were too hasty eliminating Sanchez. He would have been able to tell us who is running the girls to England. We can't wait for Duncan. If what Blake said is true, Duncan will warn his contact when he gets to shore on Monday, as soon as he learns Blake is dead. Tomorrow morning, we fly to London and find this man and his helpers before Duncan knows. Then we will settle matters for Bogdan and Pavel.'

He leaned over, took the plastic bin liner from Serghei's hands and bent down to pick up the files he had flung to the floor.

'There's something else,' Serghei said.

Potrascu straightened up.

'It's in that other room. The one that looks like a laboratory,' Serghei said. 'You're not going to like it.'

Potrascu stormed down the stairs into the living room, aware of the orchid paintings on the walls and feeling the fury coming over him anew.

Blake was tattooing people from his brothels the way they tattooed farm animals! That was all Dmitri was to him. A farm animal to be catalogued, studied and, when the time came, sent to the incinerator. And Dmitri would not even be a father when he grew up. He would be a producer of monsters – twisted and deformed babies, with multiple limbs and organs, creatures from nightmares, children kept as specimens like those floating in suspension in the bell jars! The ones Blake kept to peer at, and gloat over!

Potrascu was uncontrollable. He screamed at the bodyguards gathered in the hallway. Serghei had taken six sacks full of files and papers out to the vehicle, and was on his way back with the other driver.

They had four twenty-five-litre petrol cans, two from each vehicle, in their hands, the spares they always carried. Potrascu snatched one from the driver of the second vehicle, opened the cap and began to splash the fuel around the room, starting with the paintings then spreading it everywhere over the furniture and carpets and walls.

'Find more!' he yelled at the men. 'There must be aviation spirit for the helicopter in an emergency. Burn the fucking helicopter. Burn the orchid houses. Take that car to its garage and burn it too, and anything else in it. Spread the petrol in every room! Ten minutes. No more.'

He began splattering the fuel on the walls again, a man demented.

Serghei watched for a moment. At times like this, he

needed to make certain Potrascu didn't forget important matters. Sometimes he was carried away in his own madness.

He left Potrascu spraying the petrol around and went down the drive to where the dead pilot lay. He threw him over his shoulder, carried him back to the house and dropped the body inside the hallway. He pulled out the wallet and other items he'd taken from Blake's jacket before the *embolado* and put them inside the pilot's trouser pocket. They would burn, but that didn't matter. There would be nothing in the bull paddock to identify Blake, while forensic experts might be able to get something from the contents of the pilot's pockets. If they did, they would assume Blake had died in the fire. Finally he pulled out Blake's ring and slipped it on to the pilot's finger.

Potrascu came out of the house, pausing in his frenzy and immediately understood. He tossed petrol over the pilot's body for good measure and purred with satisfaction as the two men who had gone to the helicopter wheeled back two huge drums of aviation spirit, kept in a shed by the helipad for an emergency.

The flames would be seen for miles, like a giant bushfire rising from the heights of the Sierra de Las Nieves. There would be no way of stopping it. There was no fire station in Jorox or its surrounding villages. Bushfires in these inland regions were fought by planes, water scooped up from farm dams or direct from the coast and dropped over the flames. There would be no time for that. With the help of the petrol and the aviation spirit all would be eliminated.

Nothing would remain except fragments of the mansion structure, the burned-out helicopter and the soot in the rubble.

Fifty-six

Sierra de Las Nieves. Sunday.

Behind the wheel of the car Tabor watched from ten yards away as Anca chatted to the three Guardia Civil officers standing beside their two vehicles, barring access to the road. Another was inside, smoking a cigarette and running his eyes over her legs.

About half a mile away Tabor could see tiny spirals of smoke rising from where the mansion would normally be hidden by the folds in the hills and the trees.

It was a change of plan.

They had examined Potrascu's Marbella mansion and decided it was impregnable. The fallback position was the brothel where Emma had died, and which Tabor believed might be Potrascu's headquarters. He would need to give more thought to that and decided instead to return to Blake's house and try to get him to identify the tattooist, without waiting for Duncan.

They'd pulled over here when they saw the police road-block, and now he tapped on the wheel, wondering what had happened. It was obvious there had been some kind of incident and the smoke suggested a fire, but it could be anything from a bushfire to a problem at the house. Why was it taking so long?

He saw her smile at them and turn away. Two of the Guardia touched the peaks of their hats in acknowledgement, inspecting her body as she returned to the car.

'Turn around,' she said. 'I'll tell you about it as we drive.'

'Drive where?'

'Back to the coast. There's no point staying here. Blake's dead.'

'How did they identify him?'

They had stopped at a roadside bar for coffee. There was no rush and he wanted to think things over in the quiet of the countryside. The sudden death of Blake in a house fire was too coincidental for him.

'He was the only person at the house.'

She'd ordered the coffee and a *zuso*, a kind of doughnut, saying she couldn't race off every morning without breakfast. The doughnut was her concession. Tabor wanted only coffee.

'When the Guardia arrived the gardener was already there. He'd seen the fire from the village and went up on his scooter, but there was nothing he could do about it. The house was a burned-out wreck. Fire investigators poked around when it was light and found the remains of the body. There was a gold ring that the gardener identified as Blake's. The rest was only charred bones. The Guardia said Blake was supposed to be in Sevilla, but he'd obviously come back unexpectedly. They're trying to find the helicopter pilot to ask why, but he's also missing. He's well known locally, he likes to drink a lot when he's not on flying duty and Blake had given the staff time off until Monday. The pilot could be anywhere. The gardener said the gates were open so he'd obviously gone out.'

'The helicopter?'

'Destroyed too, along with the orchid houses, and a couple of other vehicles.'

'Arson?'

'The orchid house didn't self-destruct,' she answered with a hint of irritation. 'Of course, it was done deliberately, but the Guardia think Blake did it. They think he burned down the orchid houses, destroyed the helicopter then the house with himself inside it.'

Tabor stopped his coffee mid-sip. 'Why would he do that?'

'I asked them. The locals thought Blake was crazy. No one liked him. He never spoke to anyone in the village except the gardener, cook or cleaner and I gather most of the time he insisted they only speak to him on the phone. In their book that's odd behaviour. The Spanish are a gregarious people. They like to talk to each other and they don't have any class complexes. A cook would talk to the president or the king if she felt like it, but she wasn't allowed to talk to Blake and that was incomprehensible to them.'

Tabor stared at the barman cutting wafer thin slices of Serrano ham from a full leg and layering it neatly on a plate as adeptly as a *charcuterie* chef.

He brought his attention back to Anca. 'I don't believe it. Blake wasn't crazy. He was fanatical about his orchids. Why would he destroy them?'

'You used the same word as the Guardia,' she answered. 'Fanatic. To them that's the same as crazy. Paranoid. They wouldn't say anything at first, not until I flashed my Romanian police pass and they seemed interested in that. They talked more about Romania than about Blake, but they became friendly enough after a few minutes. I told them we'd been talking to him about orchids and that you were a journalist. They thought Blake had gone off his head and used the pretence of going to Sevilla to give him the opportunity to destroy everything with no one else around. They think he wanted to die and wouldn't want his orchids to be left without him. It's twisted reasoning, but I've come across it with maniacs before. It holds water as far as they're concerned and the death of a foreigner like this is something the Guardia prefer to have over and done with.'

'I still don't believe it.'

'You said Blake was nervous and worried about you seeing the Ghost Orchid. Someone who was fanatical about his flowers and the destruction of his reputation could have let it prey on his mind and driven him over the edge.'

'That's manufacturing an excuse.'

'No,' she corrected firmly. 'It's providing an answer. If the Guardia knew about the Ghost Orchid, that would close the lid on it entirely. Suicide brought on by the worry of being humiliated around the world. The bigger you are, the harder you fall is likely to be their answer.'

'And *you* believe that?'

'It doesn't matter what *I* believe.' She finished her *zuso* and drank the coffee then put down the glass and leaned over the table closer to him. 'Look, Simon. Blake is dead. That line of investigation is over. We have to find another way.'

'What if Blake was murdered because he *knew* who did the tattoos?'

He couldn't let go. The idea of suicide didn't fit with his conception of the man. Blake was arrogant, hostile and, yes, fanatical, but he wasn't a candidate for suicide. Not in his opinion.

'The one who did it could have killed Blake. Wouldn't that be a logical explanation?'

'It might be.' She reached across the table and took his hand. 'Which is why we have to pursue Potrascu and his brothel operations. It's the only thing left for you now.'

Tabor felt the warmth of the hand and heard the softness of her voice and the strength beneath it. Hers was the voice of reason, his was the voice of doubt, fuelled by unreasoning emotions. Anca was right.

He left his hand where it was, in hers.

'I'll go to the brothel tonight. I've been in that block. The private offices are probably on the top floor. I've climbed harder things before.'

She squeezed his hand and pulled hers away then stood up. 'So have I.' She smiled. 'We'll go together.' She saw his look and held up a finger to silence his response. 'Not another word. I can do it. If there are any documents in those offices they'll be in Romanian or Spanish. I know what to look for, you don't. Dani will stay outside and watch. Agreed?'

He stood up with her. 'No,' he sighed. 'But I don't suppose I have any choice.'

'None at all.' She smiled sweetly. 'You can pay for the coffee and cake. The barman seems to speak English.'

Fifty-seven

Fuengirola. Monday. Early hours.

By Tabor's estimation it was about seventy feet high. The building rose five storeys and all around were similar mini-towers, most of them now unlit, with residents at home in their beds, although the tourists were still out in the bars.

They parked the car where Dani could see the building but sink into his seat, hiding in the darkness.

On their way back from Jorox, they had stopped at a large sports store in a Marbella shopping centre to buy climbing equipment. Tabor needed dynamic rope, for abseiling down the building in a hurry if they had to, and both wanted tight-fitting rubber-soled shoes to make a descent more comfortable. Anca bought a pair of gloves. She'd experienced rope burn in the past and didn't want to risk it now.

Both wore casual seasonal clothing. It was a warm night and Tabor was wearing a close-fitting T-shirt and ragged cut-off blue jean shorts. Anca had chosen something similar, a snug top that showed her figure off to perfection, and tight shorts, the kind that thousands of tourists on the Costa del Sol wore, day and night.

Tabor had to force himself to concentrate on the climb ahead. A lack of attention because he was diverted by her appearance could prove disastrous.

He stood in the shadows, studying the building. Ascent would be no problem. There was a drainpipe that could be climbed on a side shrouded in darkness. There were chinks of light between the curtains on the first four storeys, but nothing visible on the top floor. If there were offices there, as he thought, any documentation would be there too. If they couldn't find anything he would go to Plan B.

Plan B was simple. Find Potrascu and use whatever methods were necessary to get him to tell Tabor what he wanted.

He checked the rope over his shoulder and they crossed the road then climbed the wall into the gardens. No one stirred.

He could hear music and singing inside, and the clink of glasses came through an open window but there seemed to be no one at the rear of the building. The bouncers were inside, watching those who approached the entrance, not contemplating an attack from the back.

He didn't unfold the rope. There were balconies if the drainpipe proved difficult. They could climb them one by one.

But there was no need. Anca followed as he led up the drainpipe and pulled himself over the parapet. She rolled over the top to lie beside him. For a few moments they stayed there, listening in case anyone had heard a noise, but there was no indication that anyone had.

He attached one end of the rope to a steel plate in the flat roof and put the remainder of the coil ready for later. He was banking on there being an unlocked access from the rooftop to inside the top level, but just in case he had brought a glasscutter with him. By hanging over the parapet with the rope, he could cut out enough glass to get a window open.

But luck was riding along with them.

There was a small housing near the parapet, covering machinery associated with the lift mechanism, and the door was unlocked. They descended into a central corridor with six doors on each side. It was unlit so they left the roof door open, waiting for their eyes to adjust to the gloom inside after the moonlight and glow of the street lamps. Tabor pointed to the doorknobs and with Anca working the opposite side of the corridor they edged along, checking doors, trying to make no sound.

At the far end Anca felt the knob turning and the door opened. She could see a large bed and a shape under the blankets, lying still and breathing regularly.

She went to close the door, but as she did the figure moved and a light came on from the bedside lamp. Anca kept moving forward. She reached out and spoke quietly, kneeling at the side of the bed as she did.

It was a boy.

Sitting upright in the bed, surprise and curiosity on his face, but no fear as he replied to her. She touched his shoulder, smiling at him. Then she pointed to Tabor behind her and spoke again, and the boy shook his head.

She turned to Tabor, speaking quickly. 'He doesn't speak English. His name is Dmitri. He's from Romania and Potrascu is his second cousin. He's not afraid, in fact he seems eager to talk now he knows I'm Romanian. I told him we're security people and he didn't seem surprised. He said other guards had moved him in here from the Marbella house for safety. I told him he should have locked his door on the inside. It's the kind of advice a security guard would give. He seemed impressed, but perhaps you should stay outside while I talk to him. There's a chance some real guard could come up here to check on him.'

'Make it as quick as you can.'

*

'I've seen lots of the other guards,' Dmitri said. There was no hint of suspicion in his voice. 'I haven't seen you before.'

'It's the weekend. We sometimes use different people then.'

'Even women?'

'Haven't you ever seen a woman security guard before?'

'Only in uniform.'

'None of us here has a uniform.'

It was a guess but the guards she'd seen outside the block had worn ordinary clothes.

Anca pointed to the box on the table beside his bed. 'It's a security alert button,' she said. 'Push it if you're worried about us.'

'I'm not. Costel wouldn't have you here if he didn't trust you. Not after Edinburgh.'

'Is Edinburgh a nice city?' she asked. The boy needed to be coaxed.

'I didn't see enough of it. It was fine at my father's house, then they killed him.' He said it in a matter-of-fact way, no tears in the eyes. 'Were you one of those looking for me in Edinburgh?'

'No. I live here in Spain.'

She couldn't be dragged into anything he might know about Edinburgh. She knew nothing about it herself. Stick to things she knew.

'What's your name?' Dmitri asked.

She told him.

For a thirteen-year-old, Dmitri was remarkably self-assured. A grown-up's world, a grown-up's nightmares, had left none of the little boy in him. His childhood had come and gone and he hadn't noticed it passing.

She spent a few minutes telling him about places they both knew near Rogojel. He told her a little about his life in Spain before he joined his father, but mostly he talked of the killings in his father's house and the other building in the city, about running from the police, with men looking for him, and how he hid out in the abandoned warehouse.

He made no attempt to embroider the truth. His manner seemed to say there was no need.

She asked him when Potrascu would be back.

'I don't know exactly. I think he's gone to find out who killed my father and my other cousin, Pavel.'

'What happened to Pavel?'

'Don't you know?'

A slip, Anca cursed herself silently. She was supposed to be a guard and she would know everything associated with what had happened to the boy.

He was staring at her, waiting for an answer.

'No,' she said. Honesty was the only approach. Dmitri was too bright to let her get away with excuses.

'That's all right. I didn't know either until Costel told me when he brought me back here. Someone killed him too but I don't know how. He hasn't told me yet.'

Through the open door, from the corridor Anca heard Tabor shuffle his feet slightly.

It was a reminder that the more time they spent in this building, the more likely someone was to come to check on the boy.

'Maybe he'll tell you tomorrow?'

'Oh, no. He's gone off, back to London or Edinburgh.'

'So soon?'

'He said the business over there wasn't finished. He had to go and see the doctor first, then he came back very angry and told me he was going away. That's why I was brought here. He didn't like to leave me on my own in the big house by the beach. He said he could protect me better here. You know that.'

'Of course.' Anca could feel the stirring of excitement within her. 'Who's the doctor?'

'I don't like him much, but he does wonderful tattoos.'

It hit her like a blow in the face. She could barely control her voice, but she forced herself not to let her anxiety, *her apprehension*, show. 'Do you like tattoos?' Anca asked, trying to make her voice as calm as she could. 'I know someone who has one. The best. Tattoos are cool.'

'You're wrong,' Dmitri flashed back instantly. 'I've got the best!'

'You?' Anca tried to sound dismissive. 'Let me see.'

Dmitri lowered his eyes. Now he was a little boy again, caught in indecision, eager to tell her but afraid. So different to his earlier self-assurance.

'I don't think so,' he said nervously. But pride was tugging at him like a heavy fish hooked on the end of a line. It overcame shyness because he was eager to let people know. It was simply that she was a *girl*. He couldn't show *that* to her, but he could talk about it.

Again the hesitation. Then he made up his mind. 'I won't show *you* but your friend outside can see it, if he wants.'

'He has to stay there,' Anca said swiftly. Get everything while she could. 'He's on guard. Tell me about it?'

'It's a flower,' Dmitri said proudly. Then he added hurriedly, 'But it's not like those you see on the men and girls at the beach. It's more like a painting. It's better than anything on a football player. Costel looked furious when he first saw it. I think he went to see the doctor to tell him to remove it.'

'Where was that?'

'I don't know. He didn't say. '

Anca leaned a little closer to him. 'Can you describe him? The doctor?'

'He looked like a vulture. He had a hooked nose and a bald head. He wouldn't talk to me about it, or say anything but it took a lot of sessions.'

Anca's face dropped. From the doorway Tabor saw the

change. He wanted to know why but he had to wait and stand guard. He could see from her expression that she'd been shaken to the core. It had to do with the tattoo, of that he was certain.

She wanted to go over to him, but there was no time. *Get it all. Get it now.* She held back the tears building up in her eyes and smothered emotions of rage and anguish as she spoke. 'Why did he put that kind of tattoo on you, Dmitri? Flowers are for girls, not boys. Did he do the same tattoo on girls?'

'I know why,' Dmitri admitted. 'He told me it was a reward for having to go through the other treatment. I haven't seen anyone else with a tattoo like it.'

'What other treatment?'

'Inoculations. He said they hadn't given me everything I should have in Romania so he made me stay in isolation for a long time. Sometimes there are allergic reactions to inoculations. He gave me lots of awful things to drink as well.'

'Did your cousin actually *say* the doctor would remove the tattoo?'

'I don't want it removed! I want to keep it. Costel looked very upset and I was afraid to say anything then, but I'll tell him when he comes back.'

'When is that, Dmitri? How long will he be away?'

'Until the business in Britain is finished, I suppose.'

He lay back on his pillow, yawning. 'I've talked too much,' he said with a quiet sigh. 'I want to get back to sleep. Can you come back and talk to me later? It's easy to talk with you.'

She pulled the sheet up around his shoulders. 'I like talking to you too, Dmitri,' she answered softly. 'Get some sleep now.'

Dmitri smiled at her. The woman was pretty, he thought and he had enough money. Perhaps some day he could buy her the way his father had bought those other women, but he didn't have the nerve to say it. Not yet. It would take a little more time.

Tabor picked up the rope and dropped it over the side.

'Tell me about it in the car,' he said. 'We have to get out quickly. Abseil. Don't bother taking the rope after us. They'll know we were here as soon as the boy talks.'

Without waiting he gripped the rope and dropped off the roof, his legs out against the side of the building, shoving himself away in giant leaps that took him to the ground in three halts.

Anca made it in two.

Fifty-eight

London. Monday.

Ruth Hartley awoke with a start at the sound of the phone ringing on the table beside her bed. She glanced at the clock next to it. *This early?* She shook her head to bring herself around, aware of the insistent tone of the phone and reached over to pull it closer and check the caller ID.

She picked up the receiver. 'Sir?' she asked in a puzzled voice.

'I know it's early,' Landon said. 'But it's urgent. Get to the office and I'll meet you there. Maybe you should get Rogers and Field out as well.'

She sat up in bed and swung her legs from under the covers. Her mind was instantly fully functional. 'Do I get told what it's about first?'

'I had a phone call fifteen minutes ago,' Landon replied grimly. 'My source in Spain. There's a Romanian gang leader called Costel Potrascu who's flown to Britain to sort out the murders in Edinburgh. I'll tell you more at the office. I've got a couple of things to do first.'

'What's happening?'

She was already reaching for her clothes. No time for a shower. Dress first, ablutions later when the flap was over.

'World War Three in miniature if my guess is right,' Landon predicted. 'Pray I'm wrong.'

Hartley was already there when he walked in.

'Sorry I'm a bit late,' he said, taking off his coat and hanging it on a stand close to the wall. There was no one else in the office.

'I waited before alerting the others,' she said. 'At half past three on a Monday morning, there's not a lot we can do unless it's an all-hands-to-the-wheel thing and you'd have called out armed response teams if that had been the case.'

He sat next to her, acknowledging the comment. 'Is there any coffee around? I didn't have a chance to get anything yet.'

She picked up the phone. 'I'll have some sent from the canteen.'

He'd obviously been hurrying, she thought. His face was drawn, his eyes tired. The lines around his eyes were strained and he'd clearly had little sleep for days, but he was alert and the job was taking over from his domestic concerns. He hadn't mentioned Helen and it wasn't the time to ask.

'I need to fill you in,' he said. 'Felix Blake was murdered on Saturday. His house was burned down around him. The Romanian, Potrascu killed him after he found the missing boy in Edinburgh. The boy has an orchid tattoo in his groin, similar to the ones on the girl washed up at Burnham and the one under the train in Edinburgh. Blake did it. He's been experimenting on children, we don't know exactly why, yet, but the tattoos are part of it.'

He paused and Hartley waited. Months of waiting, walking the streets, looking for information and now it was coming together, but there were lots of questions left.

There was a knock on the door. It opened and in came a canteen lady with two polystyrene cups of coffee. She smiled at them, laid them down, took the money and left, closing the door firmly behind her.

Landon picked up the coffee and drank it, black, hot and without any sweetening.

'I needed that,' he said, placing the cup back on the desk before he went on. 'Potrascu is here now, in the UK, looking for the people who did the Edinburgh killings. He flew in yesterday, but I don't know which airport he left from, or what time. Most likely Malaga. Equally I don't know where he landed. I called Immigration before I left and they're running names of passengers on flights from Malaga to all UK destinations from four a.m. yesterday onwards.'

'Do we have a photograph of Potrascu?'

'No, that's up to you. Romanian police may help. He may be on Interpol files.'

'How about Beech?'

'As far as I know, there's no link.'

'If Potrascu is going for the people behind the killings in Edinburgh, he'll need more manpower than just himself.'

Landon put his hand in his pocket for his wallet and pulled out a slip of paper. 'He has someone with him. A man called Serghei Lacatus. You may want Romanian police to check on him and get a picture too, and there'll be a Romanian gang in Scotland running the remaining brothels. Potrascu will obviously use them.'

'*I* may want to do it? Does that mean you're not taking the case back?'

'I can't, Ruth. I'm bringing you up to speed on what I've got and I've tried to set some of the wheels in motion, but it's still yours. I came in to avoid Helen overhearing what I was saying. She doesn't need any more distress. I'm going when I've answered any questions you have.'

Hartley breathed in deeply. It was all very sudden. 'Superintendent Murchie,' she said. 'Have you told him yet?'

'No. If Potrascu flew to Edinburgh, he could have signed into a hotel and Murchie may be able to find him there, so give him a call, but remember, as far as police are concerned, he's done nothing illegal. Spanish police think Blake's death was suicide. The orchid houses at the property were burned down and the Ghost Orchid is only ash now. No trace left.'

'Immigration. Are they reporting to you, or to me?'

'You.' Landon halted, remembering something. 'There's another name.' He had forgotten it in the activity of the moment. 'Potrascu had a brother, Pavel, living in London. Someone also killed him, according to my source.' He stopped and Hartley saw the look on his face.

'The pig farm?'

'Could be,' Landon replied. 'There's no identity to the body but you said the man had possibly been killed with an ice axe. The timescale would fit. You might want to check up Pavel Potrascu in the records too.'

'Sir, isn't it time you told me where all of this has come from? Who your source is?'

'No,' Landon snapped, then relaxed. 'Maybe soon, but not yet.'

She breathed in deeply. 'I wish it were otherwise,' she said, picking up the phone. 'I'll get Field and Rogers in after all, and they'll want to know how I found out about this.'

'Lie,' said Landon. 'Say it came direct from Murchie, or from Spanish police. Rogers won't question it. Jack might, but if you're firm enough he'll do what you want and ask questions later. By then it may not matter.' He looked tired. 'Right, I'm off home. If anything breaks maybe you'd call me, but that's not an order. I've got an interest in this one, that's all.'

He picked up his coat. Tabor was uppermost in his mind.

The voice-phone call was surprise enough, but it was the final part of their conversation that worried Landon.

'That's it then,' he said, when he'd listened to what Tabor had related. 'You can come back now.'

There had been a small silence. Then Tabor answered 'Not yet. There's a detail to be wrapped up. A wrong to be righted. My business, not yours.'

'Don't do anything you'll regret,' Landon warned immediately.

'No regrets, no tears. Potrascu was behind what happened to my sister.'

Then he hung up.

A wrong to be righted sounded ominously like a threat. If Tabor killed anybody and was caught in Spain, the police would never release him.

Tabor would be lost for good.

Rogers and Field checked electoral rolls for Greater London, looking for the name of Pavel Potrascu, but found nothing. Either he wasn't there, he'd registered his property under another name or Greater London was an insufficient catchment area.

They'd gone back to working the known prostitution haunts, covering ground they'd trodden before, but without the specific name. They checked in every hour but so far had hit a blank wall.

Murchie had called, saying Potrascu was no longer registered in Edinburgh, but he'd been at the Sheraton Grand a few days earlier, at the time when Amanar was murdered. He had brought in more men, and surveillance on other

Romanians was being increased immediately, but Passport Control insisted Potrascu had not flown into any Scottish airport over the weekend.

She found someone in Bucharest police headquarters who spoke English. There had been mention of a Potrascu about three weeks ago and he would get back to her with details in a few hours.

It was half past five when she got a call from the contact in Immigration.

Potrascu and Lacatus had flown into London Luton airport on the Sunday morning, a flight that landed before noon. By now they had vanished into the unknown.

They had found the road but it had led into a dead end, among more than 60 million people in the British Isles.

Fifty-nine

Puerto Banus. Just after midday.

They parked the car in the underground section of the El Corte Ingles superstore in Puerto Banus and walked across the square to what had once been a tiny fishing village but was now a large Marbella suburb, packed with expensive restaurants and high-class boutiques.

The pavement cafés were crowded and along the edge of the quay expensive cars nuzzled each other while tourists ogled them and the yachts beyond. Most attention was not focused on the sailing vessels or the smaller motor yachts, but towards the west, under the lee of what had once been a lighthouse.

Every step they took closer to it the yachts grew bigger in size, elegance and price. At the far end lay the *Blancanieves*, gleaming in its white livery and adorned with electronic devices for everything, from satellite television to navigational aids, bristling from the top. At the stern, where one might expect a sun terrace, was a helipad and strapped to it an equally brilliant-white helicopter, its blades folded.

Duncan was at the rail and waved as he saw them approach.

Almost immediately he was striding across the deck to the gangway, rolled out ready on to the quay. Anca and Tabor had to push through crowds of sightseers, who only parted when they realised they were guests on the yacht.

'Like her?' breezed Duncan as he helped Anca onboard and turned to pat Tabor on the back.

'I don't think I've ever seen anything sleeker,' Tabor muttered.

'Yeah, the low profile is stunning, isn't it? They come bigger but not as pretty.' Duncan grinned. 'This one's only a sixty-five-footer but I like style and pace in a boat as well.' He indicated the exterior of the ship. 'Six cabins, cruising speed nominally twelve knots but we've tweaked it to go far higher. There's loads of extra gear. A couple of Seadoo wave runners, a fully equipped gym. All you need to make life tolerable at sea. The helicopter's a Cayuse that my people back home had a go at. Its range is over 1,000 nautical miles, and top speed has been raised to over 200 miles an hour, faster than a production chopper for the military.'

Anyone else might have been impressed. To Tabor the spiel about the yacht only underscored how shallow Duncan could be. Shallow, vain. Self-important.

Duncan called out and Tabor stared at the man approaching him. Taller than Duncan, equally tanned and with a physique that spoke of a training regimen.

'Jerry Ferdetta, my senior VP in San Diego,' Duncan said. 'I called Jerry on Friday and he flew over to join us. I decided on a change of schedule. The fishing's not much good in the Med right now but there's an unusual influx of manta rays out there and I thought we'd use the chopper to scout them, first thing in the morning. I've given the crew shore leave, but Jerry can handle her for an hour at sea while we fly. Tonight we'll laze offshore. Pot luck on dinner, but I'm not bad with *huevos rancheros*. Is that OK with you?'

'If you say so.' More spiel. The man can crew yachts, the man can cook. The man can fly his helicopter around on a joy ride. Tabor turned to Anca and she shrugged her shoulders. It all depended on the next few minutes, her look seemed to suggest.

'Nice to meet you,' Ferdetta said, holding out his hand. 'And don't worry, San Diego is a sailor's paradise. I've handled this one in the Pacific lots of times. In the Atlantic too. The Med's child's play, even single-handed.'

'Where's Teré?' asked Tabor.

'She's in the master cabin, doing what girls do,' Duncan answered. 'She'll be out in fifteen minutes. Meanwhile, the champagne's on ice. Why don't you go inside while Jerry and I get the boat through the harbour, take her out a little way and settle before it gets dark.'

The interior of the yacht was as luxurious as the exterior. The lounge ran the full width of the boat, its fittings were in white leather and polished wood. A glance showed Tabor a top-of-the-range Nakamichi sound system, settees with deep cushions and a fitted sideboard on which was standing a silver bucket filled with ice, surrounding a bottle of Bollinger Vielle Vignes Françaises. Standing beside it were five champagne flutes.

He heard the gangway being rolled in and moments later felt a shudder as the engines burst into life and the yacht edged out stern first, before turning around to head for the harbour exit. It took a few minutes to manoeuvre through the crowded port but he heard the change of note as the engines picked up once they were past the harbour walls. There was hardly the slightest sensation of movement, other than the blur of the waves as the yacht slipped through, beyond the vast windows.

Five minutes later Duncan came into the lounge, whistling happily and rubbing his hands together in pleasure.

'Jerry is topside, running the place.' He walked over to the sideboard. 'Not had any yet? Anca?' She smiled and he picked up the bottle and thumbed open the cork, then filled her flute. 'And you?' He turned to Tabor. 'What will you have? The champagne? Or there's a supply of soft drink there.' He pointed to the bottles along the back of the sideboard. 'I remember you don't take much alcohol, but have whatever you fancy.'

Tabor picked up a cola in a small bottle. 'Is there an opener?'

Instantly Duncan delved into a drawer, brought one out and slid it over to him.

'Get settled in,' he said. 'I'll round up Teré, check on Jerry and I'll be back.'

He watched with satisfaction as they both picked up their glasses and drank. Then he waved and left the room.

Tabor was holding on to the top of the settee, but his mind was wandering. Waves of dizziness washed over him and his legs felt weak. On the settee Anca had already blacked out.

He fought to keep alert but it was a losing battle. It was an ingrained rule never to accept drinks from anyone dangerous, but the bottle was capped and so were all of the others. They must all have been doctored, he realised through his haze. Why take the risk of missing? Dope the lot of them.

'Bastard,' he hissed as the cabin door opened. Duncan was framed in the doorway. Tabor saw him as if through a mirage, shimmering waves around his face and grinning features. Then he collapsed.

Sixty

The Mediterranean.

His hands were bound with duct tape behind his back, and his legs were tied. On the table in front of him lay his gun and hunting knife, his passport and other documents.

'You came well armed, Ransome,' said Duncan softly, as Tabor came to on the settee. 'That's not a nice thing to do when you're paying a social visit.'

Beside him was Anca, also taped, still unconscious. Also on the table were her police handcuffs, her gun and her wallet with her police pass.

'A little arsenal.' Duncan laughed. 'The handcuffs were a great touch. I'll throw them into the sea before we leave.' He picked up the guns and put one in each pocket. 'I'll replace your passports and papers. The guns might be too much of a temptation.'

'How long have I been out?'

'About five hours.' Duncan looked at his wristwatch. 'It's closing on six right now.'

'Drugs?' Tabor could hear the thickness in his own voice and the slight slurring.

'Sure. Gamma hydroxybutyric acid, better known, perhaps, to you as GHB.'

'The date-rape drug?'

'It doesn't have to be for rape. One of the side effects is that it loosens the tongue, makes people more responsive when they're questioned.'

'How did you get it into the bottles?'

'An offshoot company of mine has a bottling plant. The GHB is in all of the sodas and beers. The champagne I fixed using a hypodermic needle. A waste of $750 bucks, but you're worth it.'

'Why?'

'Detail.' Duncan's manner had changed and, although he was still smiling, there was no warmth in it. 'Blake's dead, but of course you know that.'

Tabor said nothing. Why supply information at this stage?

'The guards at the brothel found the rope. One of them is on my payroll and he phoned me to say Blake was dead and the boy was there. I came back right away and talked to the boy. He liked your girlfriend, but thought you were a bit strange.'

Tabor remained silent. His mind was confused from the drug. *Fight it. Wait.*

Duncan shrugged. 'Don't talk if you don't want to. No skin off my nose, buddy, but, just so you know, I've got a first-class security unit in San Diego and they checked out Aron when I found the passport and handcuffs. She's in a unit investigating illegal-immigrant running. That's what you were after, isn't it? A story on people trafficking. Somehow you found out about the tattoos and connected to Blake for advice on orchids and the girls. You were after an exposé.'

Fifteen, perhaps twenty minutes, Tabor thought. Then he would be functional, but despite his training the drug was forcing him to talk. *Use it*, Tabor's mind said. *Ask but not reveal. Tell him some of what he wants to hear.*

'I was trying to find out who did the tattoos,' he slurred. 'Not trying to expose Blake. Then I learned he was experimenting on kids from brothels run by Romanians and tattooing them.'

'The boy was proud of his tattoo.'

'Why did he do that, Duncan?'

'Identification. Blake identified his test subjects by tattoos, not names. He was nuts on orchids and liked demonstrating his expertise. That's all it was. Identification.'

'Like the Nazis did on the Jews?'

'Exactly. Instead of a number, Blake gave his experiments a picture. Each one an orchid because he was obsessed with the damn things. He was crazy, Ransome, but he was a genius too. They say the two things are as close as Siamese twins.'

Tabor tried to concentrate. 'What were his experiments, Duncan? Identify them for what? Why children? Why the boy? Why Teré?'

'Questions, questions.' Duncan laughed. 'Trust a reporter.' He went over to the sideboard, picked up a tumbler and filled it with whisky, then poured the champagne he had opened earlier down the stainless-steel sink set under the bar.

'I'm not much on champagne, doped or otherwise,' he said, coming back with his whisky to sit closer to Tabor but beyond reach of his legs. 'Teré liked it.'

'Then why let Blake experiment on her? She's got a tattoo.'

A frown crept across Duncan's forehead. 'How do you know she has a tattoo, Ransome? Only Blake and I knew that.'

Tabor's head was clearing with every minute.

He'd had trouble focusing on his thoughts until now but every time he forced his brain to ingest information things became a little clearer.

'She's cleverer than you know, Duncan,' he said. *Concentrate!* 'She sneaked out a letter to a friend and the friend told me. That's why I went looking for someone who tattooed orchids on teenagers. Why did he want Teré?'

'Because she was a virgin,' Duncan said, taking a large slug of his whisky. He felt the smooth malt in his throat, the burning, the kick as it hit his stomach. He sighed with satisfaction. Life was good and about to get better. 'A couple of years back Blake was using any girl from the brothels as long as she was white. Among other things he was a racist. He believed in the purity of the strain. He insisted white people are the essence of human development. Crap maybe, but genius needs its idiosyncrasies.'

'This drug muddles the mind, Duncan. You'll have to start from the beginning. Make it simple. Or do you have a reason for wasting time?'

Duncan laughed again. 'I could do with using up another hour,' he confirmed. 'But it's not an imperative. OK, I can do simple. Basically, Blake stumbled across a great idea. A daily pill to ensure a woman of child-bearing age delivers only a kid of her choice, let's say pink for a girl, blue for a boy. It doesn't get much simpler than that.'

'It can't be done.'

'That's what everyone thinks. Everyone's wrong. Blake managed it, or as near as dammit. My hired help brought me Blake's files from Fuengirola, along with the boy. I'll use the files to get someone else to finish Blake's work.'

Tabor tried to concentrate. *Simple? Too simple! Too many answers, not enough questions. Think!*

'Go back,' he said. 'I got lost somewhere between blue for a boy and pink for a girl.'

'It takes time to sink in.' Duncan chuckled. 'And getting to where we are now has been a tortuous route. What do you know about Thalidomide?'

'It was before my time,' Tabor said. 'About all I remember is that they said it was the greatest medical tragedy of all time.'

Landon had mentioned Thalidomide when they talked in London.

Duncan nodded agreement. 'Between ten and twenty thousand deformed kids,' he said. 'Strange you mentioned the Nazis earlier. They developed it in 1944 as an antidote to nerve gas. The German pharmaceutical industry revived it after the Second World War because it has a load of therapeutic uses. One is that it's an effective antiemetic and helps ward off morning sickness in the early stages of pregnancy. That's why they used it in the late fifties. What they didn't know then was that it also gets into the womb and attacks the foetus. That caused the mutations, the so-called Thalidomide Babies.'

'Is that what Blake was doing? Using Thalidomide on pregnant women?'

Duncan checked his wristwatch again. 'You'll soon be fully recovered,' he said. He walked over to Anca, still staying out of reach of Tabor's legs and examined her. 'She'll be another twenty minutes or so. It varies with each metabolism.'

He sat back down. 'Many people don't know it, but Thalidomide's still widely used. It's a powerful anti-inflammatory. It can help with myeloma, muscular degeneration and prostate cancer. In particular it's helpful for treating AIDS and leprosy and that's worth a billion dollars a year to the pharmaceutical companies. Blake had been experimenting with Thalidomide for a long time, on and off, trying to develop a pill to use instead of a vaccine in places like the Brazilian jungles. Vaccines need refrigeration.

That's not a common commodity in the jungle. Pills would be easier to deliver, and Blake's basically a pill-maker. But AIDS wasn't his thing – the homosexuality hang-up, back to purity of the race. Thalidomide's a tetrogen, linked to Crohn's disease. Crohn's affects the gastrointestinal tract. The external symptoms include arthritis, skin rashes and so on. There's no known drug or surgical cure and all modern medicine can do for a victim is control the symptoms.'

This time the whisky was going down far more slowly, but Tabor noted that, although Duncan had downed what most people would consider a lot, he showed no sign of intoxication.

'The financial return on developing a pill for remission on Crohn's would be enormous.' Duncan said. 'But Blake didn't want the money, he wanted the kudos for doing something no one else in the world could do, like his orchids. That's when he got lucky. He developed a medication for Crohn's and started to test it on rats. The first results showed awful mutations, but two or three test subjects produced normal offspring and they were always male. He tinkered with his ingredients and came up with a couple that produced only normal females. He kept at it for over a year before he came to me. He knew he had something but it wasn't a cure for Crohn's. It was a contraceptive and he didn't know how to proceed. Contraception is a politically tricky business, and the next step should be testing on humans. Even he could see that was an orthodox no-no. He'd heard in the industry I took risks so he came to me. Am I boring you?'

'Close to it,' Tabor said. 'But I get the picture. As you said, bugger messing around with rats, or wanting a cure for skin rash. Go straight to using humans to test a contraceptive pill that produces only boys or girls.'

'Brilliant,' said Duncan, standing up with a wide smile on his face. 'A Choice Pill. Blake's pill kills off all the sperm cells of the sex that a woman doesn't want. If she needs a girl, the pill kills all the male cells so that eventually she gets her wish. Think of it, Ransome, a pill a woman can take every day that will allow her to get pregnant and ensure she produces only the sex she wants. I'll earn a fortune in China alone. The Chinese government will buy blue pills by the ton to distribute free and stop the production of girls. All over Western Europe you've got women who already have a kid and only want one more of the opposite sex. What choice do they have? Abortion, if they get pregnant and the foetus shows they're going to have a girl instead of the boy they wanted, or vice versa? Millions of women won't have abortions, for moral or religious reasons, or simply because they're afraid. The very thought abhors them, or terrifies them. Others can't afford it. In the States cosmetic abortion costs a small fortune. What women *do* want is the right quantity of kids of their chosen sex, without abortions, preferably cheap. I'll give it to them. No abortions, no mistakes, guaranteed! Fully patented and only companies who lease the licence from me can produce it.'

'You're insane,' Tabor breathed. 'As mad as Blake!'

'Sometimes making history needs a little insanity, Ransome.'

'You're trying to play God. The Vatican will denounce it. Any Catholic woman who takes it will be committing a mortal sin and get automatic excommunication.'

'They do it already with the contraceptive pill,' Duncan scoffed. 'The Vatican says God has given man freedom of choice. I'm showing the way to exercise that right and, believe me, they'll take it. The Choice Pill is a no-brainer.'

Tabor's mind was whirling, taking in the implications, trying to find the loopholes.

'Back up,' he said. 'You also talked about mutations. Did some of Blake's test girls produce deformed babies?'

'Didn't I say that? I should have. We broke a few eggs making the omelette.'

'We're talking human babies, not eggs, Duncan.'

'Commodities,' Duncan said. 'That's what we're talking. Eggs or babies. Commercial products. We could have done it in Latin America but I had my clinics established here and Blake was here. It was easy to bring in equipment for the lab and the hospital and hide the cost in the bills for my company in San Diego and the clinics here, but I needed human test subjects. I put Potrascu on the payroll and at first we used his whores. Blake fed them boosting treatment, injected some stuff and Potrascu kept them off the Pill so they got pregnant. The first half-dozen went wrong so Potrascu had them disposed of in the Med, but then his Guardia contact warned him it was too risky. Sooner or later, a body would wash up and questions would be asked, so then he started to ship the failures to his brothels in Britain to use for a few weeks and recompense his losses, before he got rid of them. But stupidly he sent one to his cousin in Edinburgh, who handled security badly. He let her pregnancy run because he hadn't got enough girls to go around and she earned big money. Some men really get off on riding pregnant women.' He paused for a moment. 'Talking makes you thirsty,' he said, finishing his drink. 'A pity you can't have one. Not that you're saying much any more.'

'I'm listening to you, Duncan. It's what I do, remember. Listen to what people tell me. What happened to the girl in Scotland?'

'The girl found herself a deregistered doctor, one who worked with the street women. He did a scan and showed the result to her. She went berserk and threw herself under a train. About then, Blake decided the mutation problem wasn't the Thalidomide base to his medicine, but some complex interaction between the medication and clients or whores with the pox or another STD. So from then on he demanded virgins for his tests and said he'd only impregnate them using IVF.'

'What about the risk of multiple births. You get that a lot with IVF, surely?'

'Not as much as people think. Besides, he was willing to accept that to get perfect products. His attitude was that first you iron out the boy/girl side of it. Produce perfect specimens for a time and, if a multiple comes along, deal with it then.'

'Surely there was an autopsy on the girl in Scotland, even if was a suicide?'

Duncan went over to the bar for a refill and came back, checking on Anca as he did. She was still unconscious.

'Costel's cousin found the street doctor,' he said. 'Inside a couple of hours, the doctor was dead and his back-street surgery burned, along with the records. Of course, there was an autopsy, but we've got a cop in Edinburgh who does what we ask. He got rid of all the evidence as soon as it was convenient, and fixed it so the pathologist never spoke about it again. Always oil the wheels, Ransome, and don't spoil the way the train runs by penny pinching.'

The haziness in Tabor's brain had almost gone. 'Why did you do it, Duncan?' he probed. 'You're risking the death penalty in the States.'

'Excitement.' Duncan peered pointedly at Tabor's tied feet, but didn't get close. No movement. 'Life is dangerous, Ransome. Or at least it should be. Until lately mine had become tame and humdrum. Excitement makes things happen. It's the creative force of life.'

'So what now?'

'I've got Blake's notes. I've already got a shortlist of biochemists in Asia who'll take over where Blake left off, and I've got a lab and hospital set up. Life goes on, Ransome.

Tatú – my name for the project – goes on as well. Blake may have gone to hell in that fire, but his ideas didn't.'

'Maybe.' Tabor tried to sound sceptical, but what Duncan was saying made sense. Once someone had all the notes, reproducing the combination of ingredients for a pill was simple for a decent chemist.

'A couple of things I don't have straight in my mind,' he said. 'One is how Blake knew the tests had gone wrong at such an early stage.' He remembered Landon's briefing. *There was something in the blood our pathologists couldn't identify.*

'Blake did Caesareans and took the embryo from some of the early trials to examine. Somehow from that he came up with a blood test that can be used at the first missed period to indicate if a foetus will be deformed. That shows how brilliant he was. No one else can do that. As I said, I've got his notes and I'll make a fortune from that alone.'

He paused, then grinned again. 'I'll bet I know what else you want. You want to know about the virgins and what Blake did to them. That's the kind of story that would make you big bucks, friend. Not a groundbreaking blood test. I'll indulge you. You're a captive audience anyway.'

He swallowed more of his drink. 'Like I said earlier, Blake got the virgins from Potrascu. He had to build them up for IVF and that involved mostly drinks, and injections in the arm or butt. But he also had to probe the uterus and the womb, and use instruments to take scrapings from time to time. He put injections into the stomach and others in the groin. The tattoos covered up the holes. That's why he put them there, although I also think he got a sexual kick out of it. Then he used IVF to impregnate them. When the post-first-period blood test showed positive for mutation he gave them to Costel for disposal. In the beginning Costel let special S&M clients use them in Fuengirola – ones who wanted young kids for bondage and stuff. He was letting them go to three months, but then one client got too rough and killed the kid. One of the risks of the business. So for the past couple of years he's been shipping them straight off to London, and using them in his brothels for no more than a month. The mutations have been fewer each time, and the latest one's over a month pregnant. Blake's last test showed she's OK, so far.'

One got too rough. One of the risks of the business.

It hammered through his brain like a never-ending echo.

One got too rough. One got too rough. One got too rough.

Emma.

He closed his eyes and forced himself to deny his tears, deny his rage. There were still questions. *He had to know!*

'How did Blake get the male cells to use in the IVF procedures? From the deep freeze in one of your hospitals?'

Duncan chuckled. 'Hell, no! Personal donations. From me to them.'

'What about your escorts?'

'They were all pregnant when they came to me. I used them for a few weeks until Blake told me they had to go. A fringe benefit for the money I paid.'

'You said one of the experiments got killed. Was *she* impregnated by your sperm?'

'She must have been, but I don't remember.'

Ignorance is no excuse. It was Emma.

'Teré is one of your virgins,' Tabor said softly. 'That means she's pregnant. She's the one you say is the latest, and still OK.'

'Got it at last.' Duncan smiled. 'It takes a long time, but I knew you'd get there in the end.'

'And Dmitri? Is he the only male guinea pig, or are there more like him? Why a boy anyway? I still don't understand about him.'

Duncan stood up and placed his last untouched whisky on

a nearby table. 'I'm getting bored with this,' he said. 'And I can hear Jerry throttling back on the engines.'

Tabor listened carefully. Suddenly the quiet throbbing of the engine vanished and he realised that the yacht was at a standstill, only lapped by the gentle Mediterranean waves.

'We've come to a halt,' Duncan said. 'It's riding on the sea anchor. Time to go.'

'Go where?'

'For a swim.' He started to walk towards the door then halted. 'You asked about the boy. Blake's final idea was sperm that would only give a male or female. He thought he could turn that into a daily pill for men. It wasn't as promising as the Choice Pill for a female, but it had fallback possibilities. So far, Dmitri's the only one. Blake was too particular. He wouldn't take the Moroccans from the brothels, and not many white boys came into his ambit. Dmitri's sperm hasn't been tested yet because no one except Potrascu could find him after his father was killed. Potrascu's bringing him here was an unexpected break. If Costel hadn't toasted him first, Blake planned to collect the boy's sperm this week.'

Now all semblance of his earlier affability faded.

'That swim,' he said. 'I forgot to mention you get a chopper ride first. Enjoy it, Ransome, but I don't think you'll see much of the view.'

Sixty-one

London. Evening.

'Nothing,' said Field. 'He's gone to ground.'

'Keep at it,' Hartley replied. 'He's here for a purpose and we have to find him. The Romanian police sent us pictures of Potrascu and Lacatus. There's one of the other man too, Pavel Potrascu. Stop by here and I'll have copies ready for you to show around.'

'It's been a waste of time up to now,' Field reminded her. He and Rogers were in a pub in the East End and he was checking in.

'If Potrascu knew who killed his cousin, he'd have gone after them right away. He's had days and there's been no report of any retaliation. I think he's still searching for someone. We've got to find him before he finds whoever he's looking for.'

'He could have hired a car and driven anywhere. Taken a train or an internal flight,' Field argued cautiously. The noise in the bar was intense and he was straining to listen.

'I've got people working on that and I've already faxed pictures to Edinburgh. It's a question of time, Jack, and we don't have much of it. Once he gets the information he's after he'll round up muscle and settle this thing. It's going to be very bloody.'

There was a second's silence.

'We'll be back in half an hour,' Field said.

'Make it fifteen minutes,' Hartley retorted, and put down the phone.

Sixty-two

The Mediterranean. Evening.

Anca and Tabor were sitting on the settee, both still bound, but in the couple of hours that Duncan had been away she had regained consciousness and was now fully functional.

'Bastard!' Anca shouted at Duncan, standing up to get to him as he returned through the door, a pistol in his hand. Ferdetta was behind him, a rifle cradled in his arms. 'What have you done to my sister?'

'Your sister? Teré?' His eyes widened and he began to smile, but he pointed the gun at her and she halted. 'So that's what this is about after all. You're not helping Ransome here with an exposé. You're after Teré!'

'Her name is Dorina!'

'Dorina. Teré. Names are conveniences. I gave her pleasure and the time of her life.'

Anca's voice was full of hate. 'She's my sister,' she spat at him. 'My fifteen-year-old sister.'

'If they're big enough, they're old enough,' he said softly, but his mind was working rapidly. 'I guess it means you're not a journalist either, Ransome. What are you, another policeman? No, no force would send someone to another country to chase their sister. Too personally involved. So she's here of her own accord and you're with her for another reason. Money?'

'*Your* mind would work that way, Duncan, but there are other things in life.'

Duncan shrugged. 'Should I care?' But now his eyes were cold, his joviality vanished, and Tabor finally recognised him for what he was. A killer. Duncan would kill for fun and enjoy it.

He pointed to the settee. 'Sit down,' he said firmly. 'I need to think.'

'Bastard,' Anca screamed again, struggling to get to him despite the gun. She lashed out with her feet as she got near him, but he grabbed an ankle and flung her to the side. She landed heavily on the carpet, taking all of the force with her shoulder.

She shoved herself awkwardly back on to her feet, but as soon as she was upright he moved fast, smashing her in the face with the barrel of the gun, knocking her backwards on to the settee again.

Blood began to flow from her nose.

Duncan ignored it dripping down her face. 'Teré never said she had a sister. For what it's worth, she was an exquisite lay and a priceless companion. Now you have a choice, Aron. Allow Jerry to bind those feet, or I shoot you. What's it to be? Jerry or a bullet?'

She spat at him across the space between them, but the spittle fell on the carpet.

'I thought so. When all else fails, abandon manners and spit like a common slut. Don't try that with Jerry,' Duncan said. 'He won't like it and he's not as patient as me.'

Defeated, she did as he told her, wincing as Ferdetta roughly secured her legs with duct tape.

Duncan turned to Tabor. 'No comments, Ransome? Don't you want to say you'll kill me when you get your hands on me, or something naïve like that?'

'Why waste breath?' Tabor answered, seething at the way Ferdetta pulled the tape tight. 'What I *would* like to know is why in movies villains always kiss and tell to impress a victim because they think he'll never live.'

'I wasn't trying to impress,' Duncan snapped. 'I was giving you a glimpse of the future, since you don't have much of that left.' He turned towards the door. 'Make peace with God, both of you,' he shouted over his shoulder. 'There won't be any time later.'

There was no vessel of any kind, nor sign of land. A breeze blew across from Africa, warm but without strength enough to cause movement on the yacht as it lay with the sea anchor holding it steady in the water. The air was redolent with the scent of olive and orange blossom, mixed with the gentle tang of salt from the sea.

They went for Anca first and as soon as they were near she lashed out with her bound feet, kicking Ferdetta in the face. In a second he was back beside her, lifting her head with his left hand and smashing into her jaw with his right fist. Unconscious, they carried her to the helicopter and shoved her inside on the back seat, behind the pilot. They went back for Tabor, ready for any further attack, but he stayed still as they carried him to the door and shoved him in alongside Anca. He made no attempt to struggle. It would have been a waste of time.

Duncan gave a thumbs-up sign as the ignition fired. The rotor began to whine and Ferdetta backed out crouching, holding his bruised face where she'd kicked him.

The helicopter rose inches at a time until it lifted off lazily into the air, the blades diffracting. It kept climbing until its lights were no more than specks in the sky.

The first thing Anca was aware of when she regained consciousness was that the tape around her legs was hurting and her feet felt numb from hampered blood circulation. Tabor was awake, sitting silently beside her.

'Glad you're with us,' Duncan called back. 'You've been out a long time. I warned you about Jerry, but it's been a great night for a ride.'

Between them and the front of the cockpit was a sliding clear screen. He had opened the passenger side to call out to them, but with his own side closed there was no possibility Anca would be able to lean over and try to hit him.

'What are you going to do?' Anca had to yell at him above the noise of the engine, but her voice was steady and showed no fear.

'I think that's obvious,' Duncan shouted back. 'A little more inventive than shooting you.'

'Where's my sister? Let her go. She's only fifteen. She's done nothing to harm you.'

'I admit I was tempted. She's got the performance of a twenty-year-old, but your kid sister isn't around any more. Her or Potrascu's brat. You'll never see either of them again. That's the way the cookie crumbles, Aron. I guess I could have brought her finger or an ear to show you, but I didn't think you'd appreciate it. Put it this way, you won't have too long to grieve.'

Tabor felt her body stiffening and he nudged her. She looked at him, pain and anger evident, and he shook his head.

'Control it,' he said. His voice was low and over the noise of the engine Duncan would not hear it. 'Don't let him faze you. Stay focused.'

Anca choked back her words, but he could see her eyes, already filled with tears.

She leaned forward, closer to the open side of the partition. 'Where are you taking us?'

He glanced down but the only thing to be seen was the shimmering moon reflecting from the waves. There was no sign of land or traffic. The helicopter was carving through an empty sky.

'There's about twenty-five minutes of flying time left with the fuel,' he yelled. 'But I lied. You won't have to swim. There's a black-ops gadget fixed to the runners on the chopper that explodes on contact with seawater. There'll hardly be enough of you left to feed the sharks. You'll never know what hit you.'

He put the steering column on lock, felt down between his legs and came up with a parachute before opening the door to the pilot's side and half-turning around. 'That's it,' he shouted over the even louder noise of the engine and rotors. 'Enjoy what's left of the ride.'

He leaned over, slid the far partition closed and pressed the lock to prevent her getting through. Then he was gone, tumbling backwards out of the doorway, heading swiftly towards the water while the helicopter roared steadily on.

Tabor did his best to watch him down.

But until he vanished in the darkness Duncan's parachute didn't release.

Ferdetta opened a fresh, untainted bottle of champagne and poured a flute for himself, then strolled outside to the deck and leaned against the rail, watching the wavelets sparkle in the moonlight. He had switched on all of the lights and the yacht was ablaze with the fire of a thousand bulbs.

He drank the champagne without haste, savouring the flavour and thinking of the future.

Duncan had kept his word. The documents had been signed that morning in Marbella before the 'guests' arrived at the boat and were already winging their way across the Atlantic, courtesy of Fedex, to his own lawyer in San Diego who would take it from there.

He took out his phone and called Cytek. The finance director, who handled things if both he and Duncan were out of town, answered immediately.

It took only minutes to explain what was happening and say that he'd be back as soon as any police enquiries in Spain had been settled. He'd organise a memorial service to Duncan when he got home. In the meantime, the finance director was to run the company.

'One last thing,' he said before he snapped the cover of the phone shut. 'Take that abomination off the top of the building. What's a fucking giant golden armadillo ever had to do with bioengineering anyway?'

Ferdetta went back to the champagne. The yacht was riding beautifully, hardly causing a ripple in his glass. All he had to do now was drink, sleep and wait for Duncan to call. Then he'd contact the Spanish police and tell them Duncan's helicopter flight was overdue. That would start an air-sea hunt.

He smiled to himself.

Among many other things, Duncan was an expert skydiver.

He could fly until someone believed the parachute would never open, then coast for miles. More than a decade ago an American had covered two hundred and sixty miles paragliding over Texas, more than Duncan would need to land in Sicily. Once he was down he'd call in, then make his way to Palermo and get a flight to Malaga with a different passport, under another name.

The idea was perfect. Duncan would be 'lost at sea'. The

verdict would be accidental death. Duncan's estate would be in order and the inheritance would pass down as instructed in his will.

Everything, including the US$200 million insurance payout, would go to Edward Beech, of Guildford in Surrey, England.

Arranging your own death was something businessmen did from time to time.

But Iain Duncan did it with more flair than most.

Sixty-three

The Mediterranean. That night.

Tabor swung his bound legs and used his feet to smash, with all of his force, at the divider in front of the cockpit. It shattered into a dozen or more pieces.

'Lean over and pick up a sliver,' he shouted to Anca above the roar of the rotors. 'Cut the tape off my hands.'

As he spoke, he was twisting around to make them visible for her and in seconds she had picked up a short length from the pilot's seat and was cutting at it.

She stopped. 'It's not glass,' she shouted back to him. 'It's polycarbonate.'

'Shit,' said Tabor softly to himself. Unlike glass, polycarbonate had no truly sharp edges.

But Anca wasn't waiting. Instead of cutting at the edge, she began to score the tape with the point of the sliver. The tip slipped and ripped into Tabor's arm. Blood began to run down his hands, but she kept on working at it.

Twenty-five minutes, Duncan had said. Twenty-five minutes of flying time.

Tabor began to count in his head.

Anca jabbed at the tape, trying to steady the 'dagger' of polycarbonate and use it like a regular pointed tool, but her tied hands wouldn't grip well and it kept falling to the floor. Each time she retrieved it and began again. Although the shard wasn't sharp, it began to cut into her fingers. Her blood mingled with his on their clothes.

Tabor was still mentally counting. By his estimate it had been nine minutes.

She picked at the edges of some of the frayed tape, her fingers trying to find a grip and she pulled it back a short way, but they had bound Tabor's hands tightly over several layers and it was taking time. Too much time. She jabbed again and kept on jabbing.

Fifteen minutes.

She ripped another strip of tape free and Tabor felt it loosen around his wrists. He flexed his muscles and pulled and in another moment the weakened tape tore free.

He turned to her and pulled the tape from her wrists. Anca rubbed them for a few seconds, trying to get the circulation moving, then clambered over into the pilot's seat, ignoring the pieces of broken divider around her, lifted the pilot's door from its hinges and threw it into the sea.

She took hold of the controls. It was a very different helicopter to the one she'd used in Bucharest, but the basics were the same.

Tabor freed his legs and looked behind the back seat where parachutes were normally kept. There were none. That left everything up to her. Anca was the one who had taken flying lessons. Tabor had no experience at all. It was her show.

He took out the other piece of the sliding divider and clambered over to sit beside her.

She was holding the helicopter steady. Ten more minutes.

'The radio won't work,' she shouted. 'Duncan must have done something to it. He thought of everything.'

'So we think of something different.'

She reached out and grabbed his hand, and squeezed it tight. 'Simon, can I ask you something?'

'Whatever,' he shouted back, putting his hand on top of hers.

'Tell me about yourself,' she asked. 'There's only minutes left. Tell me about Emma. Share it with me.'

Share it? Tell her my life story, while she's fighting to control a helicopter that's going to ditch and blow up any moment? That's senseless! I've never told anyone that before.

But it was what she seemed to want.

She wants what I've never given anyone. She wants to strip me bare.

The thoughts struggled in his head, trying to persuade him to speak out.

Tabor was fourteen when his mother died giving birth to Emma. He had never known his father. When Tabor was old enough to understand, his mother told him she couldn't marry the man. She wouldn't say why, but frequently she reminded Simon that the father loved them both.

They lived in a little terrace in Ambleside that he paid for, but it was the next-door neighbour, Davey Reed, who taught Tabor everything he knew. Once he asked Davey about the real father. Davey said Tabor should mind his own business and he would mind his. It was Davey's way of teaching the boy the realities of life.

Tabor tried to concentrate on the helicopter.

Beside him, Anca seemed calm, with everything under control, her eyes fixed alternately on the instruments and then the horizon, searching for any sign of land.

She didn't pressure him about his life any more.

If he didn't want to speak, that was his choice.

But Tabor's thoughts wouldn't go away.

The first time Tabor ran away was when his mother told him she was pregnant. He didn't even take warm clothes. He went out on the moor and found a cave. He was terrified of the noises in the night, but wouldn't go back, even when he heard the search parties calling. Then, in the morning when he was frozen, he went home and knocked on the door. They both cried. Tabor sobbed that he'd thought he was going to die and she told him something he'd always remember. 'You'll live, Simon,' she said. 'You'll live because you're a survivor.'

How can I tell anyone things like this, he tried to tell himself.

The thoughts were there, he couldn't deny them, but did he have to tell anyone about them?

He looked away from the instruments.

'How long?' he asked quietly.

'Eight minutes' flying time,' she answered.

She glanced momentarily at his face, but she could read nothing in it. She switched back to her continual check on the instruments and the search for land or a vessel below. There was nothing. To the right of them was Africa and most of that coastline would be deserted. To the left would be Sicily, Italy or Croatia.

She turned the helicopter into a steep, banking left-hand curve and dropped the altitude.

A few months after the running-away incident, Tabor was called out of school and taken to the hospital in Kendal. The doctors had delivered the baby by Caesarean but his mother died. Davey told him later she'd had terminal cancer of a hereditary kind.

The baby she wanted christened Emma was premature and was placed in an ICU.

'She looked like a shrivelled guinea pig.' The memory filled him with anguish but hammered at his mind until he admitted it inside. *He had asked himself at the time what there was to like about her.*

A few weeks later Davey told him a couple from Aylesbury were going to adopt baby Emma, but Social Services were sending Tabor to a home. Davey and his wife wanted to keep the boy, but the authorities said they were too old. That was the second time he ran away. He stayed out a week, living off the land and hiding out in shepherds' huts. By the time police found him he was almost dead from exposure and hunger. That was when the Aylesbury couple went to see him, talked for a time, then asked to adopt him as well as the baby. He said yes.

Emma grew out of the guinea-pig stage. She was a bonny infant, blonde pigtails, flouncy dresses, pretty grins, laughing all the time. She was happy. Tabor went to uni, dropped out, joined the army. The SAS. Then the Tabors were killed in a car crash.

'Four minutes,' she shouted. 'Get ready to jump when the fuel runs out.'

She squeezed his hand again.

The Tabors left Simon and Emma everything so he sold the house, put the money in trust for the little girl and used the remainder to enrol her in a good boarding school. Most of the time she was growing up, he was in the army, doing well, and didn't want to give up what he'd got to look after a sister he hardly knew.

On one of his rare weekend visits to see her, she said she was going with a school friend on holiday to Morocco. Tabor gave her spending money, told her to have a good trip and thought nothing more about it until the C/O called him in to say she was missing, and the girl she'd gone with had been found raped and abandoned near the Atlas Mountains.

That was when he went to find her, and everything ended when he did, in that place with the naked man astride her. He tried to blot out the memory.

Memories. Thoughts.

Never admit them. Not even to yourself.

That way you avoid reliving the agony, every day, every hour, every minute.

Things he hadn't done. Things he could never do now.

Was that how it had to be?

'We're going down,' she shouted. 'Fuel gone.'

The wind whistled past them, through the open cockpit. The roar of the rotors and scream of the engine dinned his senses. He watched the water as it came up to meet them.

No more than thirty feet above the waves, Anca took her hand from his and used both to pull the helicopter out of its dive and hold it steady.

The fuel light kept flashing, but the helicopter continued to charge forward. She saw lights on the horizon and looked at the gauge. It was registering empty, but there was still enough fuel to keep the engine running.

The lights grew brighter and longer across what was clearly a shoreline.

She held the stick steady, waiting for the engine to fail.

It did.

Not a cough or a sigh as the fuel ran out. The rotors kept whipping around, driven by the force of the air, but they would only last that way for seconds.

Anca jumped. On the other side of the helicopter Tabor went too.

The helicopter stayed on course for another fifteen or twenty seconds then fell out of the sky like a stone, more than a hundred yards away from them.

The explosion as the runners hit the water shattered the helicopter into tiny fragments, scattering wreckage around them.

A spume of water twenty feet high shot into the air and Tabor felt the shock wave throw him back in the sea. The salt water flowed over him making him choke. Anca trod water, trying to pull her shoes clear, hampered by her clothing.

Tabor popped up beside her and looked at her with an amused smile.

'It turned out to be a nice night for a swim after all.' He laughed. 'Now we only have to stay afloat for the next few hours. The last I saw it seemed to be about fifteen miles to the shore. I've never swum more than four.'

She leaned across and kissed him, as hard as she could on the lips.

Then she fell away spluttering, as seawater splashed into her mouth.

She came back laughing, reaching out to hold him by the arm. 'Four miles or fifteen, Simon,' she called out to him. 'It doesn't matter. You're a survivor.'

'Believe it or not, that's what my mother told me.' He gripped her under her elbows, as she closed up to him. 'I ran away on to the moors once when I was a child and I thought I was going to die. She told me it wouldn't happen like that because I was a survivor.'

He tried to pull her closer, then laughed as the bobbing waves pushed them apart.

'Find a survival kit,' he shouted. 'With that and my mother's mojo, we'll get there.'

The survival kit was the helicopter's seat cushions that bobbed to the surface.

They dragged four of them together, knowing they wouldn't last forever but while they did it would save their energy.

Fifteen miles? Five hours? Tabor asked himself. Probably more. If they didn't drown first.

*

Dawn was layering a pale-pink light over the horizon when they came to the rocky beach, riding the cushions on to the pebbles. They crawled up to a grassy bank and there they huddled together, exhausted, allowing the emerging sun to dry out their clothes, and give their muscles time to relax.

He wrapped his arms around her, as if trying to protect her from any other dangers. She snuggled closer and kissed him again.

'We made it,' she whispered. 'Both survivors. Your mother would be proud.'

'She would,' he agreed softly. 'She was a wonderful woman. You were right. I need to tell you about her, about Emma. About me.'

It took twenty minutes then she kissed him gently on the forehead.

'We all make mistakes, Simon,' she said, running her hands through his hair. 'Perhaps now we can make them together.'

Tuesday.

The sun was high in the sky when the dog found them and began to bark furiously. As they sat up, a man came over the bank and halted, looking down at them, then he spoke. They stared at him without understanding. It was no language either had heard before.

The man saw their puzzled look. 'I'm sorry,' he said, switching into English. 'Are you in any trouble?'

Tabor and Anca looked at each other; understanding dawned and they laughed simultaneously.

They'd been thrown up in Malta! An English-speaking oasis in the middle of the Mediterranean.

Sixty-four

London. Tuesday, mid-afternoon.

'DI Hartley,' she responded automatically as she picked up the phone.

'Sorry it's taken so long,' the voice at the other end answered. 'Things get to overwhelm you in this town.'

'I'm sorry,' she said, the voice not registering. 'Who's calling?'

'Shit!' the man answered with a hint of exasperation. 'I'm so tired I forget who I am. Sam Daniels.'

'Daniels?' Then it dawned. 'Agent Daniels? The FBI in Washington?'

'That's it, for my sins. Al Landon told you to call me. Can the Agent. The name's Sam.'

Hartley laughed lightly. 'Thanks, I'm Ruth Hartley. To tell you the truth, I'd forgotten you promised to call me back. It was about a man called Iain Duncan.'

'That's the one. Well, the way the workload is at the moment it could have taken me a lot longer to get back to you but I picked up the *Wall Street Journal* today and solved your problems. Duncan's dead. It's buried down there on page ten. CEO of an outfit called Cytek out of San Diego, or rather he was. Now he's probably on somebody's breakfast plate, courtesy of the fish in the Med.'

'Run that past me again?'

Daniels chuckled. 'Sorry,' he said, then picked up. 'Iain Duncan, former CEO of the Cytek Corporation, one of the leading bioengineering companies in California, died Monday night in a helicopter accident in the Mediterranean. That's a straight quote from the *Journal*. His chopper went down off the Sicily coast. The 'chute didn't open and he didn't pop back up to the surface. There's been an air and sea search by the Spanish and Italian authorities but nothing's turned up. The company has been taken over by his number two, a guy called Jerry Ferdetta. No one is saying how much Duncan had in the bank but the *Journal* suggests it runs Fort Knox a close second. You said when you called me that it had to do with an investigation Landon has running. Does it affect us? Duncan's death could make a noise if he had political connections we don't know about.'

'Wait a couple of seconds, Sam.' Hartley was thinking it through. She'd all but forgotten about Duncan until the phone call. 'As far as we know, there's nothing that concerns you. It wasn't a strong line of investigation, only something that cropped up in a local case. Is there anything suspicious about the death?'

'Not that we've heard. I called a guy in Madrid and he said it all seems above board. Then I contacted the Attorney General's people and the Internal Revenue Service. Duncan was blue-eyed in everybody's books. I checked the Pentagon because Cytek has contracts with them, but they said the man was a business genius and his company has the best brains in the industry. He should have run for president, or maybe governor of California.'

'Was anyone else on board the helicopter when it crashed?'

'Not a one. Duncan and Ferdetta were out there having a

break from business and Ferdetta doesn't like choppers, so Duncan went off for a joyride by himself. They've looked for the helicopter but can only find fragments. It seems to have been smashed into pieces. Duncan was the last of the big-time adventurer playboys. Flew a chopper, hot-air balloons, big mountaineer, hang-glider, did transatlantic ocean racing in his yacht, probably wrestled alligators with his bare hands. He'd got the money and the thirst for danger. He might have tried to loop-the-loop in that machine of his. It's the kind of reputation he had – more money than he could spend, so push the limit.'

'When you made your calls did anyone mention a man called Felix Blake in relation to Duncan?'

There was another pause. 'Doesn't ring any bells,' he said after a moment. 'I'm flicking through the databanks on the machine while I get the brain into gear but there's nothing there. No flashing lights. No thousand-dollar payout. Does that wrap it up?'

'I guess so,' Hartley said. 'Could you fax me that article from the *Wall Street Journal* and a background CV?'

'Sure. I've got a brief background here in front of me now. Age forty-two, son of the late Colonel Warren Duncan – he was a bird colonel shot down in Desert Storm. Mother died a few weeks later. There's one thing – Iain Duncan had dual nationality. Colonel Duncan was with the USAF at a place called Mildenhall in the UK. Not a colonel then, though. He married a British girl in Norfolk but Iain was brought up mostly in the States. Ivy League, Cornell. Bachelor. No other family. Whoever benefits from his will is set for life. It's all here and I'll shove it down the wire to you. Say hi to Al for me. Tell him he owes me a bottle of Six Roses for this one. Nice talking to you, Ruth.'

'Was he certain it was an accident?'

Field perused the cutting that Daniels had faxed. He'd been back in the office for only half an hour.

'It's concerning me that he died when we were trying to run a check on him, and his friend Blake died around the same time,' Hartley said. 'But we found nothing suspicious about Duncan while he was alive. Daniels said the man liked danger. Perhaps he had a death wish and let it take over. There's only one other thing. I had a call from Beech while you were out. He's back in touch, in Scotland.'

'What prompted that?'

'He was being his normal smarmy self. He asked if he was still under investigation. I told him to keep in touch regularly for the next few weeks. I couldn't do any more.'

'We don't seem to be able to do much about anything,' Field said. 'Everything's gone cold on us. There's no sign of Potrascu and the Romanians in town won't say a word. Any ideas?'

'None we haven't tried before.'

'You know what the DCI says.'

'What's that?'

'Try again.'

It was nearly seven o'clock when Hartley called Landon but the line couldn't connect.

They'd read the reports again, plodding down avenues already trodden a dozen times, rehashing old theories. At six she told them to go home and start afresh in the morning.

Now she wanted to let Landon know that the Duncan idea had also ended in nothing.

Ten minutes later, with his mobile still reporting no connection, she rang his home landline. She didn't want to disturb Helen at home and there was always a chance Landon had gone out, but she had to risk it.

He answered on the third call.

'I'm sorry, sir,' she said hurriedly. 'I tried the mobile but got no answer.'

'Is there something urgent, Ruth?' he asked quietly, not commenting on the mobile phone.

'It's just that the FBI man in Washington called me. I wanted to let you know. Duncan died in a helicopter crash at the weekend. The FBI said there was nothing suspicious, but I thought you'd want to be told.'

He said nothing for a moment then answered, 'Thanks, Ruth.' His voice was flat. 'Thank you for trying.'

'Sir, is everything OK? You don't sound your normal self.'

There was the strained silence again.

'Helen died on Monday,' he said. There was no trace of tears. Only of sadness. 'I went in to take her morning tea and she was dead.'

Hartley sensed the misery eating away inside him. 'I'm so sorry, sir. Is there anything I can do?'

She waited for him to answer. She could sense he was making an effort every time he spoke.

'Sorry about the mobile. I wanted to let her rest.'

'Is anyone with you, sir?'

'There never has been.' She could feel him shaking himself, trying to rid himself of the ache he was feeling. 'She didn't have any family. She had a sister once, but she's been dead for years. There are neighbours, but we didn't socialise with them. So there's only me.'

'I'll come around,' she said, reaching for her handbag.

'No. Helen's body is already at the undertakers. I want to be on my own for a while.' He hesitated. 'There is one thing, though.'

'Anything.'

'The cremation is in the morning. Nine a.m. Do you think you could be there with me? Golders Green Crematorium. It doesn't seem right to have only one person to see her off.'

Sixty-five

Burnham-on-Crouch. Evening.

Kelly McGlynn turned the sign on the door to read 'Closed' and pulled down the blind. It had been a long day, sitting in the office alone.

She read newspapers, sorted files and called a couple of cleaners but there was nothing of importance. October weekends most yacht owners stayed in their permanent homes, preferring the creature comforts of London and its surrounds to the bleakness of the River Crouch.

But she remained at the office until regular closing time because, for some perverse reason, she'd convinced herself people expected it of her. Now she could lock up and leave. She was reaching for the handle when the door opened.

She held on to it firmly with one hand, putting the other against the edge of the door, barring any entry. 'We're closed,' she said shortly. 'I'm leaving. Sorry.'

Serghei looked at her with an amused expression on his face. He shoved hard and McGlynn staggered back from the doorway, the door wrenched from her hands as she fell into the office. He stepped inside and Potrascu followed, closing the door then pulling the toggle to lower the Venetian blinds that covered the main window. He was wearing a dark, heavy overcoat, keeping out the wind and cold.

McGlynn shoved herself upright, using the edge of the desk as a lever, and rounded on the men, her eyes angry and her face flushed. 'What do you think you're doing?' she demanded, glaring in turn at both of them. 'Get out of here before I call the police.'

Serghei leaned down and ripped the telephone jack out of the wall. 'Call,' he offered.

McGlynn hesitated. *This was wrong.* Burnham was a peaceful little place and this kind of thing didn't happen. She looked beyond Potrascu to see if there were anyone on the street she could call for but the blinds were down, no one could see into the office and Burnham was deserted.

She backed against the desk. There was no weapon of any kind, not even a paper-knife. Her raincoat was hanging on a hook on the wall, but there was nothing in it she could use. She'd toyed in the past with buying and carrying a pepper spray, but there had been no reason for her to carry through with it. Robbery didn't happen in Burnham. Not in the main street. The yachties might get a bit rowdy with too much alcohol, and there were plenty of burglaries, but violence was hardly in the regular Burnham make-up.

'There's no money in this office,' she said nervously, sweeping her hair back from her face. Her eyes were darting from one man to the other, waiting for one to move. 'All the money is banked in the early afternoon.'

'Sit down,' Potrascu said softly, pointing at her vacant chair. 'We have no need of money.'

The softness was a mistake. McGlynn looked at the man and felt defiance rising in her. 'Get out of my office,' she said loudly.

Serghei was fast. He took one step forward and hit her

with his fist, ramming it into her face. She slammed back against the wall and slid down to the floor, her skirt raising a little as she did. Blood began to trickle from a cut lip and fell down on to her blouse. Her eyes glazed and she could feel the pain in her face. Tears flicked at her eyelids. She reached up and wiped her hand across her face. It came away covered in blood.

Potrascu tossed her a box of tissues from the desktop, and it landed in her lap as she sat on the floor. She picked it up, pulled one out and dabbed at her mouth. It was a deep cut and the blood was flowing strongly. She held it to her mouth and stared up at him.

He was inspecting her as if she were a piece of merchandise on display.

'You own a boat. The *Wanton Lady*. Who sails it for you?'

Her head was already starting to ache. She kept the tissue pressed against the cut on her lip and looked again at Serghei, hate in her face.

'What business is it of yours?' she spat, trying to make herself sound braver than she felt. *Who were these people? Please God, send someone to knock on the door right now.* She was shivering, afraid of what was coming, unable to do anything yet needing to appear in control.

Serghei stepped closer and instinctively she raised her arms to protect herself, all defiance gone in the one gesture.

Potrascu held up his hand. 'The woman will tell us politely very soon, Serghei,' he admonished quietly.

He glanced at McGlynn, noting the long legs and thighs showing where the skirt had ridden up. She saw his look and tugged at her skirt. More blood dripped on to her blouse with the sudden movement.

It had taken days to find her. All over London, across to Belgium until finally a man who came up to them in a Soho club four hours ago told them about the *Wanton Lady*. Then they had to find her name and address from the Small Ships Registry and drive here. It all took time. Time he did not have. And certainly none to waste on this woman.

'The man who runs girls across from Belgium in your boat. Who is he?'

She struggled upright, pushing herself against the wall and dabbing at the lip with more tissues. The streaks of blood showed on the pale-blue blouse like drips of claret-coloured paint. Automatically, she smoothed her skirt, freeing the wrinkles and covering her thighs.

She looked first at Serghei then at the closed door. Beyond its blinds there were people somewhere. 'I can scream,' she said in a tight, uneasy voice.

'No one will hear you,' Potrascu sighed. He swivelled in his seat and picked up a pencil from the tray on the desk then began to tap it, clicking like a metronome, on the desk top. He smiled across at her. Now she was standing, he could take in her features and figure more completely. Adequate, he thought, but he had seen and tasted better.

'There's no one in the street,' he said. 'And the wind will cover the noise. Simply tell me what I want to know. Who is the man?'

She switched her attention to Serghei. He was less than three yards from the door. Three yards and a few seconds. But he was too close and he was huge. She breathed in deeply. Time. She needed time. Time for someone to walk past and see the blinds drawn but take note of the lights inside. Perhaps the noise of people talking. Any indication of that and she could scream. *Time. Make more time.*

'I sail the boat myself,' she snapped.

'Perhaps, but there's also a man who goes with the girls. I want to know who he is. It's not so much to ask.'

'I don't know anything about anyone bringing girls from Belgium. I never go there.'

'Someone does. The girls are prostitutes. They're being run to England illegally and that could get you in a lot of trouble. You could save yourself time and pain by telling me who the man is and where I can find him. It's a matter of some concern to me. In fact, I might say it's the most important thing in the world right now.'

Make time.

'I told you. No one comes with me. There are no girls.' She lifted one hand annnd pointed at Serghei. 'And if *he* hits me again I *will* scream.'

Potrascu indicated the door near the corner of the office wall. 'What's that?'

'The bathroom. What of it?'

'No one will hear you screaming in a bathroom.'

He replaced the pencil tidily in its tray and inspected his fingernails before laying his hands back on his lap. 'You're wasting my time,' he said tiredly. 'We've been in here nearly four minutes and you've told me nothing but lies.' He indicated Serghei standing alongside him. 'Serghei has no sexual leanings, male or female, but when he requires fulfilment he makes use of either, in quite inventive ways. Show her, Serghei.'

Serghei grinned and unzipped his trousers, pulled down his underpants and slipped his penis into his hand. McGlynn blanched. The penis was huge and already starting to harden. She looked around wildly. There was no way she could get to the door. The fear rose into her mouth and she could taste it. Bitter like bile, rancid and foul.

'No,' she said, her voice starting to shake. 'You wouldn't!'

'*I* wouldn't,' Potrascu agreed. 'Not tonight anyway. I have other things on my mind, but Serghei would. The choice is yours. You can give me the name and address of the man who brings the girls from Belgium or you can entertain Serghei.'

'No!' Her voice was rising. 'Please!'

Her eyes were agitated and her face was twisting every way. She pushed back against the wall, trying to edge away from the bathroom door, as if there was safety in the bricks and plaster behind her, but it was a small office. There *was* no safety.

Potrascu put his hand in his overcoat pocket, produced a roll of tape and handed it to Serghei. 'It's to put across your mouth,' he said, still watching McGlynn. 'I have no doubt whatsoever that you can scream very loudly, but not with that across your face. Besides, you might like it. Serghei has a variety of positions. He can –'

'Winters!' she shouted.

'Winters is dead,' Potrascu said in a resigned kind of voice. 'It was in the British newspapers. I want the other man who was with him. Serghei is getting impatient.'

The dam broke. She needed to get away from these men, to be out in the street and in the pub with people and freedom and life. Her tartness had gone: her pride too. All she could do was tell them what they wanted and get out of here. 'His name is Edward Beech. He has a boat called the *Pesadilla*. It's moored out in the river.'

She realised she was blubbering through her tears. Stains from the tears and the blood on her face dripped on to the carpet.

'A boat with a Spanish name.' Potrascu smiled, ignoring her crying. 'How interesting. Where does this man Beech live?'

'A few hundred yards away.' Now she couldn't contain anything. Not her tears, nor her fears, not even her dignity. She was shaking with terror, stammering to tell him everything. 'On the left. Chapel Road. A house called The Limes but you won't find him there. He's away.'

'You said his boat is at its mooring.'

'It is. Beech is at a house he has in Scotland. He'll be there for a week or more.'

'Whereabouts in Scotland?'

'I don't know.' She couldn't move any further and Serghei was standing there, grinning at her. He was peeling the edge of the tape free.

'No doubt it's on your computer.' Potrascu touched the laptop on the desk. 'Are you going to find it for me or do I have to do it myself? It shouldn't be hard to find.'

'If I tell you, can I go?' Her legs were weak and she wanted to sink to the floor.

'If you don't, then you'll know more pain than you've ever known in your life and I'll get the address anyway.'

The legs gave way. She slumped on to her knees and buried her head in her hands. She knelt there for a minute, then slowly shoved herself back up again. Potrascu could see it in her eyes. There was nothing left. No hope.

'I don't have an address,' she cried quietly. 'It's an isolated house in the north, about fifteen miles south-west of Thurso but there's no clear road, only a track. It's a short distance from a lake called Tum Broch.'

He smiled at the woman. 'You lied about the girls, didn't you?' he said softly. 'You worked with Beech in his business. You helped him handle trips with the girls. You have been to this place in Scotland with him.'

McGlynn nodded silently. She was shaking with fear. All she wanted was for these men to leave.

Potrascu waited.

'I organised his schedules,' she whispered. 'Arranged the moorings in Blankenberge overnight when it was needed. I had to make certain the girls arrived safely and were sent on to London with a Spaniard Beech used.'

The phone in Potrascu's overcoat pocket rang. He pulled it out, spoke for a moment then stood up and walked into a corner, facing it as though trying to hide the conversation.

He slapped the cover shut and turned around.

Serghei knew instantly there was trouble. He raised an eyebrow.

'Dmitri,' Potrascu said, his voice ice cold. 'He has been taken again. They think he may be dead. A bodyguard who was looking after him has been washed up in the sea.'

He turned to McGlynn. 'It's better when people tell the truth,' he hissed. 'It saves time and trouble. If you'd done it first time, things might now be different.'

He looked across at Serghei, standing there with his trousers open. 'Use a condom,' he ordered. 'Then bind her mouth with the tape. We don't want her screaming like a stuck pig.'

Sixty-six

London. Wednesday morning.

Landon was waiting outside, hands thrust deep into the pockets of his raincoat.

She paid off the taxi in Hoop Lane. Landon wouldn't be alone. There were at least a dozen cars parked outside.

'Company?' she asked as she reached him.

'Unexpected,' Landon answered. His face was drawn but seemed mingled with relief, either at her being there with him or because in another half an hour or so it would all be over. 'The doctor's inside, the wives of neighbours are in there, and a woman from the public library that I didn't know about. I think a few of the cars may have brought professional mourners, dragged in to make up the numbers and have the place look more comforting. Let's go in and get it over with.'

She took his arm. 'Done,' she answered. 'Then I'll take you for a stiff brandy.'

The pub was almost empty, which was understandable given that it had only been open for about twenty minutes. He fetched coffees for them and they sat in a window seat overlooking Finchley Road.

'How are you feeling? Or is that a stupid question?'

'You know it wasn't a marriage of love, Ruth. We got trapped in it when we were kids and couldn't break out. When you got engaged in those days you went through with it. I was only eighteen when we married and in the first few years neither of us wanted to hurt my career by divorcing. The hierarchy wanted a stable wife at a senior officer's side. It was wrong, but at the time we thought it was best for both of us. Play Happy Families to the outside world and try to get along together inside the house.'

'And now?'

He sipped at his coffee. 'You've never asked me why it fell to pieces at such an early stage,' he said, staring at the brown liquid swirling around halfway up the cup. He hadn't answered her question. Perhaps he didn't want to say how he was feeling. Not now or later.

'It's none of my business, and you're my boss.'

'Life is full of wrong turnings, do you know that?'

'Don't get maudlin on me, sir.'

He breathed in deeply, as if letting regrets flow through him. 'Even before we married I was having an affair with another woman.' Landon hesitated for a moment, thinking about it. Remembering it. 'There was a child born only six months after I married Helen. I asked Helen to let me divorce her so that I could marry the mother, but Helen wouldn't let me. She said it would ruin my career if I confessed to adultery in those days. I was only just in the force, but I loved it and I was ambitious. I knew I was going to make it, so I made excuses for myself, and let her convince me. It didn't take much persuasion. After she'd won she refused to have anything to do with me sexually again. My penance would be to stay married to her, but have no life together. I could have done things differently if I'd been man enough. I took the easy way and life eventually demanded its payment.'

Hartley reached across the table and took his hand. 'How about that brandy now, sir? What you did in the past is your own business. What you're doing now is moping. You've got to snap out of it. Why keep sitting in the house on your own? Come back to the office. It would take your mind off it.'

'I don't need alcohol. It doesn't help.' He pulled his hand away. 'It's your case, Ruth. I told you that. I don't promise one thing and take it back like an Indian-giver when it suits me.'

'There are other cases waiting and this one could be over soon.'

'Not just like that. From what I can tell, there are lots of suspicions but no evidence. You need that to go to court.'

'True, but there's . . .' She broke off as her phone rang. She reached inside her handbag and took it out, looking at the number, then at Landon. 'Sorry. I'd better take this one.'

She listened for a couple of moments then said, 'Give me an hour or a little bit more, sir. Things to do.'

She closed the mobile. 'It should have been for you,' she said. 'That was DCI Ellis in Chelmsford. McGlynn is dead. They found her in a bathroom in her office this morning. She'd been raped. The pathologist thinks someone smashed her head in with an ice axe.' She saw Landon look up. 'That's not all. Beech's house has been ransacked, and his boat set on fire.'

'Did you say ice axe?'

'It's the pathologist's first thought. He'll need an autopsy to confirm it. Are you coming, sir? I need to get to Burnham right away. Field might as well pick us up here on the way.'

Landon's face eased into a smile. 'Like I said, I'm doing nothing except shoving aside cold coffee. It's still your case but, if you can stand having me around, I'd like to come along for the ride.'

Sixty-seven

Burnham-on-Crouch.

They stopped off at Chelmsford morgue to meet Ellis and see McGlynn's corpse.

'It isn't pretty,' Ellis said, his face impassive. 'She wasn't just raped. It was an anal intrusion by someone pretty big. Then whoever did it smashed her skull and left her propped on the toilet seat with her legs splayed and her head against the wall.'

'Semen?'

'None. He must have used a condom.'

'Did anyone see anything?'

'No,' Ellis answered. 'Most folks had gone home or to the pub. The pathologist thinks it happened around seven o'clock last night. The killer stuck tape over her mouth to stop the screams. We're having it examined, but it looks like common or garden commercial tape from any hardware store. There are fingerprints all over the place, but I don't hold out much hope.'

'What about the ice axe – if it was one?' Landon asked.

'I think it was,' Ellis replied. 'I tossed the idea to the

pathologist and he said it would need an autopsy, but it could fit the wound. That's why I called you.'

Hartley looked at the body, feeling almost as sick as she had at the pig farm over a week ago. The shock was almost as bad. The axe had split her skull but McGlynn's eyes were wide open and all that Hartley could read in them was stark horror.

'Have you tried to contact Beech, sir?' she asked.

'We don't have a contact number.'

'We do,' Hartley answered, nodding at Field who went out of the morgue into the corridor to make the call while they carried on talking.

He came back minutes later. 'I spoke to Thurso Police. There's a howling blizzard up there. It started in the night and there's already about a foot of snow. The phone lines between Thurso and Beech's house are down, and there's no mobile connection. I asked about getting in by air or four-wheel-drive and they said it's impossible at the moment.'

Hartley turned back to Ellis. 'What about Beech's boat?'

'It's fibreglass so it didn't burn except for the wooden fittings, but there was some type of accelerant used because it buckled and twisted below deck and melted a hole, so it sank. The arson experts think someone splashed paint thinners around and set fire to it.'

'It was moored in the middle of the river,' Hartley said. 'How would they get to it?'

'It's Burnham. Yacht Heaven. There's no shortage of dinghies lying around. Someone in the pub saw the flames and called 999 but they had to bring out the fire boat because Beech's yacht was too far offshore.'

'Why would anyone burn a boat?' she asked.

'Wait until you see Beech's house,' Ellis said grimly. 'That may give some ideas.'

*

Tables were overturned, chairs smashed and pictures ripped from the walls, the glass in their frames shattered on the carpet. Trophies from past yachting series had been crumpled with heavy blows.

CSIs in their white coveralls moved around the house like ghosts, but most of their work was done by the time Landon, Hartley and Ellis got there. It was obvious that someone had rampaged through the house. The back door was smashed in and there were breakages everywhere.

'He must have been crazy,' Hartley said, shaking her head, as she scanned the debris.

'They,' corrected Ellis. 'There are footprints inside the back door. It was raining earlier in the day and the lawns were muddy. They came in that way and left marks. We've compared them with shoes in the wardrobes, but found nothing.'

Hartley knelt down and picked up one of the smashed photographs. It was a full face of Beech with Tom Winters beside him holding a trophy. There was a huge cut where the face of Beech had been.

'Another ice axe?'

'Nearly all of the photographs are like that,' Ellis said. 'The cups and other trophies could have been crushed by one as well. The crime-scene officers are taking stuff away but it's doubtful there'll be anything for forensics. In any case, what's one ice axe among millions in the world?'

'Beech is in danger,' Landon said. 'They've taken it out on his possessions, now they'll want to take it out on him personally.'

Ellis turned to him. 'Any more thoughts?'

'If it's the ice-axe killer, it's DI Hartley's case,' Landon said firmly. 'I'm officially on leave for the moment. If you've got reason to think it's anything else, it's your jurisdiction.'

'Are you going to look for Beech?' Ellis asked her.

'You heard what DS Field said,' she replied. 'There's no way to contact him, but he needs to be warned and told to get back here to check the house as soon as possible. Do you want to see any more, sir?'

'No. Carry on as you see fit.'

Hartley turned to Ellis. 'Please let us know if you get any further news.'

She took one last look around the devastated house and shook her head.

She was still shaking it as she climbed into the car.

Sixty-eight

London.

'Well?' she asked. They were sitting in the office in New Scotland Yard, and Field had gone to the canteen. Rogers was hovering on the periphery, waiting to join in, but with nothing new to offer.

'It seems pretty obvious to me,' Landon answered. 'Potrascu checked out Beech's house and the way the photographs were mutilated suggests he knows Beech by sight. I'd say it's as sure as eggs is eggs Beech has been running the girls from Spain. Now Potrascu wants Beech's head on a platter. That makes it imperative you find him quickly.'

'*Us*, sir, not me. Beech is in Scotland. We don't have jurisdiction and I don't think Superintendent Murchie is going to take orders from me.'

Landon smiled. 'Right,' he said. 'Your case, my authority.'

Field returned with tea for them and black coffee for Landon. 'The way I see it,' he said, putting the cups on the desk, 'the Romanian isn't in Britain only because he believes Beech is behind the cross-channel trade. We know from the boy that Potrascu's looking for the people who killed his brother here in London and his cousin in Edinburgh. The prostitute ferrying, the massacres at Blackhall and the other brothels tie up. My guess is Beech has been running the prostitutes from Spain, but now he wants the whole caboodle. When he's got all the Edinburgh brothels, he'll head down here.'

Rogers was standing beside Field, now drinking his tea. 'What puzzles me,' he said, 'is why they did that to the McGlynn woman. I just can't believe it was because she was ferrying prostitutes. Potrascu *must* have had another reason to go berserk.'

'He did,' Hartley said, the coin finally dropping. 'He went berserk in Spain too, burning the house down around that orchid doctor. Potrascu did that because he saw the tattoo on the boy. The tattoos are the connection. The tattoos *and* Beech.' She looked across at Landon. 'Potrascu is going for Beech because he thinks Beech is behind everything. The tattooing and the massacres. Mostly he wants revenge for the boy!'

'And he knows where Beech is. He'd have forced it out of McGlynn before she was killed,' said Field grimly. 'Beech is resourceful. Just because I can't get through to him doesn't mean he's left himself without communications. He could have a private satellite arrangement. He doesn't strike me as the kind who lets weather interfere with his ability to contact people he needs, and we've got to assume he already knows about McGlynn, and expects Potrascu to go up to Scotland after him. He won't be sitting inside his Scottish mansion surrounded by bagpipes, haggis and sprigs of heather. He's got a private army, the ones who attacked the brothels. Tough bastards with guns and they get a kick from using them. If Potrascu reaches Beech before us, it will be wholesale slaughter.'

Landon was thinking as he listened. 'You're right,' he

said. 'That means Potrascu's got a day's start on us, but if he has to get men from London and Edinburgh they'll have weapons so they'll need a truck. That will have taken time to organise, but by now he's on his way to Scotland. I'll ask Murchie to have an armed response team move on that house before Potrascu and his troops do.'

He thought about it a little more. Flaws. Think fast but examine the flaws. Any omissions? Anything else forgotten or overlooked? Think!

He turned to Hartley. 'You said Beech has staff on his payroll. Do we know how many or who they are?'

'We've got names, but no details. There are about twelve, the bulk in Scotland.'

'Get the names. Run them through the files. They know guns and tactics. Cross-index them all. Then I need to check with Murchie. Jack said there was snow. We need to know if the ART can even get in there. Who's an expert on weather and terrain up there right now?'

He didn't wait for an answer. Instead, he took out his mobile and immediately swore in exasperation. It was dead. He hadn't thought to charge it since Helen died and now the battery had run out.

'Lend me your mobile,' he said to Hartley.

She handed it over and he punched in the message. 'Urgent,' he wrote. 'Voice call back this number. Imperative now.'

Then he stabbed in the number and they both waited.

'What's the hurry?' Tabor said. 'You said no voice contact.'

'I changed my mind,' Landon snapped. 'I need advice right now. What kind of weather conditions can I expect in Caithness?'

'Why?'

'Potrascu's there. He's going after a man called Beech, the

one who ferried the girls from the Continent to here. We've got to get to him before Potrascu does. Somewhere called Loch Scye.'

There was a long silence at the other end.

'Tabor,' Landon shouted into the phone. 'I'm in a hurry!'

'Get a chopper,' Tabor said, his voice now cold. 'Meet me at Wast Water in an hour.'

The phone went dead. Landon handed it silently back to Hartley.

'Well,' she asked, putting it on the desk 'Who's Tabor?'

'My source,' Landon said quietly. 'My moment of truth.'

The Lake District.

Anca stared into the fire, the flames flickering over the logs he'd brought in from outside, watching a thin film of smoke vanish up the stone chimney. It had been less than a day since they arrived in Britain. The man on the beach took them to the Romanian Embassy after they said their sailing vessel had sunk offshore. The Embassy hushed up everything once Anca's identity was confirmed.

They returned to Malaga on the next plane while Dani went home to tell his family about Dorina. It was in Malaga that Anca read in the Spanish newspapers about Duncan's death. They picked up their belongings in Fuengirola and caught the next plane to Manchester.

Anca was hiding her grief, trying to come to terms with Dorina's death. What need was there for her to die? But she already knew the answer. Duncan couldn't let his 'escorts' live after he'd finished with them. They might have learned things they shouldn't and they'd be able to identify him later. Dorina was as good as dead the moment Duncan chose her.

But reasoning had no part in emotion and she couldn't get

over the sight of Dorina's face at the casino, or forget how she looked when she was a little child, in the hills outside Rogojel, picking flowers, singing songs, dipping her toes in the mountain springs.

The memories haunted her. Those of Dmitri too. She'd only been with him a few minutes, but the boy had been so full of life, so trusting. Why did he have to die? Blake's experiments. Blake's *monstrous* experiments.

She sat in front of the fire, absorbed in her thoughts.

Tabor sat down in an armchair near to her. 'A couple of minutes,' he said. 'Then I have to get ready.'

'Ready? For what?'

'Potrascu is in Scotland. Landon will take me to him.'

'I'm coming too.'

'No.' He shook his head. 'It's wild country up there, Anca. Some of the worst in the world. I just checked on the Internet. It's blowing a blizzard. That's why Landon needs me and why he won't refuse to take me, but it's no kind of place for you right now.'

Anca got up and moved to the armchair. She knelt in front of him, hugging him towards her.

'Let it go, Simon,' she pleaded gently. 'Let the policeman handle things now. Emma's death is eating at you, but this is Britain. The country has laws. If you kill Potrascu here, it's still the same as in Spain. The police will arrest you and you'll spend the remainder of your life in prison.'

He took her hands away. 'It doesn't work like that. Not for me. An eye for an eye.'

'Then let your policeman do it for you, legally.'

He shook his head again. 'I fight my own battles.'

She stood up. 'Then we should get ready.'

'We?'

'Of course.' She smiled. 'If you're going to chase Potrascu, I'm coming too. Potrascu is a legitimate Romanian target.

I'm the police. Like you, I do what I have to do.' She leaned over and kissed his head. 'You blame yourself for not doing more for her,' she said softly.

'I did nothing,' Tabor answered bitterly. 'I paid money. I gave her no love or attention.'

'That's why you feel you have to kill Potrascu. You hate him and I understand, but hate clouds reason. That's why I am coming with you, whether you like it or not. I'll reason for you.'

Sixty-nine

The Flow Country.

The snow was like a plague of ants flying past the copse: the flakes hard and gritty, pecking against their faces. They couldn't even see the mansion, although it was only a couple of hundred yards away, at the edge of the slate-grey lake that was only a fly-speck on the large-scale Ordnance Survey map that Landon gave them en route to Scotland.

Beyond it, amid the bogs, the wild tough heather and bleak low-lying hills of the Flow Country, Potrascu and thirteen men were battling through the blizzard.

The last report DS Murchie had received was that a truck had been found wrecked on the moor, after hitting a sheep in the whiteout that covered a hundred miles around them. Potrascu had left a man with a broken leg behind, a bullet in his chest.

Half-frozen by the time a police patrol car found him, the Romanian readily told them Potrascu had taken all the others, including one man with a broken arm, on to the moor.

Murchie believed they were miserably huddled behind a

clump of boulders somewhere, shivering and waiting for the storm to die.

Murchie was wrong! Tabor *knew* Murchie was wrong. Potrascu didn't care about the snow or the moor, he didn't care about injured men. Landon had explained everything in the helicopter on the way to Wick. Potrascu's hatred of Beech would be as all-consuming as Tabor's was of the Romanian. Potrascu would *not* let go.

He was insane when he killed Blake. Now his insanity would be fermenting. Duncan had betrayed him, manipulated him with his easy smile, his laughing words and eyes that lied with every twitch of a muscle. This man Beech had done the same in Edinburgh. Both had used Potrascu as an inconsequential pawn, unimportant except to the mechanical functioning of the operation.

The Romanian would have nothing in his mind but payback. It would sustain him through this blizzard, it would force him across this desolate moor, it would drive him to attack this mansion and the mini-army waiting inside it.

Beside the reality of Duncan's evil, the weather was insignificant. Potrascu would *not* hide. He would break into a moorland cottage, occupied or vacant, to get warmth and perhaps food and rest, but well before dawn he would start out again. He would already be close by.

But he could have no idea about the reception waiting for him.

They had spent half an hour in the house at Wast Water while Landon showed them the video of Amanar's execution in Edinburgh and discussed what faced them. Tabor had immediately identified the two killers as Rory Brodie and Sean Flynn, both SAS men who had once been in Tabor's unit. Now, clearly, they were working for Beech and would have hired companions of equal calibre.

Potrascu was riding into an ambush. And a massacre.

As Tabor lay in the snow on a tree-covered knoll overlooking the house, he also knew that Anca and Landon would be caught in the middle.

Both had insisted on coming with him, although Murchie remained at Wick, with an armed response team, only fifteen minutes' flying time away, ready to attack when the weather cleared.

Anca argued that they would need a Romanian speaker at the spot. She said she had trained in the Romanian mountains and could quite easily handle the Caithness winter. Landon refused to stay behind. As he saw it, this was *his* case and he had a vested interest in seeing it through. Murchie finally agreed. The ART would wait at Wick until Tabor had reconnoitred a suitable landing spot close to the mansion, and radioed with details.

Tabor pulled over the radio. He had carried it here himself, along with a backpack and their weapons, including a crossbow.

Anca was huddled inside her sleeping bag, tired but refusing to admit the Flow Country was worse than the Vladeasa mountains. Landon sat upright, sleeping against the trunk of a tree, almost exhausted. Several times he fell flat on his face after being tripped up by heather, and once he sank in a bog and had to be pulled out by the others. Each time he wiped himself down and pushed on behind them, stubbornly saying nothing.

Exhausted or not, Tabor knew that soon dawn would creep up and they would have to leave here. For the moment he let them sleep. They needed every minute. Their only rest since leaving Wick was the hour's drive through the snow in a four-wheel-drive to Altnabreac Station.

While they slept, Tabor investigated the immediate vicinity, in particular a range of stone outbuildings close to the house.

That was where Tabor's apprehension turned into a reality nightmare.

He had been away nearly an hour when he lay down in the shelter of the trees on the knoll, and turned on the radio.

'Hold the choppers,' he snapped quietly into the microphone. 'There are half a dozen heavily armed guards inside a stone outbuilding protecting the approach. They have an L115 long-range rifle, the kind used in the Gulf to down Iraqi helicopters. If you fly in before I can get it, they'll bring you down half a mile from the target.'

'Understood,' Murchie said curtly. 'Suggestions?'

'I'm working on it.'

'Work faster. What about Landon?'

'Resting.'

'Remind him this is still an arrest operation,' Murchie said, the metallic voice through the microphone flattening any nuance of emphasis. 'Tell him to keep you reined in.'

'I'll do what I have to,' Tabor answered, restraining his immediate reaction. 'You do what you think is right. Out.' He switched off the radio.

A sliver of light was peeking through the greyness and the snow had slowed.

It was time to go.

Seventy

Tum Broch, near Loch Scye. Thursday, almost dawn.

Beech came down the carpeted staircase into the lounge where Rory Brodie was sitting in front of a roaring fire, a balloon of brandy in his hand.

'Are the lines still down?' Brodie asked.

'I got through on the Internet phone.' Beech sat down in another chair nearby, pouring himself a glass of the malt whisky from a decanter on a small table alongside. 'Life's about to get interesting. McGlynn's dead. Potrascu paid her a visit so he'll be on his way here now.'

'We're ready,' Brodie said laconically.

'You've handed out the MP5s to everyone?'

'Aye. You're like a lad wi' a new toy wi' those automatic rifles.'

'It puts a whole new slant on the word orgasm,' Beech answered with a chuckle. 'When Potrascu comes, we'll finish what we started in Edinburgh. Clear out the whole trash barrel.'

He had met Brodie when he was paragliding in Sutherland. At that time Brodie was still in the army but thinking of getting out to make real money. Beech supplied it. The money was the original lure, but now Brodie was in his element. Money was good, but what he actually enjoyed was killing people.

In the fireplace the flames danced a ballet of colours, blues and yellows, oranges and the occasional green. Beech drank heavily of his whisky, watching the artistry of the fire.

'I liked the touch with the eyeballs,' he said, after a minute's contemplation.

'It's nae original. Someone in Glasgow a few years back took the eyeballs out of a kid.'

'But you did it with more style, Rory. Like that theatrical stuff at Blackhall, putting the bodies in a circle, naked. The police psychologists must have had a field day trying to figure that out.'

'You have to keep the polis happy. You didn'ae seem upset about the woman in Burnham?'

'McGlynn? Just another lay,' said Beech. 'There's more where she came from.' He dismissed all thought of her. 'We may have to bring up a chopper later to collect Potrascu's body and dump him and his men in the Atlantic off the Outer Hebrides. Do something good for the environment. Clean up human trash and feed the fish.'

'Aye, right,' said Rory. Conversation bored him. 'Are you ready?'

'Five minutes,' Beech replied. 'One last drink then we'll do it.'

Seventy-one

Tum Broch. Dawn

Although the snow had slowed and sparse flakes drifted lazily in the sky, the mist was still hanging over the edge of the loch, making it difficult for Tabor to determine much other than the dark shape of the house and a light showing in one of the upper windows.

Anca knelt beside him in the corrie, Landon lying down behind them, waiting to be told what to do next.

Tabor pointed in the direction of the lake. 'They'll come from the west,' he said. 'On the map there's a dense clump of trees at the lake edge. Can you get there before this mist clears?'

She nodded.

He delved into his pack and brought out a walkie-talkie that Murchie had provided.

'The instant you see anything call me. Don't try to tackle anyone on your own. Keep your head low and don't do anything stupid like shouting out, "Lay down your arms, I'm a police officer."'

She smiled. 'My mother didn't bring me up to be stupid,'

she whispered. Then she put the walkie-talkie inside her anorak, picked up her rifle, whispered 'good luck' to Landon, and made certain she had spare ammunition before she vanished in the mist.

Dawn edged its way like a thief, poking fingers of light wherever it could until it pierced the greyness. Slowly the mist retreated to the lake and the house emerged in stark light. From where he lay, Tabor could see it in all its splendour. At least fifteen bedrooms on three storeys, he thought, the kind of house Victorian Englishmen built to host their friends at hunting parties.

Thirty minutes later, the walkie-talkie in Tabor's pocket squawked. The volume was set to minimum and no one could hear more than a couple of feet away.

'About a hundred yards,' Anca whispered. 'I count thirteen. A couple appear to be limping and there's one man with an arm strapped to his chest. A huge man, bigger than all the rest.'

'Whereabouts are they?'

'There's a flat approach to the house and at the far end there's a corrugated hut, probably storage for equipment or fuel. They're coming up to it now.'

'Flat enough for helicopters?'

'Easily. It could be a light-plane landing strip under the snow.'

'Stay there,' he ordered. 'I've got to get inside that building.'

He edged down on his stomach, shoving the radio set ahead of him, Landon following behind. It took them ten minutes to get to where the corrie petered out. Tabor was weighing the chances of a dash across the gap between the corrie and the outbuildings without being seen when he heard the roar of machinery. He peered off to the west, but the building was blocking the view.

The walkie-talkie in Tabor's hand exploded into life.

'They've got a bulldozer from the hut,' Anca said, speaking rapidly. 'One of them is carrying a rocket launcher.'

'Jesus,' Tabor breathed. 'Stay hidden in those trees. We'll call Wick to land on the strip. Don't show yourself and don't try to stop them.'

'Take care,' came back Anca's worried voice. 'That's all I ask.'

Tabor turned to Landon. 'I'm going for the rifle,' he said. 'There's no point in stealth now. Call Murchie about the landing strip, and that bulldozer and RPG.'

Without waiting for a reply, he rolled over the top of the corrie and kept rolling until he was on the blind side of the building. The roar of the bulldozer was almost deafening. He scrambled to the door and shoved it open, his rifle up, ready to fire at the guards.

The building was empty.

No time to think why. He put his rifle on the table, took the crossbow, drew it and fitted a quarrel into the slot, ready. Then he went for the sniper's rifle standing against the far wall.

He felt the wind and saw the shaft of light as the door was thrown open.

Tabor flung himself backwards on to the floor, reached up to the table for his rifle but came away with the crossbow. He twisted around. In front of him was Sean Flynn, staring in disbelief at the man on the ground.

Tabor didn't wait. He pulled the trigger and the bolt flew across the six feet between them, shoving Flynn backwards and upwards, the quarrel passing through his shoulder, pinning him to the wall.

Flynn screamed, but no one heard. The trundling rumble of the bulldozer and the staccato hammering of shots coming from the building next to him drowned out everything.

That was where the other guards were, Tabor realised. The next-door building. Flynn had probably come back here to get the L115.

He picked up the long-range rifle and his own, slung the crossbow over his shoulder, then paused at the door to examine Flynn. The quarrel had lifted him up on to the tips of his toes and driven a couple of inches into the stone. Agony showed in his eyes, but he was alive. Tabor smashed him across the face with the stock of his rifle, knocking him unconscious. Flynn wouldn't suffer as much that way and he'd be there later if Tabor were able to return.

Outside he hugged the wall and squawked Anca. 'What's happening?'

'Chaos,' said Anca. 'At least three of Potrascu's men are down, but the one with the RPG has blown away the main door and put a couple of rounds through the windows. It looks as though the bulldozer is going to ram the house. They've got the blade up and Potrascu's men are now in the cabin, hiding behind the blade.'

'Don't come out into the open,' Tabor shouted above the noise. 'If they ram before reinforcements get here, anything could happen. I'm . . .'

But he stopped as two helicopters roared over the top of him, men in flak jackets standing in the doorway, waiting to jump before the machines landed.

'That's it,' Tabor shouted into the walkie-talkie. 'I'm going in.'

In a second he was running alongside the protective wall of the range of outbuildings, heading towards the mansion. Landon jumped out behind him, leaving the radio in the corrie. Twenty yards from the blown-away door both came to a halt. One side of the building was smashed in and the remains of the bulldozer were at a drunken angle half inside and half outside the house. Brickwork and windows had been flung aside and flames were rising from the top left-hand corner of the building.

'Too late,' Tabor screamed bitterly. 'We're too bloody late.'

Seventy-two

Rubble littered the steps. Tabor jumped over it, through the opening where the door had been, into a hallway. Dust was hanging like a curtain. Vague figures milled around in confusion. The air was thick with the smell of cordite, his throat was choking from the cement, broken mortar and plaster. He shoved one man out of the way and went directly for the staircase in front of him

The top floor, he thought. That's where the flames are. That's where Beech will be and Potrascu right behind him. Ignore everything else.

Men tumbled down the stairs in their hurry to get out. He could hear the engine of the bulldozer racing, the cries of those wounded, and noise from falling bricks, but no longer any firing.

He passed the first landing and was halfway up the second when he stopped.

What remained of Rory Brodie was lying head first down the stairs, one hand still holding an MP5 rifle, most of his kilt riding up over his chest. But almost nothing remained from the hips down. It looked as if a grenade from the RPG had gone right through him, shattering his hips, tearing off both of his legs and throwing them aside. His eyes were wide open, staring at the ceiling.

Tabor climbed over him. The grenade had hit the landing wall and brought down most of it, but the stairs were still intact.

He clambered over the rubble up to the top floor. He whirled towards the left, where he had seen the fires. If Beech were destroying papers, that was where Potrascu would be.

He wasn't.

Although flames were rising from behind the desk, papers burning everywhere, there was no sign of Beech or Potrascu.

He turned back to the first door he came to and kicked it open.

For a moment he was stunned.

It couldn't be!

But it was!

Dorina was strapped to a bed wearing only a nightdress, unconscious or dead, not even moving her head as Tabor stepped through the doorway. He moved to the bedside. Drugged! Totally unable to do anything to help herself, or him.

Landon shoved in behind him.

'Who's she?' he asked.

'Anca's sister,' answered Tabor curtly. He looked around. The curtains! He tore them down, and ripped the heavy drapes into wide strips, then knotted them together to form a rope. The safest way out with her now was down the outside.

'Help me,' he said, but Landon was ahead of him. As Tabor released the straps to haul her upright, Landon had opened the window wide and was checking that all was clear.

Tabor ran the makeshift rope expertly under Dorina's arms, fashioning a sling to support her beneath her buttocks, then lifted her on to his shoulders and carried her to the window. Together he and Landon lowered her swiftly but gently down the wall.

Tabor could hear fresh sounds. Men calling to each other in co-ordinated fashion, the whine of helicopters running down. He felt the weight of the girl's body ease as she collapsed on the ground. He turned away, his thoughts racing.

Dorina was here! Duncan had lied about her and he might have lied about the boy too.

He ran back into the corridor leaving Landon by the window.

Dmitri was in the next room, oblivious to the noise, also still under sedation.

Tabor was moving towards him when, out of the smoke, Duncan stepped in front of him. He had a rifle in his hand pointing at Tabor's stomach.

'Ransome,' Duncan hissed in astonishment.

The light in Duncan's eyes blazed with a different emotion. Neither hate, nor anger nor fear. It was excitement but it was also madness. Duncan was over the edge. His suave manner had always trodden a fine line between sanity and genius and he had slipped. Now he knew nothing of what was happening with him, or to him. Nothing was left in his mind but destruction for himself and everyone else.

'You,' he whispered. 'You're behind it all.'

He moved a step closer to Tabor.

'My nemesis,' he said. 'Wreaking retribution. It was all fine, Ransome. Everything was fine.'

'Your premature obituary said Ferdetta's taken over your company.' *My gun*, Tabor realised. *I left my gun on the bed by Dorina. Play for time. What's Duncan doing here? Why were*

Dorina and Dmitri here? 'I guess that means your Choice Pill project's been abandoned.'

'*Tatú* won't ever be abandoned,' Duncan scoffed. 'I told you that! *Tatú*'s here at the end of the corridor. My laboratory. My hospital. Identical to that I built for Blake at Jorox. Here, Ransome, with the girl and the boy.'

'Not for much longer.'

He was watching Duncan, waiting for a chance.

'Until I decide to get rid of them,' Duncan said, his voice steady.

Think, something inside Tabor urged. *Learn what you can while his mind is in control.*

'Blake's papers,' he said slowly. 'Where are they, Duncan?'

'Where you can't find them.'

Tabor moved abruptly. Although he didn't have his gun, he never went into a battle situation without a back-up. He reached for the 15-inch khukuri combat knife, in its scabbard on his belt, at the back. No time to figure things out. No time for 'guilty but mentally unfit to stand trial'. Duncan had to die.

He moved to one side, pivoting for a kick to the stomach, trying to bring Duncan closer so that he could rip the knife across his throat, but Duncan's gun was swivelling to cover him. *A bullet is faster than a knife. No time. It had all run out.*

He knew he was going to die.

Anca was safe. Dorina was safe. Things left undone. Emma. The bastard made Emma pregnant then sent her to die.

A shout. A warning.

Tabor had no idea who and no time to look around, but he stopped in mid-pivot and fell against the wall.

He saw the flash of light reflected from the window. A chrome-steel axe buried itself in Duncan's skull, splitting it from forehead to chin, embedding itself in the bone and brain, splattering it over the walls and carpets.

The shout. He turned around. Landon had followed from the other room. Now he was on the floor, dead or unconscious it was impossible to tell.

A mad house. Everything is insane. I'm in the middle of a Hieronymous Bosch world of dreams and nightmares.

Potrascu was framed in the doorway, with a huge man behind, one arm strapped across his chest. Probably Serghei, Tabor realised, mental details filling in automatically. Like Duncan only moments earlier, he was holding a gun pointed at Tabor's stomach. Unlike Duncan Tabor doubted Serghei would need it to kill anyone. His one free hand was enough.

Potrascu stepped over the unconscious Landon, took the knife from Tabor and indicated the boy. 'You were going to kill him?'

'No. I was going to release him,' Tabor retorted. His earlier rage at Duncan and Potrascu had abated. Emotion is wasted effort. A moment would come.

'No need. The boy is mine.' Potrascu crossed to the boy and started to unfasten the straps.

'Potrascu!' Tabor demanded. The smoke was now swirling around them, biting at Tabor's throat. *Time was running out. Duncan dead. Only Potrascu left.* 'What's Duncan doing here? Where's Beech?'

A mirthless grin slid across Potrascu's face. 'You are a fool,' he sneered. 'You are the journalist. I recognise you from Blake's gate. I should have killed you at the bridge.'

'Beech!' Tabor repeated, registering the information that Potrascu was the BMW driver, but there were other matters. 'Duncan's dead, but where's Beech? Have you already killed him?'

'Very economically,' Potrascu hissed.

He pointed to Duncan's body on the floor and smiled, then turned back to Dmitri. He unfastened the straps, saying something in Dmitri's ear, but the boy didn't move. Potrascu lifted him gently from the bed, wrapped him in a blanket, pulling it over his face to keep away some of the smoke, then strode past Tabor without speaking, nodding to Serghei as he did.

Serghei kept his eyes fixed on Tabor as Potrascu vanished into the smoke like a phantom. The acrid fumes were now biting into Tabor's brain; his head was spinning and he was starting to choke and cough.

On the floor beneath him Landon groaned and stirred. Serghei looked down.

Instantly Tabor flung himself forward, his hands reaching for the broken arm, hoping pain would slow the huge man down. For a moment it worked. The gun shot from his hand, skidding across the room and under the bed, but simultaneously Serghei lashed out with the free arm, yelling in anger and agony, smacking Tabor in the face, slamming him against the wall.

Tabor slid to the ground dazed and choking, seeking fresher air close to the floor, needing it to fill his lungs and turn back to where Serghei was moving for the kill.

But Serghei was no longer there. Just like Potrascu, in the smoke and confusion he had vanished.

Tabor staggered over to Landon and felt the pulse in his neck.

He was still alive.

Seventy-three

The smoke was so dense all he could do was blindly stagger through it. He tried to be rational. Flames were licking around his feet. The staircase might be unsafe.

What would Potrascu do? Carrying the heavy boy in his arms, where would he go?

He headed for the door at the other end of the corridor, fifty-fifty that led to Duncan's hospital. He slammed into it with his shoulder but it didn't move. He tried the knob. It wouldn't turn.

Locked.

He turned back to the nearest door along the corridor and hit it at a diagonal run, not even trying the knob. It flew open and he fell through, hitting Potrascu who was by a bed where Dmitri lay, trying to fashion a rope from the bed sheets, as Tabor had done with the curtains.

Tabor's tumble knocked Potrascu away, but he came up fast, launching himself from the floor, his head aimed at Tabor's stomach.

At the last moment Tabor moved aside and grabbed

Potrascu around the throat with his right arm, locking it, pulling it tighter and tighter.

He heard the gurgle in Potrascu's throat, felt the Romanian's fingernails digging into Tabor's hands, ignoring the pain. Blood poured down Tabor's hands, but he dismissed it, squeezing ever tighter.

Potrascu's feet kicked out helplessly in reaction to the slow, determined strangulation. His hands scrabbled to release the stranglehold.

The Romanian's face was inches from his own. The eyes were bulging, the tongue hanging out. Tabor squeezed the stranglehold on his right arm, and simultaneously reached for Potrascu's head with his left hand.

One swift tug and his neck would snap. The gurgling would stop forever. The hate would stop forever. A red flood of rage roared over him. Nothing now mattered. Duncan was dead. Only Potrascu left to die, then it would be over.

He could see Emma's face in his mind, hear her voice calling, pleading with him.

'Please, Simon,' she cried desperately. 'Please!'

He let go of the stranglehold, breathing hard and Potrascu dropped to the floor, rolling out of the way towards the window, his face almost purple, his eyes glazed.

Tabor turned to the doorway. Anca was standing there, tears running down her face.

Behind him Potrascu shoved himself upright, wheezing, trying to catch his breath, physically damaged, but his mind still functioning. He pulled out the gun he had stuck inside the back of his belt.

She screamed.

Tabor turned around, saw the gun and dived across the room, clutching Potrascu around the legs, just below the knees.

Out of control, Potrascu staggered back, hitting the

window, feeling the panes and woodwork shatter. He grabbed at the curtain for safety.

Déjà vu. Tabor stared in disbelief.

Just as it had been in Fuengirola two years ago, the man was too close and it was too late. Potrascu was falling through the window, the shattered glass of the panes scoring across his back. He was off balance and there was nothing for him to hold on to except the curtain.

The rail ripped out of the wall and the drapes twisted and turned around him as Potrascu fell.

Tabor walked over to the broken window, the smoke sucking out of it around him. He looked at the body below. The curtain was wrapped around it like a shroud.

Anca knelt beside the stretcher holding Dorina's hands, her face close to her sister's, the tears dripping down her face and falling on to Dorina's cheeks.

A medic came up. 'She'll be OK, miss,' he said softly. 'She's been sedated, but she'll come out of it in a few hours. All her vital signs are stable and she seems to be a strong lass. A few days in hospital, some hot broth and warmth, and she'll be right as rain.'

Anca looked up and smiled her thanks, as the medic hovered.

Right as rain? An odd British expression. Most people hated rain. Why should it be considered right? And would Dorina ever be right again?

What of the baby she was carrying? Would it be right, or would there still be effects from what Blake had done to her? Only time would tell. It was something she would face later. She, Dorina and hopefully Tabor, but that was not her decision.

All she could allow herself to feel now was relief that Dorina was safe. The blackness of the past month had gone.

There were thunderclouds in the distance, but for the moment the emotional skies were clear.

She kissed Dorina gently on the forehead and stood up.

'Get her to hospital, please,' she said. 'Hot broth and warmth seems to be, as I think you say, what the doctor ordered.'

Seventy-four

Landon exited the building, down the steps to where Tabor was sitting on the plinth of a stone statue of a lion. Police were spread out around the grounds, semi-automatic Hechler & Koch G36 rifles at the ready, checking the terrain at the lake edge and the gardens behind the mansion. Black smoke was still drifting from the top floor but the flames had been doused.

The helicopters lay squat in the snow a quarter of a mile away with a group of prisoners sitting on the ground, armed policemen standing over them.

Landon sat on the plinth next to him. 'Some news,' he said. 'Murchie got it before the ART flew in. Two days ago a plane from Spain landed at Inverness with two children on board. They were supposed to be going to Raigmore but the hospital's got no record of any patients being booked in or admitted. They were taken away by ambulance and the number plate is on CCTV. They found it dumped in Cromarty Firth. I think it's safe to assume it was Dorina and Dmitri. The plane also offloaded about ten boxes of cargo.

Police have already opened them. They seem to be full of medical files, and notes of various kinds. First guess, they're the files that your doctor in Spain used in his experiments. I'm thinking maybe it would be possible for a good specialist to go through them, discover what Blake was doing, and if possible reverse the effects. It may be too late for the girl, but the boy could have a chance.'

Tabor nodded understanding.

'Ruth's just told me she's confirmed Duncan and Beech were the same person.'

'I think Potrascu was trying to tell me that, in there,' Tabor said. 'I didn't understand at the time.'

'Last of all, Murchie doesn't think there's any paper evidence in the house left to salvage.'

'It doesn't matter. Duncan and Potrascu are dead.' Tabor glanced at Landon. 'Flynn's pinned against a wall in the last-but-one outbuilding.'

'Dead?'

'I don't know,' Tabor said soberly. 'I used the crossbow and it took him in the shoulder. It was a lucky shot. I intended to kill him.'

Landon called a policeman crossing the lawn. Seconds later the man was running towards the outbuilding, talking urgently into his radio.

Anca came down the steps, followed by Murchie and Hartley. Anca's face was stiff and she looked pale. She might be accustomed to police work in Romania, but what she had seen today was a little more than she'd experienced before.

'Inspector Aron is coming with me,' Murchie said. 'She'll take statements from the Romanians. The helicopters will come back for the bodies.'

Tabor put his arm around Anca's shoulders and led her a few yards away, out of earshot. 'Are you OK?'

She shivered a little. 'There are five or six dead men in the house, two Romanian. How about you?'

'Fine.' Tabor saw the concern in her eyes. 'I didn't kill Potrascu deliberately. Landon's not taking any action. He just told me Blake's medical files are at Inverness.'

'Do you think I'll be able to use them to help Dorina?'

'We'll talk about it,' Tabor said quietly. 'On our own. Go check on her. She needs you by her when she wakes up. Then we'll talk about you, and your sister and the baby.'

'And Dmitri,' she replied, letting go of his arm. 'I want to look after Dmitri. I feel responsible for him.' She looked away. So many things to say. So many things to be put in order. She turned back to him. 'They will bring you and DCI Landon out next trip.'

Hartley came across, looking apologetic. 'Sorry,' she said. 'We're ready, but I wanted to brief you first. One of the Romanians speaks English and he'll give us details of the London brothels, and Murchie's leak in the Edinburgh force, in return for asylum. It wraps up things all round. A couple of minutes ago we confirmed Duncan and Beech were definitely one and the same person. The FBI had already sent a picture but we took prints off the body upstairs and confirmed it. There's no doubt. Agent Daniels from the FBI said Duncan senior had an affair with a woman called Glynis Beech when he was in the US Air Force at Mildenhall. She had a baby, and registered it under her own name. She called him Edward. So he got a birth certificate, National Insurance number, everything. When Major Duncan was posted back to the US, he married the girl and acknowledged his son. He incorporated the child's name into his own. Iain Edward Beech-Duncan. He only used the Iain Duncan bit in America, but over here he got his original birth documents legally, then a passport in his original name, along with driver's licence and what-have-you. That's why it checked out when our people investigated Beech. Ingenious though. One man, two identities.'

'Did Duncan have any other links to Scotland?' Landon asked as he joined them.

'Glynis Beech was born in Thurso,' Hartley answered. 'Duncan went back to his roots.' She smiled wearily. 'I need to contact Daniels again. He's holding Ferdetta on conspiracy to defraud because of the company insurance coming from the fake helicopter crash. Ferdetta's offering to trade information for a reduced sentence, but Daniels thinks he'll be able to add aiding and abetting attempted murder and kidnapping. He says, when he has the full story from us, the FBI should be able to march into Cytek and sort everything. Ferdetta will go down for life, thanks to both of you.'

Tabor turned back to Anca. 'I'll see you soon,' he said quietly. 'Then we'll talk.'

'I know,' she answered. Without saying more, she threw her arms around his neck.

Tabor pulled back instinctively then relaxed, following into her arms. He kissed her, folding her body into his, saying everything that had to be said without a word being spoken.

He let her go and she fondled his face.

Then she turned on her heel and walked quickly away to where Murchie and Hartley were already clambering aboard the helicopter.

Prisoners capable of walking were herded onboard the helicopters, engines roared into life, rotors began to turn and in seconds the machines lifted into the air.

Landon had been talking on the radio but switched off as Tabor went back to sit on the plinth.

'They've found about twelve bodies,' Landon said. 'We've got fifteen prisoners, roughly an even split between the Romanians and Duncan's men. The big one is Serghei Lacatus. It took six of the ART men to get him to the ground, even with his broken arm. They've had to shackle his legs to hold him.'

'That's what happens when bosom buddies fall out,' muttered Tabor. Suddenly he was also feeling tired. Not of action, but of the strain of his past life in general. Too much left undone. 'I want something from you,' he said. 'I didn't ask for anything when I went to Spain, but I want something now. Permits to set up a real survival and training camp, preferably in the Lake District but, if not, anywhere remote. I want it legal, and I want documents for Anca to come here and work with me, and for her sister if necessary.'

'Work with you? Or something more?'

'We'll play it by ear. Work first. Wait and see. I want the boy too, unless there's someone in Romania who can look after him.'

'Take it as done. Is that all?'

'For the moment. Why? Is there something *you* want?'

Landon hesitated. Tabor could see the agitation in his face. Something's troubling him, Tabor thought. Something big.

His face was drawn and grey, but his normal calm features reimposed themselves.

'I've been lying to you,' he said, making his decision. 'A small lie but with major consequences. I have to get it off my chest. Did you ever see a pathology report on your sister?'

Tabor went cold. 'No,' he replied stiffly. 'No one ever sent anything about her to me.'

'Then I have to tell you that I don't know if she was pregnant or not. The Spanish police wouldn't allow me access to her documents either. They claimed they couldn't be found. Maybe Duncan had them paid off. Anyway, that's it. I lied to make certain you went to Spain. I needed you so I used your sister's pregnancy to make certain I had you.'

Tabor sat where he was, disbelief etched in his features. The pictures flashed through his mind. Emma on the bed, her dead eyes staring at the ceiling, his agony at what he had allowed to happen because he hadn't been strong enough to reject his career and look after his only sister. The months of loneliness and brooding over his neglect of her, his impotence afterwards.

The anger flooded back. Then he curbed it. Landon did what he did for *his* reasons. If Tabor had acted on the lies, that was *his* fault, not the policeman's. Tabor had been duped, but that wasn't a matter for anger. It was for self-inspection later, for talks with Anca about the future. Her future, his future and that of Dorina and Dmitri. Those responsible for what had happened to them were mostly dead, but the poison lived on in them. Store the anger. Turn it into action. Find out if anyone, anywhere, could help them. Do it for Anca. Do it for Emma. Do it for himself. Blake's papers would be a place to start.

Yet there was something else. He could see it in Landon's face.

Landon was *still* lying.

In the distance the helicopters landed again and police began to move bodies into the two machines. He watched as they collected those around the landing strip and finally entered the house to carry out the remainder.

A policeman came up to them. 'Time to go, sir,' he said to Landon. 'There's a CSI team ready to fly in when we get back. The superintendent said for both of you to come with us.'

Landon nodded to him. 'We'll be there in a minute. You go ahead.'

He waited until the policeman was out of earshot. 'I'm sorry.' He turned to Tabor. 'It was a lousy thing to do, but I did it for what I thought were good reasons at the time.'

'Good reasons? Telling me my kid sister would have had a baby if that motherfucker hadn't killed her? Telling me she could have been carrying a mutated child with a couple of heads? Telling me my sister was creating monsters and I could do nothing about it? What kind of sicko thinks that's a *good* reason? What are you *not* telling me, Landon? What game are you playing now? Why are you still lying?'

Landon could smell the smoke of the fire, feel his guts twisting at the emotions boiling inside him.

'It's the game of life, Simon,' he said. 'The lousiest kind there is.'

He stood up, dusted the snow off his trousers, and started to move away towards the waiting helicopter. He had gone about five yards when Tabor called out. Landon turned.

'You're a lying bastard, Landon,' Tabor said evenly. 'And I'll not forget nor forgive. I'll come back for you one day, when I find out what you've been up to. Meanwhile, make certain this time you do the things you should. Anca, her sister and the boy.'

Landon nodded.

Tabor levered himself off the plinth. 'Now piss off,' he said in a cold voice. 'There's nothing else you can use me for.'

Six months later, a postcard arrived on Landon's desk.

It was a drawing. In simple black outline it showed what appeared to be an extraordinary flower. A slender stem was affixed to nothing and the 'flower' floated in space. Five curving slender pointed leaves reached upwards and outwards. From the centre stretched what could have been a wide, flowing mouth, drooping two enormously long, curving 'legs' more slender even than the leaves above.

Simple. Gracious. Eerily threatening.

Landon turned it over. The identification read: *Dendrophylax Lindenii, formerly Polyrhizal Lindenii.*

The Ghost Orchid.

There was no message or return address but someone had added four smiley faces.

Underneath them were the letters S and A and then two Ds.

The stamp was Romanian.

The postmark was *Rogojel.*